The Social Worker

a novel

Michael Ungar

Pottersfield Press, Lawrencetown Beach, Nova Scotia, Canada

Library and Archives Canada Cataloguing in Publication

Ungar, Michael, 1963-

    The social worker : a novel / Michael Ungar.

ISBN 978-1-897426-26-5

    I. Title.

PS8641.N43S63 2011   C813'.6   C2010-907958-2

Cover design by Gail LeBlanc

Cover photo by iStockphoto.com

MIX
Paper from
responsible sources
FSC
www.fsc.org FSC® C013916

Pottersfield Press acknowledges the financial support of the Government of Canada through the Book Publishing Industry Development Program for our publishing ac-tivities, and the ongoing support of The Canada Council for the Arts, which last year invested $20.1 million in writing and publishing throughout Canada. We also thank the Province of Nova Scotia for its support through the Department of Communities, Culture and Heritage.

The Canada Council Le Conseil des Arts
for the Arts du Canada

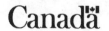

Canada

NOVA SCOTIA
Communities, Culture and Heritage

To Shirley,
and the many other social workers like her

I resolved – I was necessitated – to pit my strength and abilities against that system, to fail in no duty to myself and to my country; but at the risk of my life, or my health, and even my understanding, to become thoroughly acquainted with its windings, in order to expose and unravel the wickedness and the folly that maintained it, and to unmask the plausible villainy that carries it on.

– John Perceval,
Perceval's Narrative:
A Patient's Account of His Psychosis

one

I'M BURNING DOWN MR. JEFFREY'S HOUSE to be helpful. I'm his social
worker. That's what I do. Help. You have to trust me, this is a far
better solution to his problems than anything anyone else has done for
him.

My clients, like the Jeffreys, live in weedy gardens of nonsense and
bureaucracy. Their days are so tangled up with disappointment that just
getting themselves unwound from their dirty bedding takes more umphf
than most can manage. I'm somewhat of an authority on umphf. I
know that feeling of creeping resignation which can extinguish every
bit of hope that might talk back to the fact you're just a file number.
You have to be vigilant if you want to survive. And a little self-centred.
Appreciate the snug warmth of your own body before the draft of cold
institutional dorms and homes with empty oil tanks take from you
the one thing you can give yourself right to the very end ... heat. I
remember there always being that small sense of accomplishment
I could hold onto before escaping my ratty blankets, not because I
wanted to stand naked and shivering, but because someone, maybe even
my social worker, told me I must. Not should, or could, or might, but
must. That was their job, their vocation.

But what does it mean to help? That's the question that makes my brain do backflips. Help? It's a strange four-letter word. All those social workers, offering me the help *they* thought I needed. That was the problem. Say help in reverse and it sounds like you're being barfed on ... *Pleh!* I know it sounds cynical, and I'm still too young to be a curmudgeon, but to my mind, the one doing the helping gets nourished first. And the one being helped? If he's not careful, and a little independent minded, he's left with the bile of another's contempt dripping from his shoulders. Truthfully, now, isn't that the way it is? As professionals, there's the suave conceit of knowing that we're just a little better than those who shuffle or scream their way into our lives.

So what about me? I'm plotting to burn down a poor man's home. Sure, it's the right thing to do, but you've likely already guessed that this isn't going to be the selfless act I make it out to be. I can't lie to you. I'm fixing two problems at once. Mr. Jeffrey needs a new home. I need revenge.

I know we social workers aren't supposed to talk like this. It's professional porn. I could dress up what I'm about to tell you in the frilly lace of a chaste matron doing her good deeds on Wednesday afternoons in Halifax's North End. Or I could tell a story of some heroic ascent of a wayward miscreant who claws his way out of mismanaged care and botched supervision. If you hear me telling you either of those two bullshit stories, don't buy a word of it. Neither is true. I did what I did for my own good. To show everyone up.

Now, I imagine that someone could give of themselves unselfishly. Or that someone like me could grow past the injustices done to him. It's just that if there is someone like that around, I've not met him.

So I've hidden myself among the social workers. Like a little boy's game of hide but no seek. I used to love to pretend to be far away amid strangers before they took me away and the hiding started for real. I felt so important then, and the world so gleefully full of danger. There was just me and the G.I. Joe I'd gotten for my fourth birthday. We were all that mattered as we peered out from below a pile of dirty laundry. We would remain so still my mother didn't know we were there until she went to toss the laundry in the washing machine. Then we'd surprise her and run away quick. But not before I'd learned how important it was to watch adults closely. That's why I know so much about surviving behind enemy lines.

No one at the child protection agency where I now work knows that I once lived next door to the Jeffreys. I'll never tell them either. Never explain that I might have my own reasons for sneaking out to the Jeffreys' old place on the edge of Spryfield in a borrowed agency car. One of the plain white ones with the dented side panel where some kid landed his foot. I'm wearing gloves that I bought at Walmart. As I drum a nervous rhythm on the steering wheel, the cheap leather chafes between my fingers. I keep the radio off and drive slow enough that the cars following me all pass. On my feet I'm wearing a pair of bargain sneakers, one size too big. I found them on the discount rack, too ugly even for the welfare moms to inflict on their teenaged boys. If I'd been given them to wear I'd have dumped them in the trash out back of the shabby house the city gave us after my father died. Worn my old ones until I could get myself out to the Salvation Army on Strawberry Hill and steal a better pair.

I'll throw the gloves and sneakers into a green garbage bag and place it in the dumpster behind the pizza place near my house when I'm done. I won't even keep the old black leather jacket I bought at Frenchy's. I have enough money these days to buy a new one at one of those brightly lit stores at the mall. Not that I would. I'd feel like a traitor if I did. I still belong among those who rifle the bargain bins. I know the difference between the stressed look of experience and the superficiality of slum fashion. I promised myself that I wouldn't turn my back on who I really am.

Driving towards Mr. Jeffrey's house, I feel like I've found myself again. This mischief is wonderfully familiar. So too is the subdivision where Mr. Jeffrey lives.

I park by the mailboxes at the top of Mr. Jeffrey's road where I waited for my school bus when I was a boy. I remember I liked waiting for the bus. It was safer out by the narrow highway with its two congested lanes of traffic and the salty spray of wet slush that would splatter my worn winter coat. I can't remember any driver ever slowing after whooshing through the dark puddles that filled the deep potholes forever growing in front of me and the other children. Mostly it became a game. One child pushing another to the very edge of the unpaved shoulder, then all of us running from the next muddy face-washing. I took my turn on the line as often as any other child, but I always secretly hoped that someone would one day slow and stop and come back to apologize for splashing us. I promised myself that when I grew up I'd take that extra moment on my way to work to veer my car around the puddles. I guess I always wanted to be just a little better than everyone else around me. Or maybe I just hoped to meet some-one who was. Someone who would care enough to notice me, without asking anything in return.

I chase that thought no further, turn off my lights and get out of the agency car. Then I lock it and walk quickly past a dozen houses before standing in front of Mr. Jeffrey's. It's two a.m. when I break the back window of his house. I steal a quick look to my right. I can see my breath just a little in the moon's half light. The house my father built is there across an unmowed patch of lawn, an empty black space under the night sky. The rusting hulk of an old truck shows dull and tired in the driveway next door. I shake my head. More disappointment to add to the pile I've been collecting. My father would never have let any car of his sag into the ground like that. I can't help thinking that our old place deserves better.

I grit my teeth, then focus on the shattered window. I shine a flashlight through the broken glass, then carefully reach in and open the door. It soon won't matter if my coat snags or leaves traces of leather. I find the woodstove in the kitchen. Then, with the light extin-guished, search outside for Mr. Jeffrey's woodpile. There's plenty of dry maple, and even a box of kindling and newspaper under the porch be-neath a piece of badly warped half-inch ply. I fill my arms and go back inside. I get the fire going strong. Let the flames heat the chimney so hot I can hear the creosote burning. It's not long before the place is pleasantly warm. That's when I open the stove door. Lay in front the old newsprint I found and let the red sparks from the seasoned hard-wood launch themselves like shrapnel. The first few do nothing but smoulder. The house is too damp. But by the fifth or six large pop, enough sparks have landed to get the newsprint flaming. Still, as driven as the fire is to consume, the linoleum under the paper smoulders but doesn't light. I know better than to use anything like gasoline. Know the fire inspectors will suspect arson. They'll be looking for clues. I need to make it look like some runaway fell asleep, left the door to the stove open for heat. I need something more flammable.

I go into a back room where the stove light doesn't penetrate. I can hear mice moving. I point my light into the corners and find an old mattress, so dirty even Mr. Jeffrey has abandoned it. I haul it over by the stove and sit down. I want to leave it creased, leave no question that someone was actually here. Even in the ashes, I want the inspectors to find a story they can tell with confidence. I even think about pissing up against the wall, to let them know it was a boy. But I don't want the smell so I just sit there until the mattress begins to catch, and next to it the pile of paper I've laid beside the stove. Then the sticks of kindling at the base of the stove's knurled legs begin to smoke. I take off my Frenchy's jacket and make like I am trying to put the fire out, trying to smother it, until the flames get too big and I leave the stressed leather smouldering on the mattress.

That's when I run.

To the back door, then out to the road, where I do a quick three-sixty to see if anyone is watching. I know there's not going to be anyone to see my revenge. No audience. But I bow just the same to honour what I have accomplished. Still no one sees me. The street is as empty as it has been in my memory for a very long time. I turn and look again at my childhood home and Mr. Jeffrey's. They appear as sibling shadows, my old two-storey a big brother to Mr. Jeffrey's bungalow. Between is darkness stirred by a gentle breeze that carries with it the hint of the scrubby forest behind. The two houses with their black silhouettes are mismatched bookends to my life. I'd like to watch the flames liberate Mr. Jeffrey. I'd love to stare at the orange sparks and see my home again as I remember it. Licked by the hot red abrasion of hope. A future of coarse struggle. Remember my father's many beer-inspired lessons about what life owed me and what I needed to do to get what I deserved. But I can't let myself be caught. I'm still a social worker and my work isn't done.

I jog very quietly back to the highway where I left my car. I still can't see any flames when I look down the street. It won't be long, though, before the neighbours will rush to the house, call the fire department. They'll try to help like they always do. They'll say in the morning it was for the best, but not tonight. Tonight, they'll go, "That poor son of a bitch," and worry what Mr. Jeffrey will feel when he hears the news. I know that's what they'll say because they would expect the same from their neighbours. Know their homes are as vulnerable as the one soon to be in flames. It makes them look like good people. Strong people who want to help if only to hide their sense of fragility. I'm not so different, but my disguise is much better.

two

JOHN TELLS ME, "GET REVENGE" but he's not sure if I'm listening. My breath is shallow. If I had a mirror, I imagine I'd see a child's face that was all eyes. Pupils large. They don't give us mirrors in kiddie jail, only polished sheets of stainless steel screwed to the cinderblock walls. I fix my stare at the base of the toilet in the corner of the cell.

"Are you hearing me?" John sounds irritated. He swallows. I think to myself, I hope you choke. I shift my weight with the thought, wiggling away from it. If I were lucky enough to be here when he did start choking, I'd likely get up and perform some miraculous mouth-to-mouth chest-thumping rescue on him. Then he'd know what I'm really about. Know he isn't the only one who can help someone. But he doesn't choke and I just keep staring. His voice has a taint of anger underneath a thick spread of compassion. Like molasses over toast. Sweet and bitter. It's hard to know whether to bite or shove it back in John's face. He has a right to be angry, of course, after what I did to him.

He says, "You need to remember this. Living a good life, that's the best way to get revenge, the way you get back at them." He turns his voice gruff but friendly. Still loud, though. "Now sit up," he says. It's an order, but not one I have to obey. When I don't move, he tells me, "I'm not gonna give you the time of sweet f'ing day if you don't hear this. You understand?" He's not quite yelling, just sounds like it. It's a small cell. His barrel chest is all I see when I look up at him from the cement platform that is now my bed, concrete encased in a thick enamel of dull blue paint. I've been in this room many times. The first time, I was just thirteen. I tried to chip the paint with my fingernails, had hopes of leaving my initials by making the empty spaces spell "Joey." But the paint wouldn't fleck off and I wasn't stubborn enough to worry about it. Besides, I liked the way the paint makes the surface pleasantly cool. The bubbly texture suggestive of something softer.

John bends down to place his enormous face in my line of vision. My expression remains blank. I can out-stare him because I'm not really doing the looking. I'm watching everything like the camera mounted in the ceiling above that will be on the whole time I'm in here, when I shit, jerk off, or just sleep. John's words mix with the din of hallway noises and curses from my unit-mate next door. I don't want to hear any of it. I just want to envelop myself in the white noise of dull cement echoes.

There are two more guards just beyond my sight. I know they're there because I can hear muffled stories being told. They're likely all worried I'm going to do something. What they don't know is I'm not even thinking about leaving, now that I'm here, safe. I want the quiet they're promising. I want to be ignored.

"Why don't you all just fuckin' leave me alone?" I mumble. John says nothing. He's heard this all before. And to be fair, nobody I know can fake calm like John. That's why it's his turn to stare. I know even before I look at him that there's no point trying to disrespect him with a glance. He can bear the sting of our eyes meeting much longer than I can. I don't even try to look at him.

If I did, I know what I'd see. He's always been built like a fridge. Even has six-pack abs, which I found out the first time we met and I tried to kick him in the balls but missed and landed my toes in his gut. My foot hurt for days afterwards, but I'd known better than to give him the satisfaction of saying I wanted to see a doctor.

He grabs me with beefy arms, but he does it gently, and I let him set me upright though I still let my head slump against the wall. I make like I'm not paying any attention, but I must be because later when the magnetic locks click shut and there is nothing to do but sit there and think, I can remember exactly what he told me: *Revenge.*

Though John's a former nationally ranked heavyweight boxer, I'd never known him to be anything but big and gentle, with a piercing stare I swear he must practise. No wonder he expects kids like me to listen. Still, when he first became my worker, I'd given him the gears. I hadn't wanted him, or anybody else, thinking they'd got me figured out. So I made like I didn't need him. I'd ask other workers for advice right in front of him. I wouldn't laugh when he made a joke. I felt sorry for him when I did that, though. John wasn't too good with jokes. Always screwing up the punchlines. Instead, I told him jokes, ones that I knew he wouldn't like. When one of the older kids told me John's father lost his legs in the war, I told John a joke about a woman on a cruise who has no arms and legs but who keeps asking men she meets to fuck her, until this Newfie picks her up and throws her overboard. "There, now you're fucked," he says, and I made like it was the funniest joke I'd ever told and just kept laughing and laughing until my guts hurt and my eyes went teary.

John mostly ignores anything I do like that to put him off. I like him for that. Besides, I can't tell him what he has already figured out, that I don't have it in me to really hurt him. I just feel more comfortable dancing around, as if I'm in the ring with him, without ever risking the opportunity to stop and feel or being nailed dead centre. Boy, John keeps his poise. Happy to give me the satisfaction of thinking I'm an opponent when I'm hardly worth his spit, much less his sweat. "You're just saying that stuff because you want my attention," he'll tell me with a little chuckle. "You need me because you got squat else. When you gonna see that?" And then he'll laugh big and loud. Not at me, but just in a happy way that says to everyone he really likes his work. I didn't think I could like anybody who spoke to me like that, but I do, even if I don't show it. He is the only one in my life who really says what he means.

It has never been like that at home. My mother thinks of truth like it's a diaper. Don't like what's inside, just change it. It's the same when she cooks. She never sticks to what works. Never measures ingredients. Growing up, pancakes were dry with too much baking powder one weekend, then soggy oily messes the next. Soups were bland for want of salt and spice. Stews were a runny brown. If we boys ever tried to avoid her cooking, she'd tell us that what she cooked tasted how it was supposed to taste. "My friend Mary makes her stew exactly the same way." My mother had a long roster of "friends" like Mary to draw on for support. All of them experts. There was Mrs. Christianson, a nurse, who my mother had coffee with at IGA. (Mrs. Christianson insisted that sitting too close to the television would make children cross-eyed.) There was Mrs. Wilensky, my mother's bridge partner, who was a retired teacher. (She said reading to your children is much overrated.) I've never met any of them. Never heard her chatting on the phone, seen her gossip in the grocery store, or counted more than one dirty mug in the sink when I come home from school. I've only ever seen my mother exchange words with one neighbour, Lou, and even then it was only to beg a favour. Afterwards she'd always make a point of telling us boys that something wasn't quite right with Lou but she wouldn't say what.

The really strange thing is that I never remember my father telling us boys anything besides "Listen to your mother." I wonder if he knew my mother was crazy, or was he crazy too?

After he was gone, there really was no one else to rely on for a straight answer to questions like those. Except John.

I know I'm not supposed to disrespect my mother like I disrespect John. But you have to trust me, I've got my reasons. Which is why I'm not all that embarrassed to tell you that if my mother died, I honestly wouldn't miss her. No one else would either. Listen, her funeral could be held in a pup tent. There would just be my brother Stevie and me. My mother would be as quickly forgotten as the clothes from her closet that some anonymous person from the department would come and bag up and dump in the metal box out behind the Salvation Army. Her house would be readied for the next needy client. I could picture them doing that. Just like my mother did when she boxed up her mother's belongings from the small finished rec room down below the kitchen where my nanny had gnawed away her last years. I was only five but I remember watching bits of Nanny being put in a green garbage bag. I'd seen her just before she died, in hospital, though the old lady who groaned didn't look much like the grandmother who snuck me cookies before dinner or told me how lucky I was to still have a younger brother. I never understood what she meant by that. I could never remember a time when Stevie hadn't been in the bed beside mine. But when you're small you don't correct old people. I just looked at her funny and let her give me a hug.

I prefer that memory to my last one of her, which is of translucent skin pulled tight across her cheeks and down her bony arms that stuck out from the white johnny shirt. Then a big wooden box where I was told she was sleeping.

It confused me to see Nanny's clothes being stuffed into the garbage bag but no Nanny to wear them. I wanted to climb into the bag for one last hug.

That was Monday. Two days after the funeral.

I remember the days of the week because you couldn't shop on Sunday in Nova Scotia and my mother thought we should buy some flowers and go back to the gravesite and check that the hole had been filled. Then she could lay some flowers, she said. Only we didn't because IGA wasn't open. My father said it was better the stores weren't open. Better for the workers. My mother forgot all about getting flowers after that, though we stopped on the way to the gravesite to pick up pop and chips at the Kwik Way near our house.

Then the next morning, after the bag was stuffed, my mother put it by the front door. She never did make the donation to the Sally Ann. Instead, on Wednesday she took the garbage bag with her mother's clothes into the kitchen and emptied our breakfast leftovers into it. "No point wasting another bag," she said when she caught me watching. Then she told me to drag it out to the road. When I came back in she gave me a handful of Smarties from the stash she kept in the meat bin in the fridge. Handing me the cold candies, she looked so tired. That's the picture I carry in my head of her. A cow-like face beneath wispy greying hair that made her look the plump overripe witch I thought her to be that day.

It's different with my father. I have almost no memory of what he looked like except his paleness the day he died.

three

JOHN IS THE ONLY CONNECTION to who I really am. He has written me a letter every few months since my release. I occasionally send him back a short note, a line or two about my leaving home. About university. I've been meaning to write him about the new job but haven't had time. His letters still keep coming. His latest, like all the rest, is scribbled on institutional letterhead. "Dear Joey," he writes, "I get tired of watching people forget why they come to work ..."

I imagine he writes me late at night when most of the lights on the unit are turned off and it's quiet. There would be just the lonely glow of his desk lamp pushing back the velvet shadows cast by the security lights. I like thinking of him sitting there behind shatterproof glass. Thinking of me. Becoming every bit as cynical as I thought he should be years before he had good reason to abandon hope.

At the agency, my clients pass through a locked glass door as thick as the ones on the living unit where John writes to me. The similarity between one institution and another goes unnoticed by my colleagues. But I see it. Every morning I come to work I experience the flashbulb pop of a recurring image, an incarcerated childhood and the longing for someone to really know me. Reach beyond the cage with their touch. If a smile creases my face as I greet Patsy, our receptionist, it's not congenial, but the twisted acquiescence of one who feels violated. Neurons fire along old pathways and I am left wondering how it is that I was discharged from one prison only to put myself willingly into another. There is a difference, of course. This time, I hold the key.

Patsy deserves better from me. She means no harm, just works a no-name Admin-2 position that pays far less than I earn fresh out of university. She does what she can to make the place feel welcoming. She even wears pastel pantsuits with crisply ironed creases that gives the office the feeling that clients matter. Makes the reception area feel corporate, like a law office, or bank. Maybe it gives the place an air of possibility, as if clients are here by choice. I want to believe the façade is real, but it tires me. Within days of being hired, I had begun to let the illusion slip. Would have moments where I'd think of Patsy as Dante's receptionist. She is our window dressing, a taut plum-coloured smile that diverts attention from the black panic button positioned by her right knee.

To be truthful, Patsy needs it. Her most important function is to operate the electric lock that unlatches the door and allows workers and clients to pass beneath her maternal gaze. The annoying buzz reminds you to enter quickly. Once inside, if you're a client and you behave, she'll ask you with her Newfoundlander's lilt, "And what can I do for you, luv?" The innocence never fails to disarm. You might be excused for thinking for a moment that you've come to an old-fashioned shop where a clerk is offering to serve you like a valued customer. A new deep-fryer? A lacy bra? Perhaps a lovely pair of comfortable shoes? Anything you might need. All the worry you felt while riding the bus, the gut-churning that made your breath short, will for a moment be forgotten. Then Patsy will ask you to take a seat, if there is one. "Wait, please," she'll say. Always the eternal wait.

We social workers enter the building through the same reception room but exit quickly through a white door with heavy hinges at the side. A small black sensor with a green light is next to the handle. To open the door, workers wave identification cards hanging from red lanyards around their necks. We come back through the door when Patsy calls us.

Wednesday afternoon, the reception area is so full that Mr. Jeffrey's daughter, Joan, is having to stand by a table stacked with old copies of *Chatelaine*. She huffs a little as I take her through the white door to an interview room. She carries the scent of tinned tobacco with her. Its pungent taint fills the narrow corridor of closed office doors. Near the back of the building, I show her into a small room. I snug the door shut. Joan settles on one of the soft stackable chairs. The fabric on the arms is worried into a tangle of blue threads.

"What now, eh?" she says before I can sit down and talk about the weather (sunny with a high of twelve, a perfect fall day for Halifax) or her bus ride here (traffic on the rotary is slowed because of construction, again). Joan tries folding her arms in front of her but her large chest makes it difficult to make the cross. "You probably been givin' my girl three great fuckin' meals a day in tha' home you put her in. Ain't tha' right?" I'm sitting now, but Joan doesn't wait for an answer. "And what about me?"

When I got this job, Joan and her family were among the fifty-three families who became my caseload. It was thirteen above the union-recommended quota. Joan's file stood stacked there among the others in a huge pile on my desk, my office chair still creased from the last worker who Shirley had reluctantly dismissed. Starting me with such a large caseload right out of school was Shirley's idea. Shirley is the office matriarch. She's been here for thirty years. She started before there were security doors and interview rooms. Back then it was home visits and lunches in your car.

The large stack of files had meant late evenings reading binders of process notes. They were like novels with inky plots arranged chronologically. Except Joan's story I knew after reading just the intake form. Joan had been my neighbour when my father was alive. I used to ride my bike across Joan's front lawn, with its crabgrass and brown patches. I stole bottles from her back porch, and was beaten for my mistake. And I thought of her as selfish and called her names before I understood the difference between selfishness and need.

Over two months at the agency and I still feel like I'm on the wrong side of the white door. When I waded through a stack of three-inch black binders that chronicle Joan's life, my fingers became sweaty.

What Shirley doesn't know is that I'm hidden there among the characters. There are two Joeys. Joan doesn't recognize the boy she once
knew either. Her life is too full of passing workers to take note of last
names or faces. Too full of neighbourhood kids to remember one from
the rambunctious pack.

Leafing through those volumes, I read stories about Joan and her
father, Mr. Jeffrey, her daughter and her son all piled encyclopedia-like.
The workers' stories are Homeric. The incident reports, psychological
tests, home visits, doctors' reports, evaluations, case reviews, case con-
ference minutes, contact recordings, demographic data, progress reports,
annual case audits, placement reviews and endless narratives have all
been swept together into a chronology of disjointed moments. I read
about dirty bedclothes, brown water, disability pay, a back molar that
needs emergency removal, a broken stove, the sexual abuse of Joan's
girl by her uncle, three cats and three dogs that eat too much, and a
bowel disease of some sort.

There was a period when workers called Joan and her family a
"priority." Then everyone sat back and watched. It was nobody's fault
that Mr. Jeffrey never got a new house, or that Joan's government
cheque was never enough to keep her out of the food banks at the end
of each month. There was no one to blame. Shit happens. John taught
me that, even if he never said it out loud. Social workers happen too.
I learned that life lesson myself. Each worker tries to grow a family in
his own image. Isn't that right? We're messiahs with clipboards, though
awfully shy to admit it. "Just follow my instructions and you'll be
saved," we tell our clients. Despite my being here, and looking success-
ful, being on the brunt end of years of intervention never really worked
for my brother or me. If I'm here in this office now, it's mostly because
I had the good sense to screw up so badly that I landed myself in jail.
It was jail that saved me, and maybe John. If the size of the Jeffreys'
file is a testament to anything, it's that a river full of downstream helpers haven't done much to stop the effluent from further upriver making
a mess of their lives. Joan might not word it like I just put it, but she
knows in her bones just what I mean. Which is why she's angry. I'd be
too. In fact, still am.

By the time I get involved, Joan's daughter Vivian is turning fifteen and in a foster home, temporarily. Joan's son, Cameron, is more fortunate. He's still at home. I don't remember Joan having children. A quick look at the file tells me why. Vivian was apprehended at birth. Placed with another family until Joan was ready to parent. Cameron was born after my family had moved.

When Vivian turned two, Joan's workers thought she was ready to have her daughter back. By the time Vivian was fifteen, whatever parenting skills Joan had acquired were long past their best before date. On a sheet labelled "Reason for Intake," I read that Joan had punched Vivian in the head in plain view of the neighbours. Another flashbulb pop, only this one doesn't funnel me into any institution, but back to a home where I am cowering from a mother with a short fuse. The memory causes me a heavy sigh. Ah, Joan, you don't make it easy to show you the compassion you deserve. That fist ...

The image evaporates with a wince and I keep reading the dry prose of the professional who investigated. The intake sheet tells me that after Vivian fell to the ground Joan just kept yelling that she was going to get Cameron's baseball bat and teach the girl a real good lesson. Mrs. D, two doors down, had the good sense to call the police. When they came, Joan was still kicking Vivian, calling her a slut, yelling at her to get up off the ground, that she was embarrassing her. It took two police officers to pull Joan away from the girl. "Tsk, tsk," I hear myself mutter, and chuckle to think that's likely exactly what Mrs. D. said afterwards too.

Of course, Joan was never charged. Vivian said it was her fault. She'd told Joan where she'd been all day instead of at school. Told her about the blow jobs she'd been giving boys. About the money she'd earned. Had said things right there on the street that nobody heard but that Joan was afraid everyone knew. Of course, Joan never denied kicking the girl once she was on the ground. Even the police saw that. She still insisted she was the victim. Said raising daughters was more difficult than sons.

"What would you do?" she'd yelled at the social worker who'd investigated. The worker's notes recorded every word of Joan's defence. "My girl had just threatened to kill me. Told me she was a prostitute.

A fuckin' whore! Wouldn' you lose it? Even jus' a little?" The worker who wrote the case notes made no commentary.

Vivian was invited into care for a few weeks. A voluntary care agreement was signed. Respite really. Joan's signature is a child-like series of terse printed letters. Shirley told her, "It looks better when it's all voluntary." Cameron was left in Joan's care. Mr. Jeffrey and Mrs. D. both said Joan never seemed to have trouble with the boy.

Vivian's apprehension may have been voluntary but Joan's file number is P1341-04-Z. The Z, a warning. Shorthand for an angry client. I'm wondering if Joan will lunge at me. I hope not. If there is one mercy about this job it's that I don't have to take the punches. That's for the police. I've never been a fighter, just a thinker, the one who could anticipate the street fight long before it happened. Most times, knew when to scram quick, or turn the chaos into an opportunity, a cover for some misdeed that needed a distraction. Always made myself look good that way. The one who could coolly steal a shopkeeper blind while he was busy dialling 911. Only this time, in this small meeting room there is no distraction. Maybe even no street fight. Just Joan and her anger. I decide it's not likely she'll hurt me and relax. Decide I'm not here to talk about the beating. Discuss Vivian returning home instead. Focus on solutions. At the university, I was taught to call these "preferred futures." But first, I guess, you have to be really certain there is a future. And that you have a place in it.

All my jockeying for position is pretty much for nought, though. Joan isn't letting me say anything. "Goddamn workers. Every one of you!" she yells. I squirm uncomfortably. I'm supposed to convince Joan to like me without blowing my cover. It would be easy to just say, "I know what you're living," but then I'd lose her as a client. There'd be a conflict of interest. And I'd never be able to worm my way deeper into the system, to make it work better for Joan than anyone else. To give her the help she really needs.

"Joan, please," I say instead. "I don't want to be like all those other workers. Maybe our work together can be different." It's a lame effort to distract her from the cardboard cut-out of the useless professional, which is all she can see in front of her.

"I'll have none of your stupid tricks," she tells me. It makes sense that she resists. I know where the anger sits. I still have it inside, even if I'm beyond the reach of the professionals now. I don't want to trick her into anything, but I do need her to follow my lead, just a little. Just like I did when John caught me up with his expectations. How did he do that? I remember his manner so genuine it frightened at first. It was months before his earnestness warmed the distance between us. I don't know if Joan will be as generous with her time. Besides, I'm not John. I'm uncomfortable in the rectangularity of this interview room. To be truthful, its white walls remind me of my cell at the centre. My mouth fills with the acid taste of a half-digested breakfast. I had sworn I would not manipulate. And yet here I am recreating with Joan the very same crap that swallowed me. I want to spit my failing words. But Joan gives me no space to flail hopelessly.

"Would any of you give a shit if she'd clobbered me with a baseball bat? Would you, now?" Joan glares at me. Her voice never once chokes with tears. There's just an angry breeze that billows her flared nostrils. "No, it's all about Viv. Always is. Never about me or what I need."

Finally, there it is. A bit of truth. And an opening. Joan reaching out as best she can and making me an offer. Another pop, and I recognize this grizzled bit of emotional rubble. Like a spark from an old toaster, I feel blood seize behind my temples. More sluggish neurons recapitulate. I look closer at the space Joan fills. She's outlined now. Her life a subtraction of the area around her. Watching her, I can sense fully my veiled purpose. Something John told me. Something that makes tenuous synapses break their connections and twist comfortably back into old patterns better suited to street life than white-walled boxes. I do what I have to do. I shred the gauze of my professionalism. Roll up my shirt sleeves. Lean towards Joan as her conspirator. Think, *"Maybe she is my salvation just as I am hers."* Who else will have compassion for a woman whose dress makes her look fat? A dress that makes one notice the badly aged face of the one wearing it. Joan looks to be in her early forties but is really much younger. Just thirty-three. She wears thick heels and lots of makeup to cover sallow cheeks. Blonde highlights work hard to suggest something they're not. I'm ashamed to admit I find her ugly, unmotherly. I push these thoughts aside and do my darnedest to like her. Not to solicit her compliance as I'd been taught but to show her that she and I are fired from similar clay. Except that her disrepair is visible while mine is patched over, hidden.

With a seething conviction to be different from those who abandoned me, I look hard into Joan's face. I will offer her no platitudes of professional practice.

"Let me help you, Joan," I say, interrupting. "*Really* help you."

My sincerity startles her and she pauses for just a moment. "Why would you wanna help me?"

"I don't know," I say with a shrug. But of course I do know, and so does John.

four

ABOUT THIS REVENGE THING John is as serious as he can be. It's like this is some eleventh commandment that Moses brought down from the Mount, like the missionaries tell us on Sunday mornings. And John's got the God-blessed truth or something and he's going to straighten me out with it. I'd like to tell him to worry less, but then realize it's his job to worry over kids like me. That softens me a bit. "What a job," I mumble, only I don't quite know if I say it out loud or not.

He'd begun to share this bit of truth-according-to-John stuff an hour after I'd been dumped in the safety cell. By that point everyone had calmed down. John and five guards had carried me here, log-like, from the housing units across the centre's grassy courtyard. Two units cemented side by side. They call them cottages, as if that will make us kids feel better about ourselves. Make us forget we're really in a jail with humid walls and the sterile smell of disinfectant.

"You got the brains to do something with your life," John drones on. "Why are you so convinced you're gonna be a loser?"

"Go fuck yourself," I say back, quietly. I know it pisses people off more when I don't yell. They want me to get riled. Except being riled on the street makes your brain seize. That's how you make mistakes. It was a stupid thing to say, though. I should have rolled my eyes. Now I've let on that I know he's right. The dumb fucker, he catches on right away. His eyes get a little brighter. Not angry like most of the workers here who light up a little when they get all excited and ready to thump someone. John's eyes get brighter when he feels compassion. I guess that's what it is because for a moment it's like his looking at me makes my spine tingle and I sort of know he and I are saying something to each other without words.

John has always confused me. Even when I was two years younger and in on silly theft charges, he'd picked me up and put me in this same isolation cell all by himself. He would never hurt me. He would even wave off the other guards who stood there twitching, waiting for a fight. John would just speak to me, "You've gotta calm down, right down, you hear?" and then put his arms around me and squeezed so hard that my arms couldn't do anything but sit numb at my sides and my feet flail helplessly as I was carried to the cell. I was much smaller then, a teenaged baby. I'm no longer such a baby.

"You're a fuckin' loser," I tell John, with a viciousness that's deeply satisfying for a moment. John does nothing but grin. Listens. "You have nothing but a piss-poor job, you fuckin' asshole." I shout the words at him. "Like I'm gonna listen to you. Like right, and your life is so fuckin' full of hope, right? You and everyone else can just frig off. Got that? Just fuckin' leave me alone." With that, I'm done. John keeps grinning. I know he's thinking, *At least I've got him talking.* But he still won't leave. He just keeps a latex-gloved hand held up in front, floating just above his knees. It makes his hand look almost white. It's there in case I lunge at him. The latex barrier protection for him from my body fluids. Maybe a bite. John has been through this with other kids.

"You can have your bedding back when you're calm," he says. He pats the hard surface of the raised platform with his outstretched hand. "Okay, Joey?" I don't respond.

John wears the latex gloves when he has to transport us kids bodily down to the safety cell. Or any other time there's a risk someone will get hurt. You really only notice them when he touches the bare skin on your neck or on your arms. Maybe he thinks they make his touch softer. It's weird how I can be flailing away, spitting and angry, and still a part of me will notice the clammy feel of the glove though the other workers are there all over my body with their sweaty grips. It's not fair. I'd never bite John or purposefully scratch him. He should know that.

All the guards carry gloves in little velcroed packs hanging from a belt loop at their waists. But John is the only one who wears them whenever he risks getting cut. It's like we're dirty. Like he's keeping us away. I can't figure out why because everything John does says he likes us kids. Even John's voice is gentle when you hear him gravel his way through orders to tidy up, or when he tells you you're in your room for the night. I just want him to touch me, like I imagine I'd want an older brother to touch me. The reassurance of knowing there's a shadow big enough to hide you from the bullies, and an arm on your shoulder that tells everyone you belong somewhere. Instead, when I'm my most angry self, I can only hold John's voice. At least that comes without a latex barrier.

They'd stripped the cell of its mattress and sheet before they threw me in here. I understood why. I'd have just trashed them anyway. Or maybe even used the sheets to hang myself. In our own cells back on the unit you can fake it. That gets the guards real worked up. There's a grate in the ceiling and if you work at it you can twist the sheet through the holes. You can make like you're hanging there but really have it so the sheet is also down your shirt and under your arms. Get yourself positioned, then kick a chair from under you and let your tongue loll out and whole body just swing. I've never done it but another kid did last year just before Thanksgiving and lost all his home privileges when they realized he was just messing with them. "No worries," he'd said. "Who wants to go home and be with a bunch of drunks anyway?"

Time out in solitary means John and I have time together. John makes sure he sits with me each day. He pulls in a chair from just outside the cell door, as if it were there just waiting for him. He always turns to one of the guards beyond my sight and says, "I'll stay a while," and sits himself down, his butt so large the chair disappears beneath him. Each day I wait for some lecture, but what I like about John is he says nothing most times he visits. He's said his bit about revenge. Said it once. Knows I heard him. Instead of talking, John rocks in his seat, back and forth like he's listening to some music, and soon I find myself breathing along with him, a mutual rhythm, pacing out the minutes until some other crisis must take him away, disturbing our silent detente.

*   *   *

I wouldn't be in jail this time if Jeremy hadn't taken a beer bottle and smashed it across the taxi driver's head while we were still moving. A big left-handed *swoosh*. Bits of brown glass everywhere and Jeremy with a wide grin like he hadn't expected the bottle to break. The taxi lurched to a stop in the middle of the road as the driver slumped sideways onto the Impala's front seat. Jeremy and I, and Carrie, a wispy wannabe we let hang out with us, slammed up hard against the front seat. I could see the driver lying there, moaning just a little. He was probably scared we'd do something else to him. That was the strange part. I wasn't sure what we were going to do. We weren't even supposed to do what we did. We were just going to stiff him for the fare. Run away when he pulled up to some stranger's house a few blocks from the neighbourhood where we live.

My house is on Herring Cove Road, Jeremy lives on Circle Drive and Carrie nearby on Cherry Lane. A social worker had moved my family and me into a subsidized storey-and-a-half after my father died. Public housing with peeling green paint and a rotting porch. My father had keeled over on the toilet after coming home from work and shovelling us out from a huge snowstorm that had left my mother stranded at home with us kids all day. That was when we lived next to the Jeffreys, on a dead-end street at the edge of Spryfield. The city was just beginning to creep out and claim the boggy forests that surrounded Halifax's southern edge. My father was able to build a house on an unserviced lot. The townies would tease us we had to pump our own water and use outhouses in the winter, but none of it was true. Houses were still sparse enough that patches of wild blueberries grew mid-summer on the empty lots in our subdivision. Our neighbours were also poor but every one of us owned our own homes. My father made a point of reminding us of that every Saturday when he'd sit and stare past the television and loll back in his chair. Cans of Canadian would make him fart. My younger brother and I would smirk but never tease. You didn't tease my father.

Weekends during the summer when it got hot enough for the crickets to whine, my father would spend lots of time out front fixing car engines and mowing grass, drinking more beer, often trying to do all three things at the same time. If you stood on our gravel driveway and looked north you'd see a small bungalow with pastel blue aluminium siding, stained by rivulets of rust. That's where Mr. Jeffrey and his daughter lived. Mr. Jeffrey's wife left him before I was born, left him to look after Joan by himself even though the arthritis in his hip made it damn near impossible for him to cook or clean. Poor man, my father always said. When I was real little, and some kids from the next subdivision over, the one with the big houses and large treed lots next to the lake, teased me and my little brother about being poor, I politely corrected them that at least we weren't cripples like Mr. Jeffrey. That's why my father would push his mower right across the Jeffreys' lawn anytime he had it out. He said it didn't make much sense to be cheap with being nice.

In winter, the snow blew in from the coast and gathered in high piles on our lawn and across our driveway. I was eight and three quarters the day my father came home and had to leave his car on the road and stamp his way through drifts up to his crotch. All the while, as he's coming through the door, violently shaking the snow off his feet, he's screaming that my goddamn mother hadn't sent either of us boys out to clean even the walk up to the front door, but that all we did was sit inside and watch television when we should be old enough to know better that the walk needed shovelling, and here he was having to do it after working all day at the warehouse opening up boxes of towels from India while lame bastards with shit for brains swept the floor, pulling dirt onto their shoes with three-foot wide push brooms. We'd all tried to ignore him, though my mother had run to get him dry socks before sending him outside. All the while the television had blared and my younger brother and I had moved a little closer, worried which one of us was going to be picked up by the hair and dragged outside with him. But he'd just said to hell with the lot of us and went out by himself.

We'd listened to the scraping of the plastic shovel with the steel edge as he cleaned the steps, then a pause, then more scraping. I remember thinking it odd that he kept stopping, worried that he was reconsidering his decision to go out in the first place while we sat inside watching our shows. But the scraping and heavy thump of snow continued until the door was shaken to loosen the snow from between the summer screen and the glass and he'd come back in breathing heavy. I'd mostly kept my eyes on the television set, but glanced quick over to where he was taking off his boots in the entranceway. And then he'd headed off to the bathroom upstairs, only he was in there a long time, and when supper was ready my mother told me to go get my father, that his food was getting cold. I knocked on the door but didn't get an answer so figured he was really angry and came back and told my mother he didn't want to come to supper yet. We all ate at the table, but she soon took her food out to the television, something we kids weren't allowed to do. She gathered all the bones from the pork chops she'd cooked. She didn't mind cutting the meat off the bones for us. That way she could enjoy the grisly bits. She'd slide them onto her plate with a heap of potatoes and a few cooked carrots for colouring. We finished our meals quick and went to join her, by which time her hands were greasy from the brown sauce she'd smothered the chops in.

Our show finished. My father still hadn't come down so I was sent up again to go and check on him. This time I knew I couldn't lie. I knocked on the upstairs bathroom door and then pushed it open when my father said nothing. He was there with his pants down and very white. He was slumped against the wall, a Barbie doll crocheted toilet roll holder next to him. He hadn't even knocked it over. It looked like he'd leaned over and went to sleep. But I knew that wasn't what had happened because his eyes were open.

I tore out of there and ran screaming to my mother, who I collided with at the bottom of the stairs. She was running, knowing by my screams something was wrong. She swatted me aside, her greasy hands leaving a trail of fingerprints on me and the wall as she heaved herself up the stairs two at a time. Those marks were still there when the paramedics came to take my father from the house. Their rescue vehicle, lights flashing, telling the neighbours we were in trouble. And all the while the cartoons kept playing on the television and I just wished my family was normal and we could all be invisible instead of having an ambulance announce to everyone that we were just as unlucky as they were.

The night we got arrested, I knew those same rescue lights would soon come for the taxi driver. And police sirens, too. Except, with the top of the broken bottle still in his hand, Jeremy seemed to want to keep the show going. He leaned over the front seat, his large ass swinging in my face. I turned my head and there was Carrie beside me, wild-eyed. I remember thinking how quiet it had become. Even the radio that was babbling away with calls and static was silent.

I leaned over the seat and yelled at the driver, "Run!" a volley of spit landing on his head. But he didn't run. Maybe he was thinking, Don't move. Maybe this cab was his home. Maybe he had nowhere to run. I knew he was afraid of what we'd do next. Who the hell knew what we'd do, but right then I wanted him to run away so we could have some time to think. But he just stayed there. And I landed one good punch on his spongy shoulder, but still nothing. And that's when I saw his wallet hooked by a chain to his hip. I was at it before I could think twice and tore at the zipper and took out the few bills that were inside. There was a twenty and three fives and a few coins. Even being robbed he didn't stir.

Enough of this, I thought. "Out, man, out!" I said to Jeremy and reached past him to push the door open. But he wasn't moving, nor was Carrie who was telling Jeremy, "This is *sooo* cool!" I couldn't see anything cool about it. I just wanted out. "Let's go, guys," I said. We're sitting in the middle of the goddamn road. "This ain't good," I shouted. And that brought them both back to reality. Jeremy said, "Yeah!" and we all tumbled out of the taxi at once. I stuffed the smaller bills into Jeremy's back pocket and put the twenty into mine.

Outside, I could feel a dull thunk as a cog caught a gear somewhere in my head and I could see what the cops would see. It made me stone sober and I found my legs and began to run. As I tore off I looked back just for a moment to see Carrie still freaking beside the cab, too stunned to move, but at least Jeremy was pushing her and yelling at her to follow me. That was better. Carrie might get away, might not snitch. And as I ran it came to me that there had been silence in the cab after the driver slumped over. He must have picked up his radio that was on the seat beside him. He must have clicked it on. His Dispatch would have heard everything we said.

Run, run as fast as you can,
You can't catch me, I'm the gingerbread man ...

The song chases itself around my scrambled brain. It rides on memories of afternoons spent on my mother's knee when she still knew me. After my father's death, I cut my mother's meat. My brother and I also cleaned, and if my mother was tired, we cooked. We shovelled, too. At the slightest dusting of November snow, we were outside with scoops and brooms.

I missed her. Or someone like her.

After school, I found my own glass of milk. At bedtime I reminded my brother to brush his teeth. I knew my mother only by her angry grip which pulled me by my hair into the kitchen where a wooden spoon was a substitute for my father's more disciplined hand. The older I grew, the more I imitated my parents. I disappeared. Tore out the front door after curfew without a backwards glance.

I'm running now, again, but don't know where I'm going. When we'd hailed the cab, we'd said we were going home. I thought it loony the driver even stopped for us. Three kids, one holding an open beer, and this guy actually stops.

Run, run ...

We'd told him a fake address and he'd bought it. Three kids in the middle of the night and he lets us in his cab. He must have been desperate for the fare. "It'll be seven or eight dollars. That okay?" he'd said. He'd even smiled at us, fatherly-like.

Run, run ...

We'd said, "Yes, sir," or at least Jeremy had. I was mellow with the booze and grass we'd had in old man Ross's basement. He'd let us do what we wanted as long as we brought girls along.

Run.

The ground moved beneath my feet, the slap of my sneakers on pavement, then concrete, and finally dewy midnight earth. I was in a park. It was a warm dark night. The fog from the harbour laid an inky mist over everything. Made the air soft. The grass combed the dew. It rained upwards as I splashed across a field that had been neglected, the weeds growing high and wild. I was headed towards the trees I could just make out behind a ball diamond's backstop. I wanted to blend in with the shadows. I didn't feel safe, didn't stop running until I found a spot under a big maple, with a damp picnic table next to it. I waited for Jeremy and Carrie to catch up, if they could find me.

I've done nothing, I kept telling myself. Not that anyone would believe me. They'll have good reason to dump on me, to smugly say, "See, I told you so," and the cops, my family, even my goddamn family, teachers, everyone would think I was the screw-up they imagined me to be. The fatherless welfare brat. "Screw them," I whispered into the night, my voice raspy and hollow.

That's when I heard footsteps a ways off but didn't see anyone. I was alert like the hyped-up kids in my class who resist taking their Ritalin. My thoughts raced. I knew the driver would have no trouble identifying us.

The footsteps were getting closer. Cat-like, they'd start, speed up, then stop suddenly. Then I heard a quiet, "Joey?" but didn't answer. I put my forehead quick to the bark of a tree. The thud felt good. I did it again, only this time so hard it made me dizzy and a touch nauseous. I leaned over and puked up crusty bits of chips and the brown sludge of half-digested beer. The puke splattered on my shoes.

"Joey?" They were closer this time.

I lay down on the picnic table. Let the damp soak through my t-shirt. My legs were now jelly. I was on the edge of thinking something important, about aluminum-sided houses with cripples, and forest behind. The time before flashing lights and brown-stained walls. Before I was old enough to know when walks needed shovelling and grass mowed. Before blank staring eyes changed everything. Shouted their disappointment.

But the thought eluded me. And then I noticed Jeremy sitting quietly on the other side of the picnic table, breathing heavily. Carrie on the seat at his feet. We said nothing for a few minutes. Then rose and started to walk home. We were leaving the park when the police approached us with their guns drawn. We were just walking, at night, three kids. Carrie was the only one who started freaking. Crying. Yelling, "No, no, not us, it wasn't us." Jeremy and I were too tired to resist. I tried hard to filter out Carrie. All I wanted to do was enjoy that last precious minute, the pause before our apprehension. I took a breath and looked at the police officer whose gun was trained on me. And I thought, if only he knew me, he wouldn't be so afraid.

five

JOAN TURNS HER FACE TOWARDS THE WALL. Thankfully, for the moment, she's stopped yelling at me. Her eyes move upwards. She scans the flat topography of the meeting room for something. I can only guess she's searching for signs of blood. Or clues to how to avoid the trap that trusting a social worker puts you in. There's nothing to see except a dull print of an old house with a widow's walk atop a rocky shoreline pressed onto a chipboard backing. There's no frame. Nothing to contain the scenery or suggest that this is art. The white wall behind becomes part of the picture. An Atlantic fog bank that repels the portrait's promise of connection. Joan looks away, down at the industrial blue-and-gold flecked carpeting beneath our feet. Says calmly, "I don' need help. And I didn' come to ge' Viv back either. You keep 'er for now. But I need her cheque. The family allowance. It didn' come this month."

"I'm sorry, Joan, but that comes to us. Just while she's in care."

If there was any thin veneer of pleasantry here, that strips it, like a large Band-Aid, ripped off with a loud and painful tug.

"Who the fuck do you thin' you are?" Joan is shouting again. I really couldn't care less what she says to me, but I work with others who might. I gently remind Joan where she is, but she just looks at me and huffs again, as if coughing back phlegm that remains caught in her throat, something she would rather just hork up and lay in my lap.

"I'm really sorry. The cheque follows Vivian. There's nothing I can do."

"And you said you wanted to help. Like you know anything." Joan puts her hand to her lips and takes a deep breath. The imaginary cigarette she draws does its work. She relaxes again slightly, leans back in her chair. Her eyes jump again to the picture.

Joan says, "I wan' my kid back. Tha's what you wanted me 'ere to talk about, so talk."

I look at her and want to say, "Perfect," but instead just stare and say nothing. The truth is I don't know what to say. John would. Shirley would. But I don't. At least not as Joey the social worker. If it was just me, on the other side of the room, I'd tell her, "Sure. Viv will likely do better with you than in care." Tell her that the stats are on her side. That most kids in care do worse, much worse, than kids who are left with abusive parents. Only I wouldn't say abusive. I'd describe her as a parent facing lots of challenges. Truthfully, I'd tell her what should happen if there was any justice. But of course, you know I don't. Can't. I'd be out then. This has to be a covert operation. Save Viv, get Joan her cheque back, and keep myself safely hidden among the files. I stare at Joan. Plead with her. Soften my gaze. I could practically fake a tear, I'm feeling the sincerity. Silently, invite her to wait. Just a little while. Tell her without words, "I'm dancing with you, Joan, even if you don't know it. Please, just give me the time I need to scope out this unfamiliar terrain. I won't let you down. But don't ask me to do anything too fast. Not yet."

Joan must mistake my long silence for a ploy. My posture, confusion, or practiced condescension. She'll have none of what she supposes I mean. Slaps her hands down hard against her thighs and gets up. Throws the office door open and storms out. "Joan, please come back." No answer. "At least come back and meet with me and Vivian next week."

She's heard me, but keeps walking, yelling at a hallway of closed doors, "'Fuck, Fuck, Fuck' is all I hear from that girl. And now you wan' me to sit in a room and listen to her say things to me tha'll make her sound like she's the fuckin' good one?" Joan only stops and faces me when she reaches the white door. She deflates, realizing her anger isn't winning her back her daughter or her cheque. I feel a pang of guilt at her resignation.

"Fine. Wha'ever. I'm fed righ' up with every one of yous."

I catch up to her and reach to open the door. She looks at me as I lean over. Our eyes are on the same level now. Joan says, "This ain' no differen' than when I was a girl, you know. I had no use then for all of you, God knows I have less use now." I straighten up, the door still shut. Joan tells me, "It's me who's go' the problems, the god-damned worries, but no' one of yous ever thin's abou' me." Her face flushes red and for a moment she stops breathing, like smokers do at the end of a long draw. "Breathe, Joan," I want to tell her. I let my breath match hers as she finally exhales. Slowly, I back further from the door, leaving her some space. I'm hoping she'll be enticed to return to the interview room. I can get her a coffee. We can be friends.

"My kid should come home. With her cheque. She's my problem, not yours," she says and then without waiting for me to answer grabs the door handle and yanks it open. By the time I follow Joan through and into the crowded waiting room Patsy is craning her neck our way, her right arm down straight below her desk. I raise my hand, and like a traffic cop, signal stop before she can panic, then wave with a con-ductor's softness towards Joan's back as she approaches the glass doors which are now unlocked and buzzing her release.

*　　*　　*

I sign out an agency car to get to the group home where Vivian has been placed. On the way, I stop at a Tim's drive-thru for two hot chocolates and think about what John would say to a kid like Vivian. My mind goes blank and I'm left to do this on my own. John may have inspired me to be here, but his memory is proving pretty lame when it comes to what comes out of my mouth.

Fortunately, I like Vivian the moment I meet her. It's hard not to smile when the first time we speak she tells me, "That's a pretty shitty lookin' shirt." It was a crappy shirt. I felt stupid wearing it. I'd worn the shirt to try to look older, more professional. I'd bought it at the Sally Ann.

"I'm not too keen on the way you look either," I joke back, then hand her a hot chocolate. She doesn't even smile. Just another nerdy guy, I guess, kidding with her, then offering her a bribe. Trying to be her friend. "Besides," I add, "I have to wear fuckin' shirts like this to make people like your mother respect me. Think it's workin'?" That gets her attention.

"Not likely. Tell her she's got nice tits. Or maybe say how cute my younger brother is. She'd like that too."

This wasn't the Vivian of official reports. The emotionally, physically, sexually violated child. At the office, in sacred verbiage, my colleagues had called her a lot of different things. Simpler to call her what she was: fucked up. Vivian would eventually tell me the beating on the street was just more of today's shit. That shit included having to get her head half shaved so the doctors could get at the wound. She ranted that if they were going to shave her head, they'd have been better to shave it completely. When her scars healed a bit, that's exactly what she'd done. Made herself into a bald fifteen-year-old.

"My mom was pissed. My friends thought I was dying of cancer."

A week later, Vivian joins her mother and me for a meeting at the agency. Vivian is a lot quieter. She sits with her hands stuffed into the front pockets of her skin-tight jeans, or at least her fingertips. The pants low on her hips, suggestively leading eyes down to her pubescent crotch. Skinny legs and a face darkened by tar black make-up. The gaunt emaciation of a Calvin Klein model. And the smell of cigarettes. Joan, across from her, has set an uneasy truce today with Vivian's untamed sexuality. She says nothing.

Joan herself tenaciously holds on to some sense of herself as not quite finished as a woman. There's a sterile beauty that leaks away amid the loose flesh piled under sweaters and worn jean jackets that are her imitation of chic. No dresses this time. Stretchy pants shape her bottom into something round.

"I know what I can do and can't do as a parent," Joan says. "I was in the system, taken away when I was Viv's age and before that too. All because my dad's a cripple. Put with some old couple who taught me nothin' except tha' the whole goddamned system's a big fuckin' revolvin' door the likes of which Viv and I can twist. Exceptin' the fact tha' there's those fags they call judges who won't let a parent parent. Like whose business is it anyways when I tell Viv what to do? Like whose fuckin' business is it if I get her to listen by threatenin' her with the back side of my hand?" Her arm goes up, threatening me instead of Vivian. I lean away.

"You're too young to know, aren' you? Lots of ideas but look at her. Them boys hanging around her and she just ups and goes at night even if I tell her she 'as to stay in. I even tied her to the bed one time. Proud to have done it too. No one else had any great fuckin' ideas, did they? And none of this would be any of your business if one of my shit-ass neighbours hadn' got all righteous. I think I know the one. Probably the one whose husband left her, the one I'd say good riddance to if I was a guy, horny or not. Who'd want to live with tha' cow anyway ... "

"Stay focused," I say to myself and let Joan's torrent flow until I figure Vivian will think me stunned if I don't interrupt.

"Joan ..."

"You be quiet. I've still got more to say. I'm no' near done."

We both sit there for the next ten, maybe fifteen, minutes while Joan goes on. I figure it's not costing me anything. She has her right. And it's all part of the dance. After a time my head nods and my grunts of affirmation become mechanical, as steady as a clock. Timed to correspond with her inflection. Her words douse me into an underground river of filth and despair so powerful that where it boils to the surface it can't be dammed.

But eventually I have to tell Joan we need to wrap this up. "Go on then," she says. "Push me ou' the door. Again. See what I care." She doesn't get up from her seat for a moment. I begin counting. When I reach seven, Joan asks, "And what abou' my daughter? I can have her back? And her cheque too?"

"What do you think, Vivian?"

Vivian's bangs slide down over her eyes as she nods. "Yeah, sure, whatever."

I don't need much more. There's not much point keeping a fifteen-year-old like Vivian in care. Definitely too little too late, not that earlier would have done her much good either. I get up from my chair, which makes it clear to both of them it's time to leave. They stand up uneasily, Joan's rise a slow twist from her chair. She looks behind her and reaches to pick up the handbag she's placed on the floor. There is the abrasion of cheap cloth. I want to help her, but she's already off-balance and almost topples over with the effort. Vivian grabs the arms of her chair and flexes her pelvis up first, then rises, a lot of effort to make it look like she doesn't care what happens next.

I see them both out. Vivian returns to the care of a youth worker who is waiting to take her back to her group home. I give Joan a taxi chit. I'm supposed to give her a bus ticket. Taxi chits are only given to clients when the weather is foul and today's weather is sunny. But what the heck, Joan deserves the luxury. She can celebrate her victory while being driven home. She's still without her daughter, but I'll make arrangements for Vivian's discharge after I speak with Shirley. I'll see where her supervision leads me. But that can all wait. Right now, I just want to forget the lingering memories Vivian and Joan provoke of the time I spent warehoused in an institution. Maybe I should write John? Instead, I sit staring out the window at an old oak tree whose leaves are twisting dull green in the wind and wonder if it's going to rain after all.

six

As a kid I didn't do connected very well. Connected was just an excuse to feel like you're one rung above everyone else. Except, even one rung up, there was still always someone bigger who was ready to remind you just how shitty life can be by making you lick a toilet bowl or walk through a crowd in your underwear. Why? Because you're too young to know the word for bully and too stupid to know that fighting back is the only way to survive.

I figured out early it was best to just avoid sticky connections. I didn't want anyone to pity me, not John or my mother or my grade six teacher who thought he was so cool that he could tell us tweens that "Soap is your friend" and expect us to clean up and smell right so we could fit in. He liked to pull me aside after class. "You're very bright, but you don't do your work," he said many times. "Maybe your mother should come in to see me?" That he said only once.

"She works long hours," I lied. He was a good eye-roller like me. He knew I never gave her the notes he sent home, that I was forging her signature. Our phone had been cut off the year before so unless he was willing to risk his middle-class ass visiting our subsidized housing in Spryfield, he was not likely going to be able to convince my mother how bright her son was.

We moved there eight months after my father died. The whole neighbourhood is the dull grey of cracked tar and dirty siding, splotched with rash displays of red and yellow graffiti. Our 'burb is close enough to a new bit of four-lane road that the dust hangs in the air and snow is so black it's crusty. The highway came after many of the homes were built. During summer, exhaust chokes the few tufts of grass that manage to compete with us kids in the small garden out front of the house where the city put us, our rent taken from the welfare money Mom receives. That's pretty much the only green I see, and then only for a short time in the spring when the grass bravely pushes up. I'm amazed those small tufts survive at all. They never need mowing of course. Plenty of roughhousing children see to it that none get a decent chance to spread.

Our neighbours, those who had lived there before the decline started in earnest, didn't know me. There was a lingering sense of community, though, that reminded me of life on our crescent. In my new neighbourhood, I could walk into anyone's yard and take anything lying there and people would assume that it was meant to be borrowed, or if a neighbour saw me, maybe think, "You're the new kid who moved into that house on the next block," the last family likely evicted or moved when some parent did something they shouldn't have done. It was just assumed I was as unlucky as every one of the other newcomers. My anonymity meant that for once I had a whole collection of great street hockey gear that I splashed old paint on to make look like it was mine. As long as I hid it away for a few weeks I swear even the kid I stole it from couldn't figure it out. Besides, he likely had a dad who visited now and again with enough guilt to replace it, usually with even better stuff. That's what fathers do.

Jail is a better place to be. In jail you can dream and think things can actually change. John was good at opening space for dreams. He only left my holding cell after my breathing was as casual as his. He always knew when to move on. Knew when your breathing and attitude had fallen in line. It was something you just couldn't help doing, matching your breath with the whisper of his as it flowed from his nose down into his massive chest then back out through gently pursed lips. When I'd be in sync and feeling relaxed, he'd rise quietly. Not like other middle-aged people who I'd notice have to breathe out heavy to get up after they'd been sitting a while. John seemed to levitate, then make the chair he'd been sitting on leave the floor and float between his arms out of the cell and land noiselessly on the beige parquet floor beyond my door. Then he would push the heavy door shut, shouting to the front desk to "Lock 'er up." It was always that shout that made me feel melancholy, because I knew I was about to be given the silence I wanted but feared. When I heard the click of metal plates connecting, I lay down and closed my eyes, threatening myself with grey moving images of everything I'd promised I'd forget.

*   *   *

When I wake up, it takes me a few moments to focus, to realize the off-pink walls are a cell. I'm in fuckin' jail again. I begin to recall my arrest as a slow methodical process. Sit here, stand there, sign this, undress, bend over, flare your cheeks, turn, lift, dress. Life had calmed way down. Come into sharper focus.

Jail is familiar. That was a problem. The guards were all edgy around me. There was a rumour one of the kids had heard that I had AIDS. The sexual games that I'd played last time I was in just added to the guards' confusion and worry.

"Back for more?" John said with a smile when we first connected. It had been two years, but he was still every bit the massive man with the huge gentle hands I remembered him to be. My first time in, I'd been scared of course. That fear just made me more determined to cover what I was really feeling. John, the rest of them, they had no idea what I was going to do. No long pre-disposition report came with me. No one had yet seen my file from my school or Social Services.

At first, they'd given me a worker who was all by the book. I nicknamed him B-boy after he'd been stung on the face while we were outside on work duty and he'd hollered like a little kid. The sting made his face swell up like a melon. He was strict, moved with

45

a swagger to his little butt that made us all laugh, call him "Faggot" behind his back. I made it my personal case plan to put B-boy in his place. It was easy enough. First I took my toothbrush and sharpened the end, working it all night against the cement wall. By the morning it had come to a nice point. I left it on my shelf. I knew he'd find it during morning room checks. When he did, he pulled me right out of English class. Made me identify it as mine.

"Never saw it." I looked B-boy right in the face. He said nothing. Tried to act tough, but what he missed was that I was already one step ahead.

"Looks dangerous, though," I said.

I was locked down for a day. Then given another toothbrush. Each night I handed it to the night guard before going to my room. B-boy kept asking me in roundabout ways if there was any need for me to have a weapon. "Anyone on your case? Planning anything we should know about?" He opened that door many times, but I just kept ignoring him. To give him the satisfaction of even one little jibe would have let him convince himself that he was in charge. Instead, I preferred to just let him carry on with the illusion that he was The Man. The fear in his eyes, the way he always kept a hand close to his walkie-talkie's panic button, told me everything I needed to know about him.

Next it was the plunger. That was more fun. I took the toilet plunger from the bathroom, separated the handle from the rubber end, and stuffed the handle down the leg of my sweats. It meant I walked with a very slight limp, but it was surprisingly easy to still move around. That night I sharpened it. Quietly, under my blanket. All that back and forth motion, I'm sure they just thought I was jerking off. They had instructions never to enter our rooms if we were masturbating. Might lead to allegations of abuse. So I could rock, scrape, and make the handle into a nice point without anyone the wiser.

The next morning, B-boy was on again. I let the limp increase a bit. Just enough to get noticed.

"Something wrong with your leg?"

"Nah." Then I pulled out the plunger handle. Right there in the middle of all the boys. "It would be easier to walk without this, though."

The other residents were taking it all in, leaving their reruns of *The Cosby Show* for something that promised a lot more action. What a hoot. And B-boy there without a thing to say, except, "You give that to me." I handed it to him, smiled, then went without a word and sat down by the television. Of course, he and a second guard came over and ordered me to my room.

"What for?" I asked. Well, that got them going and they reached down and picked me up by the armpits and carried me to my room, where they dumped me on my bed.

It was all good. I had my audience. Nine sets of eyes all staring at me from across the unit quad. All waiting to see me do something else. Instead, I lay down and turned my face towards the wall. I'd decided enough show and tell for one day.

That's pretty much how I am. I like being looked at. It's the same in front of a mirror. I know I take a little too much time to look at myself. When I know I'm really alone, I'll even pull an erection and just stare. See what I look like, all primed. Leopard-like, sleek and strong. I like leopards. I've never seen one live, but in movies they're always just hanging out on tree branches. Sneaky buggers, too. Even when they're relaxed, you never quite know if a leopard is going to spring up and attack. Now that's power.

I've never liked being the star attraction. Even when my body had begun changing, and the black peppered skin around my balls had signalled other changes that made girls like twelve-year-old Roselyn notice me, I tried to remain out of sight. I liked stealth. Until I'm ready to pull something big from my pants. With Roselyn I was never ready. She kept following me. She was very pretty, of course, with a full chest already and a tiny waist. She would often drop a pen in front of me, or let her binder slip, then bend over to pick them up, one eye always on me standing behind her. She liked pink underwear. I mostly looked the other way.

Before puberty, I could never quite figure out what all the fuss was about when my friends told jokes about girls and sex and made a big show of laughing extra hard to make sure everyone else knew they got it. I knew the plumbing. Easy enough to figure that out by looking at the pictures we'd pull out at the back of the schoolyard. Some even reminded me of my mother. I'd never tell the other boys that. Instead, I'd just look and listen, hoping I'd understand why they talked so much about it. My first wet dream helped explain it. It hurt. It was like I'd pulled a muscle. I wanted to run and tell my mother, but something told me that this wasn't something boys shared with their mothers. But I was still all worried that maybe doing it would be painful like that every time. It wasn't. I'd get a hard-on just about anywhere. Walking home, in class. Now I made jokes like all the other boys. There wasn't one of us in my grade seven class who liked to be called to the board. A part of me was totally beyond my control. I had to jerk off two, three times a day just to keep things manageable. Like first thing in the morning, washing up, I'd reach down with a soapy hand and pull away, watching myself and imagining I was in some slippery cunt like I'd seen in the magazines. And somehow the sleek line of my own narrow hips swirling, pushing, even that would excite me. And then I'd let the come splatter across the mirror. I'd just leave it there for my mother to clean up. I wasn't like other boys. It didn't embarrass me letting her know what I was doing. As if somehow it was her fault I'd made a mess. She never said anything. It was our dirty little secret.

Those were the good things I saw when I looked in the mirror. If I'm honest with myself, there were lots of other things I saw that I didn't like as much. Times when I was so out of it and couldn't get a hard-on. Times when I'd come home green from drinking too much and nobody at home would really care. Times like that I'd stood at the mirror, my hair all tangled and sweaty, and there'd be this big splatter of brown chicken soup vomit across my chest where I'd heaved on my way home. But I'd be too wasted to do anything about it. So I'd just rip off my clothes and leave them in a pile on the floor then crawl into bed naked.

I hate it when I look into a mirror and see nothing but an emaciated gazelle. A wild-eyed loser, ready to vault in fear. Maybe that's why I don't do as many drugs as Jeremy.

In my room with B-boy hovering, I knew nobody would see a gazelle. B-boy was the weakling. Even I could do his job better. How difficult could it be to keep one little kid safe?

It was ten days before I was back on regular programming. For a while it was fun having extra staff escort me everywhere. Trouble for them was they just couldn't figure out if I was a danger to the other residents, to them, or just to myself. That was why they changed my primary worker to John. He had more experience with kids like me than B-boy. Or maybe B-boy was just fed up. It was John's idea I go see the centre's therapist, Ms. White. She was this angular thing with straight brown hair, a wrinkled face and quick little gestures, like you'd use to swat a fly. Though I knew little about sex at the time, she was clearly not getting any. I could just tell by the way she kept her legs crossed. Tight. I sat right across from her where I could look up her skirt if she let me. She didn't. Not that I'm really the type that would do that. If she'd opened her legs I'd have probably jumped up and run.

When she was sitting there with me, I could feel this sad energy about her, like the bank of drizzly fog you can see at the mouth of the harbour if you're still up at dawn drinking on Citadel Hill. Ms. White looked tired with dark circles under her eyes made worse by the black mascara she wore. She was always scratching her left arm. And she had this bad breath thing happening. That's why we called her Skunk-lady, though not to her face, mind you. She looked too sad to insult. I could just tell she was unhappy. She had to be, with so many strikes against her. What kind of worker chooses to spend time in a lousy kiddie jail, anyway? I guess her job was like the guys who put on wax and dry your car down at the Baby Duck. They have to wait until almost everything else has happened before they can do their bit. The other social workers, the ones I'd already known, had done the cleaning. Or at least tried. I wasn't exactly shiny.

I actually thought about trying to help Skunk-lady feel better about herself. Let her heal me a little to increase her own self-esteem. Maybe then she'd open up. I could have done that. Encouraged her to speak. Said, "Yes, yes, yes, poor dear. My, my, what life has handed you." I could let sweetness roll off my tongue as easy as a kiss under mistletoe. It would mean nothing at all. Just a show. One big performance. Like a circus. Maybe life is just a circus. And me, the Master of Ceremonies.

That first session we didn't talk much. She showed me a stack of tests to fill out and handed me a newly sharpened pencil to colour in the little round circles. She told me they were to help *us* understand *me* better. "Uh huh," I groaned and stuffed my hands down my sweats to keep them warm at my crotch. I could tell she noticed what I'd done and felt a little uncomfortable doing it.

"Here, now, you can begin with this one, all right?" she said, looking up rather than down. Then she handed me something called a WISC-R and another paper with BDI in bold print across the top. She never told me what the letters stood for.

The pages were full of questions that were supposed to help her interpret my experience. At least that's what she said. She used a lot of phrases like that. Then she'd explain, she was there to help make sense of what I was feeling. "Uh huh," I groaned again. I had tried to sound condescending. That's the word my grade seven teacher liked to use. Whenever I gave him a big eye roll, or commented on his mismatched socks, he'd say things like, "You are trying hard to be condescending, mister, but it only belittles you." The strange thing was that I could understand him when he spoke like that. I usually understand adults, even when they're trying not to be understood. Even when Skunk-lady tries to be professional, I know exactly what she means. Only, I don't usually let on I understand.

Skunk-lady seemed to ignore my groans. Promised she wouldn't do anything *to* me. Everything would be *with* me. "That's what social workers do," she explained. "We help people. I'm not a psychiatrist, you know, a shrink, so I can't give you any medications. Do you understand? I'm here to talk with you about your problems."

I yawned. She smiled.

"These tests will help make you better," she said.

"Better than what?" I asked, but she didn't answer, just wrote down what I said and nodded. So I shut up and had fun chewing on the pencil, making like I was hard at work answering all the questions on each piece of paper she put in front of me. I even had fun looking at inkblots and telling her the mysterious creatures I saw in each. I knew from television I should say things sexual, so I faked a blush and said that one of the scrawls made me think of my girlfriend touching me, "You know? *Down* there." She liked that and wrote more notes. All that happened on a Monday.

On Tuesday, we met again. I remember it was Tuesday because she made me late for lunch and Tuesday was taco day. I love tacos. It's even more important in jail than at home that you keep track of the days or else you're liable to miss things like taco day. It was the only meal we felt we'd made ourselves. Trays of food were placed at each table in the cafeteria and just like a normal bunch of lunatics, rather than the incarcerated kind, we would get to decide what to eat. Skunk-lady didn't seem too worried about my missing tacos. She probably never worried about eating. Or, I smirked, being eaten. She had no idea why I was suddenly smiling. She probably thought it was because she'd just told me that I'd scored high on depression.

"Have you ever thought about harming yourself?" she asked, as matter-of-factly as she could. The little quiver in her voice gave her away, though. Hell, she wanted me to be suicidal. For a moment I thought about answering yes. Letting her feel like she could rescue me. But then I thought about the consequences. The lock-down, no eating in the cafeteria (there are knives there), which means no tacos, and of course more meetings with her.

"No," I said, dashing her hopes. Still, I was pleased that I'd managed to answer all the questions in ways that made me seem a little bit crazy.

Though I was missing tacos, I still liked my time with Skunk-lady. It was time off the unit. Like going to church service on Sunday mornings when some clergy would come from one of the do-good churches and try to make us understand our place in the cosmic scheme of things. I'd go and hear things that I didn't know, which I liked. I couldn't have cared less about the religious crap. It was the other stuff I craved. The preachers were learned people. With university degrees. I realized that early on. I liked looking at the books they brought, which were full of pictures of paintings in museums and church architecture. Some of them were really different than what I'd expected. There was a whole book of what they called inspirational sculptures and paintings. Rodin's *Thinker*, which didn't seem very religious. And the ceiling of the Sistine Chapel, which was. There was also a strange looking

Adam and Eve, done by Bodero. I liked looking at that picture best of all, the rounded obese sculptures made the figures look so strong and full of life. I'd always thought really large fleshy people ugly, especially my mother, but Bodero's sculpture makes you want to put your arms around Eve. Feel the warmth of her big full hugs and lay your head between her humungous breasts.

I never thought about laying my head on Skunk-lady's breasts. They were too small, uninviting. More like kiwis. Besides, my relationship with her was not about hugs. It was supposed to be serious. Once I started going to see Skunk-lady regularly, I was permitted back into normal programming. B-boy even let me back into shop class, which was the part of the institution he was responsible for. That's where we made birdhouses for Christmas presents. If we were behaving we could use the shop tools. Bandsaws and routers, drills and grinders. Good, solid destructive tools. None of us boys ever purposely fucked up in shop. We liked doing something that actually seemed to count. Like when they took us out to a bush camp in the summer and let us use chainsaws to clear cross-country ski trails for the locals to use the next winter. I liked that too, even if the mosquitoes in central Nova Scotia are vicious enough to drive you mad. They'd spray us down with some lemony-smelling skin stripper and push us out into the forest. We'd never complain, even when John, B-boy and the rest of the guards stayed inside the centre's truck to avoid the swarming little beasts.

Mostly, though, our education was pretty lame. It wasn't really the fault of the teachers. I had to try hard not to let on that I was brighter than most. Shit, all the other kids would have had me pegged as some creepy outsider, a complete psychopath. As long as I was just a dumb fuck-up, then we all got along just fine. After all, what kind of loser goes to jail when fortune and fame are there for the taking through legitimate means? Or at the very least, why would anyone who is book smart let himself get caught? Being smart would have ruined my time inside.

So I farted around. Messed up assignments. Did just enough to get by. I had no reason then to think that school would play a bigger part in my life.

Skunk-lady, I think, knew the truth. She kept trying to show me some attention. But what she never got was that it was her, not the counselling, which was the problem. She was sure she could help, but as I'd read her, she was a gas pedal stuck. After that first session, she talked more than she listened. She had a theory about everything, which included me.

"We talked to your mother today," she told me weeks after I'd been diagnosed. The label depressed was sticking now that she'd written it. Skunk-lady told me, "Your mother would like to visit but says she can't get a ride." I was sitting on the brown weave couch in her office. My eyes drifting around the room. Someone had decorated to make the space look almost homey. There were curtains with tassels strung over a wooden rod. There was a television too. Sometimes you got to watch it alone if you were doing real well and Skunk-lady was away for the day. You could control the flicker. Surf. Lie on the green carpet that smells of deodorizer. Be alone without it being a punishment.

"We were wondering if that was part of the problem? Maybe, like when you're feeling sad, depressed, you're thinking about her?" She accentuated the word depressed, making sure she let me know just how much she understood how I felt. "Maybe you really want to see her."

I was listening. I had no choice. There wasn't a lot to distract me. I could hear the drone of her words from as far away as I could keep myself. If I sat up straight I could see out the window into the courtyard and watch the other residents moving between buildings. The windows in Skunk-lady's office were tinted grey from the outside. I knew I could see out, but no one could see in. There was a whole unit of kids out there, plodding along as slowly as they could towards the dining hall, kicking tiny pebbles from the paved walkway worn smooth by their shoes. It was a blustery spring day, another Tuesday, with a wind strong enough to come over the fifteen-foot walls and billow their light coats that hung open around their shoulders. I could tell they were hesitant to come back indoors, tacos or no tacos. On the far side of the track John was walking sturdily into the wind with Michael, another resident, at his side. I could see Michael leaning a little forward, straining to listen to John, the worker's big strides difficult to match. John was Michael's Primary too. I stared. Envious of his being out there rather than in here. My diverted eyes gave me only a weak moment of freedom from Skunk-lady's expectant gaze. A few breaths later, I relaxed and slumped down on the couch. Skunk-lady waited for my answer but I gave her none.

"Is it," she stuttered, then bit her bottom lip, "... because she doesn't give you enough attention? Is that it?" Under the fluorescent lighting I could see her eyes glistening. I felt like celluloid, a chick flick gushing towards a teary ending. I pitied Skunk-lady. Pitied her for being so ineffective. If Skunk-lady had lived what I lived, she'd have known better than to try so hard. She'd have felt awkward in how naked she'd made herself. She'd see how much a part of her own story she'd made me, the one about detachment, loneliness and dependency, and whatever other big words she'd learned at school.

"Wouldn't it be nice to have someone show you how much they love you?" she prodded again while I sat there wishing she'd give it up. I looked around her office to avoid looking at her. There wasn't much to see. Behind her desk there was a poster about sexually transmitted diseases with a picture of a mechanic holding a big wrench at his waist with the advice "Handle With Care." There was a wooden toy on her desk, a do-nothing they call them. You turn the handle and two pistons move in opposite directions. A way to waste time, or channel nervous energy, I guess. I wasn't sure if it was there for us residents to use or her. There was also a picture of two dogs in a plastic five-by-seven frame. A black weiner dog and a chocolate Lab were posed against a pastel pink and blue background. The picture looked like it was taken at a Sears studio. I wondered how many she'd bought? Was there a large eleven-by-fourteen over her bed? My attention shifted as she tapped her fingers on her pad of paper and checked her watch.

I told her, "Um, no," squeezing in a bit of sarcasm with each syllable. I thought the sarcasm made me sound more confident. It was a slippery slope there. Say too much and I'd convince her she was right. Say too little and she'd think I was an emotional wreck, overcome with longing for attention.

Her questions convinced me she hadn't seen my file either. Done her homework. Hadn't spoken to the child protection worker who took me into custody for a second time when I turned nine. My worker at the Spryfield Child Protection Office would have had all the dirt on my family. She was a large buxom woman. I have no memory of her face, though I sometimes think I remember her voice, but not really. I just remember her tone. She spoke sweetly to my brother and me. She spoke to us like we were important to her even though I never understood why. And she asked for a picture of each of us. So she could remember our names. She had this old Polaroid camera. She took two pictures. Kept one and gave the other to us to put in the small photo albums she'd bought. "Your lives are stories," she said. "Everything about you is worth remembering." My mother threw the albums in the garbage when we came home.

She was always angry at our worker. Stevie and I never understood why. We came back home when my mother got better and they let her out of the institution. It's not like anyone wanted to keep us. But none of that mattered. My mother didn't like our worker and that was enough to make it wrong for us to ever say anything nice about her either.

I was beginning to see why my mother didn't like anyone snooping in her life. I liked that Skunk-lady and my worker hadn't spoken. Liked the freedom it gave me to maneuver for a while longer. I could make up my life as I went along. I could play any part I wanted in this little soap opera that I'd been placed into by the courts. I knew my file would eventually be shared. It always was. I imagined my old worker rooting in dark dungeons of moulding paper, looking for me. I couldn't imagine being remembered except in text.

Skunk-lady wasn't sure what to say next. The best she could come up with after a long sterile pause was, "Are you sure? Sure you don't want your mother to tell you how much she loves you?" I waited while Skunk-lady made another note on the pad of paper on her knees. She used a cheap plastic ballpoint with something engraved in black on the white shaft. Seeing her writing about me like that swelled my anger. I had no more pity left for her and vowed to sit stoic. I wouldn't say another word that day or maybe ever. Why couldn't she see she was drowning under her own theories? Maybe she was in some state of euphoria like the one I hear you reach when you're suffocating. Just before you pass out for good. Drowning is supposed to be orgasmic.

I suppose that gives some comfort to people who have to think about someone they love dying. I dream a lot about drowning.

That's where we ended that day. There was nothing more to say and outside Michael was now waiting his turn to come in and be probed. I knew I'd return to my unit and joke with Jeremy about what Skunk-lady had said. Tell him everything. Skunk-lady was lucky it was me she was messing with and not Jeremy. Jeremy wasn't like me. He liked hurting people.

seven

I MET JEREMY A MONTH AFTER I was in custody for the first time. I
wandered on to the unit one morning, toothbrush in hand, and there
he was, impossible to miss. He was gobbling a large breakfast of eggs
and toast. A pile of five slices was stacked next to him, with one slice
already in his mouth. I could see he made B-boy nervous. But then
B-boy wouldn't much like having to look up at a child who stood a
fleshy six-foot-two, weighing in at well over two hundred pounds. A
bigger out-of-control baby than the rest of us combined.

No doubts about it, Jeremy could be one mean kid when he
wanted to be. Normally I'd have written him off as an overgrown
clown. But I'd heard from Peter who'd been on our unit a lot longer
than me and who knew Jeremy on the outside that Jeremy was loy-
al. And, as my father would have said, dumb as a bag of hammers.
He was in jail because he'd been running drugs for his older brother.
When the police caught him he refused to rat.

Looking at Jeremy, I figured he knew he was never going to be
the quarterback in the game of life. Not that Jeremy couldn't make
his own mayhem. On a night shift three weeks after he got there, he
had his fun with B-boy. We went to bed dutifully at 10:00 p.m. But

57

on shift that night was B-boy, who Jeremy liked to torment, and a lady we called Whodunit because she was well along in her pregnancy and didn't wear any rings. She wouldn't tell us anything about her life outside either. She always seemed nervous when we asked her about her pregnancy.

That night Jeremy was in a foul mood over being denied his phone privilege. He was supposed to call home. He'd even set it up to have his girlfriend at his parents and to have his mom pass her the phone. Normally he wasn't allowed to speak with her. She was on probation and there was no contact allowed between residents and kids who were in trouble with the law. That always struck me as odd given that we were housed with some of the worst delinquents I'd ever met.

Jeremy had lost his phone privilege because he'd made a rude comment to one of the female staff during the day shift. We'd been watching TV and a Playtex ad had come on and he'd made a show of sniffing the air and looked right at her, like he was smelling to see if she was on the rag. Then the staff went all ballistic about him being rude and inappropriate. That was the word they always used. As if fifteen-year-old boys are supposed to be appropriate.

He was called away from the television and sent to his room. Locked down for the night, the foot-long magnetic lock on the inside edge of his door snapping solid wood to metal door frame. That dry clunk signalling imprisonment pissed him off enough to make him tear his bedding to shreds. But they'd left him in there. Kept shouting through his door to calm down. He'd finally calmed down enough to have some food brought to him. But it was all an act. He was just biding his time.

When it was 10:15 and all quiet he did what was rumoured could be done. He threw all his two hundred-plus pounds at his door. With complete disregard for the shoulder which he badly bruised, he made the door fly open with a loud *Whump!* It snapped around and tore the doorstop on the floor from its mooring. When I heard the sound, I rushed to the narrow window next to my cell door and looked out onto the unit common.

There was Jeremy, just standing by his door. B-boy was the first to get close to him, coming out from the office where he'd been sitting like he did every night. I could see through my window the way B-boy took a few steps forward, then thought better and turned around to reach for his radio, which was still back on his desk. I have to say, Jeremy looked as surprised as the staff. But he smiled and then started calling out, "Whoa, ho! Fuckin' free! Yeah!" and just kept taunting B-boy and Whodunit to just try and put him back in his room. While B-boy was calling for backup, Jeremy just sauntered around the unit. He even turned on the television. That's when Whodunit thought she could reason with him. It was a fair bet. She looked sort of vulnerable with her swelling belly. Jeremy didn't have that violent a history and was in on drug charges. Except, now that he had his audience, that made things different. She came out of the office and looked him straight in the face, or at least up into his face, which was the best she could do considering she was just a tad over five feet tall. She told him how his behaviour was "Not helpful." As if he cared. It was some paradoxical shit she was trying. Her language kept getting words out that had a positive ring, but she was really telling him what he should do. It was like watching *What's My Line*, one actor's improv trying to outdo another.

"We all care about you, Jeremy," she said, "and we don't want to see you in more trouble. Things were just getting better for you, weren't they? If you Go Back To Your Room Now! then we can get past this quicker. That's What You Want! isn't it? You really have to go back. There is nowhere to go. You Know That! Right?"

But Jeremy was already where he wanted to be. And he knew it. He went right over to Whodunit and grabbed her arm before she even knew what was happening and dragged her into his room. She was so surprised and afraid, she barely resisted, just said to him, "Stop!" real lame like. But of course he didn't. It all happened so quick. Then with her on his bed cowering, Jeremy came back out and grabbed his door and shut it with a loud *thud*. Well, that set everybody going. There was thumping on windows and catcalls from all the residents.

Funny, but Jeremy never did say much about what happened in that room. B-boy finally got it together enough to figure he'd better rescue the lady. He went over to the door but didn't have it in him to open it. He just stood there fidgeting. He didn't even say anything, maybe afraid he'd make matters worse. Jeremy had pulled his curtain so for what seemed like a very long time, he was completely in control.

And then the cavalry arrived. First two other guards with cuffs, and then two more with full padded body suits, shields and mace. They were followed a few minutes later by three police who had everything but their guns on. And they all stood there waiting to do something. And that's when Jeremy decided to come out. He simply walked out. Gave himself up. He wasn't as stupid as I thought. It was a great manuever. He'd won. They couldn't thump him. No way they could hurt him and argue it was self-defence.

Up to then, I hadn't thought him that clever.

They still put him down on the ground, cuffed him and then six of them carried him down to a holding cell in the main building. Then out came Miss Whodunit, escorted from the cell with a blanket around her and a paramedic at either side. She looked scared, and both her hands were cradled over her baby. But her clothes were all on. I remember thinking how sick it would have been if he'd done anything dirty to her.

After that, Jeremy got to see Skunk-lady as well. She seemed to have less time for me now that she had a new kid to measure and probe. Jeremy loved the attention. "You're nothing but fuckin' jealous that I'm more fucked up than you," he liked to tell me. Then he'd chant, "I'm more fucked up than you, I'm more fucked up than you," in a girly sing-song kind of voice. I ignored him or at least made like I did. Mostly, I liked having someone I could compare notes with about Skunk-lady.

"She doesn't smell too good, does she?" I said to Jeremy one day as we played euchre out of earshot of the guards.

"All the fuckers who work here are losers," he told me.

"That new one, she looks like she just got out of school." I was talking about a student on some sort of training program at her university. She worked our unit two days a week. "She could be my older sister," I said. Jeremy meanwhile started to lay down a card, but pulled it back. Too late, I'd already seen what he was holding. "Never have seen Whodunit back on the unit," I said. "Not likely to, are we?" I looked at Jeremy, but he was concentrating hard on his cards. He led with a low heart. Trump is diamonds so I knew he had squat.

"Miss her?" Jeremy taunted, then he smiled and told me the story of what happened one more time. He was so into it that he barely noticed when I laid down the diamond ace. "She was so surprised when I grabbed her." He laughed. He always laughed when he told that part of the story. "Skunky wants to know all about it. Must be the way she gets her jollies. Sometimes don't it feel like we're these zoo animals? I'm not complaining. As long as I get to be the fuckin' king lion."

"Yeah, right." I gave him an eye roll.

"Yes, way. I can be king. A fuckin' Lion King."

"In your dreams, loser." I laid down trump and played out, taking the hand. "Maybe a knight in shining armour, but a king needs brains."

He didn't answer back after that. Just took the abuse. Then said, "Let's see what's on TV. It's nearly dinner and I'm fuckin' starvin'," and he got up and lumbered across the room.

I stayed where I was for a few more minutes. It was better if it didn't look like I was following him. When he looked back at me from his seat in front of the television, I ignored him, picked up a magazine from the shelf next to me and read about some kid with ADHD who'd become this superathlete. Makes something of himself. My mother would like that story. About a kid who succeeds. If that was her son I know she'd feel proud, cling to him to make herself look good. That's just how she thinks.

When I next looked up, Jeremy and the others were ignoring me, zoned out, not laughing or smiling or anything. I could hear the laugh track from the show they were watching begging them to follow. But it was like they were watching nothing. So calm, you'd have mistaken them for dead.

eight

MY MOTHER TELLS ME as I dress for school, "A boy like you can make it." It all sounds so Hallmark, but really, I know she's pissed at me for what I did at school. When I roll my eyes at her, she yells, "Listen to me!" half hysterical, half in tears. It's not her yelling that startles me, but the tears. "I know what I'm talking about," she says, crying. "I didn't get a lot of education. Your father didn't either."

With the mention of my father her tears begin to flow in earnest. "Hell," I think, "'none of this is really about me, is it?'" It's all about doing right by him. Proving that she's a good mother, maybe even a good wife. Making up for not knowing my father was exhausted.

She cries a bit longer, weak sobs that streak her round face, then she blows her nose on a tissue she pulls from her bra, and barks, "Get yourself ready for school and don't forget your homework and be sure to comb your hair. You understand?" She shoves at me the reader I left beside the television unopened. Tells me to put it in my backpack. "Get!" she says and goes to kick me from behind. I leave the room, narrowly avoiding a bruise.

She says all this the day I return to school after a three-day suspension from grade four. I was sent home after slamming Tina

Sposcek's face into a window. It had been three months since my father died. The lupins had just begun to push their way up out behind our house. At school, we were allowed to open the windows and let in the fresh spring air. It was still only ten degrees most days, but no one wore a coat or boots. Grade six girls appeared outside in t-shirts that were just a bit too tight over their new training bras. Slushy piles of snow remained piled in the corners by the doors to the school, black with the sand the janitor spread to control the ice that two weeks before glazed our schoolyard.

Tina stood a head taller than me and loved to tease me about being short. "You're just a wee little mommy's boy," she'd sing and then strike a chesty pose just like she'd seen the grade six girls do at recess. Only she was still flat as a chalkboard. But the way she teased me would get her girlfriends giggling. I wasn't too good yet at fighting back, which is probably why I did something so stupid. Tina was just standing there, looking out at the playground through the classroom window. I had come up next to her and was looking at her pretty face reflected in the glass. I didn't plan to do it. But on an impulse, I reached up and grabbed her hair and threw her nose-first right into the window. So quick, she hadn't expected it. There was this low fragile *bump* when she hit and then the next thing she's on the floor crying, "Miss, Miss! Joey ..." *sniffle*, "Joey just ..." *sniffle*, "hit me with the window." Yeah, I thought, like if you are going to make up stories at least make them sound real. How could I hit you with the window? That makes no sense. No teacher was ever going to believe that.

"I was just trying to look out the window too, Miss. Tina is lying." But Miss had had enough of me all year and I'm sure was looking for an excuse to get me out of her class.

"You go to the office right this minute, young man," she said, obviously flustered. She came over and pointed a finger at the door, then bent down and cooed at Tina who was still sitting there in a lump sobbing with her hand covering her nose. Hell, it wasn't even bleeding.

I arrive home with a pink note in my jacket pocket telling my mother I'm suspended. My mother looks at it, then grabs me by the hair like she's done before and gives me a good kick in the ass before she drags me upstairs and throws me into my room. Stay there, she says and then huffs her way back down to the kitchen. As I cower on the floor beside my bed, I want her to have a heart attack or a seizure or something from the stress. "Fuck," I say to myself, though I know I'm not supposed to swear, "she never even asked why I did it."

My teachers say I'm precocious. And impulsive. They say that's a bad combination for a kid without a father. I've heard them say that between themselves, when I'm in the principal's office being accused of manipulating kids out of their lunch money. Not stealing it, just making them want to give it to me. Helping them see that if they do, I'll let them play with the slingshot I promise to bring to school the next day, but of course don't bring because I don't really have one. I don't think my mother would know what precocious or impulsive means. Not that the school ever tells her what they think.

Maybe it's all the hair-pulling and slaps, but I just can't see why she had kids. Maybe it was my father's idea. I guess they wanted to make like they loved us. They must have had moments just before Christmas, or maybe around our birthdays, when they liked having a family. I wonder if they ever thought we were something shiny and clean, something you'd be proud to show off like a new car. If they had memories of our childish hugs and other things like that then we never heard about them. I was left to dream up my own stories about hugs, hugs given so strong that my father's arms locked around me in an embrace that wouldn't loosen even when he stood up. I longed for stories like that, about love tangy as wine. As bubbly as a beer cold from the fridge. A child on my father's knee who brings with him a feeling as smooth as a third shot of whisky, the *ahhh* I used to hear my father exhale.

But those are the stories I made up, not the ones I heard.

Mostly I knew about my parents' longing to be somewhere besides where they were. With us kids. They talked lots about the money they'd have had if they didn't have us. They'd talk about the car they'd own if it wasn't for us kids eating away every nickel my father brought home. "Not some crappy van," he liked to say. "That's for sure. God, I hate that fuckin' van," he'd repeat over and over again. He hated the sticky remains of peanut butter sandwiches, the mouldy smell of wet upholstery kept that way by wet bums encrusted in snow all winter long. He hated the endless repairs he had to do keep the thing running and all its dents from the careless way Stevie and I dragged groceries in and out. This was no commercial with the happy well-polished family loading up to go play hockey. We lived in the shadows of those picture-perfect images. We were the used-car lot. The tenth rerun.

As the oldest, I made feeble attempts to cover Stevie's ears when my dad spoke like that. I'd bend down with him on the couch, and try to make us both as small as possible. Stevie would bend down with me, but I'm not sure he really understood why I bothered trying to make us invisible. Stevie never said much his whole time growing up. He was all eyes. Just eyes, big brown orbs that floated above the back of the couch staring into the dining room and out beyond the patio door to the forest beyond. Eyes at night that remained open in the dark when there was arguing in my parents' room, and then a rhythmic knocking against the wall. Like our hamster on its wobbly wheel. A steady whirling clunk.

Stevie just never seemed to need to say anything, at home or at school. Sometimes, even as I would put my head close to his and whisper important things, I'd envy him the place he'd go with his thoughts. If he had thoughts. It was weird, but you could never startle Stevie. He could hear just fine if I said there were cookies in the cupboard over the stove, hiding. But I could jump out from the closet in our room and growl and he'd just look at me, then hold his Action Man by its arms again and go on pretending he was flying.

At least the van and the rest of our problems gave my father lots of excuses to swear. I think he loved to cuss, only my mother wouldn't let him say anything that would show disrespect to religious people. I grew up with him always going on about "JesusMaryan'Joseph," slurred together so fast that I never heard it quite right. I knew who Jesus was and I'd heard about Joseph, but who the heck was Mary-Anne? I knew better than to ask, not sure if I'd get a swat or, if it was a good day and he'd had his beer, maybe a slap on the back. Or he'd tweak my cheek, leaving a hot hickey that I'd rub to make feel better. Any cuss that was not religious, though, was fair game. Mom couldn't care less, and, come to think of it, could even keep pace with him in the "Fuck this, fuck that" department. It got a little confusing at times, because

Dad would mean to say "Fuck," I think, but then feel guilty for swearing in front of us kids and instead change to religious language. Only when Mom was at hand, he'd be stuck there too. So he'd have to say things like, "Jesus Murphy!" By the time my brother and I were old enough to begin beating up the bullies who beat us up, we were also street smart enough to know that my father had really meant to say "Jesus fuckin' Christ!" or something like that. Only, by then he was dead. I guess I'll just have to remember him more for what he said than what he meant to say.

I'm sure my father had a lot more to tell me but I wasn't old enough to hear it. What I did hear was that he deserved better than all the bad luck he'd had. He'd tell us, "I was the sharpest nail in the bag growing up." And then he'd shake his head. "Now look at me."

He wasn't like that all the time. If he had money left over after paying the mortgage and an unopened two-four in the basement, he'd seduce us with his bravado. "When I snap my fingers," he was proud of boasting, "there's a chicken on the table. I want a pop, I just snap my fingers and your mother gets it for me. That's what it means to be a man. You two understand?" Stevie and I would nod, only I could tell Stevie was distracted by something in the backyard, a bird or the sound of a chainsaw in the distance. We could both see out behind the house when we looked at my father, whose favourite chair was placed between the living room and the rear patio door. Stevie knew enough to nod at anything my father said.

"But you also have to be nice." We nodded again. "You have to be ready to give, sometimes more than you think you'd ever give," my father told us, his words sour with drink.

My mother hovered out of sight when he'd rant like this. I could hear the water running in the kitchen sink and the fridge open and close. Then my father would take another drink. He never guzzled like some fathers. He drank slow and steady. He'd have fit in well at any Irish pub in Halifax, only he wasn't Irish, he was half-Jewish.

"Your mother never goes without shoes now, does she?" he liked to tell us, insisting we nod again. If we didn't he'd cup our chins and make us look him in the eye and agree. Then he'd point at my mother's feet as she brought him another beer, being sure to take the empty from where he'd left it on the floor.

"I'd do anything for your mother." He'd look right at her when he said things like that. His stare frightened me. His mouth snarled and threatened, but his eyes were open so wide I thought he had a question for her. Only there was no question, just more rant. "That's what we men do. Protect ... You boys understanding me?" To be honest, I didn't really know what he meant. My mother wasn't in any danger so why did he need to protect her? I never interrupted him with a question, though. Not when he was drunk.

"I fuckin' get her new boots whenever she needs them, don't I?" my father yelled when we remained mute. I never knew whether my mother agreed with him or not because by the time he'd said what he had to say she'd have retreated to the kitchen again. "I let her go to the Sears Outlet any time we have the money." He'd paused to belch, the stench of undigested beer floating over us boys. "Fuckin' hell, nobody should have to walk about with cold feet, now should they? You boys remember that, when you got a wife, you got responsibilities." His words slurred together, a stream of adult nonsense to our ears.

You'd never really know my dad was half-Jewish by looking at him. Or hearing him speak. Though on Christmas Eve he wouldn't show up till late. When I was real small I thought he was hiding from Santa because his father was Jewish. As I got older I realized he just never really cared much for the holiday. He used to say he was part of the Chosen People and that made Stevie and me Chosen People too. I'd asked him, "Chosen for what?" and he'd slap me hard on the back, and tell me, "God has chosen you as one of the lucky few who gets to have his weenie half chopped off and would happily give you a free ticket to the gas chambers. That's what Chosen means." I didn't really understand what he meant. I didn't know weenies could look different. That I was different.

That was just like my dad. He was good at hiding when he had to. Never told anyone about his being Jewish if he could avoid it. Nor about his criminal record. Odd, but despite all his manly shit, he never gave us kids his last name either. Mom said later it was so that when *They* came for us we'd be more invisible. As I walked with my parents on the downtown streets, I would wonder which of my neighbours was Them. Which was going to take us away? I knew we'd been taken from my parents once. By social workers. But that was a long time ago and they gave us back so I figured They, whoever They were, couldn't be all that bad.

Just in case, though, I did like my dad and worked hard to fit in. It wasn't really that difficult. Where we lived, pretty much everyone looked the same except the Tangs from Vietnam and they were okay, my father said, because they'd experienced "hardship" just like us. And the Lebanese family who lived at the corner by the highway in the house with the two round pillars framing their front door, we still thought they were White, even if they all had hair that was blacker than anyone else's. You'd even have been hard-pressed to know who was on government assistance and who wasn't. We kids all came to school dressed much the same. We all wore at least one piece of Gap clothing, though in our case my mother fished our T's from the bin at Frenchy's. Only the really rich kids at school bought theirs new and had one for each day.

None of them lived in our subdivision.

If we were short on money, we made do with ingenuity. And our own laws. Like bars to go drinking in. There were none close by. Just bootleggers, which were just as good. Friendly community pubs, completely illegal, that most everyone, even the police, seemed to ignore. Maybe that's because the bootleggers like the Hornes proved themselves to be good citizens. They even sponsored the local baseball team. Horne's Aces we were called, though our rivals would call us "Horny Arses," which doesn't make a lot of sense if you think about it. Not that anybody did. Mostly, we'd just threaten to beat up the kids from white-bread communities who said that to our face.

Nobody said anything about where the Hornes got their money, of course. They paid their fines pleasantly enough when ticketed. My father said the Hornes took it as their way of paying their community improvement tax. He was proud of saying we all knew how to get along. That was my father's way. To shut up and get along.

I preferred to fight back. I never accepted that I had to stay put on the crescent where my father had built the house we lived in until his death. I loved to ride my bike down the edge of the highway to the winding streets of the planned subdivisions closer to the city with their snaking paths and sidewalk-lined streets. Though we all went to school together, I knew this was where the better-off kids lived, the ones who teased me about having to pump my water from a well or use a shithouse, none of which was true. I'd push hard on the pedals of my used Supercycle five-speed, with the rusty chain and corroded handlebars. I may not have had the chrome those kids had but I knew my legs were stronger than theirs. I'd ride by their garbage cans, placed just so beside curbs, and knock them over one by one. Or yell at boys my age that they smelled like horse piss. Sometimes they'd jump on their bikes and tear off after me, but they were never allowed to go through the intersections with traffic lights. I was. I'd race across on a yellow light, or if they were really close, even on a red. Nothing but a quick glance right and left.

The one time a car clipped me the driver got out and was so angry I thought he was going to explode. Like a firecracker. I told him to go fuck himself and picked up my bike with the bent pedal, straightened my handlebars real quick and took off towards home while the two dorky kids who'd been chasing me just stood there on the other side of the street with their jaws dropped. I had a bloodied elbow and knee, but didn't care. I just popped up on my pedals and showed them all my ass and went home where I lied to my mother about falling off coming over a sidewalk. "Go wash yourself up," was all she said. Then added, "You'd better take a bath." I argued it was too early for a whole bath, but she just glared at me and pointed in the direction of the tub. I was only eight and too young to keep fighting. She'd have just slapped me if I did.

I was all stripped down and dipping a toe in the hot water when she walked in and went for a pee. Her white panties down around her knees. And while she's peeing she tells me to stand in front of her. And I'm all cold now that I'm naked, but she makes me stay right there while she examines the cut on my knee, then gives my weenie a little pull. "You little pisser," she says. Then she holds me against her, cradling my head on her shoulder while she's still sitting on the toilet. Then she pushes me away and takes my penis in her hand again, turns it up and down. "Stand still," she says when I start squirming. Her voice is matter-of-fact, like the doctor when she puts the cold stethoscope on my back. My mother is staring so hard I think something must be wrong. Then she stands up and I can see the double folds of fat beneath her blouse where her waist disappears into her legs. And then she turns me, hits me sharply on the bum and tells me to get in the bath.

"It's still too hot," I tell her.

She pulls up her panties and pants, then trawls a hand through the water, using it as an excuse to wash her hands with the bar of Ivory in the soap dish on the edge of the tub. "That's not too hot. Now get in there," she says.

And so I put myself into the steaming water and feel the red scald of my flesh as my calves ache. I'm always anxious about getting into baths. Baths aren't safe. You could drown. I remember the first foster mother I had telling me that. And she looked so sad when she said it, she made me think drowning was what happened to just about everybody when they took a bath. For some reason, some dark thought told me to be careful. That you can get into bathwater and never come out again.

Maybe that's why when we were placed back home I'd scream and fuss about having to take a bath. But no matter how much I resisted, I'd be made to stand in the water as it got colder and colder. I'd refuse to sit down and wash my hair and my mother would get so frustrated she'd say, "Fine, stay in there till you do." And stubbornly, I would, until I got so cold and bored I'd lie down quick and dunk my head back, ears plugged with my fingers, and shake my head twice side to side, then put the smallest trace of shampoo into my little hand and soap myself up. Then rinse, and race from the tub into the wet clammy towel my mother had left me because she'd used it to wipe the floor after Stevie's bath.

But that day, the day I had my bike accident and lied, the bath is extra dangerous and hot. I crouch very slowly, letting my buttocks grace the top of the water, making like I'm sitting down but not really. My penis dips below the surface and there is a sudden pain but it takes away the feeling of her touch and so I stay like that, burning. Then I slowly lower myself and feel my skin recede from the water, all my little pores opening wide, exposed. Then my mother leaves the bathroom, satisfied I've immersed myself. When I hear the door click shut I get back out of the water and wait. Wait for something to change, all the while dabbing at my still bleeding elbow and knee with the dirty green towel that has been on the rack for days.

Later, when I'm dressed again and Stevie and I are watching a rerun of *Family Ties*, my mom storms into the living room and pulls me off the sofa by my hair and drags me back to the bathroom. Stevie never even takes his eyes off the TV as my mother keeps yelling and I scream, "Get away from me," kicking as she pulls me along. In the bathroom she shows me the towel I'd ruined with my blood. "You stupid kid!" she keeps saying while her grip on my hair tightens and she shoves me towards my room. Then she goes back to the kitchen and clanks the kettle onto the back burner of the stove to make herself a cup of tea while the laundry machine clunks its way through its first cycle and the television drones on.

I liked that at least my parents were honest about everything they hated. Us kids included. Their beatings were never deceitful. I knew that if I woke up and had to squint because my left eye was swollen shut from where my mother had hit me the night before, there would be no sympathy for me that morning. I'd deserved it, they'd say. Deserved it good.

My bed was safe, though. At the end of each day I could always count on being able to pretend I was asleep. That usually got them to leave me alone. I'd pull my blanket up over my head and imagine my stuffed animals and I were gunners in some World War I adventure like I'd seen on television, our weapons ready to shoot anyone who breached our hideout. In the pale light of my room, with my brother asleep in the bunk above me, I'd peek out and think to myself how nice it is to be hidden. And that would make me feel all warm and tingly, like you do after you come in from the cold and drink something hot, or a teacher says your picture is the nicest one in the class.

From under my itchy wool blankets, I could point my finger and fire round after round at intruders. Some mornings, when the heat was still turned down to save oil and no one was yelling at me to get up,

I would rouse myself awake just to play my game. I'd feel like those veterans we heard about who survived time in the trenches. Only they were cold and it was muddy and there were no sheets so it wasn't really right to think it was the same. But that feeling of peering over the edge, of danger being there just beyond my sight, of looking out and seeing my worst nightmare, so close it could make my bladder loosen, that was all the same. I was sure of that.

Though my mother often swiped the palm of her hand across my face during the day, the worst beatings seemed to happen at night. There was something about the dark and the tingling mix of dream with shadow that added more fear to those beatings. I seemed to always have to pee when I woke up and heard my parents fighting or, worse, making up. I never remember Stevie waking. He slept log-like through it all.

Once, I walked in on my parents all naked, my mom on top of my dad right on the living room couch. Dad's beer bottles all over the place, and mom's pair of large grey underwear thrown on the floor. And this big white woman, who I couldn't even imagine as my mother, rocking back and forth on my dad who had his eyes closed, at least until I arrived, and Mom, grabbing for some clothes quickly, became my mother and her face went from that smile that adults have for each other to the kind she reserved just for me when she was about to hurt me bad. And I'd have gone back to bed, but I couldn't move and she was coming at me and that's when all the pee I'd been holding, holding for a long time because I didn't want to get up, that pee just couldn't wait. I made a puddle there at the bottom of the stairs on the green carpet because the upstairs bathroom was all clogged with a dump from my brother. The stench had made me not want to go in there. I was headed to the little bathroom in with the laundry machines off the kitchen. But now I'd peed right there in the hallway to the living room, its cooling stink on my bare feet. By the time my mother reached me and grabbed me by the arm so tight I gasped, I was already shielding my face. I knew eight-year-olds shouldn't have accidents. I figured somehow the beating that was coming was the right thing even though I was still scared.

Strange, but she never really hit me that night. Maybe that's why I remember it so well. It doesn't blur into all the other beatings. Instead, she marched me along with her hand squeezing my arm tight, all the while yelling, "You stupid little fucker, can't your father and I have one goddamn moment to ourselves without you horde of pests at us. And now this, THIS!" And she'd given me a bit more of a shake, and I worried my arm was going to rip right out of my shoulder. And then she put her other hand on my back once we were in the kitchen and pushed me into the corner by the sink against the oak cabinets with the busted centre panels that Stevie's ball hockey games had destroyed. Destroyed like most everything else my mom had liked about our house when we first moved in. And while I cowered with my arms over my head once I was on the floor, and pulled my legs in to avoid being kicked, I watched as she grabbed a wet cloth and went down the hallway and got down on her knees to wash out the stain, her housecoat a pink blob bouncing in and out of view as her hips moved back and forth, scrubbing. And I stayed there cold and worried until she came back and threw the stinky cloth at me and told me to put it in the wash, but I was still afraid to move so she kicked me and said, "Go."

"And while you're in there strip off everything you're wearing and then get your ass back up to bed and if I see you again tonight I'll murder you, you hear!"

I did what I was told, running so fast back up the stairs naked after dropping my dirty pyjamas into the washing machine that I all but missed seeing my dad, who was still lying there on the couch naked, smiling.

I shivered my way back into bed and hugged Scamp, my stuffed dog, trying to find my special place under my covers. Only this time I imagined firing the bullets at my father. The stupid idiot. Making my mom all embarrassed like that and without her clothes. I could feel the sharp prick of tears welling, but no tears came from then on. Just anger. And so I peeked out again and imagined my father being crushed by a big German Tiger tank, even if they didn't have tanks like that in WWI, but there was a Tiger tank just the same rolling over him in a trench, his head smushed like a melon, and my mother in tears as she picked up his dead body.

I fell asleep minutes later. I must have because I remember nothing more. I was always good like that. I slept, shut down, used my dreams to sift through my thoughts slowly. Sleep was as good a sanctuary as warm sheets. Even better. Asleep, the only danger was imagining something worse than what I was living and that seemed unlikely.

The next day, everything was back to how it should be. No stain, dry pyjamas folded in the laundry basket. Maybe I had been asleep when I thought I was awake. It was one of those strange thoughts I'd have now and again, out of place for someone my age. Thoughts like that made my head ache with the possibilities. Another day, another dream.

Except my dream was my parents' daily nightmare. I'm sure we embarrassed them. They never came to any school concerts, any parent-teacher interviews. They never saw me play ball. Stevie and I would spend our time walking or biking the streets or sitting on our back steps. We might run down to a vacant lot where the year before I turned five a fire had destroyed a house and left an eight-foot foundation that was bleached white at the top by rain, snow and sun. At the bottom it was a soggy pit black with mud, haunting with the smell of human urine and cat feces. It provided a place to hide and some old piping that had miserably clung to the cracking cement which Stevie and I discovered made a great set of monkey bars.

But mostly we sat doing nothing much at all, having no place to go, and no one to offer us a refuge. We'd sit outside after school even when the weather was nasty, watching the dandelions blow puffs from our lawn onto Mrs. D's manicured "Bit of Heaven" next door. At least that's what my father called it, sarcastic, and angry. "Useless way to waste a Sunday afternoon, if you ask me," he liked to say, boasting that our crabgrass was a sign of a healthy family with time to spend on important things. But he'd still resent Mrs. D's dirty stares whenever she was out pulling weeds and he had to be outside at the same time fixing our van, beer in hand, trying hard to ignore the fact that our front lawn was really just a tangled weedy mess that made us different from our neighbours in a bad way. Dad might mow it, and Mr. Jeffrey's besides, but it still was in bad need of care.

I never remember him spraying anything on it like Mrs. D. "I get enough of that toxic shit every day I work indoors," he'd tell anyone who'd listen, like Mr. Tang who'd come to get his Impala each time my father fixed it. Mr. Tang would politely chat with my father for a few minutes before slipping him a brown hundred dollar bill. My father always offered him a beer but Mr. Tang just smiled and bowed slightly like you'd expect him to and said, "No thank you." Then my father would go back to work on our van, coming in only after he'd got it working again.

When we heard the engine roar, we'd wait tensely for him to enter and find his chair. And he'd sit down dirty, thumbing his money, and let rip about how we should never have built here. "Nothing but a bunch of uptight shits for neighbours," he'd say. He loved to criticize, loved to play up the part of the curmudgeon. Even if he'd been well fed and there was nothing to complain about, he'd still walk through the kitchen where my mother was hard at the dishes and take a toothpick from the green ceramic frog we kept on the counter next to the Cocoa Puffs and Raisin Bran. He'd poke at his teeth and make like he was sucking back spit from between pursed lips. Make himself look fed up.

I guess our dandelions were his idea of revenge. Somehow it seemed right our lawn should be as prolific as my mother, spreading its own unwanted seed across the neighbourhood.

nine

THE BUILDING IN WHICH I WORK is a converted estate home of a shipbuilder from a century before, donated to the county to provide a residence for abandoned and incorrigible girls. Girls like Vivian. It was later handed over to the local Children's Aid Society. Despite its size, it has always made a homey place to live and work. Still makes you feel welcome when you arrive early in the morning and pick the local newspaper from the front stoop that leads up to a wraparound deck. Inside, if you look past the security doors and one-way mirrors there is fine woodwork, ornamental baseboards, wainscotting, staircases with well-worn oak banisters, and window nooks where modern sofa chairs have been placed but nobody ever sits. Our offices are portioned from old dormitories, now converted into noisy thin-walled spaces. In mine, a fireplace has been split in half between two rooms, its brick front cemented shut. On dark winter mornings with their leaden skies, the building is crypt-like in its stillness, the smell of decay floating in the air amid the earthy scent of the green mould that grows between the floorboards. Still, my office feels seductively like what I imagine a home should feel.

Shirley supervises her team from a corner office that has an ocean view overlooking the Northwest Arm. It gets the southern exposure and warms nicely during the day. I envy her the sun. Her office is quaintly appointed with mahogany floors and a chandelier of small electric bulbs that creates ambiance around the impressive oak desk Shirley must have wrangled from some past executive director. But it takes several visits to Shirley's office before you even notice her desk, or the pile of children's toys, books and gift-wrapping paper stacked unevenly in the back corner. When you enter, your eyes are instead drawn to a large bulletin board on which she has tacked the pictures of the children she has had under her care and protection during her twenty-eight years of service. A montage of hope. There are other social workers who do the same, but no one at the agency has a board as big as Shirley's. Her three-by-four-foot corkboard is mostly full except for a couple of gaps near the centre where the red bristol board shows its original blood-red pigment. Perfectly square holes missing their pegs.

If you ask her about the rest of the faces that stare at you she will happily explain each child's fate. She will even tell you that in some cases the children are the children of some of the faces already on the board. If you look closely, you see resemblances and hope that's all they share. Shirley tells me, "Mostly people give me the photos voluntarily, but sometimes, if I think the darlings haven't had many pictures taken of them, I'll take a photo myself." The children usually like that. "The ones who send me their photos, well, I guess they think of me as their mother. Their grandmother even. Isn't that sad?"

Though I'm sure she has told this story a hundred times, her voice betrays the pain she feels each time she looks at her gallery of innocent faces. It must have meant something to those children that they'd found someone who actually valued their gift. Saw them as more than the afterthought from rough and hurried sex between inexperienced teens or warring parents. Tainted children right from conception.

The photos only add to Shirley's reputation as our matriarch. She is as full-figured as the other women here but she carries herself differently. Like other seasoned workers who must survive on fast food eaten during late-night calls, Shirley has grown stout, but her work has hardened her. Push her and nothing jiggles. It is like meeting one of

Bodero's sculptures, images of which I still remember from my time in jail. Big-boned bodies without necks. Top-heavy two-dimensional figures. One could never think of Shirley as anything but strong. Held together by a centrifugal force that spins her tight. Maybe her size is only a measure of others' problems, her mass leftovers from their groping handholds.

I tell Shirley all about Joan and Vivian. About what I am proposing to do. She nods and tells me to go ahead with my plan. For a moment, it feels like she is proud of me, not just in the way of a supervisor, but in the way a mother is proud of her children's independence. The feeling makes my skin flush. I feel suddenly more capable than I thought myself to be.

ten

THE FIRST CHRISTMAS I SPENT away from home was the first spent in jail. The week leading up to the holiday was a pretty calm time on the living units. There was some great food, lots of visitors, even a concert with a Christian rock band. By that point in my sentence any entertainment was appreciated. I could live without the message of how much He loves me, but then, it was electric and loud. And we could scream as much as we wanted.

The numbers were low after that. Several kids on each unit had passes to go home for the holidays. They'd be watched, with workers reassigned to go around in vans and do surprise visits. I'd have gone home but my mother said it would be difficult for her to be there all the time and supervise me. She had a busy schedule of things to do for my brother and she couldn't be changing everyone's schedule just because I'd gotten myself in trouble again. She said she wouldn't be babysitting me all the time now that I was almost an adult. It would be best, she said, if I just stayed in jail for the holidays.

Just as well. At least in kiddie jail people could fake a holiday. At home Christmas and the gifts from the Sally Ann, and the turkey from the Kinsmen, all of it was a thin scab over our poverty. Still, sometimes there'd be something extra nice in one of the gift baskets. Even a candle, with a pretty scent, could leave us with the hint of good memories well into the New Year. Take away the smell of nasty farts, and the mildew of wet socks drying on the rads. One year someone had placed into the basket a Chinese fan. Why in God's name, I don't know, but it was pretty and for some reason since I was the one who opened the box it came in, I insisted it was mine. "Give it to me," my mother said. "You fool, what the hell are you gonna do with that?" I didn't know, but I was ten at the time and there was something about having this pretty thing all to myself, something from far away that smelled different than anything I'd ever smelled. It caught my imagination and I fought to keep it. I couldn't see why my mother would want it either. She'd just set it in some drawer somewhere. I wasn't feeling that generous. I yelled, "It's mine" a dozen times, and she'd slapped me to shut me up. But she'd let me keep it. "You're a stupid boy," she'd said.

In jail there were presents. Donated. The only real ones came from our primary workers who, John said, were allowed by management to bring us something small. At least that was supposed to be the only real gifts we got. That Christmas, besides the gift I was expecting from John, there was another. It was beautifully wrapped with a flouncy red bow and happy Santa paper. If you looked real close you could tell it had been opened and inspected. But whoever had wrapped it must have known that was going to happen because of the way the paper was taped to each half of the box, top and bottom. That way it could be opened and resealed. A second layer of tape just barely hiding the remnants of the first. For a paralyzing moment I thought it might be from my mother. Except she had never shown much interest in fancy wrapping paper. I left it on a shelf in my room and watched it.

John wasn't supposed to be working the first Christmas I was incarcerated, but he came in just the same early Christmas Eve to give me his present. It was a small heavy box wrapped in blue and gold paper. I couldn't imagine his big hands tying the ribbon so it must have been one of his kids, or maybe his wife. He never spoke about his family so I had to guess who he had waiting at home. John put an arm around my shoulder when he handed me the gift. Things were so calm between us that day there was no need for a latex glove. "For the holidays," he said.

"Thanks," I said. "I got another gift too."

He looked like he was trying hard to feign surprise. Put both his hands up in defence. "I don't know anything about that," he said, touched my shoulder again, then left.

I didn't really expect him to stay. Not with his family at home, waiting. I put the box on my shelf in my room next to the other gift, a luxury in itself as we residents weren't usually allowed to have anything in our rooms that might hide contraband. Made it too hard for workers to do their weekly inspections, white gloves, poking and prodding every nook and cranny of our personal space. Maybe it was because I had so little, but these inspections bothered me more than when they did the mandatory strip searches we had to have done every time we came into the facility. At least then there was no pretence whatsoever that they trusted us. We had to stand there naked while we passed them our underwear and they'd take a pencil and poke around in it to be sure we weren't trying to sneak in anything like drugs or pornography. In our underwear! And if they were real hard up to know what to do to amuse themselves, the guards could have us bend over and shine a flashlight up our ass. And if they got worried that maybe something wasn't quite as it should be they could call a doctor and have her poke around just to be sure. Can't blame them, though. If they didn't do all that we'd have become mules for each other, forced to bring back from home visits whatever the biggest kid on the unit wanted. Smokes, drugs, weapons. At least this way the playing field was level. You had to make do with whatever you could find on the inside if you wanted to play bad.

That's why the presents were all the more special. They were something that wasn't supposed to be here, inside. Christmas Eve I waited until everyone was watching *A Charlie Brown Christmas*, then slipped back to my room and held John's present on my lap for a few minutes. I even smelled it first to see if I could guess what it was. There was a card, of course. I opened that first, just like I was supposed to. The front had a bleached picture of a snowfall and children sledding. And there was holly drawn around the edge. It was a big card and inside it was filled with John's loping script.

Dear Joey,

The very best to you this holiday. I know you won't be going home and that you'll be telling everyone it doesn't really matter. But I think it does. I think you'd really prefer to be somewhere where people gave a damn about you. Is it okay to use the word "damn" in a Christmas card? Who knows. Let's live dangerously, right? I just wanted to remind you that you do matter. Remember that. No matter what anyone tells you, you are important and your life can be better than this. You understand? You matter to me. You matter to your mother. Whether you believe that or not.

I won't be working Christmas Eve but I will be thinking of you. And in some ways, I'm sure your mother will be thinking of you too. And if your father was still alive, well, maybe he'd have realized by now how special a son he has. Remember what this season is really about and you'll do just fine. It's about hope. About renewal, you know, things starting over again. That's why the Romans scheduled Christmas around the winter solstice. It's the time of year when the days start getting longer again. When we move towards the light. It's a time for us all to be thinking about what comes next.

You're a great kid. I believe in you. See you in a few days when things are brighter.

John

It wasn't what I expected. Then again, it was exactly what I should have expected from John, who was always trying to get me to see myself the way he saw me. I threw the card into the corner of my room where it lay open on the floor. Then I ripped off the wrapping paper that covered a box from a Proctor Silex Dual Action Steam Iron. Inside, wrapped in white crepe paper were two books. The largest was a thick *Guinness Book of World Records*, the second a book of cheesy stupid kid jokes, the kind my brother might tell if he spoke more. I sat there with both books, balancing them in opposite hands, like the scales of justice, and wondered what John was trying to tell me. That's when I reached down and picked up his card and read it again. It made me want to cry this time, though I wasn't really sure why. I slipped it into my *Guinness Book of World Records*. Then I placed both books under the pillow on my bed.

I reached for my second gift. This time I threw the card aside without reading it. Tossed the gift in the air. It was light. Made no sound. I used my thumbnail to slice the wrapping paper, then slit through the pieces of Scotch tape that held the box top and bottom together. Then separated the two halves. Inside there was a brown fleece hoodie from one of the shops at the mall. It was soft and warm when I buried my hands underneath it and lifted it to my face. I know I must have looked pretty stupid nuzzling it, but it felt so good. Smelled so normal. None of the institutional cleanser scent that hung on everything around me. Still holding it, I opened the card. All it said was, "Thinking of you." And then a big circle with two dots for eyes and a half-crescent mouth. And a Santa hat on top. I turned the card over, but there was no other clue to the sender's identity. I slipped on the hoodie and slid back on my bed, resting myself against the wall. Pulled my legs up and crossed my arms tight across my chest. Tried to stop thinking. About my mother, about being home, and certainly not about my father. Or my future. Or who sent me the hoodie. I just kept stroking the fabric on my arms. And for a moment, it felt fine being safe and in a place where two people remembered me. Even if they weren't family. Even if somehow I knew they expected greater things from me. Even if one was still unknown.

*   *   *

Besides the presents, that first Christmas Eve also brought with it a bad storm. We could see the snow swirling outside the metal grates covering our windows. They wouldn't let us go out and play in it, even though it was Christmas. Instead, we were told we had to change our sleeping arrangements. They didn't quite say why, but it was easy to figure that with half the staff roaming the roads doing home visits and the storm keeping others from coming in at all, they were running short. They told us to bring our mattresses to one of the classrooms built between the housing units. Each classroom had two opposing doors connecting the living units. The staff arranged us in squads of six and kept all the doors open.

But mostly we were alone. Me, Jeremy, a scrawny kid named Pete who always had his hands down the front of his sweats. Michael, from the French community and rumoured to have stolen money from his church. Jack, a hyperactive Indian whose claim to fame was having set fire to piles of white fishermen's lobster traps all because they told Jack's father Indians had no more rights to the lobster than they did. And there was Bryon, just your average stoner who was caught stealing cash and cartons of cigarettes from a corner store to support his habit. But it was Pete who was the bottom feeder. It was his role to play the crazy and keep us all amused.

We were lying there on our mattresses on the floor at midnight on Christmas Eve, none of us feeling like going to sleep even though the lights had gone out an hour ago. The demons of Christmas past muddled themselves together with the insanity of my being inside when everyone else was back with their families and the strange lingering confusion of what John had written. Something about the way we all chattered on told me that even if we all thought we didn't want to go home, we all felt our insides aching just the same. Only, we refused to stop talking long enough to notice. Strange, but whenever I'm hurting and hiding from my thoughts I get all horny. I can't do anything but dream of pulling a girl towards me while she tells me how special I am. And just thinking about that gave me a massive hard-on right there lying on my mattress. And I was thinking that the workers were only coming by every now and then. We could even hear the television blaring on one of the units.

I started off innocent enough, thinking I'd just have a little fun. I said to Pete, who was next to me, loud enough so that everyone else could hear, "Hey, Pete, why you always playing with yourself? I bet you're still a virgin." The others laughed, especially Jeremy, which is because he was still a virgin. And then I said to Pete it must be a real wee little thing if nobody else plays with it for him, and again the guys laughed. But Pete was so stunned, he wasn't getting what I was up to at all. He said back a feeble, "Fuck you," and went on moving his hands up and down his crotch. So I teased him a bit more.

"Well, how about this, how about we have a little contest. You show us your hard-on and each of us will show you his, and we'll see whose got a leg to stand on, so to speak."

And Pete was like, "Yeah right, like you guys are going to do that!"

But I said, "Sure. Hell, I've had worse done to me than being made to show my dick," so I whipped down my pants and there was just enough light coming in through the courtyard windows for everyone to see my boner sticking up, slanted over a little. And just to have some fun, I made it twitch. The guys were all laughing now but we kept it pretty hushed to avoid the guards coming in. Well, Pete saw all the attention I was getting and pulled down his sweats and there was this wee little erection and hardly any pubic hair. But he got up and danced around and made motions with his hips like he's fucking something, then even grabbed his pillow and began pushing into it. And we were all having a good laugh. Even Jack, the cool one, was lying there with a fuckin' erection wiggling in the air and it was like a flotilla of little ships, each with a mast floating on the cold tile floor.

And then I said to Pete to put down his pillow before he gets himself glued to it, and I dared him to pull my rod at the same time I pulled his and we'd see who could get his rocks off quicker. And now he was like checking over his shoulder to see if the guards were around. But they weren't. "Oh, and just to make this more fun," I said, "no catching the come. It has to splat on the floor. See if they can figure out what it is in the morning." Well, that was too much for everyone and we were all laughing now and with that much attention Pete agreed to play the game. Like why the fuck not, anything is better than doing yourself all the time, so we began this circle jerk and the other boys are hooting as I reached for Pete's little pecker and gave a few quick strokes and he sent a squirt of himself onto the floor, and I said, "You win," but held his hand on my dick with a bit of force even though he went to pull away. "Just a little more, Petey," I said, teasing like a girl.

Only then I said a little more menacing, "You agreed, right?" and it was clear that I was not really asking him. And he knew I'd changed the rules of the game. I was making him stay put. I took my time to come, making the most of his little hand job. Made him feel more and more uncomfortable the longer I waited, the more I moaned, "Yeah, like that." And then my come was on the floor too.

The boys were beginning to get a little too rowdy. We were all having a good laugh, except Pete who was right back on his bed and wasn't saying too much. And I was just laughing, loud, which is when one of the temporary guards came in who we don't really know, and he shined a big flashlight all around at us.

"Don't mind you boys talking, but you've got to keep it down, nothing too rowdy, now. You understand?" He walked from mattress to mattress and stepped on the spot where we let our wads fall. He slipped a little and said, "What the? Did someone piss on the floor?" and shined his light down, shaking his head. But he couldn't make heads or tails of what he'd stepped in so finished his inspection and left, his left shoe making a sticky splaaatt sound as he walked away. As he left we all buried our heads in our pillows laughing. "What a fuckin' moron," said Jeremy, real quiet. I didn't say anything more, just lay there in the dark, feeling confused in more ways than I could explain.

eleven

THOUGH I KNEW FROM MY EXPERIENCE as a client the brackish waters of every intervention we were asked to navigate at university, my social work profs never asked me to tell my story. Instead, they acted like high priests. I guess we were supposed to be their supplicants. I didn't mean to, but I grew cynical quick. I'd come there eager to learn how to make a difference, then do one better than my faulty workers. But it felt like I was being taught how to make myself feel a little more clever than my clients. It wasn't what I wanted, though I should never have expected it to be any different. I only wish John had warned me that I'd be roundly disappointed by what I'd find.

As the months went on, it made sense to think of my education like a monastic immersion. The school of social work where I enrolled was in a former Jesuit College that sits on the outskirts of the main university campus. No lush ivy grows up those walls like it does on the stately buildings that surround the campus quad. Instead, the atmosphere where I studied was austere. The only adornment to the square façade is a bronze plaque by the front door celebrating the donation of the building to the university. As I leaned over reading it the day of my first class, a woman in her thirties carrying a briefcase looked at me and laughed. "What it says is crap," she whispered. "Just so you know. The university got the building as part of a settlement with the Catholic Church."

"I didn't know."

She pulled the front door open. "You know those priests caught diddling kids for decades? Yup, most lived right here. I guess those kids are our responsibility now." Then she was gone, swallowed by the stale warm air inside.

In the classroom on the second floor, my classmates and I sat eight deep on plastic chairs with wraparound writing desks. There was no graffiti. We held our pens poised to write down what the professors told us. Professor Liebenitz's briefcase was open on the lectern at the front, her papers strewn on the table next to it. She was the same woman I'd met out front. Without her coat and scarf, I could see she didn't shave her arms, legs or moustache. Her hair was stringy black and unwashed. But her eyes were so big they eclipsed her face. She handed out a syllabus. And an article she wrote in *Critical Social Work*. I read the abstract, about passion, mission and pedagogy. I couldn't understand what it said. The reading list had other articles with titles just like it. "But for today," she said, "we'll begin at the beginning."

"In 1916 Flexner debated whether Social Work was 'important enough' or 'theoretically sound enough' to be given the lofty distinction of 'profession,'" she told us. My classmates and I wrote diligently each fact, though I couldn't see how any of it meant anything to anyone I knew beyond those classroom walls. Not my family, nor the kids I knew from jail, would make much of Flexner and his theory. I doubt this occurred to Dr. Liebenitz, who each time she said "profession" articulated the word very carefully. "What Flexner never considered, however, was whether helping could be a profession at all. We would have to wait many decades until others would challenge us to rethink helping as something to be regulated and codified." She paused long enough for her hands to calmly grip the lectern. "But by that point it was too late," she told us sadly. "We'd made helping an industry. People couldn't feel anything without a professional walking them through some process. Does that seem right to you?" No one answered. We assumed the question was a statement. We captured her words, if not her meaning, in new brightly coloured binders full of crisp loose leaf, all the while avoiding Dr. Liebenitz's gaze.

When I wasn't writing, which was often, I watched the other students more than I watched my professors. I pretended I was an informant for clients yet unnamed. Looking around at the privileged lives next to me, I thought my arrogance justified. Like the reformed alcoholics who came to visit us in jail. Their passion for their message vibrating with the experience of late-night puke fests. Their sweat and destitution storied as penance for the marriages they'd ruined and the children they'd abused. It was now my turn to educate if I could ever get up the nerve. I never did inside those walls of learning.

Instead, I sat mute and listened to months of sterile lectures. Words as devoid of passion as the matronly women who founded social work. Jane Addams and Mary Richmond, their faded lithographs in my text, made me think of nothing but pursed lips. Closed legs. I decided quickly there is nothing sensual about social work. It was without libido.

Only a small group of social work students proved me wrong. Only a handful offered any hope for lust. Those few students slid easily into their seats. They wore jeans and carried backpacks they bought from Mountain Equipment Co-op. Some were close to me in age. These younger ones had tiny tattoos on their lower backs that you could see from behind on days they wore tight tops. They wore their hair mostly shoulder length with hair bands. Their overt demeanour a slow, and yet unrealized, retraction of all things feminine.

There were a few young men like me as well. We were four to be exact. The first day of class, when we were asked to introduce ourselves, a young man with an eyebrow piercing volunteered to go first. "I am here," he said, "to address the oppression of other gay, lesbian, bisexual, transgendered, two-spirited, queer, questioning and intersexed individuals." I slunk down in my seat. I was too shy to ask what two-spirited meant. Or intersexed. When it was my turn, I said my name and where I lived. The lower-class address meant nothing to most of my classmates.

Of the other men, only one looked like me in the least. He had horrible acne and was painfully shy. He withdrew from class before our first papers were due. The other walked with a limp. Like you'd imagine someone who had polio would walk. Or maybe cancer. I never discovered what was under his long black pant legs.

My time in class gave me lots of time to think. It also stirred strange emotions. Memories of injustices, and the fumbling turmoil of displacement. I still felt out of place, though nobody but me would have known that.

It was safer to remain silent. Safer each morning I walked to my classroom passing three chairs that sat outside Dr. Dirk's office. No one ever spoke about those chairs. The halls were strangely quiet in that part of the building, despite the traffic in the parking lot outside. The priests in waiting must have liked that, the insulation of heavy walls, thick glass, carpets to cushion the echo of whoever passed by. The chairs in the hall were for clients seen by Dirk later in the day. Dirk saw only victims of sexual abuse and women who perpetrate abuse. In class he'd tell us all about them. Most afternoons, if you were unlucky enough to still be roaming the halls, you'd see those women Dirk told us about sitting on the chairs, hands crossed, or straightening pleats. You could tell they'd rather be outside smoking. Or maybe even in jail. Instead, they had to sit in the hall, waiting for Dirk. And so they waited. Because courts told them to. Or anxious boyfriends threatened them, fed up with their lovers' dry retorts to sexual advances. I imagined Dirk's office was a place of flashback and pain. Hatred. Men. And lots of Dirk. And kids like me who passed by in the hall on the way to class. I pretended they were invisible. They ignored me as best they could. We were both reluctant participants in the charade.

In class Dirk made like he was friendly. He was short and round and balding. He preferred to speak to us leaning back in his chair, pudgy hands crossed behind his head. Armpits slightly moist, exposed. Everything he talked about came back to sex. He told us, "Each new wave of development in human services has been an influence on the impoverished and marginalized. Each the next assault on the vestiges of relationships that disempower."

"Uh huh," I thought, and wondered why all my professors spoke in this obscure dialect of the learned.

"For example, take the development of the term sexual abuse." Dirk put his arms down, leaned forward across his desk, clasped his hands together. "There was little thought given to the phenomena before 1982."

Phenomena? I promised myself I'd lose this strange language from my vocabulary the moment I had my diploma. Even though I had just arrived, I began counting down the days of my internment. Began to understand this was going to demand of me compromise. I would have to fake these people's ways if I was to go unnoticed. Become bland and moral like them to convince others that my sanguine passion was real when in fact the oppressive push to be perfect at school muted my angrier motives. I sat there and seethed, but said nothing. Instead, I put pen to desk and doodled with zest as Dirk droned on.

Dirk told us, "My colleagues and I were pioneers. But still, we haven't gone far enough. Have we? We've been focussing only on men. What about *women who abuse?*" He relished the phrase. "We know more about the responsiveness of the male penis than about the orgasm patterns of women who become sexually aroused playing the passive victim to their son's suckling. We ignore the vicious way that young men are being systematically arrested in their psychosexual development, arrested by the invasive caresses of their mothers, aunts, babysitters. They are all sexualized in their intentions!"

His words made me feel nauseous. For some reason I wasn't the only one. I could sense pandemonium breaking out among my classmates. There was the scent of disgust mixed with sweat in the room. Dirk again put his arms behind his head. Pushed his chair up onto its two back legs. His plump legs spread, his tiny genitals creasing his blue cotton pants. His belly like a large medicine ball balanced on his knees.

"This is the next great forward thrust of our field," Dirk said. "Though unpopular with those who dress themselves in the guise of political correctness, the sexually stimulated mother will soon become a part of our language." Dirk waited for his words to land. Phallic pinpricks on soft flesh. I heard what he was saying, but was feeling strangely absent from the room. I couldn't hate him for saying what he was saying because somewhere inside a thought formed waiting to be released. If I could be honest, I would have told the blowhard he wasn't all wrong. But I didn't. Chose to dissociate rather than engage.

While I hid, anger continued to seethe around me. It erupted by rules different from those I knew at home. My classmates stopped taking notes. Except the woman sitting next to me. She doodled. Not idly, but with deep blue scratches that made one geometric design after another. She never looked up. Dirk, oblivious to us all, continued unflinching in his demand that we listen and parrot back what he knew. "When I meet a mother who has sexualized her son, who has washed her son's back for years, who has perhaps reached down, down during his teens to inspect his genitals, well, then I understand this woman's longing for a powerful male presence in her life. Can you? Can you understand her as she reaches down and touches him, handles his penis, imagines the thrill of her own penetration?"

The geometrics lady next to me kept making her incisions, each more exact, deeper and defined. She even changed pens to make her work more lethal. She scoured her page with repetitive red lines. I found my own pen unconsciously following her rhythm. My doodles imitating hers until her paper finally ripped where the lines had worn through to the desk below. Her pen nib scraped dully into the desk's lacquered surface. She glanced my way. That's when I looked down and realized my own pen has recorded scratches as deep as hers. It was the first time I felt I belonged there. But when I turned and looked at my classmate again her eyes had shifted. She was ignoring me, talking in whispers with another woman while her pen continued drawing. I was shut out before I could begin to speak.

Dirk rose to his feet and paced the front of the room. My eyes drifted down to below his belt to see if anything betrayed his enthusiasm. There was nothing.

"We have been stuck in our thinking as social workers. Stuck in a model of matronly bliss. We can think of woman as only mother, a being so sexually destitute the Virgin Mary is a whore by comparison."

Beside me, my classmate stopped her assault on her desk. Mumbled, "It's not women we have to fear, you asshole," then simply closed her eyes. Thankfully the clock over Dirk's head had come around to the hour. We all began to shuffle in our seats, pack up our binders and reach for disc players even before he had dismissed us. Then, through the classroom door and into the hallway we filed. At the other end of the hallway was Dirk's office. The chairs were still there. A woman was sitting on one. She wore a dirty ski jacket, years out of date. A pack of cigarettes was in her hand. As we approached her, all thirty of us, she looked down at her feet. Dirk's door was closed, of course. He was still in the classroom. My classmates tried their best to ignore her. Even the woman who sat next to me walked by averting her eyes. But their silence was only a slipcover for their embarrassment. And shame at not having said anything to Dirk. I watched them file down the hallway, letting them all go ahead of me. When it was my turn to pass the woman, I stopped. "Do you need anything?" I asked. It felt comfortable standing a few feet to her left.

"Oh, no thank you. I'm fine," she answered, surprised by my intrusion. Then, realizing my offer may be sincere, she leaned forward and asked me quietly, "Where can I go to smoke?" I told her there was a back door to the building leading onto a small porch that was sheltered from the wind. "That's where the staff go. I can show you." As I led her down the hall and into the stairwell, I could see Dirk leaving the classroom. The woman looked at me. Her cigarette was already in her mouth and her matches pulled from her purse. "He'll wait for you," I told her and quickly snuck her away before Dirk knew what I was doing.

twelve

IN THE SAFETY CELL, there was nothing but time and an eerie quiet to mark its passing. A place of decision. A purgatory of sorts. Just moments after John and the other guards had slid me into my cell, John had pointed a finger at me. He was a little shaky and out of breath. Told me, "Right, now stay there and calm down." His east coast twang was all but hidden under his Caribbean roots. His pointing finger changed to an open hand as he laid his palm gently on the room's heavy door and as lovingly as a parent might close a child's door at night, secured the cell, a metallic click signalling the connection of the four magnetic plates. When the door closed you really knew you were alone. I welcomed the solitude. For a few moments at least I could close my eyes and though a camera twelve feet above me recorded my every movement, I could feel safely alone. Not something I felt at home where a furtive beasty disorder gnawed.

Boundaries disintegrated after my father died. A towel became a breezy replacement for a bathroom door, ripped from its hinges by my mother in one of her rages when Stevie wouldn't let her in to see the mess he'd made after he'd slipped standing by the sink and smashed the mirror with his head. Or at least that's what he said had happened to the nurse and social worker at the Emergency Department where we took him to remove the shards of glass that had embedded in his forehead.

Inside my cell, I was free to stop the performance. There was no need to lie to anyone about anything. I knew John wouldn't be back for at least an hour, maybe two or three. I was tired and it was so peaceful. There were 162 bricks on the wall in front of me, if you counted the half pieces and spacers as full blocks. I didn't feel like counting the other walls right away, but did the quick math in my head, maybe 600, no, 550 if you take away the space I couldn't see behind the cement bed frame.

There was a forgotten smell of urine and the more present smell of feces and disinfectant coming from the corner by the toilet. Since I had no bedding I sat on the concrete slab that stood raised and built in to one side of the room. I preferred the corner, my knees pressed tight to my chest, my breathing as even as when John was there as my metronome. It was so quiet I swear I could hear the thunder of my pulse.

I thought, if I do nothing else this day or the next it won't matter because nobody really needs me to exist. It was a complicated feeling.

I had become committed to being crazy. An outsider here on the inside. I was happy to be something other than those jocks at the shopping mall with their designer labels. Like how hard is it to go to a store and say, "Hey, I want to look like everyone else"? Being crazy meant breaking the mould. It's standing in front of the world and yelling real loud, "I'm fuckin' different than the rest of you!" That was my commitment.

And it was my problem. Right then, in the holding cell with the dimpled paint and the lingering scent of every other fuck-up who'd come before me, I just wasn't ready to make that much commitment. Suicide, playing the fool, showing them all how angry I was ... No way. More effort than I was willing to give at that moment. I was fed up with trying to impress anyone. Even as the crazy kid. Sitting there very quietly, my head dropped onto my knees, I knew I'd already done enough.

Things had started to go badly that morning during math class when I got into an argument with my teacher. They sent me to Skunk-lady in the afternoon to talk about it. She looked happy to see me. She reminded me of the gazelles I'd seen on the Discovery Channel. Staring, mesmerized, unaware how vulnerable they look. A poacher's bullet and *Whomp!* The end.

"So what's been happening?" she asked. Her lips were moist and shiny.

"Not much," I said, slouching lower on the couch.

"Really? You sure?"

"One of my teachers did officially announce she's out to get me," I said. This isn't quite what Skunk-lady expected.

"How, um ... how exactly ... does a teacher officially announce that?" she asked. She measured out each word. I could hear her doubt mixed with the defensiveness of a team player. There was us and them, and I was definitely the "them." Or maybe she hesitated because she could still remember being the geeky kid nobody liked, the one who got picked on because of her glasses and being so skinny and all. And she probably remembered telling some teacher about being bullied and not being believed. Maybe some stupid old woman, an old school crone, in her forties or maybe even older, told her to go back to the playground and be nice. It's comforting thinking I might have something in common with Skunk-lady, this experience of being a victim, even if I have to make it up. ·

"She said she's out to get me. Really." I added a plaintive "Really" because I knew she'd understand it's kidspeak for "Please believe me."

"She said exactly those words?"

"Not to the whole class, but loud enough. Jeremy heard it."

Skunk-lady picked up her pen, stabbed it at her paper. "Maybe you could explain what the teacher said, *exactly*."

"It's kind of painful to talk about. Could I have a glass of water first?" Now that I'd made myself all mushy and vulnerable she was plenty willing to go to the kitchen next to her office where staff take their breaks. She came back with a Styrofoam cup full of water. She handed it to me gently, her tone now lighthearted, sincere.

"There you go." Then she sat back down on the edge of her seat where she perched half on, half off the upholstered armchair.

I took a slurp from the cup. "Well, it all started when I told Miss Simpson I thought my answer to the math question she asked us was right and her answer was wrong."

"What was the question?"

"Well, Miss Simpson was teaching us about lines and how they intersect and make angles and all that. And then she draws this line, on the board, and then asks me how many dimensions it has. And I say three. And she'd smiled right back and explained that no, a line has only one dimension, and I said that the line *she'd drawn* actually had three."

"I'm not sure I understand," Skunk-lady said, blinking, which I was pretty sure meant she really was confused.

"Miss Simpson didn't either." But she'd never even asked me why I thought her line had three dimensions, instead of one. All she did was explain that sometimes you have to listen to your teacher. "Teachers educate because they know something about something," she'd told me. But she should have listened to me. Her line had three dimensions. Skunk-lady was still not following. Only instead of thinking, "Hey, maybe this kid is brilliant or something," which would have been the right thing to think, she looked at me like I was crazy.

"She made the line in chalk," I said, grinning. "A *chalk* line has length and width and thickness."

"Oh, I see," she said, and I sat there thinking for a moment that she really could see the world the way I saw it.

"That's when Miss Simpson started telling us about how when she was in university she had a professor who asked her to do an assignment on her family history, and the professor said her assignment was wrong."

She really emphasized that too, that she was told she was wrong. All because she said her mother had owned their family land, and that her dad did the cooking and cleaning. But the professor had said that couldn't be, and if her mother and father were married, which he told Miss Simpson he was sure they were, then her mother would have sold the land to her father. And so he failed her. He wouldn't let her rewrite her paper or anything. And then she told me, right there in front of everyone, "That's why you have to listen to your teachers. That's how you get along, do you see? I'm trying to help you. But you must listen to me." And I was there with my mouth hanging open, and she just put up her hand, like she was some traffic cop, and that's supposed to be the end of it, except I wasn't going to be called wrong when I knew better, so I explained to Miss Simpson very nicely why her chalk line had three dimensions. A line, I told her, would be where two edges meet. She should have known that. Of course, she didn't like being corrected.

Skunk-lady sat back in her chair, rested her pencil on her pad of paper. Placed a finger beside her nose, massaged the little indent where her glasses sat, then stroked her chin gently with her thumb. It made her look bookish, thoughtful. "She was teaching you how to get through her course. Seems very reasonable, don't you think?"

I shook my head and took a sip of water. My eyes began to mist up, which surprised me at first, then I thought, "What the fuck," and let a tear slide down my cheek. I'd really thought for a moment that Skunk-lady would understand. But she hadn't. She was crazy-glued to this idea that us kids are the ones who are always wrong.

"I'm sure Miss Simpson didn't *mean* to hurt your feelings," she said in her kindly voice.

I leaned forward on the couch and let my head hang low towards the floor. Stared at my sneakers. Realized I needed out of this conversation. There was pain everywhere now, especially across my chest. I sucked back more tears, became stingy with my emotions again. Skunk-lady watched and dutifully made notes on her pad of paper, uncrossed her legs and leaned towards me. I swear she was close to putting a hand on my back or something motherly like that. And that made me real mad. Like who the fuck is she to think that she can all of a sudden presume to be close to me when she hasn't understood anything I'd said? And now she wants this tender moment? A breakthrough moment? Isn't that what they call it on television?

I looked up, right into Skunk-lady's face that was now only a short distance away, and smiled a big dimpled grin. "Do you really think I care what that cow Miss Simpson thinks is right or wrong? Do you really think I care?"

The magic evaporated. Skunk-lady was visibly uncomfortable now, having got caught leaning in close to me. She slid quickly back deep into her seat. Brought her knees together tight. After a pause, said, "Maybe you were out to get her? Maybe a little? Maybe you meant to tease your teacher and that's why she treated you like that."

That's what's different between Skunk-lady and John. John sees me when he speaks, not past me to the boy he wants to see.

"Yup, you're right," I said, fed up. "I'm just a crazy kid out to get my teacher." Skunk-lady puffed up a little like she was convinced we were getting somewhere. At least until I jumped up on an impulse and began flapping my arms like a chicken, bouncing up and down on her couch, shouting, *"Cluck, cluck ... cluck!"*

She tried to stay haughty and calm, but her hand was by the alarm button. "Joey, w-, w-, what are you doing?"

"You're right, Miss," I yelled happy and loud, "I am just a crazy little fuck. Ain't that right?" And I kept clucking and bouncing up and down, up and down until one of the guards heard the noise and came in and grabbed me. I didn't resist. But shook the guard off by pleading, "Wait, wait, I've got something to say." My voice low and menacing, I told Skunk-lady, "You should have believed me." Then I turned and let the guard take me away.

I might have calmed down except that back on the unit, I'd only walked in the door when B-boy told me to phone my mother. She'd finally called, a week after my birthday. Sixteen years old. So? Was I supposed to now have this warm and fuzzy moment with her on the phone? As if *I* owed *her* something.

If I called her she'd go on and on about what she remembered about my birth. About how she and my father were supposed to be go-ing to some movie, were all lined up and the tickets bought. That I'd ruined it by arriving early. The money for the tickets, gone. I think she still expects me to pay her back. Then she'd remind me, "Your father didn't really mind the inconvenience once he saw you were a boy." And like that makes it all better? If I were a girl I'd never let anyone make me feel like nothing. I'd lick my lips moist like you see on commer-cials, push my little titties out, maybe even grind my hips a bit when-ever some guy said something stupid to me. "Oh, what did you say?"

I'd say sweetly. "Something about us girls? Hee, hee, hee." Then I'd knee the jerk in the gonads. Watch him hit the ground. "Oops! Did I do that?" I'd giggle, as I watched the dork writhing on the floor.

That was some father I had.

I wouldn't make the call. B-boy went on and on insisting. I could see he'd read some psychology book because he had this theory of my need for attachment and all. I could read too. I actually liked the psychology texts on the shelves in our classroom. And other books that found their way onto our unit. Books about how *Kids are Worth It!* And I watched *Oprah* after school. I knew what B-boy saw when he looked at me. Trouble was, he wasn't really seeing me either. Just like Skunk-lady, he was seeing the me he had inside his own head. He needed more attachments, not me.

When he failed to convince me nicely, then it became, "You *must* contact your mother. She was nice enough to call and asked that you call her back." All I was thinking was I didn't want to have to pay her back again. The more I thought about it, and I did a lot, the more I figured I'm the one owed something for having been born from that stupid cunt.

"If you won't make the call, then you can go to your room." I said nothing. Just kept sitting on one of the sofa chairs by the television. B-boy wouldn't let it go, though. "We have our responsibilities, mister, and you have a case plan. Both are about you going home and not getting into more trouble. Right? Now isn't that right?"

John wouldn't have been hammering at me like this. He'd have had more respect for what I was feeling. But John was busy in the office. I could see him writing something and making phone calls. I wished John would come out. Do something. I was his goddamn job. Not a bunch of papers. Instead, there were just B-boy and me staring at each other. The other residents were there too, but they were paying no attention to my drama. They were getting their fix of after-school television before it was time for chores and homework. With nothing to distract either of us, B-boy and I were locked in battle. But staring at B-boy was turning my stomach so I decided to go to my room, at least until I got to the door. It's pastel red, like a sunset. I guess the colour is meant to soothe. It didn't work. Standing at the door, I suddenly thought, "No fuckin' way," and I turned around and paced to the other side of the quad, looking at each resident's door as I passed, none offering an escape. There are twelve bedrooms on each unit, plus a kitchen, an office, a laundry, and the mop room where sometimes you can leave hidden notes for each other under the sink. Workers are always having us do the shit work anyway so there's no danger of them finding the notes. I thought of running in there. Grabbing a mop handle. Making myself more dangerous. But I was past acting like a little kid. They'd only call for backup. Then John would never intervene. Never tell B-boy to shut up.

I was sure John was watching me pace the unit common with my back to him and B-boy. I made like I didn't care. I plopped myself down again on a heavy foam sofa on the far side of the room and picked up an old *Time* magazine donated by the missionaries. It lay on a stack of board games. This playing chicken was a live version of *Risk*. Conquer or be conquered. No reason to say *Sorry*. My life the pursuit of trivia. Endless clues but no answers. A pawn in a game that I refused to let put me in checkmate. My mind raced with metaphor.

Only trouble was, I'd played my last hand wrong. From where I'd sat myself I couldn't see the television and now all the boys were watching me instead of the television, which seemed like a waste. "It's my television time," I thought. "And it's my fuckin' life, too." I'd decided no twerp with a college education was going to tell me how I should fuckin' love my mother. So I got up and found a chair closer to the others. When I looked over my shoulder, B-boy had turned redder than any sunset I'd ever seen. That's when he strode over to the office to consult with John, who still hadn't said a word to me.

John just shrugged, and kept writing. Then made another phone call. "Jesus." He was probably doing a crossword or calling *his* mother. The thought made my stomach feel hollow. I could hear voices running around my head like a big shouting match making my ears go flush. Voices so loud I couldn't even hear the television blaring next to me. I wasn't the only one getting flustered, either. There was a scent of fear in the air as all of us teenaged boys began anticipating the next act. *Déjà vu*. It was becoming our daily ritual, this waiting for confrontation.

B-boy is not tall so when he came and stood over me and told me to get to my room, and I just kept staring at the TV, I could practically feel his breath parting my hair. "Fine," he snorted and turned off the television, then sent the other boys to their rooms. They grumbled, but not at me. They respected me for my right to resist. "Maudit," cursed Michael in French. He's returned to jail, just like me. "Leave him alone, man. If he doesn't want to call his mommy, what fucking business is it of yours?" Michael shouted all this as he went into his room. He was seventeen, the group defender now. The others hissed, "You stay put, Joey," or "You go, girl," and other shit like that. But I wasn't buying their taunts either. I was looking around for John. He was still just sitting there in the doorway to the office, doing nothing, arms locked across his chest.

B-boy said, "You have one more chance to go to your room. One last chance before I put you in safety. Your choice."

"Think I'll watch some TV instead," I said, faking calm. I got up and turned the television back on. He switched it off for the second time.

That's when John had to get up. I could see he was hesitant to get into this. He was shaking his head a little but he wouldn't do anything to let on he too thought B-boy was a loser. Paul, Jeremy, Michael, they were all watching. Their open palms high fives on their bedroom windows. Something about all this felt eerily familiar. Fear and anger. Threats. The smell of hate.

Jeremy slapped his window a few times real hard and jumped up and down. Michael followed. Soon all of them were pounding on their glass. John was now standing behind B-boy. If I were John, I'd have just swatted B-boy across the head. Told him to go pick on someone his own size. Except there's a code among the guards. Just like on the street. My worker isn't *my worker* when he's backing up another staff. Then he's another piece of the machine. A slave. The least John could have done, I kept thinking, was give me a wink. Let me know that he was still there for me. Silence the voices of make-believe which were all I had.

Without that, I had nothing to lose. I was a circus performer after all. Out there on the highwire and everyone wanted to see me fall because their own lives were so routine.

"What the hell," I thought. Even if it was just for their amusement, I'd show B-boy who he was messing with. It's really about brains over brawn. B-boy had already lost. He was the one panting. He was the one who was standing there worried about his safety. Completely unsure what I was going to do next. And I had the home team rooting for me. "Hey boys, enjoy it while you can," I yelled. "You owe me for this."

That's when John radioed for help and reached for his latex gloves. My left leg started bouncing like it does when I'm really nervous. And the voices shouting in my head kept saying, "No fuckin' way I'm calling her." And I kept wondering why John or B-boy didn't just ask me why this phone thing was pissing me off so badly. Why I wouldn't call. But of course B-boy, with his books, thought he had me all figured out. If I had an education, I thought, I would teach this scrawny twit about real kids, not textbook cut-outs. I'd burn his fuckin' books. I'd write my own instead.

Then Clarence and Janet, two more guards, joined B-boy and John. John stepped back towards the control panel next to the mop closet. Its red and green lights told him which doors were secure. The panel was all red, of course. Good news, I guess, what with the boys all thumping hard on their doors and windows. The whole scene would have been a little funny if I hadn't had such a throbbing headache.

Then B-boy did it. He put his hand on my arm and tried to pull me up, and I lost it. I reached up for his belt and with one great yank pulled him down on top of me and slammed my fist in below his chin and then reached down and sank my teeth right into his shoulder. "Fuck," I thought, "if they are going to treat me like some crazy, then I'll show them." But the whole thing was over in a few seconds. Janet plowed one at my head and Clarence pulled my arms back and even John was on top of me laying me out on the floor, crushing my head into the cold tile. Then someone was on my legs and one on each arm. And I could hear B-boy yelling, "For Christ's sake," and I hoped he was bleeding, bleeding badly. I wanted to look him in the eyes, stare him down, but I couldn't as long as some fucker was crushing my skull. That just made me more livid with rage and then I was yelling, "Leave me alone!" But they wouldn't. For sure they wouldn't.

I was cuffed and shackled. A helmet and face mask placed over my head so I couldn't bite anyone or knock myself out. And then I was carried, like a cannon is carried by army toughs practising for the Tattoo. All the way down to the safety cell. All the way, and still no one had asked me what I was making all this fuss about. Nobody, not even John.

That's when I stopped fighting. That last thought was a hot slap across my face. "It's not worth it. They're not worth it," I mumbled so quietly I'm sure they couldn't hear me beneath their laden breathing.

When we reached the main building, they threw me like a curling stone into the safety cell, then, pressing me hard against the skanky cement floor, undid the cuffs and leg shackles. Finally they took off the helmet. Like some lumbering TSN ballet, they all rose and released. B-boy was the first to the door. Then Clarence and Janet took their exit quickly. That left John, who stood there pointing at me with a gloved hand. Breathing heavily. Then he too backed his way out of the cell and I heard the dull thud of the magnetic locks. And once again I was alone with only memories to hug.

thirteen

It's strange to be part of an agency now and doing investigations rather than having my life being controlled by them. I don't tell Shirley this. I prefer she think about me only as a professional. She has no reason to think otherwise. That's not the case with Lou. She knows my past. She helped shape it, though not as a social worker. She'd retired from that role by then. That doesn't mean, though, that she didn't interfere just the same.

Her real name is Louise. She lives next door to the house Social Services found for us after my father died. My mother told Stevie and me that she's a strange woman. "She works too hard. Doesn't seem quite natural the way she looks after her own house, either." Louise can build things, which was why I liked to visit. My mother was glad to have me disappear. Gave her time to watch her late afternoon soaps.

Louise prefers I call her Lou. She's finished raising her kids. She's never said what happened to her husband. Her eldest daughter visits weekends when she lets her. Mostly Lou spends her time puttering, tells me, "When I built this house there was nothing else much here. Herring Cove Road was narrow and quiet. There was nothing much behind me either, a few houses, but mostly just forest and ponds. Then they widened the road and more people built further from the city." She points in the direction of where my old house is, too far to walk or even bike. I haven't visited since we left. The busy highway I see from my front window is a fault line between two times and two dads. This new dad would look fine in a dress, though she prefers overalls. My real dad liked overalls too.

Night and day, the traffic speeds past Lou's front yard and mine. Lou says it wasn't always so loud. I don't like living like this, so close to our neighbours. The only good thing about where we live is the view. From my back deck you can see pretty subdivisions that rim the decaying houses of my new neighbours. Expensive homes sit tight up against the Arm, which we're still close enough to smell when there's a stiff breeze, especially at this end where the sewage gathers and rots. Our neighbourhood is like an apple left at the back of the fridge, the red skin hiding the wormy middle. Lou tells me, "The city used to seem a long ways away." She exhales with an old man's sigh. Only she's an old woman. Either way, there's resignation in the way she loosens a throaty vowel, the long *ahhh* of someone who lost something but can't remember what.

Lou finds endless things to do. I grow up watching her transform her front garden, her steps, her windows, her front and back porches, into something better. There wasn't a Saturday that didn't start with her neighbour's saw eating through lumber or the *thwack, thwack* of her hammer. Sometimes my mother would get her to help around our yard. Lou never seemed that keen but would do what she had to do to be neighbourly. I wondered if Lou's hesitancy was because she heard what my mother said about her after she left. I remember my mother leaning over the kitchen sink, looking across the fence that separated our properties, the one Lou kept painted. My mother would keep repeating, "God, what have we come to now?" Then she would gingerly pick up the glass Lou had drunk from when she'd paused from fixing the drain under the sink. My mother lowered the glass into the hot soapy water and gave it a vigorous scrub. It was the same glass, full of tap water before, that my mother had offered Lou as miserly thanks for the work she'd done.

Mostly Lou kept to herself. Except that whenever my mother and brother and I were outside in the backyard, and Lou was out working on something manly, then my mother would say a cheery, "Hello," and Lou would chorus back, "Nice day, isn't it." There was never any need to say more. No invitation in my mother's voice to come to the fence and talk about the weather. Only when she needed help did she force Lou to chat. My mother's tone with Lou was as light and empty as I'd heard her use with other mothers in the grocery store before we moved here, mothers she'd met every day for years on the brief walks she made with us boys to the end of our street where we caught the school bus.

Across our back fence with Lou it was the same. Lou would look our way. But it was like she would always try to look past my mother. If I were around, she'd look mostly at me, with a real serious expression. Times like that, she looked worried. I was still too young to think about what I looked like, but now I know I cut quite a sight. My ripped jeans. The one dirty shirt I would wear every day, until I would let my mother buy the next one that I liked, then I'd wear that to threads. When I was nine my chosen shirt had a big white number seven on the back, fading to grey, the decal peeling at the edges. I forget why I thought seven made me great. Who was number seven? The only thing dirtier than the shirt was my hair.

I hated baths in our new house as much as before we moved there. Only now, with my father dead, my mother gave up fighting. It was a truce, until the teachers complained I smelled bad. Maybe if I'd changed my underwear more, that wouldn't have happened. There were skid marks on the inside, brown stains that had long ago set. Never enough toilet paper around to do a good job. Besides, I'd clog the damn toilet if I really cleaned myself. Our diet of cheap canned beans did a number on my system. And chocolate milk. And candy. My teeth were rotting. Lou noticed things like that. Maybe she was the one who eventually called the social workers. She probably did it thinking she was being helpful, but the day this heavy-breasted woman who smelled all clean came to visit I could tell that something was wrong. I was wrong. My brother was wrong. Our house was wrong. It was the way she sat. She never really let her arse settle onto the living room sofa. And she didn't even take a sip of the tea my mother offered. Her name, I can't remember, but she looked familiar, like another woman who used come to visit me and Stevie in our old house. The one who took us to our foster mother's in her car. Only this woman was a little larger, and her hair a little more grey than that other woman.

My mother was all cuddly with Stevie when she was in front of the lady. But mostly Stevie just wanted down from her knee. We were hungry and dinner was supposed to be chicken nuggets. It was Thursday. I remember Thursdays. Canned peas and nuggets, golden and greasy from the oven pan. I could make them myself if my mother was too tired to get up from the sofa. But that night, with the social worker visiting, she opened a bag of frozen corn. And there were pork chops from the freezer with this brown tomato sauce like she used to make for my dad. I remember that. But neither Stevie or I liked the sauce, which tasted burnt, so we scraped it off the chops. My mother glared at us so stiffly that we knew we had just better eat it because sure enough after the lady left, my mother was livid. "I made a perfectly good dinner, and you fuckin' ungrateful kids didn't eat it! You can all get yourselves to bed, NOW! And I don't want to see you until morning. You hear me, not until morning!" And we got away from her quick, avoiding the hair pulling. I knew she was ashamed about something, but I couldn't figure why she cared so much about her goddamn pork chops.

"We still ate them, didn't we?" I mumbled to Stevie. As always, he said nothing.

After Stevie and I had scurried up to our room, Stevie sat on his bed in the corner with his Action Man, making the sounds of bombs dropping as he flew the little man around in circles. I stared out the window because it was still only six-thirty and I wasn't the least bit tired. There was no way I was going to lie down. I looked out into our front yard and there was Lou across on her front lawn putting some water on her plants even though there was already a heavy dew that evening. And for a moment I thought she was looking past the flowers, into our yard at something, and then she looked right up at my window where my light was on. I waved, but I'm sure she didn't see me because she looked back down at her plants, and stooped to pull a weed.

fourteen

I DIDN'T WANT ANYTHING AT ALL when John came back sometime later to visit me in my cell. He was alone. No ballet troupe of officers. No B-boy. My legs had fallen asleep under me where I'd let them rest once the cuffs and shackles had been taken off. I hadn't moved. I hadn't slept. I couldn't even remember if I'd been breathing, which is funny I thought, since I don't normally think about breathing, except when John is around. John hovered. At first he said nothing, but then surprised me when he put his bare hand on my head and made me look him in the face. "Okay now?" he asked. Then he laid his usual crap on me about revenge and left me to ponder life in the quiet of my concrete sewer.

I didn't want to think about anything but the warm marshmallow feeling I had growing inside my head. I just wanted to zone out. But the idea of revenge kept pulling me back to this world, this cell, the cramp in my legs, the numbness of my left arm that had been the next part of me to fall asleep. I spat on the floor. Let my body disintegrate. Refused to change position to let blood flow back to my extremities. It was too much work to want anything, drugs, even a girl's tongue on my prick. I could feel myself go hard with the thought. Still I didn't move.

I had no energy for revenge or to resist. I watched from somewhere outside me. I watched how I shifted posture to relieve my sore muscles only when forced by some inner animal. It wasn't me who moved any longer. I watched as I slowly let urine run in a stain across my pants, then collect in a cooling puddle behind my back. I became the camera watching my fall. Anger left me. I couldn't feel anything. This wasn't suicide. It was better. It was separation, the living dead. I knew I couldn't kill myself. But I could give up. Completely. These thoughts passed like water, one stream joining others as I let go, drifted, and then finally slept.

It was hard to tell how many hours had passed when dinner arrived. By then I'd slid myself into the corner of the cell to get farther away from the camera. A foot farther. I rested myself beside the wall, my head at the base of the toilet. I was still curled up, as if this cell had become my mother's now sterile womb. The floor cold as the hospital operating theatre into which I'd fallen sixteen years earlier.

That's when I saw them come in. *Maybe they'd been in before?* I wasn't sure. Knew I didn't care. They seemed concerned about something but I didn't know what. For the first time in months, I felt blissful. Absent.

Then John came in. They must have called him because I remember they all stood outside for a time but left the door open. I stayed curled up, watching from somewhere above. There were some muffled sounds. Maybe they were threats? Meaningless parts of speech I had chosen to let pass. The words sifted together like the dry ingredients my foster mother would invite me to help her mix when she made cookies on Saturday afternoons. She was a nice lady. The social worker had come back to our house in Spryfield a few more times, then finally one day met Stevie and me at school and told us that we would be coming with her for a little while. That my mother was in hospital. That my mother wasn't feeling well. Needed a rest. I was scared to go with her because my mother always pulled my hair if I missed the bus after school. No surprise, Stevie didn't seem to care. He never minded the beatings as much, either. He'd just sit in the corner, whimpering.

Then get up and watch television. As the years went on I heard him speak less and less frequently.

Our worker had reassured me it would be okay for us boys to come with her. And Mr. Roberts, the principal, was there too and told us, "Boys, this woman has your mother's permission to take you. It's all right, boys. You'll be safe."

I guess butter and chocolate chips are what safety meant. The thick scent of baking and the warmth of a well-heated kitchen greeted us as we filed into our foster home, each carrying a green garbage bag my mother had packed for us. There in the entranceway, waiting, was a woman with an apron who told us to call her Donna. It felt like I'd met Donna before, and her smile told me the same, but neither of us mentioned it. Instead, she said, "My, how you darlings have grown," then she led Stevie and me into the kitchen with a hand on our shoulders, gave us each a spatula and our own mixing bowl. Showed us how to scrape clumps of greasy dough from the side, leaving smears of brown along the edges. Irregular spoonfuls of dough were plopped onto pans tacky with old grease and black with age. It had all seemed ... familiar.

I felt pulled to these thoughts as I lay in my cell. These thoughts which hid the chatter around me. It was easier to be lost in my mind than back with the pain of limbs that were all pins and needles.

John and the other workers eventually left me alone, there on the floor. They must have because when I opened my eyes again the door was closed and I could hear my pulse. I don't know why but I reached across the floor and pulled the plastic cup they'd left for me to my lips and swallowed something. I mechanically chewed whatever my hands reached. I convinced myself I could do this without being any part of a world where food was necessary. I was just a machine. I imagined a world of lifelike robots that whirled around, vacuuming up vomit and piss after parties.

Later that night I slowly let my bowels loosen. Feeling the warmth of fresh feces smear across my briefs. Another warm drip of piss found a place below me. Still I watched. I had only the most fleeting moment of smugness or embarrassment. Clean or dirty, neither choice seemed to have much consequence. Nor did any possible revenge.

That word again. It disturbed the peace. It made me think of John, who strangely seemed to be there again, holding me up. There were others too, who with hot breath were lifting me, swearing at me. This time, though, they all wore gloves. Then there was cold water over my naked body. But nobody touched me anywhere except under my arms. John's big rubberized hands. I opened my mouth to let the spray fill my mouth and stared blankly forward.

I was dried and wrapped again in clothes. Only this time they moved me back to my bedroom on the unit. I walked without acknowledging them. I just moved as they willed it. I said nothing. That I'm sure. I made no effort to resist. I entered my room and settled onto the mattress that had the pleasant smell of someone I knew.

Over the next two days staff tried to speak with me. It was remarkably easy to stay silent. I didn't move except to go to the toilet, to eat at irregular times from trays brought to me.

John appeared the morning of what he said was my third day on retreat. The light behind him was filtered by the mesh screen over the window. It softened John's outline, making him seem blurred, featureless. I was thinking I could paint any face I liked on the blank expanse between his dark borders. Happy, sad, cruel.

John said, "You got to eat more or they'll start doing things to you." He meant Skunk-lady. "She thinks you're crazy, Joey. I tell her you're not. Just taking some much needed time out. But she's not buying it. It's up to you what they do to you."

No reaction, though I wanted to tell him not to worry. He seemed so concerned.

"It's time to come back. If you're like this, then you're just letting everyone who ever shit on you think they're right, that you deserve it all. You don't need to be here. None of this is really your life, right?" He hesitated. Hushed his voice. "Come on, talk to me." I was sure he didn't want the other staff to hear him begging me to save myself. He didn't want them to see his genuine concern. Big burly John, with the composure of a mountain, telling me I was worth saving. Maybe saving himself along with me.

I did nothing except turn and stare deep into the painted pocks of the cement blocks inches from my face. I heard John's heavy steps retreating. The echo of the quad, the empty sound of deep voices bouncing nowhere. I was nowhere.

John came back again the next day. This time, he tried to get his breathing to match mine, but I wasn't willing to play along. I wanted him to leave. He was ruining the silence. I liked the dead space I'd found. I didn't want to be reached. I let myself slip back into my dream. But the dream was no fun either. In the blurry thought of half-sleep I saw myself running away. There was something wrong. I was trying to get somewhere, but that place kept changing. I didn't understand why I could see the front yard of the house on the crescent. Except in front of my dream house the grass was all burned. And then my neighbour Lou, who never lived next to our old house, she was standing next to my mother. Only, she's mean and pushes my mother down. She's kicking her. That couldn't be happening. I watch. Lou yells down the street to me, "Don't worry, it's fine. She's not hurt, son." And then I turn and some dogs are yapping at me and I give one a boot in the snout but the others begin to chase me and I race around the corner of this big imposing brick building that reminds me of a school, and some lady with deep cleavage and a hat, Jesus, a hat of all things, a big old lady's hat, with feathers and flowers, she begins saying to me, "It's all right," but when she touches my arm she feels like a store mannequin and the expression on her face is just as plastic, fixed.

That's when I hear John calling to me, "Joey, you there?"

I open my eyes with a start and he's sitting on the bed next to my head, leaning down to look at me. He looks all strange now that he's upside down. A big black moon, waxing. I know him right away, though. The voice, the smell of his aftershave. His ungloved hand is on my shoulder, and he's gently rocking me. His touch is warm.

"I called your mother, told her you didn't want to talk to her." I think to myself, "John, you are the king of the fuckin' understatement." Then he tells me, "I told her about how you had exploded on the unit. She didn't ask much except if you'd broken anything and then said how it was just like you to be like this. I sort of felt like we were talking about a dog or something. Is that what it's like with her? Is that why you didn't want to call?"

Suddenly my cocoon felt uncomfortable. I couldn't help letting my eyes shift to look at John for a moment before staring again at the wall. It was the first time in days I'd let anyone see inside me. He was smart enough to catch this fleeting glance. I knew John knew I was listening. He stopped talking.

I suddenly felt safe. Here buried in a bedroom-like cell in the shadow of this immense man who could rip me apart, who was paid to be my minder, I felt safe. But before I could betray myself again, John got up and left the room, leaving only his scent behind.

I'd never felt safe like that with my foster mother. There was no point getting close and letting her cookies bribe me into trusting her. We were headed home soon. That's what they said. When my mother was better, we'd return home, that's what the social worker had said. As if that promise was supposed to reassure us. Stevie never once spoke about our mother. He just ate cookies, watched more television than ever before, sat quietly during the long drives to and from our school each day. I pouted. I threw things. I swore. I kept beating up kids and getting beaten up. The school wouldn't suspend me. Instead, they had me shadowed by a young woman named Martha. She was very strict. She would make me leave the classroom if I was the least disruptive. Sit me outside at a wooden desk and tell me to fill out silly worksheets while she went outside to smoke cigarettes. The work was too easy and I was bored. So I ripped through the sheets with my pencil. Then chewed the pencil itself, spitting bits of wood on the floor.

But here, in jail, I felt safe. The thought brought a cool shiver down my spine, into my legs, even through my groin. My legs cramped from four days of inaction suddenly ached to move. I was falling back into myself. I was finding that space again where the performance and the performer are all jumbled together. I was beginning to want something. And then I knew what I was going to do. It was what I had always wanted to do. I was going to get back at them. Teach them to suffer. Show them everything they were doing wrong. Make it right, finally, for me, and maybe for others.

I stretched, my muscles resisting my will to move. I focused on the grated window as night was creeping in, the last pinkish grey licks of a sunset just barely visible. If I'd been outside I'd have searched for the moon. It would have been nice to believe that celestial bodies were actually turning on my cue. I'd have closed my eyes and faced the land breeze that comes on as evening sets. I'd have looked at the way grass lies down when storms are blowing in. I'd have looked at all this and known it was somehow all about me.

But I was still locked up. The ventilation in my room now made me feel cold. I reached for my blanket and could smell the ripeness of urine. I rose unsteadily and knocked on my door, my blanket wrapped around my shoulders. When John came, I looked at him and managed to get out one word: "Shower." It was the first word I'd spoken in days and my voice was gravelly. I padded barefoot over to the washroom while the other residents stared. It was strange seeing the whiteness of the porcelain, feeling the cool of the tile, touching the sleek silver of taps. I sat on the toilet and let my bowels move, a steady stink that I realized I'd being holding inside, tight. I even flushed and then looked in the mirror at the dishevelled head of a young man I barely recognized. I ran hot water in the shower, shed my blanket and grey sweats, underwear, peeled off the t-shirt they'd dressed me in and stepped under the heavy spray. "I'm done with it all," I thought to myself as I washed my chest, then reached down with a soapy hand and held my erect penis. That brought me back. I let my hips pretend whatever they wanted to remember, push in, be pushed, and quickly came against the shower wall. Not much fantasy. Like my life. Pushed, push back. Action, reaction. I dipped my head under the water in silent prayer and could feel tears welling inside as I became wet inside and out.

With the shower still running, I reached beyond the curtain for my toothbrush. It was still there in its holder, standing sentinel for my return.

fifteen

THE OFFICE ROUTINE IS ALL ABOUT PTA. Protect Thy Ass. Document, document again, then just to be sure, document everything one more time. Gerty didn't document enough, or pay attention to the rules, and look what happened to her. I'm her replacement. It's tough knowing that where I sit is where she sat.

The rumour around the office is Gerty was investigating a kid who begged her not to tell anyone about her sexual abuse. She just wanted some time to work things out before anyone told her mother. The kid knew what was going to happen. That the family was going to be ripped apart. So Gerty waited. Only, the bastard doing the abusing was the girl's mother's live-in boyfriend and two days later he visited the girl's room one last time. And when the girl told the courts what had happened, that she hadn't wanted Gerty to tell, the judge had a shit-fit. It also made it look like the kid wanted the guy to fuck her. The judge said it undermined the prosecution's case. The boyfriend claimed the girl was seductive. In competition with the mother. He might as well have called the fourteen-year-old a whore. After that, Shirley had to do something. It turns out kids can't make those decisions for themselves. And Gerty isn't here any more to disagree. I think I would have liked Gerty if I'd had the chance to get to know her.

"I've seen it all," Shirley says. And she has. "When I was trained it was even before systems thinking or cybernetics. It was just about common sense then. Now it's solution-focused practice, brief strategic therapy, client-focused this, empowerment that. Some of it's useful, I'll give you that, but it's begun to feel like you new workers are talking about theories like they're this month's favourite donut at Tim's. Where's the common sense in any of it?" she asks but isn't looking for an answer. "Ideas just make us workers into martyrs," Shirley says and shakes her head. She tells me to be careful. To not do anything silly. I'm guessing she's thinking of Gerty when she says that. "Just remember why you came to work and you'll be fine."

I mostly try and ignore Shirley's advice. I'm sure she hasn't figured out why I'm really here and I'm definitely not going to be the one to tell her. Instead, I try as best I can to make my own rules, quietly.

I share an office with Ellen who treats me like I'm still a student on placement. "You really replacing Gerty?" she asks the first time we meet. I assure her that I have my degree. She laughs. "Gerty had big shoes."

Ellen's feet are small. She's curvy, with more mass than sincerity. She wears Winner's business suits. I see the bags in her office where she piles them after lunch hours spent shopping. Her change in colour by season and style are as indeterminate as her weight, which yo-yoes up and down. Her desk is stacked with fashionable diet books. Her black gym bag by her desk says The Women's Place. A recipe card taped to her phone has handwritten rules on it: No eating after dinner. Exercise each day. Look in the mirror. Be happy. Give to others. I should give her a chance. See what she thinks about the clients. But first impressions being what they are, I'm pretty certain those cards have long ago lost their influence and what's left is someone who is thinking more about herself than anyone else.

We share a computer, which means sometimes our lives cross in places I'd rather remain unknown. She's a single parent. Her ex-husband is rumoured to have run off with a Russian diplomat even before their child was adopted from a Romanian orphanage. I hear she's never been in a relationship since. There's a photo of Ellen and her son on her desk next to the recipe card. It's been placed in a heavy pewter frame with a lighthouse sculpted down one side. Ellen is smiling. Her son looks startled. "I understand what it takes to raise a child by yourself, without anyone's help," she says when she catches me staring at the photo. I think she means without the help of any man. I shake my head at the thought of her comparing herself to women like Joan. As if Ellen, a well-paid, educated woman, is the same as those others who wake up only to find a baby growing in them. Silly hopeless dreams of love and boys who will bring them flowers just like in the movies. Their bodies not chaste like Ellen's. The space between their legs as easily filled as the cups you get at Subway. Refills welcome. No charge. I can tell Ellen isn't one of those women. She is more the type who make a show of ordering Perrier when 7-Up would taste just as good.

Ellen asks me about my meeting with Joan and Vivian. I give her a *Reader's Digest* version of the truth. I don't want her advice but she offers it without an invitation. "I can imagine it's tough for Joan. She's a sole parent, right?" I don't miss (nor does she intend me to miss) the way she uses the feminist version of manless motherhood. Sole implies choice. Single means Joan lacks something. Ellen says, "I know what it's like for her. Once you've done it all by yourself, you understand better."

Ellen has stopped typing at the computer and takes a long draw on a straw she keeps stuck in a plastic mug full of Diet Coke. I perch on the edge of a nearby desk, hands neatly folded in my lap. Waiting.

"Late nights, diapers. You don't have kids, right? So it's difficult for you to understand." She tells me this as her eyes drift from my face downwards, too far, and I know she is really thinking I don't understand because I am a man. Privileged by default of a dick. She takes a long *slurp* from her cup. "It's all about being tuned in ..." *slurps* again, "to another's situation. You see?"

I say nothing. Just stare out the window. She jerks her head towards her computer screen, slouches forward, mouths silent profanities as she types. "I'll be done in a second." She hits a few last keys. Straightens her dress, then pushes back from the computer table. "I guess I should know better than to expect people without much experience to understand people like me." Pausing long enough to sort some papers together into their rightful order, she rises from her seat, and tells me with authority, "I'm gone for the day. Be sure to turn the machine off when you're done. Security." I still say nothing, then sit down and begin to type my report. The silence is welcome.

I'm beginning to understand why workers burn out and the soul-numbing amount of energy that it is going to take for me to stay convinced this all matters. I might feel Jesus-like, but it's not for any miracles I do, just the magic I have to multiply paper like fishes. Paper words instead of deeds. As morning shadows fade in the midday light and the building hums with activity, my focus drifts from my screen. I begin to stare at the walls around me. No client baby pictures here. I guess no one ever cared enough about Ellen to send her a note with a little picture attached. I begin thinking, these walls need something. With determination, I roll my shoulders back and sit very straight.

* * *

An hour later I leave the computer running and grab my green portfolio. I'm supposed to see Vivian's family today, this time at their house. Vivian's moved back home. Shirley said it would be best if I visited before noon. Seems her grandfather, Mr. Jeffrey, likes to watch the soaps in the afternoon. Won't turn them off for anybody.

I take one of the agency cars again and drive out past the edge of the city to the old neighbourhood where I once lived. Our street is still a stand-alone subdivision of aluminum-sided homes, twenty to the development, a narrow road up the middle. Just behind is a deep stunted forest with boggy fields full of berries and swarming with mosquitoes. Imaginary lines are drawn between the wild brush where you can still find deer and the residential zone with rows of planted pines that are taller than I remember. Children still play on the green grass of their front lawns while fathers use chainsaws to keep the forest from casting too big a shadow over their backyards, killing the grass with their shade. I don't remember the forest being as close to the houses as it is now.

I can't recognize my house either. A garage has been added and a rickety wooden enclosure with a sheet-metal roof has been attached to the front porch. There are weeds around the foundation and the driveway hasn't been paved in years; deep ruts show where car tracks have worn their way down into the earth. An old beat-up F150 sits with flat tires on the grass. The paint on the front door and window trim is peeling. I feel nothing but hollow, as if my life here with my family is someone else's story.

Next door, there's another old car, rusting on Mrs. D's front lawn. And another on Mr. Jeffrey's. The housing lots are big enough to keep old cars parked and abandoned. These communities are not gated, but they might as well be for their isolation from the monster homes with their estate-size lots that sit in subdivisions a little closer to town. This end of the city looks like someone played jazz with people's addresses. Rich, poor, poor, rich, poor, rich, poor, poor, rich. If you drive fast enough, which is difficult in my crappy agency Grand Am, you can almost tap out a melody of sorts.

Mr. Jeffrey has had a lot of social workers work with him. He's fifty-eight, from the Island, Prince Edward Island. As if that explains everything, his backwardness, his poverty. Joan never left home. Had Vivian. Stayed a bit longer. Took care of her father and her daughter like she was expected to do.

The road in front of all the houses is potted. I suspect not too many politicians worry about getting Mr. Jeffrey's vote.

It's hard to know quite where to enter Mr. Jeffrey's house. From the outside it looks like a shed, the original shell obscured behind plastic sheeting that drapes over weathered wooden boards nailed haphazardly together as a snow and windbreak across the front. There's a year's worth of wood, five or six cord, stacked in uneven piles at the front. I find the front door behind the woodpile, under an improvised roof that slants out from the house. A lot of time has been spent keeping that wood dry, carefully stacking it so that some of it is always under the overhang. Shirley told me Mr. Jeffrey's neighbours have for years been coming by, checking in on him. Seeing to it the family doesn't freeze to death, or starve.

Mr. Jeffrey was expecting someone from the agency. Shirley had phoned. But I'm not Shirley. "You can' be my worker. How ol' are ya?" I don't answer the question but reassure him that Shirley sent me. He's aged badly. He was in his forties the last time I saw him, an arthritic old man then. Now he looks even more twisted, his stature bonsai-like. He squints, asks me, "What you know abou' any of what's goin' on wit' me? Eh? Come on now, 'fess up. What's this really abou'?"

I have no intention of telling him who I really am. There doesn't seem any point. Instead, I repeat for him slowly what I just told him, that Shirley sent me. Three dogs, all matted, one missing a hind leg, another snarly but submissive, are poking around my feet while I wait at the door to be invited in. Mr. Jeffrey has no time for formalities and turns and walks inside. His hearing isn't good, and I can see his hips hurt as he limps his way inside while he draws one heavy breath after another. There's a walker, old and battered, by the door, but he leaves it there. It must be for when he goes out. If he goes out. Shirley told me the family gets things like that donated second-hand from the Women's Church Auxiliary.

"Well come'n, then," he hollers at me with his back turned. "You can si' down 'ere." He points at a saggy old couch by the wall in the country kitchen, which is the room I've come into. The house is small, and drafty cold, even though the weather is fine that day. Mr. Jeffrey sits on a wooden kitchen chair, the white enamel paint badly chipped, the legs wobbly. He says, "Shirley promise' my wife and me a house. You any bette' at makin' tha' 'appen? Sure could use a 'ouse. This one ain' good for the lad, is it?" There's no sign of Mr. Jeffrey's four-year-old grandson. He should be here. Is always here, I'm told. Loved so dearly everyone is worried that Mr. Jeffrey and Joan will never let him go to school. "Where's tha' Shirley? Why she can' come see me no more?"

I avoid this question too. Can't bear to tell him his family is no longer a priority. Wonder again what Shirley would say if she knew I was of these people. Would she see it as a conflict of interest? Likely. There's danger, though, in working with people you know. Who you think you know. Whose past you share. Fact is, if I'm being honest with myself, I don't know everything about Mr. Jeffrey's life. His life is still a story of his own authorship. A plot that he brings to life himself. One only has to look at who holds the clipboard, who asks the questions, and who answers, to see the chasm between our lives as they have been lived.

I ask Mr. Jeffrey, "Your daughter and grandson, and Vivian, are they here too?"

He looks towards a door in the corner. I hear the sound of a four-year-old running from the back bedroom. Cameron's a small boy, with a round little face and bright green eyes. He bounces into the kitchen. He's holding an exercise book with a purple bird on the cover. I say "Hello," bending down so I don't look so tall. Smile. You have to smile when you look at Cameron. His dancing eyes fill his face.

Joan follows from behind the curtain that serves as the kitchen door. Her timing makes me think she was waiting there. Here with her father, in her own home, she is oddly shy.

According to the file, neither Mr. Jeffrey nor Joan had got past elementary school. Mr. Jeffrey not much past grade three in fact. Neither one of them could do much more than write their names. Mr. Jeffrey had let Joan stay with him all these years, happy to have her keep him company. How she ever got pregnant, twice, and with whom, is anybody's guess. And people have guessed. Have looked closely at Vivian's eyes and round features and wondered if she shouldn't be cross-eyed. There's no father listed on her birth certificate or Cameron's. Of course, this makes it simpler to collect welfare. There's no wayward male to chase down and make pay his fair share. According to Shirley, it's a strange home but somehow everyone has found what they need. By putting together their welfare cheques, they've managed to live comfortably enough. Shirley has never believed any of the bad things said about Mr. Jeffrey.

The household should have fallen apart years ago, with or without financial assistance. But it survived because neighbours looked in on the family every few days. It didn't work so well in emergencies, like when Cameron was ill or Vivian out of control. But at least here beyond the suburbs, there was more room to be a screw-up. What might be a crisis in town could be overlooked next to a scrubby forest. There were fewer eyes watching that cared to complain. At least if you didn't beat up your kid on the street.

Cameron seems oblivious to the tempest around him. The dogs all come over to give him a kiss on the face before Mr. Jeffrey shoos them away. They leave the wet muddy earth of the backyard on the worn linoleum and Cameron's little jeans. Not that one could tell. I'd kept my boots on as I'd come in when I'd noticed Mr. Jeffrey had on his. Only the boy is barefoot, his clothing nothing more than a floor mop.

"Tea then?" says Mr. Jeffrey.

"No thanks, I can't be staying too long today." I lie. I have the time. Know I won't be leaving soon, but tea is risky. I worry about how the cup got cleaned. Years of case aides coming in haven't made much of an improvement in the family's hygiene. You could smell something fecund. Maybe it's the boy? Or Mr. Jeffrey, who uses a portable toilet chair when his hips are bad. It sits there in the middle of the kitchen, slightly yellowed, its white plastic trap set askew on the tubular steel frame. I wonder where they dump it. Maybe in the sink? I try not to think about them manuevering the pan of piss and shit around the dishes that are piled high on the counters and in the basin. A plastic tub is used to conserve water. An old habit, I guess. There aren't many other dishes. Tea would mean them having to wash a cup with the dishrag Joan had just used to wipe Cameron's snotty nose.

I sit, hands empty, and watch. Cameron stands by his mother's knee, then runs into the back bedroom after she hums a little something in his ear. I catch a glimpse of a mattress on the floor that is likely his bed. Cameron comes back through the curtain with a stack of board books and a dog-eared Duo-Tang in which he's been practising his numbers. At age four, he knows all his letters and numbers up to thirty. Both Mr. Jeffrey and Joan, maybe even Vivian, must have been spending time with him reading and counting. The cover of his little exercise book is ripped. Inside there is a thin math book with a turtle on the cover juggling. It's the kind of educational material found in the discount bin by the checkout at Zellers. I'd been told they shop there once a month when a community volunteer drives them.

"In the great green room ...," Cameron reads, standing beside his mother who leans herself against the door frame at the entrance to the kitchen. His finger traces over the words of the picture book. He comes over and shows me what he can do. "Shirley gave him tha' one. Loves it. Go' the whole thin' memorized," Mr. Jeffrey says.

Shirley told me the city would like to move the family into an apartment, downtown somewhere, rather than give Mr. Jeffrey the money to fix up his place. Folks at the department thought the family should be someplace where it's more convenient for Cameron to attend school. Get extra help. That kind of thing. No one said it, but I figured the move would also make it so outsiders could watch the family even more closely. No one was thinking about Vivian, mind you. About her being in the city. About her being freer to move around.

"Is Vivian here?" I ask, looking at Joan for an answer.

"She's at school, like she should be."

I nod. Change the topic. Looking at Mr. Jeffrey again, I say, "Shirley told me she's still working on getting you a new place. More in town. She wanted me to help too. Would that be okay? Get you something closer to the city? Daycare for Cameron. Maybe a preschool?"

"Naw. Wha' would we do with tha'? Wouldn' be a' all good for the boy, now would it? All tha' crime. All them people and roads and traffic." Mr. Jeffrey shakes his head. "Ou' here at leas' you ca' see wha's coming. I though' Shirley wa' gonna get us a new house here. Tha's wha' I though' she said."

I explain, "It's a little more difficult. You see, the apartment, well, we just need to make a change in where the money you already get goes. But fixing up this house, that means money from the Housing Authority. They finance it. And the banks. It's not so easy. It, um ... it can be done, but we have to petition financial assistance. And the city. For a place in the city all you need is the welfare office to say okay. Do you understand? It's easier." I feel like such a moron. I'm even talking very slowly, like his being old and arthritic and a little deaf means he's also stupid. I almost wish Joan would start ranting. Save me from drowning in charity. Mr. Jeffrey makes it no easier. Shakes his head.

"You gonna take the boy if we don' move?" I was waiting for him to ask this. First Vivian, now Cameron. Cameron is back next to Joan, kneeling on the floor at her feet, his book in his lap. Joan's hand is resting on Cameron's head. She stares at me, cold and defiant.

"No one is going to take Cameron from you. Whether you move or not." I can almost believe my own words.

Cameron must sense the change of mood. He reaches for a colouring book from a cupboard shelf by the sink, one where the door has been pulled off, holes gaping where hinges once hung. He goes over to Mr. Jeffrey and climbs into his lap. I'm always amazed at how kids seem to know what to do. People think they can fool us social workers. Make us think their kids love them. We show up some morning to talk and there's a strategically made meal, eggs and toast, orange juice from a seventy-nine-cent can of concentrate. The kid is practically dancing and you know this isn't just another regular day.

Not Cameron, though. He just told me everything I needed to know. There's nothing lacking here. Nothing that a few dollars won't fix.

"I've got to go."

"All righ' then. If you gotta. Thanks for comin' by. Sure you won' ha' some tea? It's a col' one. Joan cou' make it."

"No, really. That's okay. Mostly just stopped by to introduce myself. Lots of workers coming through, I guess. Must be confusing for you." Mr. Jeffrey looks at the boy's colouring and ignores me. I see myself out while Joan moves to the sink and begins the hopeless task of rinsing a single dish, scrubbing hard for my sake, trying to get off the baked-on ketchup and beans caked there. I don't breathe too deeply. Just use my eyes. They're a better judge of the situation. Cameron throws me a smile and keeps on colouring.

I walk out into the fresh air and look back at Mr. Jeffrey's place. Then I glance over at my old home. Maybe it wasn't such a bad thing my father died. I never thought about it like that before. Maybe his dying was a gift after all. My launch along a dizzying path that led me to John. And finally back here.

When I get back to the office, I phone my contact at the Metro Housing Authority. "It's a real dire situation," I tell the clerk. Her name is Dale. I never get to know her last name. "You should see the place. It's ready to fall down, or burn down."

When she answers, Dale sounds tired. "That file has been activated, though it has not been prioritized for this year's acquisitions. Given that they are housed makes the situation stable. There is really nothing I can do at this time except maintain the status of the file. I thought Shirley had been briefed on all this. Would you like me to call her again? Or close the file?"

I try something different. Say, "You sound tired today." The comment is so unexpected, that Dale actually drops the front for a moment.

"Up forever last night with my two-year-old. Do I really sound that tired?"

"Just a little. I can sort of understand why you'd not be needing another crisis on your plate. It's okay, I understand."

She softens. I'm learning these clerks all have mushy centres. Just got to know where to lick to find a sweet spot. "You want me to see what I can do?" she says. "I may have some time tomorrow. All right? But no promises."

"Thanks," I tell her, and mean it sincerely. There's really no good reason not to build Mr. Jeffrey a new house. I think Dale knows that. It wasn't like it was going to cost anyone anything. The bank would finance the eighty thousand they needed to gut the place and start again. And the family's welfare would more than cover the mortgage after that. It wasn't about what made sense, though. It seemed to me to be more about whether Mr. Jeffrey and his family deserved the house. Were they poor enough to make Dale feel good about offering them the charity of her public purse?

I owe Shirley a donut. She's the one who told me I need to think about these clerks as people first. Whatever they're doing, it's all about them. "Look at the person," she likes to say. I can't see Dale but I can guess what she looks like. Drooping eyes. A nervous tic. Maybe scratches a pimple on her neck while she sits there hour after hour combing files. Balancing what people need with departmental finances. Trying to ignore how powerless she feels enforcing policies she promised herself she'd never believe in.

Maybe Cameron will get lucky this time. Then again, seeing Cameron on old Mr. Jeffrey's knee, I know he's already lucky. I fax Dale the completed paperwork later that same afternoon.

sixteen

LOU'S BACKYARD IS JUST AS TIDY AS HER FRONT. The fence that separates us is the straightest my ten-year-old eyes have ever seen. Every white picket is as neat and pretty as the vertical slats on crosses I'd seen in pictures of Flanders fields. They show us those each November when we're supposed to remember what the veterans sacrificed for us. Lou's like a veteran. She's old, but not that old.

"I have no children at home anymore," Lou tells me. "So any time you want to come over and help me with my work, that would be fine. I could use an extra hand now and again." Her saying she needs my help in front of my mother makes me happy. Like I'm the man of the family just like I thought. My mother smiles and goes on about a friend of hers, a man whom she worked with for years (I didn't know she had worked), and how he had made the same offer to let me spend time with him but somehow we'd never found a way to take him up on it.

"He lives in another part of the city," she tells Lou. Lou nods politely but I can see she isn't altogether believing my mother. It was the first time I'd seen two adults lie to each other and knew what they were doing.

"I've never had any luck changing people," Lou tells me, hammer in hand. It's a friendly fall day with the air clear and cold. If you keep moving, your fingertips stay warm. The sun warms my cheeks too when I look up. The well-painted surface of Lou's deck where I sit is also toasty warm as long as the sun stays out from behind cotton clouds. I place my palms down on the wood to draw up the warmth. I wait to be told what to do next. Overhead, jet trails scar the blue. Lou says they're from transatlantic flights. "Just about everyone who heads east flies over us," she tells me but never looks up herself. Swings her hammer with a steady rhythm.

Those make-busy afternoons I quickly learn I'm there to listen. "As far as I can see," Lou says, "they do whatever they think they're gonna do and only change when someone bigger makes them." *Thwack*. Another shingle is on the new baby barn she's building next to her deck. It's for a small snow blower she bought the year before.

"Just because you want to do some good doesn't mean it's going to happen. It's not like that. Life." She goes quiet after that. Picks up her chalk line. Reels it all the way in then has me pull the little loop at the end across to the other side of the barn. She shows me where to hold it. How to pull the string taut so she can snap the line. The purple chalk mark will be the bottom edge for the next row of shingles. The line is crisp and exact. Only a little bit of dust gets onto my fingers.

Not long after the barn is finished being built, I'm home from school during the day. Suspended again. I can't quite remember why that time. With the suspensions came beatings. And groundings. But I was always allowed to sit on our back steps if I was good and didn't make any noise or interrupt my mother if she was watching her soaps or sleeping. She didn't used to sleep like that when my father was alive. He'd have her working at something, or maybe she just kept busy to make herself feel important. She lived then like she was working as hard as him. He'd like it if he came home and found things just right. With dinner on our plates and Stevie and me in our place and my mother serving us maid-like, my father would sit at the head of our chrome-edged dining table and wait for the meatloaf to be served, a bitty pile of green peas rolling around next to it for colour and good sense. The Heinz in easy reach. Then my mother would settle and tell us, "Ground beef was just ninety-nine cents at the grocery store." My father always smiled, kindly winked at us boys. I guess ninety-nine-cent ground beef was something we should notice, or was it my mother and her service that we were being told to remember? Either way, I liked meatloaf as long as the green peas were on the side. My mother once tried putting the peas into the meatloaf. "The boys will eat more of them," she told my father when he gagged and left the table. Stevie and I had to finish our plates. Stevie ate zombie-like. I ate with my face close down to my plate so I could spit the peas back out half-chewed.

Evenings when everything was just so, my father liked to complain about his work. It was expected we kids would listen or go to our rooms for the night. "You know what 'Just on time delivery' means, boys?" We never interrupted, even to answer a question. "That means we slaves have to be 'just on time,' every fuckin' day." He'd complain, drink a glass of milk which he said was good for his heartburn, then sit with his back arched and his two hands cupped low on his back trying to massage away the knots.

It's weird, but I'm always comparing Lou to my dad, never my mom. Except Lou's hands aren't like my dad's. My dad's were rough, chapped, the nails broken, always grimed. But Lou's, even though she's older, and she's outside more than my dad, her hands have these long fingers, and the nails are cut just so. You'd never know that even at her age she still can put away a cord of wood herself, carrying armloads of quartered maple and chopped kindling spliced bone white. She walks each armful down to her basement where it dries beside the furnace. Lou says she prefers the dry heat wood gives. There's a big square woodstove next to the oil furnace, the flues snaking together in the dark above like two ghouls holding hands. When I tell my mother that Lou reminds me of my father, she slaps my face hard. "Never say that again," she warns, pointing a finger so close to my face it almost pokes my eye.

Seeing me sitting on my back porch during a school day, Lou calls over, "Are you sitting there for any good reason?" I shrug. "Not allowed to go to school? Sick? Which is it?" I'm sure she can guess.

She mutters something that sounds like "Jesus Christ." "Maybe you should be moving around a bit then, work it out of your system." I like that about Lou, the way she looks at me like I'm a good kid.

She's cut a little gate in her fence just two slats wide. A tight squeeze for my mother, but just right for me and Stevie, though Stevie never does go over for a visit. He prefers television to hammers.

The spring-back gate lets me slip back and forth. There's a latch just on Lou's side. She'll throw the slider some days when she doesn't want me in her yard, but she never padlocks it, though she could. There's a place for a lock.

She gives me a few nails and a boy-size hammer and shows me how to align the new treads for the stairs up to her back deck. The old ones that she's pulled off are lying on the lawn, which is still green from a summer of watering. The old treads don't look rotted. I figure she'll probably use the wood for something else. She's busy carefully setting the riser. I'm sitting on the deck above her. That's when I notice Lou isn't balanced. She's not wearing a bra like my mother. But she's only heavy on one side. Like she's only half a woman. It's hard not to stare. There's a little scar when her t-shirt falls away as she leans to pick up a nail. She tells me to drive the nail into the new stair tread while she holds it.

The nails are big and don't bend over too easy so I don't feel too awkward when I miss. I miss a lot at first. "Were you always a carpenter?" I ask.

"Nope," she says, but doesn't go on. I'm never quite sure if Lou likes it when I beg for details.

"What were you then?" I ask, cautiously. Maybe she was something bad? Maybe she was a criminal, or maybe she was one of Them, the ones who took the Jews away. Maybe she is a Jew and is just hiding? Or maybe her being half a woman is something she doesn't want to talk about.

"I was a social worker," she says, taking a nail from a yogurt container at her feet. Then she puts her hand over mine and helps me swing my hammer to get the nail started. "Retired early." She tells me this without looking at me. But I can see a smile crease the corner of her mouth. After a moment, Lou stops adjusting the riser, looks towards me, tilts her head a bit, squints, then pouts. I know she's going to share a secret with me. Something she'd probably rather I didn't talk about with my mother. "I was plenty ready to leave when I left. You can only try to help for so long." The quiet way Lou speaks makes me think that being a social worker is something dirty that people do.

I know the social worker who came to visit us at supper, she seemed nice enough. And I remember another lady driving us in her car. She was a social worker too. I don't really understand why Lou thinks her being a social worker is something she has to talk about quietly. But then, my mother doesn't like social workers. Maybe Lou knows that. After the last one left, my mother said, "They're nothing but wrecking balls, destroying people's families." I'd imagined a big round woman crashing through my kitchen, knocking everyone over, my mother upside down with her feet wiggling from a pile of rubble.

Lou goes back to her work on the stairs still pouting. I'm not stupid. I know how to keep a secret.

"I won't tell, promise," I say. That makes Lou smile.

A few minutes later, after another tread is nailed down, I ask in the hushed tone of a conspirator, "Did you like it? Was it a good job? I don't think my mother likes our social worker."

"You have a social worker, eh?" Lou says, her eyes flashing quick to my back door.

"I think more than one."

Lou asks me no more questions. Tells me, "It was ..." *thwack* "... an all right kind of job." *Thwack, thwack.* "Just got sort of tired of people so high on themselves, they'd lost the trees for the forest. All that fiddling while Rome burned to a crisp."

"Rome was burning?"

"No. No fire. I mean they couldn't see the trees for the forest."

"It's forests for the trees," I tell her, emphasizing each word carefully. My teacher told me that. I'm thinking this is going to impress Lou. I didn't want her to think I wasn't smart just because I get suspended.

"Is that so?" She gives me one of those adult looks, the kind I can tell is meant to remind me I'm still just a kid. Says nothing more. Keeps puttering and I hammer in another nail, only the head is sort of tilted over and Lou pulls it out without saying a word and gets another nail to track down straight, leaving the last few hits for me. Then she measures another piece of wood and goes looking for something among the collection of screws and bolts and other odd-shaped fasteners she keeps in a big tattered cardboard box wedged into the corner of her metal tool box. Eventually she finds the woodscrew she needs and carefully extracts it from the tangle with the craft of a surgeon.

"That's the one there. See, it's good and long with a deep thread. The bottom step always takes the biggest beating. That means it's the one that's needs to be the strongest."

I'm not sure I understand. "Why are you changing the treads? The old ones don't look rotted. Are you gonna use the wood for something else?"

"Never know," she says, as if that should be enough explanation. "You just never know." She's using an old hand drill to lay in a pilot hole. Then she takes the red square-headed screwdriver from her toolbox and with big turns huffs the screw in, snugging the tread onto the riser. When the head of the screw has been forced slightly below the surface of the wood, she stops and bends to the right to check to see that everything is still square.

Then she looks me right in the eye. "What do you think your dad would have said about you being out of school today?" Lou doesn't wait for an answer, not that I had one. Tells me, "Drop a plumb line through life, Joey. Figure out what counts and throw away the rest." Then she picks up her hand drill again and moves to the other side of the steps to start the next hole.

"What's a plumb line?" No answer. Lou's back with her work. She coughs a bit, though I think what she really wants to do is spit. Picks a second screw from the box and begins to force it into the hole she's made. The screwdriver slips and suddenly she loses patience and throws it down in disgust.

That's it for today, she tells me, and gently guides me back to the gate between our yards. When the fence swings closed she latches it, then goes and shuts her toolbox and carries it inside her back porch. I go back to my own steps and notice our landlord has let the wood rot. Lou's right, the bottom tread looks the roughest, its spruce veins broken, the shaft of the screws that anchored it showing through where the wood has flaked away. I let the toe of my sneaker poke into the spongy wood, all the while looking past the fence and up to Lou's back door.

seventeen

ONCE I BEGIN TO WORK AT MY PROGRAM, John arranges it so that we can walk the track inside the secure compound. Just the two of us. Low-profile housing units border the track on three sides. At the far end is the main complex with its glass windows two stories high. The sightlines are perfect. There are no shadows to hide in when you're in the compound. An imposing perimeter fence of brick and steel joins one building to the next. On summer days you can see trees poking their branches up on the other side of the wall. There's even an apartment building that's been built a little ways off. People can look right down into our courtyard from the higher balconies while they barbecue.

Seven laps of the track makes a kilometre. The centrifugal force caused by endless corners forces me to think about life as a cycle of hopeless repetitions. There is the constant monotony of reflection. Samsara. I read about that in a book on world religions. I read more and more each day.

John gets me time with him on the track most days his schedule allows it. Even cold wet days we walk. Out on the track John talks incessantly. I can't shut him up, though I'm not sure I would if I could. The contrast is jarring. It's like having two workers. "Why do you talk so much out here, but not in there?" I once asked him, pointing back to the unit. He'd just spoken for a full twenty minutes with barely a pause to moisten his lips.

He'd looked at me with a real gentleness in his eyes. "No point talking if people aren't listening," he said, like this was the most obvious thing in the world and something I should already have known.

"People always listen to you, John," I said.

"They hear my orders but they're not really listening. Out here, there's no one to take the conversation away."

He was right. Even under the bright area lights on grey winter days, when our ski jackets make us stand out against the walled backdrop, we remain remarkably private as long as we keep moving. Stop too long and others passing nearby are likely to overhear our conversation. It suits me fine to listen.

Mostly, John tells me about his time overseas. At first I don't believe him. He tells the same stories to all the boys. We share them with each other. I'm pretty certain that none of what he tells us is true. But he insists we listen just the same, to stories that make the world seem large and colourful.

"Joey, do you ever think you'll make a difference?" John is looking straight ahead. His hands out by his side despite the cold. He strides when he walks. The pace helps keep us warm. "You know, do something that really makes people stand up and take notice?"

"No," I answer and thrust my hands deep into my coat pockets.

"You should, you know. Should be thinking about the future. If you don't, life has a way of coming around and biting you. Know what I mean?"

I know he's not really looking for an answer. He's working himself into a story, like Lou does.

"You know I worked overseas for a time. I've told you that."

"Many times," I mumble, but he ignores me. John takes a long slow breath. There remains just the sound of our footsteps. They echo back to us as we get closer to the perimeter wall.

"Actually, I spent a lot of time overseas. In places like Pakistan and Tanzania. You probably don't even know where those places are, do you? I didn't when I was your age. I didn't really believe anything I did had much consequence either. It's not true. Life's a lot like a black mambo. Did you know a black mambo can raise itself six feet? It can bite you on the top of your head." John now looks at me. His massive hand pats me on my crown. "Right up there. That is some snake. A snake like that deserves to be the most deadly. Each bite can kill you a hundred times over but it doesn't just bite you once. It keeps biting you. Once it decides it's going to mess you over, it does one fine job of it." He takes another long breath, sucking air through his teeth like he's just been burned. "Life's like that too. Trust me on this, once it bites, it doesn't stop."

I'm not sure whose life he's talking about, but it doesn't matter. It's a dour cold day and I'm outside while the rest of the guys are inside.

At times like this John is much more real to me. Though he's never entirely real. My worker, a caricature of brawn and wisdom. No weaknesses. The John in my head is all positive spaces. Like that picture of the two vases and the face I'd seen in art class. John remains to me only the face. The rest of his life ... imagined. I wonder if the John in my head is the same one who must dress up to go out to dinner with his wife (does John have a wife?). Even the staff room at the side of the guards' station in the main building seems to me a portal to some other dimension. What do they talk about in there? When they cross that threshold, are we remembered?

My grade seven art teacher taught me how to see imagined spaces. She liked to make her classes stare at arrangements of old chipped teapots and flowers, the unfamiliarity of still life, artefacts of her life, not ours. Then she'd tell us pompously, "Remember, boys and girls, the teapot in your head is not the real teapot." I'd winced at the thought. "Draw the teapot on the table," she'd insist. I'd try. Feel the synaptic pop of my brain switching left to right. Then I could see the space around the teapot, the illusion of what I thought was three dimensional disappearing into a canvas of shapes and shades. The negative spaces became solid. Like John's life. Fashioned from the shapes he leaves me to tease together.

I used be good at that. My art teacher would offer me her enchanting smile when she looked at my drawings. She would put a green star in the lower right-hand corner. Told the rest of the class to come see what I had done. "Teacher's pet," the girls teased. I'd stick my tongue out at them, then hide my pictures in my schoolbag. When I got home I'd throw them away.

"I never went looking for trouble, but Christ, it found me," John says. We'd settled into a rhythm. An apprenticeship in what was to become life's dirtier lessons.

"There are towns in Northern Pakistan that are so polluted with diesel, your skin turns sooty. Blacker than me even. The dust thick like you can't imagine. The homes are cement block flats with black painted grating for windows. Makes this jail look like a hotel. In front of the homes are these fruit sellers and old ladies with bright red and yellow head scarves with sheets laid on the ground selling pots and underwear. God, the smell. There's durians and jackfruit, when it's in season, and both stink up the street. You've probably never smelled those things, have you?" I shake my head. "It doesn't matter. Just imagine something tangy and putrid. You have that?" I nod. "You smell them everywhere, except of course when you get too close to the open sewers where men and children squat relieving themselves next to the fruit sellers. The sewers reek worse when the weather is dry. Without the rain the place is toxic. You can feel the cancer cells taking you over, just breathing. And sometimes when it all hits you at once, your stomach heaves. But you just have to live with it. You understand? If you have commitments like I had, you can't just run away. I had something important to do there. I was leading this group of young people, not much older than you. We were building a school for Afghani refugees. We'd fundraised, then flown over and were actually building it, brick by sorry brick. Sounds glamorous, don't it, jetting halfway around the world on a mission of mercy, but mostly it was hard work."

I'm really not sure why John is telling me all this. The stories fill time but I'm not so stupid as to think he's not got some other purpose. I look down at my feet and keep walking while John keeps talking.

"Things like that look better from this side. Those kids I took over were all psyched for adventure. It wasn't a religious thing, but Christ, for some of them it was like they were boy scouts for Jesus. At least until they'd put in eight hours and used squat toilets that were rank with the sludge of everyone's crap. Or they'd choked back too many diesel fumes exhausting themselves unloading cement blocks from lorries. Then they'd figured out what's really important. And it wasn't helping some godforsaken refugees. It was a shower and clean sheets."

John stops walking for a moment. Stretches his big arms in a circle like he's guiding a jetliner down into our courtyard, locks his fingers behind his back and bends forward slightly. A reflective stretch summoning some greater energy. He draws a breath deep into his chest. It inflates with the effort. Then he exhales through his nose. I can hear the hiss.

"You put in that kind of effort, do without those sheets and the shower, then you've proven something. Given something back. It's all about knowing you made a difference."

A difference? Is that what John wants to make? I don't look at him. Keep walking and kicking the small stones that get tossed on the track by the ride-on mower. Sometimes we boys get to make a difference. We get to mow. But a resident has to be close to discharge before they'll trust him. They they'll make him wear steel-toed boots, and plastic goggles, and gloves. Even a reflective vest. They want us to be safe, too safe. Dress us up like grass gladiators. Afterwards, the fresh-cut grass looks so orderly, you'd think you were in the Public Gardens with their fancy flowerbeds and trimmed walkways. I know it's silly, but I want to ride the mower someday so I can be the one to make the grass look like that. Lou would like that.

"After a while you got used to being there." John is oblivious to my thoughts. "I actually used to like the chaos," he says. "There were motorized three-wheel rickshaws and bicycle rickshaws too. They're used to pull people and just about anything else you can imagine. And there's loads of mini-buses made from Toyota vans that hold sixteen, maybe eighteen passengers, each. It's complete chaos. Lawless too. Maybe that's the part you'd like, Joey?" He smiles down at me with the tease. "There were like no rules." He laughs. "At least not officially." I follow his lead and laugh with him.

"I'm sure there was a time when people obeyed the laws. There were these old buildings around with the names of British businesses that used to be there. Names like Raj Transport and Her Majesty's

Furniture. The buildings might have been nice years ago but by the time we got there the dieselly grime had blackened all the stonework. Everything was falling apart."

As we approach the jail's perimeter wall we turn.

"Well, anyway, the border with Afghanistan was just a half-day's drive. There was a flood of Afghani refugees. The war had made a lot of people flee. They survived selling drugs, and arms. Or they'd join the Mujhaddin, freedom fighters. Scrawny men with long black beards, just like you see on television. And boys not much older than you. Believe it or not, they'd be out walking around with AK-47s, carrying guns like kids here carry Walkmans." John shakes his head, cusses "Sweet Jesus" more to himself than me. "Completely mad. They loved to fire guns in the air at weddings. Any excuse they could find. And all this live ammo is going up. And when I asked them about where the bullets land, they'd look at me like I was simple or something. '*Inshallah,*' that's what they'd say. That means, 'God willing.' Complete faith that God would protect them. Like he was up there catching the goddamn bullets. I decided it was better to make my own luck and hid under a roof. But, brother, did they ever laugh at me."

I've heard the boys on the unit teasing John about this before. Making guns from their fingers and yelling, "Take cover, John!" He's a good sport, though. He knows it shows the boys were listening.

"If it was so dangerous, John, why the fuck were you there?"

John scowls. "No swearing, okay." I look down at my feet, momentarily held in check.

After a pause and another turn, John says, "Being there, we had a purpose. That's what counted. That's the really special thing, Joey. Imagine waking up every single godforsaken day and having an honest-to-goodness purpose. Can you imagine that?" I shake my head. Feel slightly stupid for paying so much attention. But still, it feels safe out here. Not chocolate chip cookie safe, but safe like being in the shadow of a really big rock when the wind is howling and you're wet.

"And we got to do things, other things than just work. Like see the Khyber Pass. That's one of those famous places where Alexander the Great, in fact all the great armies, marched through. Think about that. Thousands of years of history, all happening in one place. And we're like on this Sunday drive, only with an armed escort of six soldiers and a jeep. And this soldier who is standing on the back bumper of the truck with his gun, he's telling me that as long as we stay on the pavement, we're fine, but ten feet on either side of the road and the Pakistani government has no authority. It's all tribal lands. The local chiefs decide what to do with you. That's what we foreigners have never understood. We think we can control those people. Educate them. Make them like us. Give them democracy. Christ, it ain't gonna happen. Theirs is an entirely different world."

Now I'm listening.

"You see it as you swerve through these dusty villages. There's mud-walled compounds with stalls selling sheets of hashish. Hashish! Draped narcotic pillowcases drying on roadside lines. And the government can't do anything about it. It was quite the trip, even if the air was choking us with grit and exhaust fumes that clogged us up like old carburetors. And everything was grey, brown or black, except for the bolts of cloth laid out in front of lines of women dressed in tent dresses. They call those burquas. Of course, you can't so much as look at a woman there." John throws a playful punch at my chin. Big brother like. He's checking to see if I'm still listening. I am. Soldiers and drugs, and women. I know he's got a point to make. Something about helping. There's something he wants me to know and I'm waiting.

"Of course, we weren't supposed to be out there with the army roaming the Northern Territory. Claude, my program director, had told me, 'You can't go to the Pass.' But I made like my phone wasn't working. 'Say again?' I'd kept shouting, then hung up. I know I shouldn't be telling you this, but it's the truth. I've never told the other boys this story, but I just think you need to hear this one. You okay with that?" I nod and warm slightly despite the chilly air seeping through my clothes.

"Good. Well, then, when the lorries showed up I told the participants, 'We're breaking the rules, boys.' And they all looked confused, except this one kid, Gonzales. He was this really interesting kid from the suburbs whose family had been refugees themselves. And he gets right quick with what I'm doing. Tells the rest of the kids, 'Who gives a crap what they think. Screw the rules.'"

John's radio crackles just then and he stops to answer a call. He holds it to his ear as he listens, then answers, "In ten minutes," and looks at me. "A couple of more laps, okay?"

I shrug. It's not my decision. If it was, I'd keep walking.

"So then we're off, right. And after a while the villages disappear. The air clears as we go higher into the hills. More donkeys, stinking camels, old bicycles, an occasional scooter, but fewer and fewer cars. Only, you see these Mercedes that speed by, with windows tinted dark, both front and back. They're arms dealers, drug lords. And somewhere along the way our lorry swerves to miss a child herding goats, or maybe just to miss the goats. I don't really know. But it doesn't slow, just changes lanes for a moment, the tires catching the far shoulder. And I'm thinking, 'Just stay on the road, buddy.'

"And then we're there. The pass is nothing special. It's in a valley. There's nothing much to impress us, but we still take snapshots of what we're allowed to photograph. Barren hills. Razor wire. Stuff like that. I'm not sure what I expected to find. Maybe thought I'd step on a discarded Roman tunic, or at least see a Russian assault helicopter hovering in the distance. But there was just camel and donkey dung that kept clinging to my sandals. You could tell the soldiers had no idea that this littered piece of scrub and rock had so much history. Still, I picked up a handful of dirt, put it in an empty film container I'd brought along.

"And then I did this thing with my eyes, Joey. I blinked, like I was snapping photographs of the guns and soldiers that they wouldn't let us point our cameras at." John shows me what he means. His big face scrunches up to make his eyes into shutters. "That's the memories I still keep with me," he says. "Khaki, armoured vehicles and sunshine on tin roofs over armouries. And all these lazy men with guns. Can you imagine all that?" John doesn't wait for an answer. "Oh, and this." John pulls from an inner coat pocket a small black film container. He opens it and inside is dirt so dry a mist swirls over it when John touches it.

I'm wondering if I'm being set up. Am I really supposed to believe John is hauling around a little bit of those dusty hills and just happens to have it in his pocket? Except John looks so sincere. And no one else is watching. No one would know if he's pulling one over on me. So I look John right in the eye. "This for real?"

"Yeah, of course."

I dip a finger into the dust. It's warm even though the day is cold. For a moment, I want to believe him. Except John's smiling now. I'm still worried that this is all some stupid joke. But John says nothing. Just looks again at his dirt, then closes the small plastic container and puts it back in his pocket.

We've almost finished our last lap around the track. John says, "You know, it was the strangest thing, being there. The soldiers had all finished their cigarettes. Some of them were coming back from the toilets, scratching their privates and adjusting their uniforms. And the lorry started its engine. There was this black clot of diesel chugging out the exhaust pipe. Maybe it was the heat, or the strangeness or the danger, but as our lorry backed up, then went forward and then turned again to get around the gates, it was all sort of confusing which direction we were headed. And you know, Joey, just for that moment, I imagined that we were headed across that border, into Afghanistan." John pauses. His tone changes. He sounds so serious I look at his face, but his attention is far away. "And I remember thinking, 'Now that would be wild, wouldn't it?' To be part of something like a war. A holy war. To be so passionate about something you're willing to die for it. To make your contribution and know, really know, that you'd done something for someone."

As he speaks these words we arrive back at the door to our unit. John radios main control. "Two in from the track." The radio crackles "ten-four" and John puts his key into the unit lock. The first door opens. We slip inside a small glassed enclosure. I kick off my shoes, putting on the slippers we're required to wear. John says, "Sometimes it's okay to break the rules, Joey. You just have to be sure you're doing it for the right reasons. You understand? That you're making things better, not worse. Can you see that?"

"Kinda," I answer with a squint. I'm feeling muddled. Wondering how John ever figured that looking after kids like me was the same as fighting some war.

"You'll get it yet," he says, then opens the second door that lets us onto the unit.

I grunt, "Thanks" and am pleased the other boys are ignoring me. I don't want them to ruin what I'm feeling with their smirks. Just for this moment I want to think about a purpose bigger than getting through this day. I go over to a chair near the television. I'm invisible here. Nobody notices that I keep my right hand out at my side, one finger still dusty with Pakistani dirt.

eighteen

D<small>EAR</small> J<small>OEY</small>,
    Congratulations on the new job. Though not so new anymore, is it? I'm not surprised it's Child Protection, given all that you went through. Does your mother know? I don't suppose you have much contact with her, do you? I'm not sure she'd approve anyway. Ignore her. You're doing what you should be doing. Setting things right, aren't you? Besides, you don't owe her anything. Remember that. She owes you, Joey. You're a great kid, and it's her loss if she doesn't know what she has.

    Things here are much the same as ever, though our numbers are down. We've closed one of the housing units. There's new legislation that's making it harder to put kids away. Just as well – all we did in most cases was teach you little f'ers how to be better criminals. You're one of the few graduates who did something with his life. Besides, there aren't as many of you these days. They tell me all those programs we started (you probably studied all about them, safe sex campaigns, stay-in-school initiatives, those kinds of thing) they mean there's fewer neglected kids. I'm not sure that's what's made the difference. I think it's abortions myself. No unwanted

146

pregnancies, no delinquents. Simple logic. Not popular to say, though, but that's likely the truth. I just can't bring myself to give credit where credit's not due.

Tell me how you're getting along when you've got a moment.

As always,
John

* * *

The day after I visit Mr. Jeffrey at home, I speak with the home-makers, older women who themselves have had children and now work as case aides. I love them dearly. Each is a fountain of support without Ellen's put-downs. Sandy, as she likes us to call her, though her real name is Marilyn ("Like Marilyn Monroe"), flicks her blond hair like a little girl, laughs at every joke. She's in her fifties now. I imagine she must have been quite a good-looking woman years before.

Sandy loves my attention. I describe Mr. Jeffrey's home to her and she knows instantly how she can help. "Nasty stuff, living with all that filth. Why don't you tell the family I'll come by and help Joan tidy up. I'll even bring some new books for Cameron. They'll keep him busy while we tidy. I'm sure Joan is just overwhelmed, that's all. You tell her that, okay?"

I'm thankful that this time I can offer Joan something more than platitudes. Sandy will be my eyes and ears for a few weeks. I trust her completely.

I drive out to Mr. Jeffrey's a few hours later to quietly negotiate with Joan to let Sandy visit. "You spying on us?" Joan asks, looking at me sideways.

"No one is going to take Cameron," I reassure her. "Sandy will make it less likely you have to meet with any social workers. Ever. She'll help you get things sorted out. You can even get some sleep if you need it. She'll look after Cameron. Whatever helps, okay?" The of-

fer is too irresistible and she accepts. Even agrees to put the dogs outside so the floors can get a good scrubbing. For a second she looks
mildly hopeful, her face relaxed as she swats away a housefly that's
landed in her hair.

As I walk out their door this time, I think, "What if social workers got standing ovations when we did something right?" I should write
John about that. If I did I'd tell him how I just kept some cherub-
faced kid at home, a little safer, maybe better fed, a whole lot less
filthy, and his mother a little more connected to the world. But what
do I get? More paperwork for sure. And likely another of Ellen's ugly
lectures. I shake my head as I drive, grasping for comprehension of the
kind of humility it takes to be Shirley. Shirley's professionalism means
no accolades. She is ever the cloistered do-gooder. Maybe Shirley's just
a saint in the flesh. For a brief moment it occurs to me that not everything she says is necessarily nonsense.

I'm at the computer in my office when Ellen arrives. "When will
you be done? I've had two no-shows. I have notes to file." She fully
expects me to leave the keyboard right away.

"I'll be done in a bit. With the computer, that is."

She's angry, though I have no idea at what. She exhales while
mouthing a long and very quiet "Men." At first I can't believe she said
that. But before I can tell her about the success I'm having, and how
Joan likes me, maybe even suggest her no-show clients are trying to
tell her something, before I can say any of it she has stormed out of
the office to the staff room. A minute later, as I type the requisition
for Sandy's time, I can hear the clunk of the pop machine dispensing
Ellen's Diet Coke.

I pity Ellen. Ellen, whose walls are bare. I want something different for my life. I envy Shirley the continuity. The way she is here each
day. The way she has hung in. Her work paced like John's, steady and
rhythmic, one generation to the next.

My life feels more like a dramatic fall down an elevator shaft. I'm
a wet butterfly. My wings outstretched, they bruise against the walls of
my confinement. The light above drawing me, a flame, but my descent
inevitable. I'm never sure why John has kept in touch all these years.
It's not to watch my fall, that's for sure. And yet, what can he do to

raise me? When I look in the mirror I'm ashamed to admit I still see his client. A boy, a delinquent really, cloaked in university parchment, but a bad little boy nonetheless.

When I write John, it is usually with the unusual. I still try to throw him off balance, just like I did years ago on the living unit. I don't know why I do that. Maybe it's fear of getting too close or a reluctance to accept his invitation to be my best. To be who he wants me to be. My first letter to him during my internship at university was meant to shock. I was on placement at a children's mental health clinic where I was supposed to run a recreation program for child victims of sexual abuse. I was still so new to the work that the stories I heard could scratch at old wounds.

"I met a kid today who told me his parents are into threesomes," I'd written John. "He's only eleven and that's what he said. So I asked him how he knew that. And he tells me he gets sent to his room with a movie and told not to come out. His prick of a step-dad gives him ten bucks if he does like he's told. So I asked his mother about it later, when the kid is off playing. And she looks at me like 'So what?' She tells me she's the one who invited the other woman into the bedroom. She's like taking this uber-feminist line about how she's in control."

My pen had run out of ink by that point and I'd had to switch to pencil. I had wondered if John would read some secret meaning into that. Interpret what was purely coincidental.

"It's not the part about the parents that I don't get," I'd continued writing. "Like the part about the sex, I can reach for that real easy. That much you likely know about me. But the part with the kid? Like these parents are buying prostitutes and doing this while he's next door. He can hear most of it. He tells me they take turns. Says he can hear moans and screams. But mostly he says he just turns the volume up on his television. He told me all about it like it was so normal."

I thought I was just using the letter to John to show him I was still able to get his attention. Except the note was turning into something unintended. A confessional of sorts. I had wondered if John would get it. Understand why this story. Why this would be the one I shared.

Such a long letter from me was unusual, but I kept writing. "He blew the ten bucks once when he came out of his room for a piss and there was this woman completely naked sitting on the toilet, and he just walked in on her and she says to him as nice as day, 'Hi kid.' And like he stands there waiting to pee, he tells me, and she finishes up, then walks back to the bedroom. But when his parents heard what he'd done, his mother comes out with a towel in front of her and yells at him for leaving his room. Then he hears the mother wailing at the prostitute and somebody hits the ground and all of a sudden doors are slamming and next thing the kid knows the step-dad flies into his room, yelling, 'You just lost your ten bucks, buddy,' and slams his door so hard it shakes his basketball net that he tells me is nailed on the back. I think he was ticked that it broke. That's what really pissed him off. Crazy, eh?"

As I wrote those words I remember finding it odd that the boy could describe it all. That he had words and phrases for what he'd seen. For what had happened to him.

"You know ..." I continued to write, then stopped abruptly. I wanted to tell John more things. Sort wheat from chaff. Fact from fiction. Tell him about insides and outsides that are no longer distinguishable one from the other. About how confusing it was becoming a social worker who could hear others' stories, but still felt his own silenced. I should have just glazed over, let the boy's story be his alone. Except, stories have a way of leaking backwards into our lives. Their toxic seepage make us mistake ourselves for who we're not. Remind us of lost opportunities and moments when decisions failed us. I just sat there with the letter unfinished, worried and confused, unsure how to tell John even some small part of who I really am.

Frustrated, I crumpled the letter into a ball. I was angry. Not at John, but at myself. The light at the top of the shaft disappearing. I wanted to stretch. Tears came close to showing. I was falling. Then drowning. Until heavy breaths that I pushed forcibly down gave me buoyancy. Helped me to rise. In a gush, I committed to telling John about my abuse, about my mother, and my father's death.

But not right then.

I smoothed the crumpled letter and put it into my backpack to take home with me. It would eventually find its place among many other reflections in a bottom drawer. *Another time, John,* I'd thought to myself, then started another letter.

"Dear John," I wrote. "Everything is going well ..."

nineteen

IN CLASS TODAY THERE IS NO TALKING. B-boy has taken over for Miss Simpson so she can have an operation. We only know that because Jack was sitting on a chair outside the nurse's room waiting for a tetanus shot after stabbing himself with a finishing nail that he'd found in a corner of the courtyard by the new shed they built to house the ride-on mower. He wanted to prove to everyone his piercings were done just as he said they were, with a hot needle and lots of pain. He insisted that Native kids were tougher than us white kids. So while we're all outside watching the guards play ball with a few of the keeners from another unit, he takes the nail, which is a whole lot thicker than a needle, and rams it up through his bottom lip. I practically heaved when he did this. The other boys, too, together made this big "Ugh" which of course brought John over to us. We all looked the other way, but there was Jack with a gaping hole in his bottom lip and in his hand a nail, still bloody.

"Christ," said John, and he grabbed the nail, then lifted Jack by the arms and took him down to the nurse's station.

Jack told us the nurse was talking with Skunk-lady. Said something about her history and her rectum. Or rectumy, something like

152

that. We couldn't make much sense of what he was saying but knew it was way too much information. Our workers and their personal plumbing. None of us really want to go there.

B-boy says he's not sure how long Miss Simpson will be indisposed. That's the word B-boy uses. I think of garbage bins instead of someone in a hospital bed. Sorted by product. Would Miss Simpson be recyclable A, B, or C? Or just plain trash? Out of respect for her, we sit quietly and don't give B-boy too hard a time.

After class, there's a break and we hang out on the unit. We're not allowed to watch television until after school, so most of us just flake out on the softer chairs and close our eyes. I sometimes take up a game of chess with John if he has the time. He likes to be asked. I've even seen him refuse a phone call if we're in the end game and I'm struggling to keep my queen. If I look close at John's eyes, he'll always tell me the piece to move. He just stares. Or coughs or hums when I go to touch the wrong piece. He never says anything, though. I'm sure watching us, you'd think John was some autistic retard, making weird sounds, rocking on his chair when he is about to make some big move that's going kill me.

If time's running out, John usually rocks a bit faster and then puts me in checkmate in a move or two.

Days I'm not allowed to go to shop class, or into the gym, or anywhere near the girls, I get to do my own studying in the library, with a guard from the front desk as company. Most boys hate library time. You have to read, or at least make like you're reading. I actually like to read. The words come easy to me. Even ones I haven't seen before, like sardonic, serendipity, and ecclesiastical. There's a dictionary I can use, but mostly I just say the word and ignore the meaning. If I went and got the dictionary, the guards might tease me. They might force me back to class. Playing bad, I get to read more. I've worked my way through donated boxes of classics. Penguin special editions with red and black covers. The covers make you yawn. Feel ... how would I say it? Ennui? But inside, the stories are fine. I've taken a stab at Dostoevsky and Austen. I guess you have to be a girl to like Austen. There are other books, like *To Kill a Mockingbird*, and this really long violent poem about the Trojan war. It's weird the way I can read this stuff. I shouldn't be able to. No one else can. Mostly they read John Grisham novels. I read those too, in a single go at night. Or Stephen King. Helps put me to sleep. But I like something about a book that you open and smell stale paper and dust. If it's been read a lot, some of the pages may be falling out. Each, a loose thought. Sometimes I read the pages out of order, guessing at what happened before. Imagining my own plots. Then put the pages back in sequence. Except, some books come with missing pages. I read through hundreds of pages of *The French Lieutenant's Woman*, only to find out the last twenty weren't there. When I asked one of the workers if she could get me another copy, she just laughed.

The workers browse the magazines. Old issues of *Good Housekeeping*, *O*, and *Cosmopolitan*. The guys like that one as much as the girls.

They come and get me when the rest of my unit is moving to their next activity. If they're coming from shop class, the boys have sawdust in their hair and wood chips stuck to their socks. There's a smell of resin and paint. One time Jeremy came out wearing a Band-Aid on his middle finger. "Cut it on the bandsaw," he said proudly, then smiled. Goof. I couldn't see what was funny until he pointed the finger up and I realized he could walk around like that all day if he wanted.

"Jeremy, put that down," said B-boy, though he couldn't resist laughing a little.

"It heals better if the blood drains." The rest of us snickered and B-boy rolled his eyes.

After class, John tries to walk me around the track at least once a week. The rest of the boys have television privileges, which means the unit is quiet.

Most days, John just begins talking. But sometimes, when I've had a really good day, he'll ask me if I want to talk or listen. I mostly say listen. Except one day I ask him, "Why are you telling me all these stories?"

He stops his lumbering gate. "You'll remember my stories long after you forget me," he says. I'm not so sure, but nod just the same. Then he looks at me differently. There's something urgent in his eyes. A lick of fire. And for a moment I'm not talking to my worker, just some nice guy named John. "Sometimes I'm really afraid that when I die, that's it. I'll be forgotten. As quick as my body cools. What do I leave behind? Just you, and the other kids, and a few stories." He bends a little towards me. "Any of that making sense?" I suddenly feel very mature. Like you do when you dress up fancy for dinner even if you are still eating from the kids' menu. For an instant, everything feels different. Endless. And with a point. I wake out of my routine. Again, I'm watching myself. Only this time, I see a young man doing something right, and listening.

"I want to leave having done some good," John says. "Not just harm."

"What bad things you ever done?" I tease.

John clears his throat, dismissing my question. Folds his arms, looks at me. "You're a clever one. Good listener. You should do something with that."

I actually blush, then blink twice to wash away the moment. The compliment lands somewhere solid inside, somewhere I didn't know existed. And suddenly I want to listen that much harder.

twenty

THERE ARE GOOD THINGS ABOUT JAIL. There's more gym time here than at school. On the gym floor you can roughhouse, bodycheck, even take a swipe at someone's head when the guards aren't watching. Sometimes the guards play stick hockey with us. Or basketball. When they're playing you can almost mistake them for big brothers, or what I imagine a big brother might be like.

We walk from the housing unit down the paved path to the main complex to get to the gym. One Wednesday in January the weather is grey and wet. I remember it was Wednesday because there were greasy chicken nuggets for lunch, just like every Wednesday. The building's red brick was dyed a deep maroon by the winter rain. We could feel the wetness soaking through our crappy raincoats down to our t-shirts. It was a blustery thaw of a day, but the heavy wind that swayed the tops of trees was much lighter inside the courtyard on account of the walls that surrounded us. The rain sluiced down the roof into gutters that ring the complex. The water funnelled into a drain at the edge of the building. The drain had a large metal grate over it and two padlocks and an iron bar.

You could drive by the building and hardly know what lay behind those walls. There's no hint of anything but a government building doing whatever governments do. Tinted glass. Heat efficient. A few shrubs planted along the cement walkway to the front door. They even planted a few of those tiny evergreens by the side door where the sheriff escorts you in, cuffed, a firm hand on the scruff of your neck.

We clear the glass doors that lead in from the courtyard and Pamela, our escort, shouts to the guards at the main desk, "Six to the gym." We bank to the left like a row of geese all the while honking jibes at Clarence, an older worker who's on the desk with a crisp-looking young man we've never seen before.

"Still on, Clarence?"

"When you goin' home, man?"

"Hey, Clarence, like get a life, man."

Clarence loves the attention. He leans a bit closer to his security monitors and squints through his glasses. "Now boys," he says without looking up, "what would I do without all of you, eh?" Then he lifts his head and, with a wizened grin, shouts happily, "My time is your time, boys. Feel free to come join me down here anytime. Best accommodations in the house."

And we all laugh in snorts. Clarence is okay. When you're in the safety cell, you know he's watching, but somehow, knowing it's him you don't mind as much.

Pamela holds her hand up like a traffic cop so that a unit of girls can go by on their way to the games room. Carrie's among them. She shows me a small wave. Then keeps walking, her ass wiggling in the same grey sweats we all wear.

"Hey, Clarence," I shout, "you sold any of those tapes of me in the safety room yet? I want my cut. My actor's fee."

Clarence puts two hands on the counter in front of him. Behind him I hear the crackle of a radio and he tells the young man beside him to take the keys and go and unlock something. "Naw," he shouts, "had an offer from Discovery, you know, jungle life series, but they were only offering six figures. Thought I'd hold out for a bit more. Hell, all that puke and piss, that's got to be worth more. Right, boys?" We all laugh.

The young guard pushes past us, without so much as an excuse
me. He's headed towards the girls who are leaning up against the walls
farther down the hall. If you time it right, you can meet a girl at the
water fountain that's just outside the games room door, which is across
from the gym. You can make like you're drinking, let the water course
across your lips while you mumble a message to whoever's lined up
behind you. Sometimes the younger guards get impatient and will deny
you fountain privileges if you take too long. But the older ones, like
Clarence and John, they see no harm in it. They'll wait there as long
as you want them to wait, whistling so they don't have to hear what
you're saying.

I can hear the games room door being unlocked, then the gym
is unlocked and its big double doors opened. As we file in, the young
guard is also unlocking the equipment room. Its door is next to the
games room, just past the fountain. He doesn't actually open the door.
There's no need. The last unit to use the gym has left everything out
for us. Still, it's odd that he did that. Usually it's the unit staff who
use their own keys when they need to get the basketballs or the floor
hockey sticks.

I actually like to spend time in the equipment room. It's the only
quiet place that's not a cell. I like being asked to tidy up in there. In
there among the sticks and balls, and big blue buckets with the volleyball nets and the metal shelves full of outdoor equipment, the smell
of grass lingers even in winter. It's impossibly quiet, the way it can be
when things aren't used too often and they find their place. You feel
important when you're in there alone. A warm feeling that makes your
chest tingle. Like you're responsible enough to be doing something for
someone else.

Today we'll play volleyball. We challenge another unit who are
marched in after us. Not much chance for contact in volleyball but we
do what we can to make the game physical, kneeing each other at the
net, throwing shoulder punches as congratulations for a good hit. No
one really knows how to spike, though a few of the guys try making
leaps up at the net, their arms rubbed raw as they catch on the top
and fall backwards. Pamela plays too, so we have to rotate through po-
sitions, waiting on the sidelines every seventh turn. When it's my turn

to wait, I ask the new guard who's still down watching the game if I can go for a drink. He nods, practically ignoring me. He's watching Pamela serve, her sports bra barely holding her tits as she leaps and lands. The new guy doesn't even want to know my name. He should have radioed my movement to the front desk. I push through the heavy gym door, which slides closed quietly behind me, muffling the applause and shouts of my unit mates who are three points up and on a roll. I take my time. Carrie's come out for a drink too. For a moment, the doors to both the gym and the games room are closed and we're there at the fountain alone.

"Hey," I say.

"Hi," she answers shyly.

As I lean to take a drink, an idea flies into my head. Impulsively, I grab Carrie's hand. Put my index finger up to my mouth. "You up for some fun?" I ask in a whisper. And without waiting for an answer, I pull her willing body through the unlocked door to the equipment room, quietly closing it behind me as Carrie stands giggling inside. As the door clicks closed, I feel an excitement I haven't felt in weeks. A part of me re-awakening. Not the bad kid, but the adventuresome one. The one who knew how to beat the system at its own foolishness. There is something sweet in knowing that any moment, my workers are going to shit themselves thinking that Carrie and I have escaped. They are going to again have some great stories to tell about Joey. They'll know it was me who thought this up. No offence to Carrie, but it will be obvious to them who's to blame. I'll again be the clever kid who you have to watch. And when I walk back onto my unit in a few days, because it will take them a few days to trust me again, Jeremy and the rest of the boys will offer high fives and friendly jabs. Tease me about being alone with Carrie. Jeremy will be a bit jealous, of course. Not because I got to be alone with Carrie, but because he didn't think of this first. I put my arm around Carrie and join her nervous laughter.

At first we don't know what to do except stand there by the door, waiting. I let go of her and Carrie starts shifting foot to foot, arms folded in front of her, bouncing like she has to pee. She doesn't offer to help while I tug on a large metal shelving unit and work it over to the door. Then I take another and wedge it sideways so the door is blocked. Then I go stand beside Carrie again and wait for someone to pound.

It's a couple of minutes before we hear the dull thud of the games room door open and close, and the murmur of a worker's voice on a radio, then steps up the hallway to the front desk. They'll look for Carrie, think she went to the desk for something. Likely be angry. Probably already preparing the mini lecture. About how she is not allowed to do anything without a worker's permission. Carrie and I creep to the door and put our ears up to it and wait for the gymnasium door to open. For the new guard to realize he's fucked up bad. And while I'm waiting, Carrie seems to realize we are alone and that I'm actually every bit as clever as Jeremy, and she leans over and rests her head on my shoulder while I'm still leaning against the door. Then she kisses me on the cheek and I'm realizing that she's thinking this was all an excuse to get into her pants. The warmth of her lips excites me. It's been a while since anyone touched me. And I think, *Why not go for it?* Only not all my attention is on Carrie, because the stupid jerks in the gym aren't playing their part. I'd be more into getting it on with her if my workers would notice I'm missing. Christ, they haven't even started looking for me yet. The fuckin' idiots. I knew they were all losers, but this is a bit much. Even Carrie's workers have at least begun to make the effort to do their job. But Dork and Pamela, hell, they're so into flirting that they haven't even caught on to how much I'm screwing them over.

All this thinking is making me fuming mad. No cavalry. No angry pounding. No audience. My workers are leaving me here to wait, like I'm *that* fuckin' unimportant.

And it occurs to me the only one who is ever going to tell this story is Carrie, who's now holding my hand. So I kiss her. She tastes stale. I wouldn't say it, but I think her tongue needs brushing. She doesn't really move her lips either. Kissing her is more like velcroing myself to dry rough flesh. Then she moves awkwardly in front of me and backs me up against the wall next to the door. She giggles again. Imitates a romantic moment by craning forward and letting her head rest a bit below my chin, only she's just about my height so the effect is more like stooping than a swoon. I guess I'm the bad boy now. I feel bad. And she wants me to be the bad boy. Wants my hands to claw all over her tits. Only, it's difficult to concentrate on her, when what I'm really thinking is why hasn't anyone come to find us. It's like I'm more invisible that I ever was. Even Carrie isn't really seeing me. Just the cardboard cut-out she wants me to be.

But at least she's here. Still craning, and then reaching down into my pants, which is really appreciated and all. And she feels me hard and backs up and turns around, and takes off her t-shirt and this little white cotton bra, and then she turns back to me and goes back to the crane position. She's got cute little breasts, soft mounds with the nipples not really out, but flat. There's no shadow underneath. She's too small. I've seen girls' tits before, and felt them flat against me when I'm on top, but I usually have to work harder to get at them. Carrie's such a slut, you can see there is nothing that she won't let me do. Only, just as I'm sort of thinking I should just fuck this entire game of hide-and-go-seek, ignore the workers who still haven't noticed I'm gone, be totally here with Carrie and just enjoy this half-time show, that's when I hear the door to the gym open and two voices and then static from a handheld radio. And Carrie freezes and with a hand over her mouth, giggles again. Puts her arms over her chest but doesn't pick her clothes up off the floor. And I'm smiling too. *Finally!*

At least until I see the handle to the door turn and someone tries to push it open, except I have it so well jammed it's like it's locked with a deadbolt. Then I hear two units of boys and a unit of girls marched past us with radios beeping and workers shouting, "Six back to the unit," with an urgency that tells me I'm winning.

Then it's quiet again. And Carrie and I slide ourselves down the wall and cuddle together. We wait, again. And Carrie puts a hand back down my pants and is about to put her mouth down into my lap where my hard-on is making a tent from my sweats when I hear Clarence's voice near the door yelling at someone. Then it's his hand on the door handle and this time he pushes with such force that he can tell the door is not bolted shut as it should be but blocked from behind. "Jesus H. Christ," he shouts. "Joey, Carrie, you in there?" Carrie pulls her hand back and we both stay real quiet. We want to see how long it takes for them to figure out what's happened.

There's a bit more murmuring outside the door and I punch the air with my fist and give Carrie a silent high five. I have forgotten her advances. This other drama is a much bigger turn-on. Carrie, sensing that something's about to happen, reaches for her t-shirt and bra, and slips them on as workers' fists slam again and again against the door. Still nothing budges. We've got a stalemate. And all the attention.

I imagine lots happening right now. The cement walls in here don't let too much sound travel. The ceiling tiles up top and the ventilation opening send us only muffled shouts, and the occasional curse.

Then the door presses open, slowly, breaking the seal. "Joey? Carrie? You've got to come out. Enough of this." It's Clarence again. Calm and sincere. I feel sort of sorry for doing this to him. And Carrie looks at me obviously wondering if she should say anything. I just hold my fingers to my mouth. Then we both get up slowly and move deeper into the room, tucking ourselves in behind the large blue buckets at the back that hold the summer equipment. We reach out and pull down pinnies and a couple of life jackets to make ourselves a comfortable nest.

There're lots of hockey sticks we could use to defend ourselves, but that would just be stupid. Instead, we sit there, comfortably, and begin to whisper insults under our breath. "Idiots," I say. "Fuckin' assholes," adds Carrie. Neither of us is feeling very creative. We stare at the walls while Clarence keeps trying to cajole us into answering him. Then he sighs, and the door seals up again. We smirk at one another and stretch out. Wondering what's next.

It's only a minute and then Skunk-lady's at the door. "Oh Christ," I say, loud enough she likely hears me.

"I know you don't want to get into more trouble, Joey. Now you two really need to think about what you're both doing. Do you really want your workers to get in trouble? Just think about what it's like for all of us."

Carrie and I are laughing now. The only thing I care about is notoriety. I never thought we could keep this going for this long, but now, all I'm thinking is Guinness world record holder for biggest in-your-face lark in the youth centre's history. The roar in my ears from the excitement sounds almost like applause.

When we don't respond, Skunk-lady gives up. I put an arm back around Carrie who is tight to the corner of the room. If I'm really going to make this a story, I should fuck her. That would be something. I doubt any other kid's ever done that in here. So I reach over and put my hand right on her breast. She doesn't do much of anything. But keeps staring at the door. It's like kneading clay. I wish she'd swoon again, but now I guess she knows what I'm thinking and there's no real way she can do anything to say no. And that's when it comes to me this is turning into a rape, more than a fuck. And Carrie is zoning out, letting me do whatever I want. I could pull her sweats down, or force her mouth onto me. I know she'd do it. And that's sort of confusing, because I don't really think that's what I want. Her vacant eyes make me think of being touched too, in strange ways. Of times when touch hurt inside. I really want her to want me. Just like I want the guards to notice me gone. Only now the guards are doing their bit, but Carrie's not doing hers. So I just take my hand away and she doesn't do anything except go on staring at the far wall.

It's quiet now.

We wait long enough to get a little hungry and Carrie is squirming, which makes me think that maybe she wasn't just out to get a drink of water. Where in hell is she going to go for a piss in here? Or worse.

We don't talk. We just sit there, eventually stretching out, our backs up against the dimpled cinderblocks, staring at the ceiling tiles. Until we hear a scraping sound up above us, and squint weird-like at the sound. Then one of the tiles opens up and out drops skinny little B-boy, who as he drops to the floor tumbles over on his ankles, which give way. He yells, "Don't move," as if he could do anything about it, and Carrie has to cover her mouth to smother another laugh, because B-boy is poised like you see actors in action movies, with his right arm outstretched, and a can of pepper spray ready to be used.

Neither of us does anything but sit there. Staring.

And B-boy, who's now kneeling, glances around the room, and clicks his radio to life, shouting, "I'm in! I'm in!" Like where else would he be, I wonder?

"Took you friggin' long enough," I say, which makes Carrie take her hand from her mouth and laugh loud. B-boy looks a little confused now that he's outnumbered, even with his pepper spray. He crawls towards the door and begins to pull the metal shelving away. Only he's struggling because I tumbled several shelves on top of one another. He's really huffing what with his bad ankle, so I get up, which makes him stop what he's doing and point the can at me.

"Let me help you with that," I say, and real nonchalant begin to move the metal shelving. "That one goes here. You don't want to be making a mess, now do you?" I tell B-boy, as the door is forced open and three more guards rush in but aren't too sure what to do next. They stand there, the fabulous four. At least they're finally here, I'm thinking. I turn my back to them and kneel down and give Carrie a big kiss, with a whole lot of lip movement until I feel B-boy's hand on my shoulder and he and the other guards press me down to the ground and cuff me.

"Now gently, boys," I say to them.

As they yank me to my feet again, I take a last look at Carrie, who is still there in the corner giggling, her legs crossed tight to keep from pissing herself.

* * *

A month after Carrie and I barricaded ourselves in the equipment room, it was John, not my teachers, who began asking me about university. Every six weeks, staff held these incomprehensible case conferences to which my mother was invited but never came. I would sit there listening to reports read in monotones. Miss Simpson, my math and social studies teacher with the bad attitude, who I still hadn't forgiven for embarrassing herself, reads her report verbatim from her handwritten notes. She never looks up, leaving us to stare at touches of grey at the fringes of a mountain of jet-black hair she keeps pulled up into a bun. Her aging face reminds me of the death masks of mummies, loose flesh pulled tight at the edges. We boys were always laughing behind her back when she bent over and her underwear rode up above her polyester pants. When I'd get bored in class I'd make doodles of her in a chastity belt, with a little heart-shaped lock on the front and her big wide hips flowing over the chains circling her waist and thighs.

"Joey continues to demonstrate capacity," she reads. "He is doing extremely well with the concepts being presented and should be easily able to complete all his grade twelve school leaving credits *if* he applies himself." Miss Simpson's words meet with a chorus of feeble nods and a few cursory looks my way. Even Skunk-lady, who comes to these meetings, casts me a wry little smile. We've met more than once since the incident in the equipment room. She's told me she has forgiven me for acting so silly in her office.

Miss Simpson says she has great plans for me. "Joey could go to a community college if he really put his mind to it. There is no reason why he couldn't continue with his education." She says "education" with a slightly British accent, though she's not British. Gives the feel she is talking about something extra special. Like Lady Di. Or lace. "What do you think, Joey?" she asks, finally lifting her eyes from the page. But before I can speak, she says, "You may want to look at some of the trades or even consider becoming a technical writer, maybe a paralegal. You have great potential." She enunciates "potential" with the same flourish as "education." Extends her chin, which helps make her look like she only has one chin instead of three. Says, "Though we must keep in mind that you do tend to be disruptive in class. And incite others to disobey even the simplest instructions." She casts her eyes over to Skunk-lady, but not to John. "You have potential," she says again, "but young man, you make it difficult to teach. Anything. To anyone."

Skunk-lady takes that as her cue. "It's not that you're not bright enough, Joey. It's just that the questions you ask are often frivolous and disruptive. Do you understand?"

They weren't waiting for answers.

"Joey," Miss Simpson continues, "you need structure. The kind of thing you'd find at a trade school. Don't you agree?"

John sits quietly, biding his time. He keeps his large hands folded in his lap, his eyes cast down. I think he hates them for their arrogance as much as I do. Only he's more polite about it. "So he's doing really good then?" John asks when the ladies have stopped nattering on about my weaknesses. Offering me cautions. "What about university, then? Perhaps we could take him down to meet a counsellor, see what his interests are. Seems like college might not provide enough challenge." John doesn't ask me what I think.

Miss Simpson is obviously feeling trumped. "It's not that I can't see his potential," she says quickly, lips pursed. Sugary politeness a coating over what even I can't miss as malice. "But I think we might be setting Joey up for failure." She looks at me instead of John. Says too kindly, "No one in your family has ever gone past high school, isn't that right, Joey?" I shrug. She doesn't need me to add to her trap. "And then there are the money problems." Now she's looking at John. "He wouldn't get much funding and if he did he'd have to manage it carefully. No drugs, or drinking. Let's be realistic. Joey, you haven't exactly excelled at managing your life. You might have the potential, but we know that going to university takes more than that. It's all about discipline."

John looks at me. If I look closely, I can see him smiling on one side. It makes him look constipated.

We adjourn. It's getting late. I'm left to sit on a bench by Security until they can move me back to my unit. "All right now?" Clarence asks me when I'm unusually quiet.

"No problem," I say, half-heartedly. I feel like Gumby, stretched, held in an impossibly awkward position. I watch as my workers go to their cars beyond the security doors. They will go home to lives lived small. Television, a beer, take their kids to hockey. Sex, unlikely. A few minutes later, Clarence tells me I can return to my unit. I spend much of that night in my room by choice, plotting how I'll get back at my teachers for making me feel so small.

John calls me into his office on the unit the next morning. "I've been thinking that maybe I could get us a day pass and arrange for you to visit the university. You could make up your mind for yourself."

A day out was a day out. "Sure," I say. "Why not?"

A week later, John, Clarence and I take one of the blue unmarked cars provided by the centre and drive the two hours into the city. It is already deep fall and most of the leaves have turned. I sit in the back seat not letting on that I actually like the rock 'n' roll that they play on the stereo. Away from the centre, they talk about their cars, their wives (John *is* married), about how Clarence is building a new home. Winter is near and he and his brothers are in a panic to get the new place roof tight. Some "damn contractor" had fucked up, delivered the wrong shingles, the wrong plywood. I let all this trivia just float by.

A half hour from the centre we turn off the highway. John tells Clarence, "I have those antique door handles you asked me for." We drive a little way down a side road and roll up to a big farmhouse with an impossibly long laneway. The kind you'd need a tractor to plow. John's home is under renovation. Plastic sheeting billows on one side. "New shingles," he tells Clarence. As we pull up, a woman comes out the front door. She is brown-skinned and stands straight and tall. I guess she is Pakistani. She'd be beautiful, except that she's thin, gaunt to the point that her cheeks are sallow and her eyes look like they are glued onto her face. She walks slowly and waves at us as John pulls up and stops on the far side of a large front lawn. He gets out. He gives her a little kiss as he walks by, then disappears around the side of the house. We can see the forward corner of a barn set back on the property. John's wife, at least that's who I guess she is because nobody introduces her to me, stands there silently staring out over the fields. She reminds me of documentaries on the News channel. Of AIDS victims. And of the exotic ebony statue of a Masai woman John keeps on his desk. Her skin colour is lighter but her shape is just as elongated.

"John's a great guy," Clarence says, all the while staring at the woman.

John must have slipped in a back door because we hear him call "Fatima" from inside the house. The woman turns her head, then her body. Moves quickly through the front door. A couple of minutes later John comes out with a Canadian Tire bag, doubled and sagging with door hardware.

John hands it to Clarence as he gets back in the car. "Thanks. How's Fatima doing now?"

John shrugs. "The drugs are working." Clarence nods. And then the two men discuss the merits of cedar shakes over treated siding. "I still prefer the look of the old, even if it needs more work," John says. Clarence nods.

As we get closer to the campus, a light rain begins. The windshield wipers are on delay, periodically sweeping our vision clear. On the side of the road, fallen leaves from oaks and maples are becoming a mulched brown mass as they begin to slowly rot. The forest comes almost up to the campus that sits on a hill overlooking the city. We turn in a gate and drive by a steel and stone monument next to a platinum building. It's so shiny and new that it draws your attention away from the other buildings next to it that look like ugly cement bunkers. I'd later learn these were the inspiration of Sixties architects whose modernism meant sterility, students stationed in cubicles or meandering through halls of learning with the planned accuracy of experiments. Even that first day I had an inkling that if I came here I'd learn to be like the rest of them, to poke here and get a treat. Poke in the right order and get a degree. At first glance, it all looked unnatural.

We park next to one of these buildings, then wander behind them to find loftier older buildings that sit squat at the centre of the campus. Ivy tentacles grip their stone façades in what looks like a fearsome battle to do the impossible, climb where there are no handholds. These buildings make you look up. Ornate columns topped by the mumbo jumbo of what I knew from books were Ionic and Corinthian head-dresses. I slow my steps to look at them a little longer. I wonder if John thinks I'm reconsidering my decision. I might have reassured him, but instead say nothing, just keep staring at the sedentary, stoic grey stone. I had never been in buildings like these before. As we enter one, I trace my palm across its surface. It's cold, solid.

Inside, there is a dullish brown light. But there are also flourishes of colour. A beautiful blue skirt hiked high up a girl's thighs, magenta tights reaching down her legs to black pointed shoes. The effect slender, lean. Her white blouse folds out from her breasts, a small leather knapsack slung casually from her shoulder as she breezes down the hall in front of us. I don't see her face, just the swing of hips that are careless in their sex. I take all this in like one sorts through a menu. There are lots of items to sample.

I already know that the effect of being incarcerated makes one a traveller when back in the world. But this isn't my world. And the effect is narcotic.

As we roam the halls looking for the counselling centre, one girl after another brushes up against me. Time slows. I must look odd staring at them. Nobody gives me any notice even though I am not yet of them. I wear a black t-shirt, cotton pants, sneakers. I make no statement. I give nothing away except perhaps my youthfulness. The male students don't look as geeky as I'd expected. My life had been so full of the stranger products of such institutions that I didn't know you could look normal and be here too. T-shirts and jeans. Backpacks. I thought they'd all be marching along with briefcases and pens stuffed in plastic holders, pasty complexions stuffed in prim Walmart fashions.

The counsellor is an older woman, Miss Rivolis. Healthy-looking and oddly buoyant in her enthusiasm. This is the first time she's had such a request from the centre. She is pleasantly honest. "So if I understand, you're finishing your grade twelve in jail and you will be able to attend university next year?"

"Yes," I say politely. It all feels like a performance of an unfamiliar play, though I know there is no need to be anything other than myself with this woman.

"That's wonderful," she says, far more jubilant than I feel. "Any idea what you'd like to study?"

"I dunno," I say, shrugging my shoulders. Studying those girls in the hallway seems like a good idea, but I don't say that. Something about Miss Rivolis's sincerity makes me pull back. Maybe it is the stone walls I can see beyond her window. They told me this place endures. It survives winter after winter. I think, if the end product is someone as lithe and elegant as this woman, then it can't be all bad.

John and Clarence excuse themselves from the room. "We'll let you two sort this out." As the door closes behind them, I sit staring into a face that looks at me with expectant eyes. An engaging hopefulness. I willingly answer questions that appear in ordered lists on multicoloured sheets that Miss Rivolis places in front of me one by one. She takes up a pen and leans forward. Her bra is just visible beneath her beige blouse. I avert my eyes. She writes my name on the flap of an orange file folder and puts in a few sheets of blank paper. My life is gaining another file, only this one would stand out in a foot-high pile of them. She does all this smiling a gentle smile that creases her white cheeks, makes the tiny wrinkles around her eyes dance. I think her ageless. Not like my mother, or Miss Simpson, whose pouty jowls make them both seem to be sagging into their graves even though they are likely no older than Miss Rivolis. I like that my answers seem to please her.

"These exercises can help you to narrow things down a little. Though truthfully, most students don't make a decision about a major until they have one or two, or even three years of university successfully finished. There's really no rush, but you will have to enrol in some department. You'll also need to get connected to someone as an advisor."

"Can that be you?"

"Oh, no. I'm just here to support you making a decision. Or if there's a problem later."

"Okay, I understand."

I'd gotten as far as thinking about being at university, but not about any career. That seemed too concrete. What did I know about being anything other than who I was already? My whole life hadn't been about much. My role models nothing but a long line of professional helpers. Most of them daft rejects from life. They occupied my dreams. Tormented me. Mostly made me feel like shit, then special, then shit again. All except John.

And then it comes to me. I can feel a dark idea gather like a summer storm cloud on the horizon. My thoughts turn again to revenge.

"Is there a department that interests you, Joey? Maybe a career you'd thought about?" Miss Rivolis is being unnecessarily patient. I pause for only a moment.

"Social work," I tell her, and surprise myself with my sincerity.

*　*　*

John and I are back walking the track. It's been a few weeks since we visited the university. I finally tell John thanks for arranging the meeting with Miss Rivolis. The distance from the event is a cushion. It's John's turn to shrug. "No bother," he says. He knows better than to frighten me off with encouragement. Nothing worse than cheerleaders.

In the past few weeks John has handed me forms to complete. They appear at random. There're questions to answer and lots of boxes to put neat checkmarks in. There're requisitions to fill out too so John can take money from my personal account. My portion of my mother's Family Benefits cheque comes to me while I'm here. I know it annoys her. "I still have to heat your goddamn room, don't I?" When she speaks like that, I hold the phone farther from my ear. We talk once a month.

The centre takes a portion of the money to pay for my lodging, and the rest is put in trust for me until I leave. John uses the money to pay application fees and buy stamps. Each form is placed before me on one of the large worktables in the common room. He takes me out of class to do the paperwork. Every form I complete, he takes and puts gently into a brown envelope with my name on it. He always tells me when something has been mailed. And the cost.

He never asks me what I think it will be like. *When* I go. Worries, I think, that I'll screw up to avoid being ripped out of my skin, put where I don't belong. Most days that's how it feels. I'm molting, like those big sluggish snakes on Discovery.

After his shrug there is a long pause. Track time means John does most of the talking. Still, with my discharge coming soon, it's been nagging at me to ask John why he stopped travelling. Settled into this job? Is so careful with us kids? Wears the rubber gloves? I think, maybe if I figure out John, I'll figure out myself. Only, I'm not really sure what it is I'm supposed to figure out, about either of us. There's a mystery here that I never intended to solve. Instead, it's solving me. John's quiet kindness is a clue. Though I'd never tell him, I'm sure he knows I appreciate every one of his small gestures of concern. His behaviour, that of a caring worker. Or deceptive evangelical. Likely both. I sometimes wonder, alone in my room, if this isn't as much about him as it is about me. He behaves like my future apostle, waiting for me to emerge the Chosen One. To offer a sermon from the university's ivy-covered mount. Am I his salvation? Am I the one saved to save others?

John says, "Don't know if I can really explain why I stopped travelling." Then he turns the volume on his radio down. "What's a story without a good ending, though, eh?" My chest tingles and I realize how much I like being in John's confidence. When he tells me special things about his life I'm transported to the other side, that place where staff live their lives. Where they screw up, too.

I wait.

We walk a half lap before John raises his hands in front of him and makes one of his big sweeping gestures. The preacher warming up his congregation. Then he begins.

"Sometimes, Joey, we think we can save the whole world. And you know, for a time you can. Don't let people tell you otherwise." He spits. "You can save the world, or at least feel like you can. You ever felt like that?" He doesn't wait for an answer. Doesn't expect one. Tells me, "Ever think that if you had the chance, you could put the pieces together right, play the king and make it all better? That maybe, you could prevent others' mistakes?"

"Like some psychic?" It's like he doesn't hear me.

"Helping to heal someone. That's the biggest turn-on. Trust me on that. Being as high and mighty as Jesus. You ever feel like that?" He looks at me and I feel small. I turn my eyes to the ground. Notice the grass is losing its green. Wonder if the mower has been put away for the winter. It doesn't seem like winter is coming. This day it's warm. There's no wind. The flag over the centre roof is limp. Nothing is moving, except us.

I can feel John still looking at me. He tells me point blank, "You've got enough brains, Joey, to feel like that too. You're so close to healing the world. Don't go all shy about it. You'll see, you'll save yourself too." John points one of his sausage-size fingers at my chest. He doesn't actually touch me but it sort of hurts just the same.

We walk silently a dozen or so strides. "Anyway, there were lots of things we weren't supposed to do while in Pakistan. Like the trip to the Pass. Remember?" I nod. "The refugee camps were off-limits too. Except Saleem, my Pakistani counterpart, the fellow I relied on for everything, he really wanted to show me one of the camps. God, I was naïve." John takes one of those big breaths of his. "Saleem is one of those guys you want to trust. He looks the part. He's one of what they call 'the new middle-class Pakistani.' All that means is he's sophisticated, the kind of fellow who looks like a movie star in some cheesy Bollywood film." John realizes I'm not getting any of this. "Anyway, it's not important."

"Okay," I mumble. Like I care? I just want to know what happened that frightened John so bad that he ran back home.

"So Saleem is pushing to take me to the camps. Right? And I'm of course thinking, 'We are going to stand out.' Saleem's in Western jeans. I'm this big Black man. Saleem has on black leather shoes, which is sort of an odd contrast to me with my hiking boots and those multi-pocket travel pants we all wore. Mind you, it wouldn't matter what I was wearing. There's sometimes some pretty ignorant things said about Black men in Pakistan."

John's found his rhythm now.

"After a while, though, I figure to hell with it, that's all fine, and we drive out to the camp, but before we're too far inside, these Afghani guys drive up in front of us. They're really soldiers, disguised as refugees. And that's when it begins to all get a little weird because the young man driving the jeep that blocked our way has obviously been expecting us because Saleem recognizes him and right away parks our car right there in the middle of the road, turns the engine off, and makes me get out. I'll admit I was sweating a bit right then. And he tells me to walk over to the jeep where there's this whole line of bearded young men wearing dirty brown and grey shalwar kamize with automatic weapons over their shoulders. It's like a Taliban fashion show."

John rolls his shoulders, like he's avoiding a shudder, or maybe just stretching. "It was right weird," he says. Then he stops his story. Asks me, "How do you think you'd feel?"

"Dunno," I say.

"Damn right you wouldn't know." He laughs. "I didn't either until I was there. And that's the point, Joey. We're always thinking, 'Just give me the chance to do something good and I won't crap my pants when it's time.' Except we all feel fear when we're about to do something important. That's our human nature. We're afraid of being our best selves."

I kick some stones and keep walking. The sun's too bright. John's words are stray chords, jazz. I'm lost. Squinting. All I can do is wait and shelter myself from the sun. I keep next to John, positioning myself so that his head and shoulders cast a shadow across my face when I look at him. He takes that as a cue. Keeps telling his story.

"Anyway, then Saleem says, 'This is Mamoud' and pushes me forward. Mamoud's holding a disc player in one hand and in the other his gun. I don't know much about guns. But it looks light and easy to carry, the kind of weapon even a child could use. He puts the gun down first, leaning against his leg, then hands the disc player to one of the other boys and extends both hands to greet me. He sweeps his palms along both sides of my hand which I put out for a shake. Then he does like this ..." John shows me what he means. He puts his palms together and then flattens both on his chest. "It is a bit freaky having such a passionate welcome from someone I don't know, with the guns and all. And I just know there is something else going on. But after the welcome everyone relaxes. Two of the boys with the guns squat and two others go over to look at Saleem's car. Saleem makes me sit on a cement wall that borders the road where we're standing. Well, by this point, we've drawn a crowd. Young kids, all boys, are looking proudly at the fighters. They point at me and keep laughing and shouting 'What's your name, mista?' But Saleem eventually claps his hands, and that shuts them up.

John's radio beeps and he stops his story while he unstraps the device from his hip and answers the page. "I'll just be a minute here." He goes and stands a few feet from me, his back turned. A couple of minutes later he comes back and goes on with his story. The interruption is ignored.

"Next thing I know, I'm visiting Mamoud's father, who I figure out pretty quick is a real Mujhaddin general or something like that. 'My father,' Mamoud says, and presents me like a prize to this stocky man with a white swollen scar across his left cheek who's sitting on a cushion on the floor of his mudbrick home. It's pretty dark inside with these tapestry curtains drawn behind me. I extend my hand, just like I did before. And without getting up, the old man just leans a little forward and passes his hands lightly across both sides of mine like his son did, only his gesture is limp and he only makes like he means to raise his hands to his chest. Then Mamoud makes Saleem and me sit and he disappears behind one of the dark tapestries to my side where we hear women's voices. They're a real lively bunch, which I know means food is coming.

"It's weird, because for that first bit, Mamoud's father and I and Saleem just sit there in silence. I know better than to start the conversation, but still, it is awkward. Then the food arrives and the old man looks at me and gestures for me to eat. There's piles of it. Freshly prepared naan, which is like pitas, green beans and chillies and a mystery meat floating in a stainless steel pot of brown ghee. I choke down two servings. They keep wanting me to eat. But I'm the one doing all the eating. Saleem eats practically nothing. Just keeps waving away the invitation. The old man eats too, very slowly, forming small balls of rice and meat in his right hand, occasionally wiping his brow with his left. And we're eating for a long time but all I say is 'Very good,' and Saleem, who's playing this all just the way he should, translates and the old man nods and so does Mamoud, who has joined us again.

"When I finally put my hands up and show I can't eat any more, the old man smiles and lets out this huge belch, and then Mamoud takes the food away. That's when Saleem starts prompting me to speak. You see," John says, stopping and bending a little to look at me, "you don't know this about me, but I used to love to go on and on about politics, to anyone who'd listen. I'd tell them what I thought." John stands up straight again and walks. "We'd get news from home and I'd shoot my mouth off to Saleem about how screwed up things are. Or when we'd be going through security at the airports, I'd tell Saleem how stupid I thought the searches were. Like terrorists don't need to go to all this trouble to screw us over. Hijacking planes. There were simpler ways. And I'd let my mouth run on and on and on. Saleem never minded listening. He acted like he was writing it all down in his head.

"So Saleem wants me to do some ranting in front of the old man. We've settled down to talk. A little boy comes in from the street with a silver tray with glasses of tea on it. This strong boiled sugary brew."

I begin to notice John's eyes are wet. Wonder if the sun is too bright. His voice isn't the same booming baritone either. It goes gentler. Like he's telling me something secret, something that maybe he hasn't told all the other boys.

"Anyways, I did what Saleem wanted. And the next week, I came home."

That's it? I feel cheated and it's my turn to stop, to step out of John's shadow. "What do you mean, 'I came home'? What did you say?"

John waves at me to keep walking. "I shouldn't really tell you what happened." I pout. My silence is demanding.

A few paces on I tell John, "You don't think I'm old enough to hear this stuff?" My voice cracks. "What? Like you don't think I deserve to know. Especially since you expect me to continue my education, become a social worker. Help people. You got me here, the least you can do is tell me honestly why you're doing this work. Fair's fair. Right?"

John remains quiet for a moment, then nods. "You're right. But this has to be between you and me. Okay?"

It's my turn to nod. John checks his watch then tells me, "You know, Joey, it's all David and Goliath. Play on our fear here in the West and we're doomed. I'm not really comfortable telling you that I told that old man about some weird thoughts I'd been having. About how simple it would be to screw us over. Say three or four weeks before Christmas. Think about it, that's when people are all out shopping. The entire Western economy needs Christmas. Now think what would happen if the whole thing tanked. Imagine ten bombs. Ten small bombs in ten stores, a Walmart or two, a furniture store, a McDonald's. Maybe a grocery store. You know, in among the Christmas turkeys. I mean bombs the size of backpacks left in shopping carts. Or on public buses. In ten different places, big cities and some small towns in between. I mean, who ever notices a shopping cart left alone for a minute or two, even in a checkout line where people are all crammed together on a Friday afternoon?

"That's what I told the old man. I'm not sure he understood everything I said, but I was so full of myself, it didn't matter. I just kept talking. Told him, 'Ten small bombs and the entire Christmas season is flushed.' Completely predictable reaction. People would stop shopping. At least for a few days. Then there would be security guards everywhere. That's when they could do it again. You see, we're so dumb, like at the airports, that we only know how to react. So Walmart and the other big chains would have security, but no one else would. The subways wouldn't have security. The tree-lighting ceremonies. Children's school concerts. If you wanted to completely paralyze everything, then ten more bombs go off a week later. That would do it. People would panic, board themselves up. The Western machine would lie rusting. And then maybe, just maybe, we'd taste some of the same violence we've exported. Understand what we did in Egypt, the crazies we put in power in Iran, Iraq. Understand how people feel in Cambodia, Chile, Laos."

His lecture done, John is looking past me now, over the wall and up at an airplane's slipstream. I'm not even sure he knows he's still walking the track. He hasn't even paused to listen to the squawk on his radio.

"That's the kind of stuff I told the old man. Pure crap! With my silver cup of tea in my hand, I went on and on." John's radio beeps again but he still ignores it.

"Then the old man asks me if I talk like this when I'm in my own country. And I tell him, 'Sure' and that makes him smile, like he's listening to a child. So I tell him, to try to save some face, 'I know the terrorists will win.' Why? Because whichever army changes the rules of engagement always wins. Think about that, Joey. The American Revolution. All those polite British soldiers marching out on to the fields and the American militia stayed in the woods. Vietnam, the same thing, only that time it was the Vietnamese who stayed in the woods.

"And as I'm saying all this, Joey, there's this creepy feeling inside. It wasn't just the caffeine buzz from the tea making me feel like that because I was realizing ..." John's radio beeps again, and he stumbles with his speech for just a moment ... "Um, realizing I'd said too much. You with me?"

"Sort of."

"It takes a while to see it."

"Is that why you came back. Just that?"

"That old man, he listened politely for a little while longer, then he leaned forward and said in pretty good English, 'So the West deserves to be taught a lesson,' and I'm a bit unnerved about him speaking English, but I tell him, 'The West is weak. It can't win.' Then he picks up his empty teacup and spits into it. Says, 'Maybe you would like to help us teach them.' I'll tell you, when he said that I looked towards the door to see if it was being blocked because I was ready to bolt. I knew I was being recruited. And my first thought was, Christ, what happens if I say 'No'? But he must have seen my fear, all my bravado just leaking away and he must have known I was still just a kid in a man's body. That's when he waved me away. He didn't even look at me again. Next thing I knew, I'm back outside and headed home."

John sucks at his teeth. Scrunches the knuckles on his right hand into his left fist, then switches. "I left Pakistan a week later. Faked an illness. Came back here to do this job."

Clarence comes onto the track down by the main building and whistles at us. Makes a signal like he's talking on a radio, and I see John nod and reach for his walkie-talkie. The voice at the other end squawks away about "transport" and something else about "shift change."

"We have to go in."

As we clear the security doors, I'm wondering if that's the whole story. John shoots his mouth off to an old man and then dedicates his life to saving kids like me? To being the perfect helper? I want to tease John. Tell him he should toughen up. But looking at John, nobody would ever think he isn't tough. At least in some ways.

As I stand waiting for doors to be unlocked, I ask John, "Do you like your job?" but he doesn't answer. The rhythm is broken. I watch him walk onto the unit and notice he doesn't look quite so tall today, or maybe after all these months it's me who's getting taller.

twenty-one

I T'S SIX WEEKS BEFORE I get back to see Mr. Jeffrey. Christmas is coming. It's an excuse to visit. Vivian's still fifteen, so as her worker that
means I can get her presents from the Christmas Daddies. Cameron
gets them too. Nice old ladies hang a description of each child and the
child's wish on the big tree at the mall.

On December 23, I pick up the gifts and go play Santa. There'd
been some snow days earlier that had decayed into trenches of slush
that remained deep in the hollows next to sidewalks and in the ruts
of gravel roads. I'd half-heartedly agreed to distribute Christmas baskets
of food and toys to all the families on my caseload. It was hard not to
feel preened and pretty with boxes of food to give away.

The Christmas basket for Mr. Jeffrey and his family is a cardboard
box with Green Giant Canned Peas printed on the outside. Inside, a
volunteer has stuffed a huge frozen bird, canned goods (including no-
name peas), nicely wrapped presents for Vivian and Cameron, and a
plainly wrapped package for Mr. Jeffrey. The shape and feel tells me
its pairs of socks. There's also something in a small lacy round box for
Joan. It has a Walmart logo on it. Someone placed a bow on the flap
of the box to dress it up. The bow keeps coming unglued. As I ap-

proach Mr. Jeffrey's door, I place the bow on top of my woolen hat. Joan comes to the door after my third knock. She sees the bow and backs herself away from the door. She says nothing. Cameron curls himself around her leg when she comes back into the kitchen. He giggles when he sees me.

I wrestle the heavy box through the narrow door, the cold air following me. I put the box on the kitchen table and the bow on Cameron's head where he leaves it. Vivian's there this time. She comes out of her room at the back of the house. Plunks herself down on a couch by a small fir tree that has been tied to nails that have been carelessly driven into the wall. There's a lot of silver tinsel on the tree but not much else. Vivian has her earbuds in and is listening to something on an old Discman. I can hear the faintest buzz of gangsta' rap. Vivian looks a little heavier this time. *Good*, I think, *at least she's eating.*

"Cup of tea, then," Joan says. This time there's no getting out of it. I hesitate and check my watch, then accept the courtesy. Vivian notices my hesitancy. Pulls one earbud out so she can hear us better.

"Yeah, sure." I sit on an uneven kitchen chair. A small space heater warms my feet under the table even though the woodstove is stoked in the corner. My boots are still on. Even little Cameron wears winter boots indoors today. Vivian wears dirty pink rabbit slippers, the toes worn away. The floor is muddier and wetter than it has ever been. Thankfully, the dogs are still outside.

"I'm not much for Christmas, myself. Viv and Cameron like it, though." Joan takes the teapot from the back burner where it had been on a steady simmer. The brew looks acidic, darker than most coffee and powered with caffeine. She must be doing this for Mr. Jeffrey. Islanders. They'll keep the pot boiling all day, adding water and tea bag after tea bag. I know there's tea in the Christmas box. At least they'll have that for a few days after the turkey's gone.

"I remember I liked it when I was younger." I make polite chatter to cover the charity. Then ask, "Mr. Jeffrey here?"

Joan ignores my question. Hands me tea in a chipped mug with *Wayne's Transmissions* printed on the side. It's boiling hot, with globs of milk powder still floating on top. And lots of sugar. The cup looks clean, though. I say a silent prayer to some imagined germ god, then take a sip. Joan sits across from me at the table, Cameron on her knee now. She tells me, "Half the time my mother had to hide our presents so tha' they didn' end up all broken. Wit' my father drinkin' and all. Not tha' it wasn' sometimes good around here. A little extra like you brung today and it takes away the edge. My father and mother, if there was food and presents, then sometimes they' get all romantic, and they' put me to bed early, or at least shu' me in my room and then they' just lay by the tree, the lights all shiny and bright. I'd sneak and watch them. Sometimes my mom snuggling with my dad would keep him from getting too drunk and ruinin' everythin'. Distract him, if you know what I mean." She laughs a little and takes a long noisy drink from her cup, then offers Cameron a taste. He lets the sugary liquid touch his lips, but flinches. It's too hot.

"Not much call for any of tha' now. My father and I, neither one of us gettin' much lovin'." She looks across at Vivian, who sits with her legs splayed out in front of her, slouching on the sofa in the corner by the stove. "Your father, Viv, was a hell of a man in that way. He could ge' my pants off in a flash, be on me and ge' me a-grindin' like nobody's business."

I look at Vivian, who's listening. I blush when she looks away from her mother and back at me.

"Mind you, he knew how to ge' respect. I fel' so safe next to 'im." It's the first time I'm aware of that Joan has ever mentioned Vivian's father to any of her workers. I take it for what it is. A thank you for the gifts. I don't ask any questions. Laugh along with her. Vivian just keeps sitting there half listening to her music, hands crossed low on her stomach.

The dogs scratch at the door and Cameron goes and lets them in, then disappears out back. The dogs start tearing around, their antics threatening to pull down the Christmas tree. There's a fourth dog today, a small wiry thing that yaps at me then jumps onto Joan's lap. It's an ugly little breed with a bulbous face and short coat. A mole on each cheek. More rat than dog. It's wet like the others, but Joan doesn't seem to mind it on her lap. She pats it lovingly, then claps her hands together hard. "Get now," she hollers at the larger dogs. Instead of running away, all three come to her. The largest places its head on her knee and tries to playfully bite the smaller dog that swats the bigger brute with its paw. One of the dogs is wagging its tail so hard, I move my teacup to the centre of the table so it doesn't get knocked.

"You' never know it but these two made the nicest pups last year," Joan tells me, pointing at the two dogs playfully nipping at each other. The little one gets up on its hind legs to lick her face. "This fella is the horniest little thin'," she says. "When this other one, the big brown one 'ere, went into heat around abou' this time last year, the poor little bugger followed 'er like it was 'is only chance to lose his cherry. He kep' walking on his back legs, his little pecker makin' 'im all off balance. Wasn't that so, eh, Viv?" Vivian bobs her head side to side in tune with the music.

Joan lets the little dog lick her face. "Well, I got to feelin' for 'im and so got the bitch leashed and then lifted him up on 'er back so he could get at 'er. But like the little bugger practically gets stuck in there. So like 'ere's me all bent over with this guy between my legs and me having to ge' the brown one to stay put. Thank God I had the good sense to tie 'er before trying this or else I'd have been all over the house wit' 'hem both." Joan is laughing hard now. I keep pace with uneasy smiles. It's the happiest I've seen her. She takes another sip of her tea, pats the little dog on its head, then rambles on about other things. She tells me about the cost of turkey, about a favourite bracelet she'd had and lost one Christmas, about Mr. Jeffrey and how he'd had to slow down his drinking once the arthritis got real bad. Then she goes and gets more tea.

The light that sifts through dirty cotton sheers is fading now. It will be colder outside. Snow and slush turning solid. I think I'll wait just a few more minutes before I go. Drain my tea. Make sure Joan knows I appreciate her hospitality this once. She keeps on talking and I keep nodding.

"I've got somethin' for you," she says after a time. "Thought you migh' be by." I'm surprised when she hands me a brown envelope the size of a playing card. Inside are two pictures, school photos of Vivian and Cameron. "I know Shirley always like' to 'ave pictures of the kids. It's the only gift she' accept. Thought you migh' like to ha' some of 'em too."

I'm speechless at first. Then after a confused moment, tell her, "Thanks." I try not to sound too pleased but I think she knows she's caught me up in some emotion. I slip the envelope into my jacket. Tell her it's time I left.

Vivian never gets up off the couch. Cameron never comes back into the room. I suspect he must have found Mr. Jeffrey somewhere out back. As I leave I wave at Vivian. She surprises me when she smiles and even lifts one palm. It's almost a real goodbye. Or maybe thanks.

Three weeks later I hear from the Public Health nurse that Vivian is almost five months pregnant. How would I have known? She has what they call a high-risk pregnancy. Of course everyone wonders if she is going to keep the baby. She was too far along for an easy abortion. Not that Joan would have likely let her have one. There was nothing to do but wait until Vivian went to term. For another picture for my wall.

twenty-two

I WAS RELEASED FROM JAIL for the last time four months after John told me about his encounter with the Mujhaddin. I never did get to quiz him about his reasons for coming home so quickly. I regret that. I guess we both had things we needed to tell one another but hadn't. Somehow, the truth never came up. I haven't had the heart to scratch John for more details since then either.

It was early spring when my release came. Good timing, really. I left with my grade twelve completed and some odd looking ceramics that I'd made. A pen-holder that hooked on the wall but looked like Medusa, and a red lobster with eyes, which is sort of stupid if you think about it because by the time they're cooked and red, the eyes are just empty black pools, not the friendly inviting gaze this fellow had. But I'd made it just the same. I was intending to give it to my mother.

On the day of my release she came to get me with Lou. "Your mother said she needed a ride," Lou tells me as she gives me a hug. I don't remember her being so grey. She shakes everyone's hand. She is obviously uncomfortable. Like she was adopting me, not just giving me a lift home with my mother.

Next, my mother gives me a cold hug. She's dressed in a light blue sweater. Odd little balls of wool hang off the sleeves and in a line across her chest. Like bits of snot dangling from your nose on a winter day. It's hard for me to not think of her as a billboard for my failing.

I wonder what she said to Lou to get her to drive the two hours down to get me. I never knew Lou to be one who was bored so it's not like she needed something to do. Charity work, I figure. I am Lou's good deed. The thought makes me grimace. The two of them are like a receiving line. Shaking everyone's hands. You could forget they hated each other, looking at the way they carefully choreograph this dance.

Besides the ceramics, I have copies of completed applications for entrance to the university and copies of the forms I'd submitted for financial aid. Skunk-lady is pleasant as I leave. So is Miss Simpson. She even wishes me well. Skunk-lady mostly frowns. Miss Simpson says to me, "I'm sure you'll do wonderfully. But of course, you must remember, you will need to be disciplined. Be sure you don't get distracted." If you sniffed the air, you could practically smell her insincerity.

"Maybe you'll get out of here too some day," I say, impulsively, a smirk on my face. She hardens ever so slightly, smiles in her condescending way, then seems very self-satisfied as she diverts her gaze and looks towards my mother. She knows I'm watching her watch my mother. She pulls her chins in. With her silence, I know she's had the final word.

After that, there is paperwork to be done. My mother is guided over to a small desk off to the side of the guards' station. Lou is talking with one of the older workers who is escorting some youth to the gym. It looks like they know each other. Then Skunk-lady and Miss Simpson are over with my mother. They ask her about the drive down, interrupting her paperwork. They're vengefully dragging this out. Miss Simpson is speaking again: "A boy with so much potential ..."

I sit down on the front benches by the admissions and discharge desk. The chair is cold plastic beneath me. I wait for John to come down from the unit. The last thing I want to do before leaving is say goodbye. Or something like that. Just doesn't feel right not having John there to see me leave. I'd already said my goodbyes to Jeremy and the rest of the boys. John is different. I need him to watch me pass through those exterior doors. He's been radioed so I wait. I can see Lou's car parked in the spot right at the door where police are supposed to drop prisoners. I'd have preferred a taxi. If I am embarrassed having Lou see me here, having my mother inside these walls is completely wrong.

The longer I have to wait, the more I wish they'd just sent me home in a cab. Of course, wouldn't that be a treat? Like which driver is going to volunteer for that duty? Not likely any of them after what I'd done. Maybe that's why John was so insistent my mother make it down here. She'd never asked Lou for anything like this before.

It takes a while, but John eventually lumbers across the courtyard and swings the glass doors wide as he enters the main building. A refreshing blast of morning air follows him. I look him in the face as he approaches. I don't want to cry. I might have even asked him for a hug if all the other guards hadn't been watching. And my mother, too. I surprise myself by making a fist and playfully throwing it right at his eye, a stretch but my fist almost makes it before he snaps his hand over mine. "No," he says, "that's no way to say goodbye." And then he releases my hand and reaches down and touches the crown of my head. "I'll miss you," he says, slowly, and I swear he looks like he's misting up. But before he can see my own eyes moist under the fluorescent lights I reach for my two garbage bags of clothes and turn and head to the door without saying anything more. John lets me go and takes a few large paces over to my mother. He shakes her hand. Thanks her for being there. "Nice to meet you finally." He sounds sincere. Meanwhile I'm waiting at the door. Impatient. I want to shout, "Come on, everyone. Let's go," but stand there silent instead.

Lou joins them by the desk. John reaches out his hand to touch Lou on the shoulder. Lou shuffles her feet. *What a pair,* I think to myself. John stands a full head taller than Lou. Lou is as white as John is black. My mother eventually introduces them. They shake hands briefly. It's nice to see them meeting. I imagine they'd have a lot to talk about. Only, they don't say anything. Just look my way.

Lou claps her hands. Changes feet. "Time to go. A bit of a drive, right."

Lou and my mother join me at the security doors. Lou offers to take one of my garbage bags, but somehow the thought of her holding one of those green bags makes me feel queasy, and I say no. I think I'd do her a favour right then if I let her hold one. She looks like she needs something to do. Except this is my sad little life. I don't want anyone else sullying themselves with it. My mother waves at John one last time.

"Thank you. I really can't thank you enough." Lou and my mother go in front of me into the vestibule between the locking doors. The first door has to click behind us before they can let the second one unlock. There's this moment when I'm trapped between glass, with my mother and Lou. With John and the other workers staring at us, we're fish in an aquarium. Then John raises his huge right paw up to his chest, a quiet wave just for me. And a little frown. Like he forgot to say something. I might have waved back if only to save him feeling awkward. He looks dorky standing there, the only one of them who believes in me enough to wave goodbye. Only, I've got a garbage bag in each hand and don't want to put them down so I don't wave. Then I hear the click on the exterior door and that means freedom.

Lou quickly leaves, uncomfortable standing so close to my mother. My mother too bustles out. The act over, she doesn't even look behind her. The stale smell of the jail leaks outside. You can feel the decompression, a large cancerous lung exhaling. I'm its spore.

I suddenly feel whole. "Fuck you all," I shout back at the staff as I pass through the second set of doors, but feel immediately stupid for having said it. And with that, I take my first full breath of the cool April air.

*   *   *

On the way home, the first thing we do is stop at a Tim's to buy my mother a tea and a Boston Cream. She says she needs the caffeine and sugar to calm herself. Lou grunts as she pulls into the drive-thru. She doesn't want to stop. To make things worse, she's in the driver's seat so she has to pay. My mother makes some excuse about not having the money because some friend of hers needed help fixing his car. "An old shiny car," she tells us. She rattles on, while gingerly pulling back the beverage cover's plastic tab. She has to lean out, way out, to sip the hot tea, making sure she doesn't drip it on herself. Lou offers me a hot chocolate.

"A large," I tell her.

"Of course," she says, resigned to this entire dismal day.

Lou keeps the radio on while we're driving home. Oldies. She's doing that to avoid talking to my mother, who rides up front with her. I didn't even ask to sit up there. I like it in the back. Private.

Two hours later, Lou pulls into her driveway and yanks the parking brake. Turns around and tells me, "Good to see you home." She's sincere and all, but looks tired from the drive. I'll bet any money the old gate is locked for good.

I haul my garbage bags from Lou's back seat, say, thanks, and really mean it. Then walk around to the front of my house. My mother is on my heels, tootling away about how nice that was of Lou.

"I normally would have asked a friend of mine, but he's a mechanic. You know how it is. On a weekday. He couldn't really get away."

When I come in the front door, my brother is watching television. My mother hardly notices him. Stevie waves at me, a shy little wave. I wave back, surprise myself by going over and giving him a one-armed hug around his shoulders. I'm a head taller than him so it's easy to catch him that way. He doesn't even get off the couch. Just lists a little to the side to rest his weight in under my armpit. Then lists back as I loosen my grip. He keeps watching his show.

I go up to my room, or what I thought was my room. It's been taken over by my mother's sewing machine. There are lace curtains on the windows. Nailed to the window frame. My bed's still there, but it's piled high with pieces of fabric, women's magazines, and a make-up kit.

"Christ, Mom!" I shout but she's in the kitchen. She's probably making herself a snack. I remember I haven't eaten for a few hours myself. I march back downstairs. Tell myself, *Try not to yell.* Stevie is beside her opening a bag of salt and vinegar chips. Ruffles. He's old enough that junk food is making his face break out in big zits. I speak to my mother's back. "I need my room."

"Just put my stuff aside," she says, pulling a chip bowl from its place on top of the cupboards. "It's not like you've been here very much, now is it?" She keeps her back to me. "At least I didn't give your room to your brother."

I go back upstairs, taking the steps two at a time. I push all my mother's crap into a corner. Magazines fly like birds, settling awkwardly atop heaps of junk. But the room is still not mine. I had posters up before I left. Centrefolds from *Maxim*, and one of Shania Twain bending forward. I dump both garbage bags on the floor in a corner away from my mother's things and kick my clothes into a huge pile.

When my mother comes up to check on what I've done, she of course turns red. Just like she always does when she's annoyed with us kids. "I didn't mean throw everything on the floor, you little prick! Not home five minutes and already you're ruining everything."

Everything? I want to say, but remain mute. Just stand there looking at her. I'm too big to cower anymore.

"My friend told me you'd be trouble."

I cross my arms. I feel like B-boy doing that. I'd uncross them, but I need the posture. I'm not willing to play along with her lies any longer. "You have no friends," I say. "Not one. It's you who's sayin' I'm trouble. Right?" I move forward so I'm up in her face.

"Don't talk to me like that!" And before I know it she's raised her hand and goes to smack it across my face. Only I catch it before it hits. And then we're stuck there. Her open palm in my clenched hand. We stare at each other. I'd never seen her worried like she is just then. At least not worried about me.

My voice goes low and threatening like I imagine John might talk if he was here. "You'll ... never ... hit ... me ... again ... or pull my hair, or call me names. You understand?" My mouth froths. My brother has run upstairs to see what's happening, but stops at the door when he catches me towering over my mother, her hand frozen in mine.

I let go gently and she takes a step away. Her tears are close, which makes me feel a little guilty. I'm not home five minutes and my life is already sliding backwards. I want to ask her to stop. To wait with the accusations. To say something nice to me. Just for today. Give me a break. Then maybe I could say something kind back. Like they taught me in jail. I could tell her, This isn't what I want. But instead, I do only what I know and stare defiantly.

"You couldn't get away with that if your father was still alive. You hear me? He wouldn't let you do that to me." She pushes past Stevie, who shields his head as she storms by. He smiles at me, whistles something snappy.

I tell him, "I'm doing this for you too, you know."

The little smart-ass nods his head with a big loll and says, "Uh huh," like he doesn't mean it.

I can hear my mother in her bedroom banging drawers open and shut. Seconds later, she thumps back into my room and throws some money on the bed. "There, now get out. I got you out of jail, but I don't have to keep you. Out! You hear me? Out! I don't need this. I don't need any of this."

My brother backs down the hallway. I feel sorry for him, as sorry as I feel for myself. But what else can I do except look down at my mother and tell her, "Fine," and grab the money. Then put my hand on her chest and give her a firm shove out of my room. I slam the door shut and begin stuffing my clothes back into the garbage bags. Then I go over to her pile of crap and stomp on it. I shred a couple of magazines. But I don't touch her sewing machine. I think about it, but I know she couldn't afford to replace it. I'm not mean, just angry. Besides, it dawns on me just then, she'd just given me my freedom. Twice in one day.

In a few minutes, I come down from upstairs and head to the back door with my bags. As I march past the living room Stevie's gone back to watching his shows. I'd like to tell him, "Come on, then, pack your things, we're going." But that's just Holden Caulfield crap. I'm no saviour. I'm barely managing to look after my own sorry tush. That's the way my dad might have said it. With a touch of Yiddish. Like the scent of something exotic. Instead, I tell Stevie, "I'll come back, if you want me to." He shrugs. His eyes look in the direction of my mother who's in the kitchen. "You can come, then," I tell him.

"I can't," he says and turns towards the television. But his eyes are focused someplace else. I'm about to say something more when there is the rattle of angry pots. I wonder if something is going to be thrown at me.

"I'll let you know where I am." This time he doesn't even shrug. Just shifts his gaze to the floor, as if shrinking before my eyes. There's another loud *clang*. I take that as my cue to keep moving.

I head cautiously through the kitchen where my mother is pressed up against the sink, looking out into the backyard, a stack of dirty pots scattered over the counter. She says, "Always leaving. That's all everybody does." I almost stop to answer her. To yell back that she's the one who left first. Left me. When I needed her. But I know she'd never hear me. Then she says something else in a voice so small I can barely hear her because of the pounding in my head. It sounds like, "Leaving or taken away, it's all the same," but I'm not sure. Then she turns and shouts, "You go, now. Don't think it makes any difference." I hear her that time.

"You sorry piece of ..." I don't say it, or even finish the thought. No one is being taken this time. I'm leaving because I want to leave. I keep marching towards the back door while she does nothing more than cough. Sounds like she's drowning. The thought makes me boil. She should go drown herself. Do us all a favour. Be done with it. Lean forward into the sink. A few horrible moments, then peace. The image of water and death reminds me of something I want to forget, one trauma triggering another. And for a moment I am nauseous with the thought of her head under the water.

That's how I leave her. Me, casting silly spells. Her wheezing over the sink. As I shove the second garbage bag through the back door, I hear her say, "Nobody ever thinks about me," but she's completely wrong about that, because that's all I'm thinking about as I push through the back door and for the second time that day breathe cool April air more deeply than I have ever before.

* * *

I know before I even put a foot on the steps down from our back deck there's only one place I can go. I avoid the rotted bottom tread and head over to the fence. It's padlocked, just like I thought it would be. But I'm bigger now. I throw the bags over into Lou's yard, then go under our back deck and unlock my bike with the key I'd left hidden. I throw the bike over the fence too, then jump myself over. I march right up to Lou's back door and take five deep breaths. Like John would do. Then knock. There's no answer. I knock again, real loud and urgent. Lou comes to the back door and sees me through the door's glass cut-out even before she reaches for the handle. I can see her mouth the words, "Oh Christ," but she opens the door just the same. "You've got to be joking."

"I need a place to stay."

"I figured this wasn't going to end with the drive. Your mother ...," but Lou doesn't finish her sentence either.

She stands back from the door and this time grabs one of the garbage bags out of my hands. "You can sleep in the basement. I'm not sure for how long."

I reach into my pocket and put fifty dollars from what my mother gave me on the table by the back door, but Lou reaches for it and presses it back into my hand. "Go," is all she says, and points towards the basement door.

twenty-three

LOU TELLS ME, "You'd better get a bank account." She even asks my mother for my identification. A birth certificate. I think my mother was so embarrassed that she actually gave Lou what she'd asked for. I want to hug Lou for doing it. For all of her help, but as I lean towards her she stiffens and shifts her weight onto her right leg as if she's avoiding a punch. I hit pause before saying anything, or doing anything else. It would feel too weird embracing. I'm getting this vibe that maybe Lou's helping me is something she just knows she's got to do. She's not cold about it. Just abrupt, as if she's tolerating her compulsion but not quite letting herself immerse in the joy of giving. Maybe she's like all the rest, this being all for her own benefit. I can't quite accept this version of the truth. This time, I prefer the illusion that she's here for me. It feels genuine, no matter what her motivation.

Lou tells me a little later, as she's repairing an old toaster for no good reason and I'm drinking the last slurp of juice from a carton that Lou found pushed to the back of the fridge, that my mother said she has a friend who knows all about Tough Love. Told Lou she's doing the right thing by not letting me come back home. I say nothing but roll my eyes. Lou says, "How come her tough love has to become my problem?" She says it with a smile that makes me feel part of her conspiracy.

Lou lets me stay in her basement rent-free. "As long as you keep at your studies," she says. She even begins to let me be part of her family. Tells me her daughter, Lyla, and her family are coming over for dinner on Sunday. "They invite themselves over every six months. Since my partner, Claire, died. Now they think they have to do that. But what do you do? Right?" She purses her lips a bit while she continues to putter with the old toaster that doesn't look like it has much life left in it.

Lou's explains that her daughter and her husband are former missionaries. Back after twelve years overseas. "They were saving souls." Lou's trying to sound nice but I can still hear the sarcasm. "They were mostly on the east coast of Africa, but also in Indonesia and Afghanistan, I think." I nod. I don't know if I should tease Lou about this or not. It's like looking in a dirty clothes basket. There are things in there you don't want to see. Especially when you've had a mother who once imagined herself sexy. My thoughts go to slingshots, or horse bridles.

"Good enough people," Lou mumbles, a piece of black wire held between her teeth. She pulls and the plastic sheath strips away. "Mind you, nothing quite as arrogant as a Western missionary." She laughs with a light guffaw, obviously pleased with her sacrilege. It's an old woman's laugh, privileged. I don't usually think of Lou as old, except when she laughs like that. "Oh, they want to help for sure, whatever they take that to mean. But it's all about buying themselves a place in heaven. Fundamentalists every one of them ..." She pulls the sheathing off a white wire, then twists it into place alongside the black. She makes sure the two don't touch. "I sometimes think it's all just a way to disguise evil." Lou gives me a little wink, then returns quietly to her work. "Let's keep that last comment to ourselves, okay?"

Lou's daughter and her brood deliver themselves to her door promptly at 5:30 p.m. the next Sunday. I can hear them get out of their car, even see a set of thin calves walk past my basement window. The two kids tear in the front door and head right to the television. I can hear their footsteps. Other footsteps go towards the back door and the kitchen. The fridge opens, then closes. Then the footsteps return to the living room. At least one set. I figure that's my cue to go upstairs. I find Lou in the kitchen. Lou makes a little grunt when I ask her if she's sure this is a good idea. She stops putting nacho chips into a bowl and hands me a glass of Coke, the glass she just poured for her guests. Then she pours another. Whispers, "Don't worry about Lyla. Just keep your opinions to yourself." Then much louder, she tells me, "Oh, and you'll need to learn to drink coffee if you're going to university. I've been meaning to tell you that. Coke will do in a pinch. Hot chocolate too. But those are for kids. You'll never survive without coffee." She flashes a knowing grin. I get it. She's telling me to grow up. Fast. Or maybe saying she knows I am grown up. Just not showing it. I guess if I've emancipated myself from my family, I'm there, in the land of the mature, whether I want to be or not.

Lyla comes in to the kitchen. She's polite. Shakes my hand. I look her in the face, like an equal. Notice that her handshake is just a small bony grip. I can feel her knuckles. I may be an adult now but that doesn't mean I know what to say. We never had people like this in our home. And no one ever served me a glass of Coke so formally as I've just been served. Lyla doesn't wait for small talk. "Mom said you used to live next door. Needed a place to stay, or something like that."

"Sort of," I answer. I don't really want to get into it.

"We used to take kids in, too. Some Black, some white, whoever needed help. Most were teenagers with big problems. Though one or two of them did okay afterwards." Lou glares at Lyla, her eyes telling her to stop. I'm glad Lyla stops. I'm not a kid.

"Oh, I mean young men," Lyla self-corrects. Like one of those toys that moves across the floor bashing into walls, then rolls over and scurries somewhere else to do it all over again.

"I was always jealous of the attention they got." She laughs like the wound is only flesh deep.

When Lyla changes the topic and tells me where she and her family most recently lived, I play innocent and say, "I thought that was a Muslim country." Lou has taken salsa and chips out to the living room. I hear her lightweight voice next to a great baritone.

"That's my husband Jurgen," Lyla tells me when she notices my attention drift from her for a moment. I can also hear the television set blaring from Lou's office. I can even see the screen if I look past Lyla through the glass doors to where Lyla's kids have parked themselves on floor cushions. I've never seen Lou use the television before. There's a commercial on and I realize the kids are watching a Christian television station.

"I'd heard that proselytizing is illegal, or something like that. That they put missionaries in jail. I know someone who's spent a lot of time over there." I make myself sound concerned, worldly. John would be proud.

"Where'd you hear that?" Lyla asks, obviously pleased that I've given this some thought. She's leaning with her back against the counter.

"I heard it in church," I lie. Actually it was on television one Sunday morning and John filled in the rest of the details. That's sort of like church, I reason. John could have been my preacher.

Lyla is nice enough to not ask me more questions. I'm sure as hell not going to volunteer my life story. Besides, she has a bit of an edge to her which I like. Not like the syrupy Christians I knew who would drive us to doctor's appointments when my mother was too ill to take us on the bus herself. Or the lay clergy who preached to us in jail. They always spoke in high-pitched whines, as if their voices were meant to be an octave above everyone else's. Lyla's voice is that of a small woman who you'd never think would have it in her to live rough. Except when you look at her face. Then you see the imprint of a tropical sun. Or you look at her tanned hands that flutter like budgies in a cage when she speaks. If you squinted, left things out of focus just slightly, you'd think you were looking at someone much younger. The thought evaporates when I look past her at her two children glued to the television, bookends to her life.

"We never proselytized. Just did things that needed doing." Lyla's hands settle down. "My mother never believes me when I tell her that."

"Lou hasn't said much to me about it." The lie makes me obvious in my deceit. Lyla already knows what I'm up to. She blinks slowly, then raises an eyebrow.

"Anyway, it's like social work, but without state support. You understand? It's altruism. Helping. That's the really important part of the work. Not the part about Jesus."

She reaches into the fridge. It has the freezer on the bottom. Lou told me the day after I moved in that Claire always wanted one like that. So she bought herself one after Claire died. Sort of ceremonial. A monument in white. Lyla doesn't seem to notice the novelty. Takes out some lettuce, a long English cucumber and some baby tomatoes in a plastic bubble.

I imagine my mother would like a fridge like that. No need to even bend over to find the Cheez Whiz.

As Lyla clears space on the counter to prepare the salad, she tells me, "With all the fighting and refugees, and unsafe roads and lack of water and whatever else, not to mention children barely getting an education, is it any wonder we were needed?" Lyla's head shakes slightly. "Even with all the problems, though, I still loved it there."

"Why'd you come back?" I ask. My conversation with John is a faint echo. I always seem to meet people on the rebound. Or maybe I just want to understand why anyone gives up. Stops doing what they're passionate about doing.

"Um ... it was time." She's not looking at me when she says that. She keeps sorting the leaves for the salad, the good crisp ones in one pile, the brown limp ones in another. "The boys needed to be home for a while and get to know who they are. They need to know their grandmother, too. It was just after Claire died. She was my mother's ... friend." Lyla says this with the precision of the performer. I can tell she's said it all before, to many others. She stops speaking for a moment. Then, turning to me, she looks me straight in the eye and tells me, "Here everything is so ... dark, don't you find? Overseas, I loved our rooftop terrace most of all." Her hands leave the lettuce to dry in the colander where she's arranged the good leaves. She begins chopping the cucumber, rhythmically, her pace steady as she raises and lowers a large black-handled knife she found on the counter. Chopping, she tells me, "From that roof I could watch the whole community go by if I was patient."

She passes me the tomatoes. "Give these a rinse, will you? There's some vegetable cleaner by the sink." I'm not quite sure what I'm supposed to do with vegetable cleaner but move towards the sink anyway.

"I'd feast on pink sunsets over desert sands. It was beautiful, like something you'd never see here. My mother never visited, though. Me and the boys and Jurgen, we, of course, kept telling her to come. I'd describe camels back from long treks visiting Bedouin tribes. Things like that. Absolutely magical, but still, she stayed put." Lyla's hands freeze for a moment. Then they wave away a thought and she returns to better memories. I can see a change in her face and the tension drains away.

"No rooftop gardens back here, though. Too friggin' cold!" Her language catches my attention. She knows it too. "That's how my kids would say it, right? 'Too friggin' cold!'" She drops her voice so she can sound like a man. "Maybe I should have been a poet."

She tosses the onions over washed greens which she has placed in a large clear plastic bowl. She moves over to my side of the counter and adds each of the tomatoes I've sprayed, then carefully rinsed. I must have done it correctly because she puts them in by the handful. With her standing next to me, I notice how short she is.

"When you're on a roof you have time to think," she says. With her gaze fixed on her greens, she recites, 'The world is a kaleidoscope that changes with each turn of the clock. Each moment of my life brings a new collage.' I wrote that in a letter to my mother and she shared it with Claire. Claire said she liked it. I don't think I ever told Claire how nice it was to have my writing appreciated." Lyla gives the salad an unnecessary toss.

"Right, then." She turns and bends down to get the compost bin from beneath the sink, gently pushing me aside. "Anyway, we were on a laneway. And all day people passed by on their way to the small market at the end of the street." She stands back up. "If I close my eyes, I can still see them." And she does. She turns her back again to the sink and rests both hands on the rounded edge behind her, positioning her hips so they're practically touching my legs. When she closes her eyes I take a small step backwards.

"I can remember things like a man in tattered shorts and a torn orange t-shirt pushing a wheelbarrow of cut grass, and a woman in a red dress walking behind him, an enormous pile of twigs and branches and grass tied together with vines, the whole lot balanced on her head, softened by a tourniquet of purple cloth. Then a businessman, his bright yellow shirt and tie, polished black shoes. He always walked by with his head down while the others always walked with their heads up, eyes straight forward. I always wondered if he was looking down to avoid the puddles and the dung." She opens her eyes and turns my way but looks at her left hand instead of at me. Looks at the ring she's wearing. It's the only jewellery she has on. She closes her eyes again. "Then after him come three rappers, at least they look like rappers. You know, youth shuffling their way down the dirt road, around the potholes. They dress just like the kids here. One of them is fiddling with his Tilly hat. I remember that. And they're all smiles. And then six milking cows are herded by. The cows move from one tuft of grass to another. And a young man in nothing but a pair of shorts holds a small switch that he uses to slap their flanks if they stay too long in one place. Then behind the cattle, another young man, wearing the most outrageous orange shirt with these large black polka dots." Lyla opens her eyes. "Can you imagine all that?"

"A little."

"They were beautiful." She sighs. "All of them. And so in need of what we had to offer them."

Jurgen comes in the back door which opens into the small alcove next to the kitchen through which I'd crashed my way into Lou's life just a week earlier. Lyla's hands grab for the last two tomatoes. Something electric seems to fizzle and she stops talking. I guess Jurgen and Lou must have been outside looking at something. Maybe the steps. Lou's proud of her steps. And her shed. Jurgen puts out his hand and gives mine a rousing shake. He is very white. Middle-class, white bread white. A blue shirt and red tie. Ironed beige cotton pants. He's at least six feet tall. A big man with a sissy energy. Soft round face and a bit of a paunch that folds his gut over his belt. A receding hairline. He must be older than Lyla. Much older.

Jurgen invites me to the living room. I can count on one hand the number of times I've been in here with Lou. There's a slightly worn couch, side tables, and lamps with pretty shades, and a few ebony statues from Africa. Likely presents from Lyla. A large picture of Jesus is over the mantle. I'm sure that was a present but it confuses me why Lou put it there. Maybe it's her way of telling her daughter she loves her. Or a necessary concession that makes her home more acceptable for her grandchildren to visit.

We sit down and Jurgen tells me about a map he keeps tacked up over the mantle in his living room. The communities where his mission works, each community with a church marked by a big blue dot like a massive bingo card. "Each dot we put on that map is another victory for Jesus."

When later we sit down for dinner, two brightly scrubbed children appear from the television room. Jurgen says grace. "We thank you, Lord, for this meal we are about to receive and for bringing us this boy under your protection. We give our prayers to the unborn and the ignorant, and revel in your mercy to show us the right way to live our lives. We pray that we are worthy of the food you have given us and with it will find the strength to do your good deeds. In the name of Christ our Saviour, amen." Lou grumbles something, but I can't hear what she says exactly. I'm thankful Jurgen finishes our pre-dinner prayer mercifully quickly. Then it's potatoes and peas, salad and beef steaks. No floating turds of mystery meat in oil like John described. I was worried Lyla may have brought home with her more than just stories.

"I'm still getting used to the simplicity again," Lyla says as she passes around the salad we made. "The water is clean. Food is so easy to get. Such a blessing." She beams what looks like a smile at the boys, even though the far sides of her mouth still fold down. One of the boys chimes in, "And nothing crawling across the floor, right, Mommy?" Lyla smiles again, this time with her teeth showing. She looks so proud of her little guy. "No, nothing crawling. I never did like that part." Jurgen coughs and tells the boy to eat up. "Don't be wasting food now," he says, a caricature of himself, unrepentant for the stereotype. The boys shush and Lyla goes quiet as well.

"We're fortunate," Jurgen says. "We have been rewarded with our blessings for the kindnesses we bestowed on others and for our belief in our Saviour. Isn't that right, boys?" They answer as expected, with small heavenly nods.

Even before we're finished, Lyla begins to clear the table. Jurgen pushes himself away and goes to the living room to read. The children ignore him. Even Lou ignores him. Lyla tells the boys, "We'll be going soon." I offer to help with the dishes. Lou joins the kids in front of the television. I hear her playful banter with them as they watch some cartoon I've never seen.

Lyla hands me a dishcloth and tells me to dry the pots as she lays them on the counter. "I'll put them away. No need for you to do that."

As she hands me the first one she says, "The boys loved it overseas. I don't know if Jurgen really wanted to come home. I didn't. But we had to ..." She leaves her words hanging. Looks in Lou's direction. Swallows hard. "It's hard to know where you belong, the longer you stay away. Our lives were hyphenated. We were there, but not really there. What they call, third culture. You don't know what I mean, do you?"

"Not really." But I listen all the same. A good story is still a good story.

"For years we lived with the Masai and this other family of missionaries. That was before we had the boys. My Lord, but we confused those people. We were always the outsiders. The other family, they had teenaged daughters. That's why they had to leave. The Masai boys were always at the girls. Figured they couldn't be virgins. You know why?" I shake my head, feeling a bit uncomfortable talking about virgins. "Because they had breasts." She blushes slightly as she says the word, but only slightly. "The Masai figured a woman developed breasts because she had sex. And we would trot the girls in front of the Masai elders and the girl's father would point at the girls' chests and explain that it didn't matter if a girl had sex or not. The breasts grew anyway. But the elders didn't believe us. They were looking at us like we were the ignorant ones. They were sure the girls had simply lied to their father and mother. Can you imagine?" Lyla's pot scrubbing is on the vigorous side now. "Such ignorance needs us, don't you think?"

I shrug. She's quiet after that. Until she notices me staring out Lou's kitchen window as I dry the dishes. My mother has come out on her back deck to put garbage into a trash can that she has tied to the railing so it won't blow away. When Lyla's hands stop wiping, I know she is watching me.

"Who's that?" she asks. "Your mother?" It's my turn to redden.

"Hmm," is all I say and she steps up on her toes slightly to get a better look. My mother glances our way for only a second before she changes direction and goes back inside, keeping an old sweater she's wearing pulled tight against her body.

"Do you still visit?"

My silence must tell Lyla everything she needs to know. She drops the conversation quickly. I look at the dish rack and pick up another plate that needs drying. Lyla finishes the last couple of pots that are still on the counter. When she's done, she wipes her hands on a dry teacloth. "We'll have to do this again," she says. Then she's off to check her boys and I'm left to make my way back downstairs alone.

Though it's early, I lie down and close my eyes just for a moment. I drift into a half-sleep, thinking about my mother, then Lyla's stories. And then I'm on a rooftop. And it's warm. And I'm looking down into an alleyway that looks like something from *Black Hawk Down*, only it's peaceful. Three adolescent girls in black headscarves carry big-boned babies on their hips. They're full of smiles. The babies do nothing but stare and hold tight. I think how life for these girls is measured by the clothes they wear. First their heads get covered, then their bodies, then even their faces. But these girls aren't invisible. They're exuberant. Except, I still feel sad looking at them because I think, they are so innocent. Sex must be traumatic. A rupture with all they've been taught. To cover. To cover up what must be kept hidden. That's when I notice John sitting beside me on the roof. And he points at one of the girl's ankles. Says it's pretty. And I laugh at him. Like you have to be pretty horny to get off looking at an ankle. But beneath my tease, I feel mildly uneasy having John joke with me about sex. Especially in front of the girls. I know they can't see us up on the roof. I wonder what it would be like to touch them. John says there are couples who cannot conceive because the men keep fucking their wives up the ass. Now I'm really feeling uncomfortable. And Lyla is behind us offering us drinks, which only makes me feel stranger because she's laughing at what John just said. I suddenly want to push John away. He's being rude. I'm feeling really upset having to tell John to stop talking like that, but he doesn't listen to me. I don't want to hurt the girls. I am sitting there and it comes to me that I don't want to cause any more pain to anyone. "Shut up, John," I yell, and Lyla laughs some more.

I get all flustered and go back to looking at the babies on the girls' hips. Another image of a baby with less hope comes to me. Of a round and bloated cherub bobbing like a cork in an old bathtub. My head barely over the edge. The toilet seat is on the floor next to the bath where I knocked it off trying to stand on it. My arm is sore from the tumble I took. I reach in to the bath to try and pull the baby out of the water but she's really heavy. And the water's cold. So I let her float and watch. Just like I'm watching the babies on the girls' hips. My eyes fill with tears seeing them. They just stare up at me while the girls smile and chatter away in some language I imagine. Clicks and long vowels, throaty, melodic. I know I'm there waiting for them to help me. I want absolution from them. I reach into my pocket and take coins and shout down to the girls, "For your babies," and let the money shower them. At first they cover their heads, then when they hear the clang of coins and see what it is I've thrown, they drop the children roughly on the street and scurry to grab the money. Now the babies look startled and begin to cry. But the girls ignore them and search for more coins and then look up, hands fluttering like little brown wings, their long dresses full of air as they jump up and down. Childish. And the babies keep crying.

I wake to one of Lyla's kids upstairs screaming. I can hear Lyla's muffled words say something about, "We have to go!" There is little threat in her voice. I wonder if I'd have been happy growing up with Lyla as my mother. Lyla doesn't look much like a mother. Her hips haven't spread. She's energetic. She smiles a lot.

I try to go back to sleep, but the crying has annoyed me. And my dream lingers. I'm not sure what happened to the girls on the street. Or the baby in the bath. My uncertainty makes me afraid and I lie there as the house settles, my eyes wide open, waiting.

twenty-four

A S MY SCHOOLING ADVANCES through its first year, Lyla finds more and more excuses to visit Lou. She brings dinner, packed in square plastic containers, each perfectly shaped for what's inside. She even brings napkins. She heats each dish in the microwave, which surprises me because the food comes out tasting bland. A beautiful dinner with so much care put into it and then this final reckless act. I offer to heat things on the stove but she brushes me aside. Says it's a waste of a pot. She hates dishes.

When Lou's not around, Lyla comes down to the basement for a visit. As the end of that first year approaches, I'm forced to huddle over my textbooks afternoons I don't have classes. Mornings are for sleeping when I can steal the time.

A month earlier, Lyla brought me an old Ikea chair to put in my room. The white fabric is badly stained. A milk crate is my stool. She likes to sit in the chair and talk.

She tells me, "In India, in a place called Imphal, near the border of Bhutan, there's an old priest. Well, not all that old, really. Father George. He once told me that Imphal must be heaven. It must be where all the good Christians want to come. It's so beautiful, the fields ripe and lush, very green. You throw your seed down, and no matter what, good things grow. The people there can be as lazy as they like. It's a perfect life."

I've pushed my books aside for the moment and stretch out, putting my feet up on the milk crate beside Lyla's.

"The place looks like a postcard for heaven. You see? But the people are all so poor and there is a lot of fighting. Armed insurgents are everywhere. The fighting means the government ignores the people. The poverty is disgusting. Father George says Imphal is the part of heaven that needs renovation. Like a do-gooder's paradise." She laughs at her own joke. I notice the clock by my bed. It's nearing dinnertime. Lou is still out. She's out a lot more these days.

Lyla keeps rambling. I listen, loving Lyla's stories as much as I loved John's. "The corruption there is epidemic. Of course, there's no one to blame. The old priest told me about a village where people needed a bridge to cross the river to get their crops to market. The politicians got them the money from Delhi. A contractor was even hired but by the time the bribes were paid and money siphoned, there wasn't enough left to build the bridge. Still, a bulldozer arrived and cleared a road to where the bridge was supposed to be built. A barge was hired and sat idle for months. But instead of a bridge, the villagers were each given money by the local politicians to help them get their grain to market the old way, by pulling it six miles upriver over muddy roads to the only bridge that does exist. And it was all fine. People liked being given the money, until they realized they were never going to get their new bridge."

"That's kind of sad." Lyla nods. The more she speaks, the more depressed she looks. As she shifts in her seat, her foot accidentally touches mine. I pull back, just a little.

"Well, that's the strange thing. It is and it isn't. Somehow it works. Even the corruption. The villagers became very creative. When the money ran out, they said, 'Fine, we need more money.' So two years later, they tell the central government, 'Our bridge needs repairs. The heavy rains have ruined one of its piers.' More bribes are paid and an application is submitted and Delhi sends another cheque, money to repair the phantom bridge. And the villagers were happy again." Lyla laughs now. When she does, her eyelashes blink rapidly, so quick I think of black-winged butterflies.

"My old worker, John, he'd like your stories." Lyla grins. I feel shy for having finally admitted I had a worker. And about her foot having just touched mine. "He's been overseas. In Pakistan. Right to the Khyber Pass. He's a social worker too. He used to travel just like you."

Maybe it's the way I say "used to travel" that deflates her. Her chest sinks but her hands rise in front of her and wave slowly back and forth, as if pushing aside thoughts that only she can see, like evil spirits. Then she bends her knees to lean towards me, her toes still on the milk crate. "I was such a coward. I parachuted in and did my work, then left." She sighs. She reminds me of John. Except John said he came home to save himself from something I couldn't quite understand.

"No use lying. I wanted home comforts," Lyla says. "I like the enamel, the chrome, and everything clean." Her hands settle and she looks pensive. Dissatisfied. "I got all that, and routine. But no one to help anymore. It makes me feel useless. And besides, life here, it's all so ... boring."

Maybe John came home for the same reason. Could he have been a coward? A regular guy who got afraid? Who missed home? His stories about the Mujhaddin could be an exaggeration. A way of hiding the truth. His work with me, atonement for his cowardice, not his arrogance.

At least Lyla is honest. If not a little pathetic. She seldom talks about her boys, or Jurgen. With me, she only dreams of what could have been if she had been a bit stronger. A bit more adventuresome. Willing to really extend a hand to people and make their lives, not just their superficial souls, much better. I imagine she is looking for something to excite her. Then I know for sure she is when she stretches out her legs again. This time she purposefully places her foot so it's touching mine. She gently soothes the sole of her foot by massaging it over my big toe. She stops speaking and looks at me with soft, swollen eyes.

"I'm sorry to get so emotional." Then tears well and somehow her head is resting on my knees and I am stiff as a board confused by her lying there. A mother of two, a Christian, Lou's daughter. Only Lyla doesn't seem to feel out of place at all. "Would you give me a hug?"

I am lost instantly amid a swarm of stinging emotional bees. The only reasonable thing to do is to lean over clumsily. Think, How can I not do this for her? How can I not play the role of her consoler? To not let her touch me would be hypocritical. Unhelpful. She gets up from her chair and stands there, waiting. So I get up too and put my arms around her. I feel like a small boy next to her. The thought lands heavy enough to make me think about pulling away. Suddenly there are two Joeys. The man holds Lyla and argues he has a right to let her use him. He has a right to let her think she is directing when it is really this older Joey who decides what happens next. But that testosterone bravado is squelched by a screeching child whose anger sends a shiver down my spine. Lyla's touch as inflaming as fingernails scraped across a chalkboard. The child I still am knows better than to be used like this. I can try and convince myself this is a selfless act. Letting me be seduced to help her feel young and loved. It should be an easy illusion, except my temples are thumping and I know it's a lie. The only reason I continue is that Lyla helps me help her. She doesn't respond to me like I'm a boy at all. She doesn't play a game of show and tell, or seem to want to hurt me. She just wants my touch. If I evaporate a little and let Joey forget the manipulation, I can even sense the pleasure. I can feel useful to another human being. But I have to remain disengaged or else another thought, much darker, abusive, threatens to overwhelm. Of another time ...

I remain balanced there on a knife's edge of emotion as Lyla nestles her head into my shoulder. Her arms reach around my waist. She unfolds emotionally. Her tears soak through my t-shirt. Strange, I think, how she is as taut as any other girl I've held. Not at all like my mother. Not soft. More adolescent, which makes it easier to tilt towards being more man than boy, though my arms remain stiff while my fingers explore.

"Jurgen doesn't hold me. I miss that so much." Her words muffle at my shoulder. She pushes closer. Squeezes. I can feel myself begin to go hard, which embarrasses me even more because Lyla is so close she's sure to notice. "He's too distracted. You probably don't know what that's like. To miss seeing what's right in front of you." Her hands reach down my back and are now below my waist. I go harder and my hands begin to wander. I suddenly wonder if the sheets on my bed smell bad. If the old futon is big enough for two.

And then Lyla brings her hands around to the front of my pants and looks up at me as she fiddles with my belt, staying so close her small breasts touch my chest. "Is this all right?" It sounds more like a seductive plea.

"Yeah," I say with my voice feigning the lower octave of someone much older. My hips sway a rhythm in time with the blood still pulsing at my temples and a headache that's rushing on. There are still thoughts trying to escape that I am beating down. As forcefully as Lyla now pulls me over to the bed and pushes me backwards and doesn't look again in my eyes until she has slipped my pants off and taken down my boxers to where I can kick them off myself. For a moment I wonder if they are like the ones she spends days washing for her boys. I force that thought away only to be assaulted by others. Of underwear in a pile on the bathroom floor and folds of flesh in front of me. And then she is guiding my hands over her body. Forcing me to feel her with an urgency I haven't experienced before. Take her slacks down while she slips her shirt and bra off over her head. Her nipples are large, and wrinkled. Until I touch them, then they pop. Little towers on fruit-like hills. And she kisses me once on the mouth, then on my nipples. That's not something any girl I've been with has done before. Mind you, we seldom even have time to get undressed. Mostly it is pushes and shoves on basement sofas. Lyla takes her time. Which is a bit hard for me because the licking and caresses have made me anxious to finish. Then Lyla brings her mouth down lower and lower, only I'm not really comfortable on the bed and my calves are still hanging out in mid-air. I don't want to move for fear I do something she doesn't like. And the lower she goes the more off the bed she slides, until with a hand under me, she solves my predicament and gently urges me forward, then takes me in her mouth. I want to tell her how excited I am, but can't find the words. I feel powerless to do anything other than let myself be used. The feeling is familiar. I leave my thoughts aside. Realize I am practiced at this, at not thinking hard about someone touching me whether I want to be touched or not. My role here is to help Lyla break routine, not to speak or seduce. Not that I've ever been very good at the words. The girls neither. My first girlfriend didn't lift her legs. I guess she didn't know she was supposed to, and I didn't know enough at thirteen to tell her.

Between kisses, Lyla tells me, "When you climb Kilimanjaro you have to go slow. The guides tell you ..." she pauses to make gentle moist caresses on my inner thighs, her voice slightly dulled by the distance, "... if you're attached to reaching the summit, best ... not to try. No way to predict how the altitude will affect you ... No way to know who will make it." She plays with me with her tongue. Her hair brushes my erection. "The old make it more often than the young ..."

Her mouth descends over me again. I feel virginal as Lyla paces me. I whisper, "I'm gonna ..." and she takes her mouth off me but a bit too late and I splatter her cheek and hair. I feel stupid, like I've let her down.

She looks a bit angry but smothers the thought. "Just let me know next time." Her voice is tender, but instructive. She takes my t-shirt from the floor and wipes her face. Then she cuddles into me and places my hand on her dark curly pubic hair. There's a little swell at her lower abdomen. Lyla is vase-like, a woman now, which makes me focus as a man. She patiently guides my fingers to her, then later draws me in when I'm ready again. With her face buried into my shoulder, I hear her through heated breaths mumble the slutty dialogue of a late-night movie. A few moments later she quivers over me.

The wind outside shifts. Its sound changes the same moment I hear Lou's footsteps upstairs and notice the dirty dusk of night approaching. Lou turns on her study light, which illuminates the grass outside my window. I look out at the flash of a stockinged foot. I suddenly feel exposed. I tense but Lyla stays put for just a moment, then methodically slips into her clothes. She arranges her hair back into its bob, then walks upstairs. Her movements are deliberate.

I think about pulling the curtain closed but decide I don't want to. I refuse to be invisible here. Decide to let her see her boy playing at being a man. I hear Lyla say hello to Lou and then go into the kitchen. I just lie naked. Spent. Why not expose myself like this?

Angry, I think, what should I care if she's watching? I touch myself and lie there listening to the microwave heat dinner until the "ping" sounds and the latched clunk of the door opening tells me the food is ready.

Lyla's voice calls down from upstairs, "Come eat, Joey," and I realize just then how hungry I really am.

twenty-five

DEAR JOEY,
     Sorry for not writing sooner. I've had a few family issues that I had to attend to. Things are settled for the better, unlike at work. It's been a good eighteen months coming, but it looks like they're going to close down most of Secure. Crime is down, way down. You probably know that from all the books you've been reading. The handful of real criminals, like your friend J., all those kids together would hardly fill one ten-bed unit.

     Rumour has it I'm headed to Adult. They have some openings. There've been retirements, injuries, stress leaves, all those kinds of things. Who knows, maybe I'll meet some of our graduates.

     Thought you might like to know Ms. White left already. She went into private practice. She said the work's cleaner. And Robert, I think you used to call him B-boy? He's become an insurance agent. He did all the courses at night. He's been dropping brochures off around the Centre trying to find business. He tried to convince me I was living recklessly because I wasn't insured enough. He didn't know the half of it. He still picks up the occasional shift, though. I think he needs the money.

Who else can I tell you about? Ms. Simpson is still here. She's been thinking about getting some sort of IT teaching certificate. She says once she's trained she'll speak to her students through the computer. She seemed awfully happy about that.

And Clarence, he says he'll follow me to Adult. Young or old, they're all the same to him.

I wonder whether the guys in Adult will like my stories?

I'll write again soon.

As always,
John

* * *

Becoming a social worker meant shedding the connections that had made me who I was. It was a diet of sorts. People drifted away. I began to feel as thin and gaunt as I came to look. I could almost imagine turning sideways and appearing invisible to everyone who mattered. All I had to do to speed the transformation was catch a bus each morning to the university.

It was a long ride. I never knew where to sit, or whose conversation to listen to. There were the too-loud white Rastas with corncob dreadlocks who looked freakishly lost, and real preps with leather jackets with their names sewn on the shoulder. There were wannabe scientists, too, who stared down at the computers sitting open on their knees. The closest thing to a social worker I saw was a girl about my age with a shaved head who told her friend that she cut off her hair in solidarity with her mother who was dying of breast cancer. I stared, wondering at the dedication it takes to do something like that. Especially if you're a girl. I kept staring until she noticed me. Then I looked down at her tits and felt hugely uncomfortable, thinking that maybe her mother's cancer would get her too. I doubt she noticed, though, because when I looked up again, she was back looking at her friend, oblivious to my embarrassment.

I told Jeremy all about the bald kid and everyone else on the bus when we'd get together at his place on the weekends. By my second year of university, Jeremy lived among the suburban two-stories I grew up looking at from my bedroom window. Mind you, he wasn't there too often. Between jail time and being mandated into detox by a friendly judge, there were lots of weekends he was beyond my reach. His family had moved there after his father found a better job than working in the recycling plant. Jeremy's room was in the basement. His choice, he said.

I would bicycle over on my old twelve-speed, taking the long route, down the strip with fast-food storefronts lined up like take-out containers in a fridge. I loved Spryfield's four lanes of traffic. Especially on Saturday nights. I liked to ride hard alongside cars with their windows rolled down and music blaring. And if they gunned it, I'd push even harder on my peddles, grab my lower bars, my ass waving at whoever was behind me. I'd find the slipstream and chase the music. Or I'd slip down the centre lane, peering over the heads of pubescent girls who giggled as boyfriends revved heavy on the gas. When I had to hold up at an intersection, I'd crook my front wheel to the side and pose, erect on my two wheels, never touching the ground. And then, red or green, I'd plunge into the open space whenever I found it, waiting for the Mustangs and Dakotas to catch me.

Jeremy listened to my stories at first but after a while he would yawn when I told him things about Dirk or the bald kid on the bus. Carrie would be there too sometimes, loaded, feebly trying to look cool and sexy on the couch in jeans that were always too tight. Her top too short to hide a swelling belly that folded out over her pants.

"Sounds like a lot of fucking work," Jeremy said and lolled his head to one side or the other, or lifted a beer, stolen from his father. "What you wasting time doing social work for? Fuckin' losers every one of them."

I ignored the taunt. "You'll fuckin' need both a lawyer and a social worker," I said laughing at him, knowing full well he was up on more charges. He scowled, then lifted his head and looked at me serious. Too serious for Jeremy. Even Carrie, as spaced out as she was, sensed that something wasn't quite right.

"Yeah, like what you missed there, you fuckin' geek, is that maybe it doesn't make one fuckin' difference to me. Like maybe it just doesn't matter if I'm here or back inside."

He reached for the pouch of tobacco on the coffee table in front of him. Carrie sat up a little straighter looking for a smoke. She reached over and touched Jeremy's knee. I could tell she didn't want us fighting.

Jeremy stared at me hard. "Don't be fooling yourself, man. You're every bit as much in jail as I'll be. You just don't see it yet." He tapped the end of a cigarette on the table to settle the tobacco, then lit it with a match. I stayed quiet, and leaned back in my chair. I'd have put my hands behind my head, but the thought of doing that reminded me too much of Dirk so I kept my hands on my knees. Blew Jeremy's words away with a breath. I wanted to say something, but instead, I flushed a bit red and faked big time like I'm fading out to black. It was my turn to let my head loll.

"Soon, Joey, they'll have you thinking it's all good, like you belong with them. It's all crap. Fuck, you know it. Like is it really all so different being inside one place or the other?" Jeremy took a big draw on his cigarette and the end burnt bright. Ash fell to the table.

"You're an asshole," I told him, but regretted saying it. There was no sport in making Jeremy feel small. It made me feel sad to think how easy it was to hurt him. To leave scars that last longer than bruises and broken bones.

I got up from my seat slowly, like I was tired, and moved towards the stairs, shaking my head. "I've got to go," I said and began climbing the stairs. Neither Jeremy nor Carrie said anything. Jeremy just blew some more smoke and stared at the ceiling, making me feel eerily like I had already left. I didn't see Jeremy much after that.

I kept studying. And riding the bus. It was almost a year before the bald-headed girl talked to me. She was no longer bald. Her hair had grown back in blonde with red streaks.

"Are you in Soc 3320? With Myeroff?" she asked from her seat facing mine. Stunned she'd spoken to me, I nodded. "I thought that was you," she said.

University girls still unnerved me. They're beautiful and all, but I found myself oddly shy around them. Two years into this degree and all I could manage was a nod. I guess I felt like an anthropologist, and this woman, like the rest of them, exotic. But she had these really large eyes that pulled me across the cultural divide that separated our seats. No mascara or other make-up. Totally genuine. Her hair leaked forward from behind her ears. It wasn't quite long enough yet to stay in place. Each time it fell across her face, the effect was like watching two suns extinguish themselves.

She didn't say anything else. We sat there the entire bus ride without another word. Me feeling all exposed, like she's opened a can but left the opener stuck in the lid while she's off answering the phone or something. Completely nonchalant. She just held her bag down by her feet while white men in business suits and tired Black women with children standing beside them, their hands linked, remained solid hoodoos as the bus listed side to side from one end of the city to the other. Realities exchanged as we moved closer to downtown. Meanwhile the young woman just sat there, sometimes sweeping her eyes over me, blinking, pulling her hair back, and looking away.

As the bus cleared towards the centre of town a seat opened beside her. I knew I should move. Instead, I just remained where I was looking out the window in the direction from where the bus had come. Maybe, I began to think, it's time to see what these people are all about. Only by the time I'd made my decision, she had stood up and braced herself for the next stop. She dropped a small wave my way when our eyes met and that was it, she was gone. At least for that day.

The next day, I take my regular seat and she takes hers. Her invitation from the day before makes me take the risk. I'm still figuring out the grammar of this new text. In my world stories are written quick, without flowers. Something about this woman tells me she knows something I don't. And it smarts. Or turns me on. Maybe both.

"How did your mother do?" I ask, leaning across the aisle when the bus stops at the mall for a few minutes on our way into the city centre. Many of the passengers have gotten off to make other connections. There is a momentary lull in the morning crowd.

It's her turn to look stunned. But she catches herself quick. Answers smoothly, like I just asked her if the next stop is hers. "She's okay. In remission." A self-conscious hand rises to her hair. Pushes a wayward strand back behind her ear. On anyone else it may have looked like a flirt. Except with Sheila, there's nothing insincere at all. If anything, I think I see her eyes shine a bit brighter. I imagine the moistness of tears being held back.

"What's your name?" I ask.

"Sheila. Yours?"

I tell her it's Joey and she nods. She tells me her mother had breast cancer. I explain how I already knew. We both laugh, nervously. Her hand goes back to her hair. "It's strange having hair again," she says. Her big eyes make her seem the most sincere woman I've ever met. You can't learn enough about brain physiology to ever take away from the soulfulness of eyes.

She changes the topic. Asks me, "How you liking class?" I shrug. I still think it ain't cool to be high on school, though if I was to tell her the truth I've been enjoying the opportunity to study.

"I like the course. Though I think a lot of those theories don't work so well where real people's lives are concerned."

That makes her turn her head to the side and crack her neck. Like she's processing something. Then beams a smile my way. "Yeah, I think that too. Not that I have a lot of experience to base that on." The way she says "experience" makes me think of eating fresh melon. The effect is calming. "Except for what happened with my mother, I wouldn't say I have much experience with real people's lives at all. You know, bigger problems. Helping and all."

After that the bus fills and Sheila gives up her seat to the same stout Black woman with a child hanging from one hand who stood between us yesterday. It's been raining outside so the woman has to maneuver her way into the seat with the child all the while keeping her half-closed umbrella from hitting anyone. I wonder if Sheila's gesture is all kindness or about getting away from me? I keep watching her as the bus becomes more crowded with strangers who stand towering, their briefcases pressed against my knees, the smell of armpits mixing with the mildew of wet wool. I begin to wonder if it shouldn't have been me who offered the woman a seat. But the thought goes nowhere before Sheila moves towards the door. As she slings her bag over her shoulder, she makes a point of giving me another of her tiny waves. I secretly hope someone else besides me has noticed. I lean back in my seat and ride the next two stops tapping a tune on my knee.

*　*　*

The next day when I see Sheila in class, she invites me to join her afterwards at the student centre. "You play pool?" she asks. I don't but agree to come along and watch. She smiles slyly and I can tell she won't be letting me watch for long.

The student centre is one of those buildings that was apparently a good idea at the time. Big brown blocks and panels of glass wrapped around stairwells that appear to go nowhere except into more big open spaces ringed by places to buy subs and fries. A bookstore inhabits the basement. You tread around on well-worn carpets and tile that is never properly cleaned. The smell of stale beer lingers everywhere. But the pool tables are good quality and the lighting thankfully low enough that each time I miss a shot, and I miss them all, people can only watch if they mean to.

Sheila plays very gently. She's short enough that some shots mean she has to perch on one toe, while her other leg swings free as she lines up her cue. She makes her cue slip sometimes and I wonder if this is because of her balance or if somehow she is trying to make me feel better. I'm already her charity case, I think, but the thought passes quickly.

It's bar pool so we keep the table for a while with lines of quarters laid on the table's edge. Soon others put down their money. They watch patiently as Sheila and I mess up one shot after the other. She giggles a bit now that we have an audience. She hadn't giggled once before. Now I find her taking more shots with her cue held high and her little ass pointed in the air. If I didn't know better I'd think she was setting up the cue ball to be where she could barely get it just to make herself practice her stretch. I'm sure she lets me win, which means the next fellow who comes onto the table is going to easily take it from us. He's a larger guy, crisply cut hair. Glasses. He seems polite, but he keeps his eyes more on Sheila than the game. All the while Sheila treats me like a brother. Nothing but friendly touches and chatter. Like she's an airhead. He beats me handily, of course. Sheila lays down another line of quarters and we watch the next game between the fellow who beat me and a friend of his who was next in line. We sip Cokes. I offer to buy Sheila a coffee but she says she prefers Coke.

When it's Sheila's turn she asks the two guys on the table if they would like to play doubles. She says it with her big eyes twinkling so of course they agree. And then she giggles and next thing I know I'm trying to break and the cue ball practically misses the rack and I'm beginning to heat up with embarrassment. I find myself thinking how much I'd really prefer to be telling these guys to wipe the smirks off their fuckin' faces than take even one more shot. But Sheila is still all friendly and so I think, what the hell and do what I can. Sheila just keeps missing, but the cue ball never seems to land where it gives the guys an easy shot. It's not long before all our balls are still on the table and the boys are three shots from winning and that's when Sheila begins to rag on me about losing.

"I just thought you were better, Joey!"

"What?" I say.

She doesn't wait for me to say more. Tells me, "I know we can do it. Absolutely. I know we can. Right? Positive psychology. That's all we need." I stand there sort of stunned. Our opponents are still smiling at the little-girl way Sheila has of being hopeful. Sheila says again, "We can do it. Okay? I just know we can. We just need motivation. That's what we learned in Soc class, right?"

"Something like that," I mumble back.

And that's when she takes a twenty from her pocket and puts it on the side of the table. "Come on, what do you think?" She's not asking the other guys to put down their twenty yet. She's asking me to match hers. "Come on, you need some motivation too!" I can't really afford the twenty and think, like this will only be more embarrassing if I don't kiss the money goodbye so I lay down a twenty next to Sheila's and the two guys are smiling at all this positive psychology crap. It's not like we could win so they each cough up a twenty as well. And that's when Sheila claps her hands and begins chanting like a complete fool, "We can do it! We can do it! We can do it!" And I just want her to shut the fuck up and play pool and get us out of here, only she is really happy now.

She takes her next shot and misses. I can't believe it. She misses! Only the cue ball rolls all the way to the far end of the table mercifully far from the boys' remaining balls. The one with the glasses misses too. I'm up next and blow my shot as well, which is fine because it speeds the inevitable. The next fellow scratches. Then it's Sheila's turn and she gets one in on a long slow ball down the table. A real wimpy shot. But her next shot she misses and the boys manage to get one down before it's my turn to miss again. This goes on for a while until the boys have just one shot and the black ball left. But strangely, all our balls are getting lined up by the holes. And that's when Sheila begins to get a string of lucky shots and ties up the table. The boys of course get a little concerned by our good fortune. But eventually Sheila misses and the boys get their last ball down but miss on the black ball. It's up to me and fortunately our last ball is now hanging by a thread at the corner pocket so all I have to do is get my ball to even touch it and it is sure to go in.

I make the shot and Sheila is jumping up and down and clapping. And I smile and chalk my cue, trying to look cool, but know this is all bullshit. I of course don't have much hope of doing much with the black ball, which is snugged up against the far bank. Only Sheila whispers in my ear to not even try to get it in a pocket. "Just hit the ball head on, not too hard." I do it. The cue ball hits the eight-ball square on, which leaves it nestled up against the bank. The cue ball rolls away and back down to my end of the table. The boys are obviously pleased except they can't lift the eight-ball off the wall with any control either and instead watch it as it rolls around the table, wildly. That leaves Sheila to do one of those awkward shots where she has to tiptoe. Only this time she is not aiming at the black ball but is shooting at the opposite bank. She laughs a little and blinks then squints and pulls her hair back from her eyes and sure enough double banks the cue ball, which rolls gently up to the black and gives it the lightest of touches that sends it into the corner pocket. She jumps up and claps again and says, "See, I knew we could do it." She points at the money on the table and makes me pick it up. We all shake hands and Sheila and I are smiling and the guys are confused by our luck. As we walk away with the money Sheila looks at me and without the faintest hint of a giggle says, "Now that was fun, wasn't it!" And I think at that moment I'm in love.

twenty-six

IT TOOK ALMOST A YEAR of pool hall hustling and bus rides to figure out that Sheila and I needed each other. Or at least that I was
okay with being needed. Not like Lyla had needed me. Just that once.
Afterwards, the reserve in her voice when she said hello told me everything I needed to know. Regret. My selflessness likely being twisted
into a silly dalliance. Maybe she even blamed me for what happened. I
never asked and she never found her way back to my shoulder to tell
me what she was really thinking.

With Sheila, I was on more familiar ground, though I still felt
that somehow I was one step behind her. Just like that day playing
pool. It was weird. I knew Sheila liked having me around even though
for the life of me I couldn't say why. It was particularly troubling when
we studied together, sharing a table among the stacks on the fourth
floor of the cement building that houses our books. The air smells thick
inside. The lighting top heavy. The chairs are just comfortable enough
to avoid cramping. It is a place for efficient digestion. You can bring in
only coffee cups, never food. Oily-haired librarians in soft brown shoes
scurry between the stacks. Students methodically replace volumes that

they're admonished to leave on the carousels rather than risk disrupting the order of the shelves. There is fear here of disorder. Fear of a dropped decimal, or the misappropriation of a title. I don't mind the rules, though. It's a place I've found where I can learn. I do everything right to be allowed the privilege of sweating over words.

Not Sheila. She chews gum. She's not supposed to chew gum. Gum is as dangerous here as in the Youth Centre. It threatens the integrity of chairs and tables and floors and pages so crisp they crease like parchment. I can't bring myself to tell her to stop. Tell her I like the books more than her when I'm in the presence of both. I know that sounds crazy. I've never thought of myself even once having anything over on Sheila, except this. Just haven't figured out this other Joey person yet. But I will. Then I'll tell Sheila what I think. Then I'll have a lot to say.

For now, I just spend my time doing the research I need to do. I can find lots of canvas-clad volumes with words to cull and graft into sentences for my assignments. It's really not difficult to borrow ideas. Every now and then, my reading actually drifts into understanding. The words of ancient men and women tantalizing enough to make this exercise in mimicry worthwhile. Like a night spent at Sheila's. I love digesting a book that touches me that way. But of course not all of them do. Many remain detached like my professors. They speak theory but seldom provide the details of the individuals to which theory applies. What these others smell like. Whether they tidy the bathroom after a shower. Whether they choose bran flakes or Cocoa Puffs from the store shelves. I read each text imagining the cursory case examples as full-bodied lives. How would I ever help them? What do they really need? I doubt their endings are ever as tidy as the authors make them out to be. No one's life can be compressed and straightened into a simple case study. It would take pages, many pages, like a novel, to fully capture who someone really is. Academic texts aren't up to the task. Texts leave me confused. The shallowness of each life described only makes the social worker's intervention seem miraculous. Or else the client less than really endangered.

Whenever I tire of the monotony of my own discipline, I roam the aisles and go in search of odd titles. I will read just about anything for a page or two. The vocabulary intrigues me. My favourite is English literature. I read about dunces, then missionaries with daughters that become crows in African trees. And about little girls who ride whales. And boys who tame tigers while lost at sea. Crazy, crazy stuff like that. Ever notice, though, how many of those books are really about bigger ideas than they seem? Like religion, or God. I know I'm searching for something among their pages. Something the authors intended me to find. If I'm honest, I'd tell you I'm looking for what it means to be a good person. To give unselfishly. To really do something good for someone else that isn't just about personal payback. Not that weird New Age fluff, either, with its pages of middle-class secrets about doing whatever you want. I don't buy a word of it. Unless you already have the shoes to walk that path, there's a no trespassing sign. People like me run around in hand-me-downs, with scuffed heels, not leather Birkenstocks that make the walking easy.

I know it sounds smug, but I'm frustrated searching for the answers to questions that I can't find in my part of the library. They've got to be elsewhere. Somewhere. I just haven't found a good enough story yet. Times I wonder if I ever will. So I keep reading. I read more stories, this time about twelve-year-old prostitutes, suicide, rape, and murdered and unwanted children. It's among these other volumes that I learn much more about people and what healing means. Much more than in the HB and HV aisles of social work where tidy professional voices speak.

Sheila never follows me into the stacks. She remains chewing in the great room near the ecology journals. If I didn't know better, I'd think she likes to be seen there. She likes to be seen with me, too, for some reason I haven't yet figured out.

* * *

I am to graduate as expected after four years of university, with average grades. I could have done much better, but couldn't imagine why I should. In fact, if I make a tally of my educational experience, the pros and the cons, both lists are remarkably short. Perhaps if I had nothing to compare it to, no other adventure, then the experience would have been more stimulating. But I'd walked my way through the underbelly of the system, negotiated for privileges with the likes of B-boy and seen the suicides, the violence, the desperation of those whose lives were destined for huge case files. After all that, the inside of these academic cells had seemed lifeless. I could write beautifully about the etiology of disorders such as Tourette's, ADHD, NPD, CD, BPD, and God knows what else, but was damned if I was much closer to knowing what to say to the poor clients I was supposed to help when they were sitting across from me with blood and guts hanging from their teeth after they've gnawed their way through the tenuous strands of mind and matter that held them fixed to this unpleasant reality. In any case, graduation doesn't feel like a remarkable event when you place it next to life as it's really lived.

The best I can say is I had been taught to do no harm. To be critical. We wrote critical essays, critical analyses of theory. And we critiqued each other.

I know for certain I leave university having done no harm to anyone. Not even myself.

As graduation approaches, I begin to think about what's next. Which brings my thoughts back to what was first. I call John at the adult facility where he now works. He's busy, but I leave a message. I let him know I'm going to graduate. Tell him that next time he's in town he should call me. Maybe we could have a hot chocolate together. I think about asking him to come to my graduation, but am too shy. Too worried he'd say, "I can't." Or won't. Not even sure if he'd be allowed, his having been my worker and all.

If I were honest with John, I wasn't even sure I wanted to go to the graduation either. Walking around in black dresses? Besides, who'd attend? Jeremy was back inside, this time in Adult for brawling. Lou would come, but then Lou does things because people expect her to do them. I already owed her enough.

Who else was there? My mother? Parade in front of her the person I'd become? Force on her the truth that I'd done this on my own? My fear was that she would expropriate what was mine. Tell a story of my success that was not rightfully hers to tell. Even if the story is told just to herself in private.

I decide this performance is mine alone. I don't attend the formal graduation. Instead, I hand in my last paper and walk out the doors of the grey building which has been my school. The day is cloudy with brief washes of sunlight. There is a heavy wind that makes me lean forward as I walk. Even though it is still quite cool, I keep my jacket unzipped. I want to feel the wind envelop and lift me. I stand there on the steps leading to the path that will take me back up campus, to the ivy-covered buildings. I close my eyes. My thoughts turn as I knew they would to Ms. Rivolis. And the day John drove me here for the first time. The thoughts ignite something deep inside and it comes to me that I am about to move on. I am no longer the troubled kid. The apprentice. I will now be someone's social worker. I feel giddy with the possibilities. And vulnerable. Yet, if I can just place one foot in front of the other, I am sure I won't fall. For a moment, leaning into the wind, I feel I can almost lift from the ground. I grab the bottom corners of my jacket with each hand and hold them out, letting the wind billow my coat.

I begin to run.

Not for any reason. Just to feel my feet moving me, every buoyant stride taking me further from the madness that was my life before. My cocoon is now tattered, the threads unravelling as the bile that glued them together dissolves. In that moment I am convinced I have wings. Other students look at me and laugh and I don't care. I feel my voice swell. I let out a loud "Whoop!" and keep running. I turn only for a moment to look at that old square building which had contained me. And I think, no one will recognize me behind the papier-mâché mask of university parchment. My face now painted in rueful colour.

Run.

My coat flutters as I race through the centre of campus and out towards the main gate.

Run.

I slow down only when I reach my bus. The driver glances at my flushed face, my heavy breathing. Nods at me as I show her my pass. She is oblivious to what she is witnessing. I weave my way to a centre seat, not the back, not the front. Sit right in the middle, a single by a window, and look out over the campus. The old Jesuit college now invisible behind the imposing vine-encrusted stone walls that first greeted me.

It's then that I suddenly feel very alone, and very afraid.

twenty-seven

IN EARLY FEBRUARY OF MY FIRST YEAR at the agency I finally get an answer from the city. It arrives in a well-worn interoffice envelope. Dale's note tells me with the dryness of professional distance that it will take a while to get the Jeffreys a new house. It seems the numbers still don't add up. The family was seven percent underfinanced. They need more income to ensure the mortgage will be paid. And besides, the Central Mortgage Council wouldn't finance a home with a wood furnace, even as a secondary source of heating. It has to be oil, which means their monthly expenses will increase too. I'd made the case that Mr. Jeffrey got wood cheap. That neighbours helped him stack it and split kindling. But Dale would hear nothing of it. "This isn't the turn of the last century," she told me when I called to complain. I must have sounded exasperated. "Besides," Dale insisted, "there was a risk of fire." Dale had obviously never lit a woodstove.

I tried being polite, then sarcastic, then rude. Eventually I was yelling at her to get up off her fat ass and go visit the family. To see what Mr. Jeffrey's living day in and day out. That didn't help much either. Shirley got a call from the officers at the Metro Housing Authority.

Not Dale, but those above her who hold the vault keys. They didn't appreciate being yelled at.

"That's not the way to get things done, Joey," Shirley tells me while standing in my office. "We have to be persistent but never pushy."

I'd have listened better if Shirley's voice hadn't been so heavy. It's not like her to be tired. Sometimes when I'm with her, I hear something else in her voice. Something like an apology.

"Fine," I tell her. After she leaves, I stare at my computer, screaming, "Fuck, fuck, fuck" to myself.

By late February Mr. Jeffrey's hips are getting worse. Joan calls me to say she's having to do the shovelling herself. She's finding it hard to clear a path to the street so Cameron can make his way out to the road, then walk down to the highway at the end of their subdivision where he waits with the older kids in the cold wind to catch a van that picks him up and takes him to a subsidized play school. If the shovelling isn't done, then Cameron might not get to learn the things he needs to learn. She was wondering if we could hire her some help. I told her I doubted it, but would ask. Vivian has dropped out of school altogether.

Dale eventually visits the family but later tells me how upsetting it was. Mr. Jeffrey was on his portable toilet when she arrived. He'd made her wait outside for fifteen minutes while he finished. Then she had to sit in the kitchen next to it, with the foul smells of an old man's bowels lingering in the half-rinsed pail. Dogs sniffing and licking the salt from her boots. And the tea bitter. She'd actually drunk the tea. I felt sorry for her. She should never have drunk the tea on a first visit.

After that the city insisted the family move rather than giving them the money to fix their place up. I told Mr. Jeffrey in person the same day I got notice of the city's decision. I felt shy entering his home. Everyone was out except Mr. Jeffrey. When I knocked he shouted from inside the house to "Just come in." Maybe he'd heard my car and knew it was me. Or maybe he had just gotten used to strangers entering his house. The dogs followed me in and went to Mr. Jeffrey, who was sitting on the same kitchen couch where Vivian liked to sit. I couldn't bring myself to take off my coat, though I slipped off my shoes as I walked in. I could see the place was much cleaner thanks to Sandy's efforts. The dishes were all put away and on the floor you could actually tell where the dogs had just walked, their prints distinct on the clean linoleum. Standing by the table in the centre of the room, I told Mr. Jeffrey what the city had told me. "The house is still yours of course. But it will have to stand empty. The city's agreed to pay for the insurance while you try to find someone to buy it."

Mr. Jeffrey sat with his hands wringing a red handkerchief. He wiped his nose, then gave the large dog at his side a pat. "I understan'. You dun wha' you cou'. I'm jus' a bi' worried abou' the' ki's aroun' here breakin' in."

"Maybe I could check with your neighbours. The same ones that bring you wood. Maybe they'd keep an eye on it." Mr. Jeffrey said nothing, just kept patting the dog, massaging his arthritic hands into the animal's fur. It sat quietly, mouth open, looking back at him. "The insurance company will only cover the house for three months, so it will have to sell quickly. I'm very sorry about that, Mr. Jeffrey. I guess they know about the kids too. Too much risk, they said, to go any longer."

"A' leas' the place is wor' some'hing. Wou' giv' us all some money f'r Cameron's schoolin'."

I began to feel very warm, though the house was drafty and cool. "I'm afraid the city will take most of the money once the place is sold and use it to pay your family's welfare. I'm really sorry to tell you that, but you can be house poor and on welfare, but any cash or savings and the city claws it back."

"That don' seem righ'," was all Mr. Jeffrey said, looking down and picking at a hangnail. I asked him if he needed anything, but he just waved me away. I could see him tearing up and thought it best I leave.

The family moved two weeks later to subsidized housing downtown. There was talk about getting Vivian her own place once she gave birth. She'd live there alone. She's never told anyone who the father of her child is. I doubt Joan ever asked.

I didn't like the place the department provided the Jeffreys. Even I didn't feel safe walking outside their building. Cameron was now sure to grow up knowing less about the kindness of neighbours and more about street violence and poverty. With an address like his, it wouldn't be long before someone phoned the agency worrying over Cameron. And we'd have to respond. Find him to be a "child in need of protection." That's what we'd call it. We dig the hole, then fill it. Bury the kid alive. Blame the family. Someone, probably me, would have to inflict himself on Joan and Mr. Jeffrey. Likely remove Cameron because of neglect. The dirt. The infirmity. The potential for Joan's violence to erupt once Cameron's mouth becomes as rancid as his sister's. The danger would be obvious in the social worker's telling of the family's story. Even though it's really just a story of our own making. Our narrative, the system's contempt for Cameron's parents dressed in the guise of a capacity assessment. We will conveniently overlook our culpability.

During my weekly check in, Mr Jeffrey tells me, "I jus' knew a new house was never gonna 'appen. You never understoo'. Ou' here fightin' for us. You and Shirley. Phaw! No use, now was it? None a' all. Makes no difference if you figh' or ha' frien's in 'hem high places. Nothin'. 'Hey'll do wha' sui' 'hemselves. I'm righ', aren' I? You can' 'ell me I'm wron'."

Mr. Jeffrey is kind enough not to blame. "My only real worry is for m' boy. He's alrea'y gettin' into his head we're nothing bu' poor. Seems t' be thinkin' we' livin' pretty rough, though the apartmen', I guess, is like everyone else's. Go figure, eh? Like wha' can I do? I don' have much to give him." And then he surprised me with tears that this time he didn't hold back. Silent tears shed by a man who could bear anything but hurting his grandson. He rubbed his hip and took such a long sigh I thought his heart might stop.

Each time I visited, the piles of dishes in the sink grew larger. Most days, I'd find Joan watching television rather than playing with Cameron. Sandy told me Joan had refused her help. Not that there was much that needed doing anymore. There was no wood to chop or need for long walks to get milk. No little garden. No dogs to breed. The dogs had been given away. Cameron said he missed the dogs. The house was quiet except for the noise of the television, often turned up loud so you could hear it in every room. I'd have to ask Joan to turn the volume down to speak with her. She'd reluctantly agree. Then push herself off the sofa and go to the fridge for a glass of Big 8 pop, or make herself a sandwich though it was only mid-morning. Her hips had spread and Mr. Jeffrey looked more brittle. Soon, Cameron was being called disruptive at play school.

When I next write John I tell him, "The system sucks, really sucks." He is the only one I can safely speak my frustration to. I imagine his words encouraging caution. "Don't give up ... Remember revenge." I rant with my fingers tapping hard on my keyboard. The thought of complacency leaves me empty, stale, like the dry cold toast I'd eaten that same morning. I don't care if John responds. I write as much for me as for him. These days, all I have to share are tales of my impotence.

Riding the bus to work one winter morning a week after I post my letter, I vow to think my way to a solution. In my office, sifting through case notes, I realize that we had given Mr. Jeffrey insurance on his house while he waited for it to sell. A rare bit of compassion. It is also an opportunity. And I know of a better apartment for the family. One the department has already subsidized, but in a much safer neighbourhood.

The change of apartment is the easier of the two things I could do. I call Dale and make the arrangements. She's so exasperated with me and my endless requests, she agrees to do what I ask. Mr. Jeffrey and his family move into a half duplex beside a single mom on welfare, her son and a mad Rotweiller. The landlord, when I call him, is hesitant to have two welfare families but is desperate for the income. "Screw the neighbours," was all he said, then faxed me the paperwork for Mr. Jeffrey to sign.

Dealing with Mr. Jeffrey's old house takes more thought. I don't tell anyone, even John, what I'm going to do. He would likely tell me to play by the rules, or at least stay on this side of the law. "Which side?" I'd ask, and then maybe tell him I didn't believe in his laws. Legislated laws. Natural laws. They're not the same. We should be concerned with getting a four-year-old boy what he really needs. Not playing patsy to a system that ignores the vulnerable.

I go get my revenge instead.

* * *

I fetch Mr. Jeffrey with the agency car the day after he calls me to tell me about the fire. He wants me to take him and Joan and Cameron out to see what's left of his home. Vivian stays at the apartment. Tells us she's feeling sick. She's scratching a lot. I guess her liver's not doing too well. We leave her. When we get out of the car and walk through the burned shell of Mr. Jeffrey's house, Cameron looks confused and for a moment I feel the hot flash of self-loathing. "Where we gonna live?" he asks. The apartments were always someplace temporary.

"Like camping," I'd heard Joan tell him once.

"We'll figure tha' ou'," Mr. Jeffrey tells the boy and looks at me quickly before casting his eyes to the ground. He pauses to kick in the ash, then continues to walk circles through the rubble. "We'll figure tha' ou'," he says again.

He and Joan stay a while amid the charred remains before coming back to the car. Mr. Jeffrey says, "I'd really like t' move back 'ere. Think tha' will happen? Tha' 'ouse we've talked abou'? There's insurance, eh?" He doesn't sound happy. I know he's lost his house, but inside, I had held hope that maybe of all people, his simplicity would let him see my brilliance. No clutter of should's and what if's. I thought he'd understand my sacrifice. Find a clue, though I'd left him none. With his hand on the car door, he turns to look at the house. Says to no one, "Waste of a goo' 'ouse. All's it nee'ed was a little fixin'. Shou'n' 'av lef' it. Someone shou've stayed." Joan is quiet. She holds Cameron's hand and lets Mr. Jeffrey mumble away. She looks resigned to whatever happens next.

As we pull away, Mr. Jeffrey looks at me from the passenger's seat. "You can ge' 'em t' build us a new 'ouse now? Can you?"

"Maybe now, yes." I try to sound confident, but my voice has a small crack in it. Like it's been dropped too often to sound whole. I'm no longer sure what the right answer is.

"I'm guessin' t'at's good then," he says, and stares out the window as we drive back into the heart of the city.

twenty-eight

WHEN I GET HOME FROM WORK after showing Mr. Jeffrey his burned-down house, Stevie is waiting for me in my downstairs bedroom. Lou must have let him in. He's taller than I remember him. His face is full of acne. His hair is long and stringy, a veil of black strands that swing loosely across his eyes. Those eyes don't look so good. Red and framed by black circles, Stevie shows the signs of late nights and drugs. I've seen him out in the yard now and again, but we haven't spoken. My shame and his awkward silence have been barriers to our sharing. Looking at him close I begin to feel guilty, again. I hadn't wanted to think about what he must have had to do to survive all these years living alone with my mother. It sounds corny, but all I can think to say is "Long time no see." Stevie remains as quiet as ever.

"I'm going out west," he says quietly. "You'll have to look after her." He means my mother of course. Looks up and out the basement window in the direction of our house.

"Where out west?"

He shrugs and pulls from a front pocket a cigarette. He doesn't light it, just holds it between his teeth. "Just thought you should know. In case she needs anything. Not that you give a fuck. I know."

"Why should I care? She threw me out."

"Yeah," he says. His voice is flat. Uncommitted. Like he's not really here, or anywhere except deep inside himself.

"You have a girlfriend? Leaving anyone special behind?" His look goes sinister, but he doesn't say anything. Just looks again towards our mother's house. Keeps gnawing the end of the cigarette. I can tell he wants to light it. When Lou let him in I bet she told him to butt out. That's one thing Stevie and I share in common. We don't mind being told what to do by someone we respect.

"Is that all you wanted? To say goodbye?"

He hesitates. Fidgets with his belt buckle. Not looking at me, he asks, "You remember anything weird happening? When we were real small? I know you're a social worker now. Just thought that ..."

It's my turn to go silent. I sit down on my bed. Looking at my feet, I tell Stevie, "Maybe. Why's it matter?" I'm feeling too exposed to admit it does matter. And it must matter a whole bunch to Stevie if he's actually asking me for something. But I have no answers. I tell him, "It was all just weird. The foster homes, Dad dying, Mom. Baths." As I say the last word, he looks at me, angry.

"You too, eh?"

"Maybe."

He turns and starts to head upstairs.

"Wait," I shout. "The bath thing. Yeah, of course it happened." He turns and nods. His face is as blank as a mug shot. He betrays nothing of the pain I guess mirrors my own. Then he finishes his climb and leaves silently by the back door.

I go upstairs and find Lou watching from her study. She comes over to where I'm standing in the kitchen by the back door and puts a friendly arm around my shoulder. "He was saying goodbye, wasn't he?"

"Yeah, and a few other things." Lou takes her arm away and leans against the wall. I dig inside and find the courage to ask her questions I've wanted to ask for a long time. Not as much for Stevie's sake as for my own. "What do you know about why we were taken away? You were there, at least the second time. And you used to work in the department. I can even remember you looking up from your front lawn after the social worker came to visit. I can't really remember her. Just a big friendly woman. It's all echoes inside my head."

Lou tells me, "I wouldn't know too much about any of it. You've got to remember, I'd retired by the time you'd moved in. I reported you, though. You've probably figured that out. I don't think your mother was coping very well. Still doesn't. But exactly what they found when they investigated, I don't know." She waits for me to say something. When I don't, I can see she feels strange. Never one to be bullied, Lou stays silent for a moment longer. I guess my staring at her eventually shames her into saying more. "Nor should I have known more. It was none of my business. My duty was over after I made the call." She's looking right at me now. Says with a hint of a grin, "Though you showing up on my back stoop seems to have proven me wrong on that point." We both laugh a little, like convicted felons. "I never regret having taken you in or made the call. I learned that what makes one kid survive and another fail isn't about something inside us most times. It's about who gives a damn for their welfare. Who changes the odds stacked against them."

"Thanks," I tell Lou but she waves away the appreciation.

"Be good. That's all I ask." She pats my shoulder again, and heads back to her study while I stare out the kitchen window. I look across Lou's well-tended yard to the chaos behind my mother's house. The snow has been trampled down to make a path from the back door to the garbage can. No one took the time to shovel or pick up the rusting tin cans that are scattered across the deck. Their rusty edges show through the snow. Stevie is now sitting alone smoking on the back steps. The paint has long since peeled from the deck and the risers are showing rot. Deep furrows split the surface of the wood. Stevie sits there a long time despite the cold. Even after he finishes his cigarette, and a second one after that, he stays sitting. I get a glass of water from the sink and keep watching until Stevie finally throws a third cigarette butt under the deck and goes inside our mother's house. It's the last time I ever see him.

twenty-nine

A YEAR AFTER I GRADUATE and now working at the agency, Sheila and I spend most of our time together. Lou just smiles whenever I find my way home, t-shirt on backwards and tired. She likes Sheila. I think she likes what Sheila is doing for me. Maybe happy to see her foster child finding a new home, finally.

It's that same spring when Sheila helps to organize a Rally in the Valley. She borrows a sharecar from the local co-op and loads it with pamphlets and signs. Everyone is gathering to resist one of the big pesticide companies and the fungicides that are linked to birth defects in babies in Asia. Sheila tells me, "Now they want to spray the same stuff in our backyard." I look out the kitchen window at the tiny patch of untended grass behind Sheila's apartment. I can't help it. She catches my affront. "Seriously," she says.

The car is loaded early enough that we can make the two-hour drive and still arrive for the organizers' meeting. Except Sheila insists that before we go we vote. I'd forgotten that today is our municipal election. I never gave it much thought. I'm embarrassed to tell Sheila I've never voted. She insists, even though it might make us late.

"The election is going to be close."

I'm guessing from Sheila's tone that this is a problem that should concern me. I've been learning from Sheila lots lately about what should concern me.

"Besides," she says, "even if it wasn't, could you really live with yourself if you didn't vote and the entire country began shifting to the right, one municipality after another? It could happen, you know. It's only a short leap and our government becomes some right-wing oligarchy. Just think of that!" I think she knows I haven't a clue what she's talking about, but nod anyways. At times like this I'd like to crawl home and bury myself under my mother's decrepit porch, but then that would be copping out. So I listen and try to learn as best I can. On topics such as this we have always agreed that Sheila does the educating and I follow blindly. At least until I get fed up. Then I hold the right of last refusal and willingly pay for my transgressions with her cold stares, or worse, nights alone in my own bed. "Have you really never thought about this?" she asks, obviously exasperated with me.

"Not really. It's never come up."

She changes tactics. Cajoles. Her voice now that of the small girl again. "We have two choices. MacPherson. He's an idiot. He'll vote against anything to do with public transportation. There's a bunch of bastards just like him on Council. They'll make it so even poor people have to drive cars." Now I see her point. "Damn MacPherson," I want to tease. I wouldn't have met Sheila if it hadn't been for public transportation. The bastard.

I stand next to the car we have for the day, leaning against the door, the defensive posture of the adolescent at the end of an argument that he knows he's losing but stubbornly wants to ignore. It's all just male bravado. As empty of purpose as my father's drunken rants. "Okay, I don't want the country to swing right," I say, showing her she's not the only one with the gift for exaggeration.

"Absolutely." She is stooped down on one knee in front of me searching a backpack for the address of the polling station. She finds her voter card. I'd accidentally thrown mine in the recycling earlier that week. But I can still vote, as long as I show my identification. They're not too strict when it comes to mayors and councillors.

"Mind you," I tell her, "who's to say that I just don't go and cancel your vote with mine? That could happen, you know."

Sheila grins devilishly, still down on one knee in front of me, her backpack's guts spilled open on the ground. She looks up like she's proposing. Her expression friendly but tinged with the kind of sarcasm reserved for those she trusts. Her lover's condescension a thin veneer over the love being held at bay. I've avoided that word, Love, but her expression confirms what we both know is taking root. The playfulness of our resistance is just ground cover for a fertile bed of hopeful perennials.

"You wouldn't. I just know you wouldn't."

"Who am I supposed to vote for, then? Not MacPherson. Right?"

"You can vote for anyone you like, Joey. No point being childish about this." My expression says it all. "Yeah sure," like she really expects me to think this through myself. So I wait, silent. It's only a heartbeat before she tells me, "I'm going to vote for Betty Finke. She supports public transit. Municipal gardens. Accessibility. Things like that."

Finke? She wants me to vote for someone with a name like Finke? I nod and get in the passenger's seat of the car.

A few minutes later we park outside a nearby junior high school and walk into the gym where two women sit straight in their chairs and a tall gaunt man stands next to them with Parkinson hands. They look at us and check for our names on the voters' list. "I'm not on the list," I tell them and hand the man my driver's licence. I used Sheila's address when I got it. I hadn't wanted to make it seem that I was a permanent fixture at Lou's. They check the address carefully, then hand me a bunch of paper ballots with perforated creases. The more elderly of the women points to a cardboard screen which I'm supposed to stand behind to vote. Sheila is already behind hers. I lay before me like playing cards my six ballots. One says councillor and sure enough there are two names printed in bold letters. I go to put an x beside Finke but hesitate. My mind races to the possibilities. I would forever hold the private truth of my resistance, even if it is never shared. I put the pencil tip down next to MacPherson's name, but can't make the mark. I can see Sheila is finished and has put her ballots into the padlocked box that sits beside the clerks. I blush red with the thought that she must think I'm confused. I'm taking too much time. I imagine her saying to the clerks, "He's never voted before" and I redden. I look down at the ballot and then up again at Sheila and my imaginary story about her malice evaporates. She isn't speaking to anyone. My anger, nothing but clouds on a hot day. Sheila is just standing there looking at me with the gentlest of expressions. Her casual stance tells me there is no hurry.

I lift the pencil and scratch an x beside Finke. Leave the other ballots empty. Then steal the pencil. That much I am willing to do. Grind the machinery of the state to a standstill. It's my only authentic act of resistance that day.

* * *

We drive the two hours to the rally and though we are a little late, no one seems to mind. Sheila distributes the signs. Begins to organize people in lines. She asks me to be a parade marshal and I dutifully put on my red armband. There's a hundred of us on this sunny Saturday afternoon. It's all over in an hour. A satisfied collective of mothers and fathers with their children in strollers who hold signs they can't read. The traffic in the small town where we are is polite. They wait patiently behind as we chant our way along our designated route. There's candy to keep the children amused, and crisp cold apples given free to everyone by a farmer who tells us proudly his produce is organic. A local coffee shop, advertising fair trade business practices, has set out a table in front of their store. Coffee is poured in biodegradable cups. Everyone sips and munches and chants until we arrive at the offices of the local federal representative. Demands for controls on pesticides are voiced and a woman with greying wispy hair, solid calves and comfortable canvas walking shoes speaks from a makeshift podium of hay bales. Everyone claps while I keep an eye out for cars that need directions how to get around us while we mill in the street. The crowd disperses with hugs and promises amid songs that trail off as one group becomes many.

Before we head back into the city, we take advantage of the car we've borrowed and go further into the countryside to buy fresh lettuce and free-range eggs. Sheila knows where an organic farmer has his land. We travel a fabulous road that meanders through maple and spruce forests just starting to bud. We rattle across old bridges that ford rivers flowing into finger lakes. The weather only hints at rain on the horizon.

We get lost and never do find the organic farmer, though we pass orchards of apple trees with their white blossoms. We're determined to eat something fresh so we stop at a country market and buy from a wooden crate organic apples that have been stored all winter. Their flesh is soft, but still tasty. We eat as we drive back towards the city. I finish my apple quickly, rotating it in successive bites, the core nothing but a seed and hard cartilage. I power down the window and go to launch it into the weedy ditch beside the road when Sheila suddenly shouts a harsh, "Hey!" Gasps.

"What? It's only an apple."

"You're not going to throw that out? All this beautiful land and you think people want to drive by looking at your gross apple core? I can't believe you sometimes."

"It's a friggin' apple, Sheila. It's biodegradable. Besides, the birds or whatever are out there could use the food. Think of it as community service." The car bumps over another small bridge.

At the other side, I decide to hell with it and launch my environmental bomb. It lands amid the alders that grow in the ditch. From the corner of my eye, I see it hit branches and bounce back onto the gravel shoulder.

"What did you do?" Sheila yells. "It's on the fucking road. You just can't leave it there."

She's serious. Thinks this is some kind of blight on the ecosphere. Looks at me like I'm a mindless idiot and stops the car.

"Fuck," I growl as she turns the car around quickly, spitting gravel onto the pavement. We drive back. When we reach the spot where I threw the apple, Sheila parks on the shoulder and gets out. She takes a small plastic sandwich bag with her, one that she was going to recycle. She waits to search the road while an old school bus that's been converted into a moving house passes. It feels like the driver is frowning, not at Sheila, but at me. Then Sheila walks along the shoulder looking for the offending item. Back and forth she weaves until there, a few feet from the alders, brown and dirty, she finds my apple core and puts it gingerly into the bag.

When she gets back into the car, she holds the offending object in her hand as if it's a turd. "Now, Stupid, we can go."

Sheila's quiet the whole ride home. A Sarah MacLaughlin CD plays. I wanted to complain that she was overreacting. That here we are in our gas-guzzling car causing untold environmental damage and she's concerned about some stupid apple core. Nobly saved the world from the slight of its visible decay. It all makes no sense to me. I exhale hard, the bitterness of my shame confusing itself with the apple's lingering tartness.

That evening, with the car returned and the signs torn apart, we sit at either ends of Sheila's futon bed watching the late evening news. Finke won but only by the smallest of margins. MacPherson is demanding a recount.

"Just a coincidence," I tell her.

Sheila looks at me over a cup of tea she's prepared for herself. Smiles and lets her toes drift amicably over to mine, which she massages tenderly.

"You see, I told you, didn't I. Surprised?"

"You're sure I did what I was supposed to do?"

She blows me a smile with a flick of her bangs, then gets up to refill her tea from the pot on the burner at the back of the stove. As she sits down again, I see she has brought me a fresh apple from the basket on the counter. The apple is laid pleasantly on a white plate with a knife beside it.

"Would you cut up an apple? I don't want a whole one, just a piece. Thought you might like the rest."

I understand a peace offering when I see one. "You trying to make up?" I ask timidly.

"No," she says. "Just thought you'd like an apple. That's all. Thought you might be hungry."

Feeling a little silly, I tell Sheila, "I am hungry," and she can tell it's not for an apple. I know it's a corny, even dumb, thing to say but now it's her turn to feel the apple-red flush of embarrassment as our toes entwine.

thirty

JEREMY WAS TWENTY-TWO when John became his worker for a third
time. He was back inside the regional correctional facility for adults.
John would have volunteered to be his worker. Signed on board without a thought to the consequences.

It was John, they tell me, who pushed Jeremy to see a counsellor. He offered to drive him. Was willing to work overtime to make
sure Jeremy got to his appointments every week. The counsellor, I've
met her, is a grey-haired woman whose office is in a downtown tow-
er. I imagine she was waiting for them to arrive. Worried when they
were late, but likely figured Jeremy had simply lost his privileges. There
would have been an empty chair in her office, and another a respectful
distance from her office door. That's where John would have sat reading old magazines.

John and Jeremy never made the appointment. John had borrowed
a car from the facility. A Chrysler Neon. Fuel efficient. Anonymous. He
would have had to fold himself into the front seat. With Jeremy doing the same, they would have looked like two Shriners clowns. The
springs would have sagged. The car would have handled poorly.

I imagine John would have told Jeremy one of his stories. About Mujhaddin with guns or tribal lands where sheets of hashish are normal sights. Or maybe not. Since 9/11 John had been more shy to speak about these things. His letter shortly after the collapse of the World Trade Center was astonishingly brief. "I'm so ashamed of what happened," he'd written. "How could I have ever been so naïve? I don't know how I'll ever tell my stories again without thinking of the consequences." I think that's why John was so eager to help Jeremy. Though it was absurd to connect his boasting and a cataclysmic act of terror, I'm sure John had done just that.

But Jeremy would have been too stupid to understand any of it. To appreciate what John was offering him. Jeremy would have just been thinking about what was to come. The knife of intimacy about to be thrust into his chest by the soft and gentle prods of a kindly old woman. And that his life really sucked after all. And that he was drifting nowhere but back to jail. And that Carrie was too strung out on drugs to really love him. And that there was really no one else to whom he mattered. At all. And that I was off making a fool of myself trying to be something I'm not. And he wasn't going to become like that. But he wasn't going to become anything else either. He'd have it all figured out. For once, in that shitbox Neon, he would have known he was nothing but a make-work project for people like John.

I imagine he would have been thinking back to his glory days. The beer bottle to a taxi driver's head. The exhilaration of being someone who could lead others. The thrill of being so much more special than John, or me, or Carrie, or anyone else. And he likely had no way to tell anyone any of this before he slipped off his seatbelt and reached over towards John and punched him in the head, then steered the car deliberately into the front of an eighteen-wheeler.

I heard the truck driver walked away with nothing but a scratch. His rig damaged, a small expense to his employer while John and Jeremy were tangled amid their car's wreckage. John tumbled like a gemstone, his black skin brushed and bruised to a shiny deep purple lustre. The dark maroon of spilled blood soiled by fuel and the mud and baby spruce branches that the car sluiced through while upside down.

Jeremy was tossed through the front windshield, then crushed between the truck cab and the Neon's hood. A sandwich of steel first, then the abrasion of metal scraping skin over forty-five metres of tar. Bits of him ground beneath wheels.

I wonder if John had time to think, "Why now?" India, Africa, the Middle East. All the lost worry over what he should do or not have done. I wonder if he had time to remember his commitment to me and others. All that atonement, only to be foiled by a loser like Jeremy who unfortunately had the horse sense to know when life was done. An adult with an adult's foreclosure on the future.

Or did John see that moment as something more, even just for the millisecond before his death? Did he understand that his part in Jeremy's exit was to be his last and greatest gift? Helping Jeremy to kill himself in a way that was flamboyant enough to leave a story lingering behind him. To be a six-o'clock news item rather than some junkie in a rooming house who must overdose. Would John have glimpsed the white glare of irony that he had made a sacrifice great enough to earn him his redemption?

I'm not sure. I chant over and over, "What a waste," and just sit there in the dark of my basement room. The new nineteen-inch television I bought offering its blue glow to the walls around me. The three-minute news item done, I mute the volume and cry.

The funeral is held three days later. I insist on going alone. I don't want to have to tell Sheila all the violent details about who I once was. Before I had the education. The job title. When I arrive, there are church pews full of social workers and correctional officers. B-boy is there, and even Skunk-lady. They are all friendly with each other. I remain at the back. Clarence slips in late after the service has begun. He sits to my right. When he notices me, he reaches out to shake my hand, obviously pleased to see me there, in a shirt and looking like I belong. Then he looks to the front of the church and his face becomes emotionless, until the singing starts. Then his eyes, like mine, go moist.

I want to avoid tears. At least in public. I turn and ask Clarence in a whisper, "Is John's wife here?" Strange how this funeral has brought Clarence, John and me together again. My memories, straddling time.

Clarence shakes his head. "She died last year."

I feel something congeal in the pit of my stomach. The reflux of acid. Truth trying to escape. I mumble, "I didn't know."

"You probably also didn't know that John brought her back with him from Pakistan, did you? She was a widow. Her husband worked overseas and slept with a lot of prostitutes. At least that's what John told me. You can guess what killed him." He shakes his head. "John said widows have no future there. Especially ones whose husbands die that way. Still, can't say as I understood why he'd bring someone like that back here."

I just nod and know it's not my place to share John's stories. Not here, not now. I had always assumed his work with us kids was his redemption. Never knew there could be more. Or that John lied. He didn't come home right away. I guess his story just sounded better told with a quicker ending.

I turn my eyes again forward. Then stare down at my hands and think of John's large mitts. And the way he'd sheath them in latex whenever there was a risk someone would get hurt. Bitten or scratched. And I suddenly realize John wasn't protecting himself from us. He was protecting us from him. And the thought forces me to tears whether I accept them or not.

thirty-one

THE ONLY TIME I SEE MY MOTHER is when I catch a glimpse of her from across the fence. Or from the sidewalk when I see her sitting in her front window when I walk by her house. There is only silence. No one ever visits. At least not that I've seen. It's been almost five years since I caught my mother's hand in mid-flight. Since I drew a line, marked the space where childhood ended.

With everything that's happened recently, I'm finally feeling as grown up as I am. It's the holiday weekend in July when I have the time to catch my breath. Sheila is in New York, part of a youth forum on climate change. Lately, I'm jealous of her passion for something other than our relationship. Maybe that's good. Could mean I'm connecting. Still, this weekend I'm happy to be hanging out enjoying this time to do nothing but rent movies and feel sorry for myself. Mourning John. Thinking about Sheila. Peeling layers of thought like winter clothes in a steam room. Emotions sweating out of every pore.

Lyla and her boys are over, cooking another meal for Lou. Jurgen is away. The boys hardly seem to notice. They play in the backyard with the tools in Lou's tool chest, which she has left open on the back porch. She's on the roof, repairing shingles. She's tied a ladder so it lies

248

flat on the slope of the roof, a sturdy rope snaking over the peak to a big old maple on her front lawn. Another ladder rented for the day gets her up to the second-storey eave. She wears an old grey leather carpenter's belt that you can hear dragging across the coarse black shingles overhead. A little box on a rope lets her pull up whatever she needs. Her grandsons oblige by putting things in the box. They seldom send up the right thing on the first go and Lou good-naturedly calls down, "No, honey, not that one, the other green box of screws."

Lyla meanwhile putters inside. I'm helping her scrape potatoes in the kitchen. Every now and then we see Lou's little box float mysteriously up past the window. Watching Lyla's boys enchanted with their grandmother, I'm reminded of the sanctuary Lou provides all of us. I still don't pay her any rent. She seldom asks me about my work. Though if I tell her things, she nods her head politely. Listens, but never offers any advice. All I get from her is the occasional, "Times have changed, haven't they," and then she goes on puttering with some electrical appliance that no longer works.

She's converted her study on the main floor into a little workshop. She has a computer now, the casing off. Leftovers from some repair she'd attempted. She'd had to have some geeky kid in a new red Beetle come and sort out the mess she'd made. When I got home I'd found Lou staring at the computer. She had taken off the casing again after the young fellow had done his repair. "Just want to see what he's done," she told me as we both stared at the computer's guts. Then she went outside to tidy up her yard after a winter of wear.

Lyla tells me, "Jurgen is thinking about going back overseas." Chop, chop. "I don't know. The boys like it here. Their school's first rate. I'd love to go back, too. But Jurgen's not thinking about the boys." It's the most intimate thing she has said to me since my bedroom. I'm relieved that single episode gets almost forgotten. She has only once since that day even hinted at unfinished thoughts, when she caught me with my shirt off, walking from my bedroom to the shower upstairs. She was carrying a bag of vegetables to put down in the cold room when she passed me in the stairwell. She paused long enough to look me up and down. "Some girl will be lucky to have a boy like you," she said and continued to descend the stairs.

She shifts the cut vegetables to a colander. Puts the knife in the sink. Does this all with the deftness of the short-order cook. Always the same motions with Lyla. Only this time cubes of potato slip from the colander and as Lyla reaches to scoop them up, her hand brushes the knife and cuts a long thin line across her middle finger. She comes as close as I've ever seen her to swearing. "Fudge it all," she says and runs to the bathroom to root for a Band-Aid. By the time she returns, I've put all the potatoes back in the colander and made sure they're rinsed. She holds up her hand with the bandage, pouting and obviously disgusted with herself.

I stand off to the side as Lyla prepares the remainder of the food. Lettuce from her garden still moist with dew. And a big pot of beef stew. She's banging down the pot lid when the sound of the lid closing seems to shake the house and we both stop to listen to the *thunk, thunk, thunk,* in perfect rhythm that comes from somewhere up on the roof. Our eyes go to the ceiling, then are drawn to the window as we see the bottom rung of a ladder sail downwards and then Lou, still holding on, is travelling by on her way to the ground, her hands clutching the sides of the ladder even as she falls. The whole scene is like sketch comedy. Lou's face, as cool as a cucumber as she flies past the window. Then there's the hard compression of aluminium sinking into soil and the ladder tilts back away from the window. It takes us a moment to react. Lyla, hands clasped to her face, with "Oh my God!" I'm half-laughing, not because I think it's funny, but because I'm scared thinking what I'll find as I tear out the back door to check if Lou is okay.

Lyla's boys are standing on the deck dumbfounded. And there's Lou, hopping on one foot, examining the ladder, saying, "I don't think it's broken." Lyla makes her sit down and orders the boys to go and get their grandmother a chair and some ice in a plastic bag. "Don't just stand there," she yells at them. Her anger just makes them more mute and they remain frozen to the spot. I don't think they could do what she wants them to do even if they tried so I run inside instead and make the ice pack.

When I get back, Lou is muttering away, "The rope just let go. Must have rubbed on the peak a bit too much. Lucky not to have broken the ladder."

Lyla looks pale next to Lou. As I give Lou the ice pack, Lyla excuses herself and runs back inside, pushing one of the boys aside. "Move," she shouts at him. I can see she is covering tears with her bandaged hand.

Lou takes the ice and I help her inside. She sits on one of the kitchen chairs and puts a foot up on another. She calls outside to the boys, "That's all for now. Put the tools away for me, please." Then to me, she says, "Don't worry about Lyla. She's always thinking I'm going to die. Always living in the future."

Lyla comes back to the kitchen a while later. I've finished preparing the dinner. Lyla serves everyone, then sits saying nothing and ignores her food.

When the dishes are cleared and Lou is with the boys watching television, her foot up on a stool, I sit with Lyla on the back porch in the half light of an early June evening which is quickly turning cold.

"If I smoked, I'd smoke now," Lyla says, then adds, as if only as an afterthought, "I'm just so tired of being good."

It's not what I expected her to say. Lyla pulls her sweater tighter, retreating from the night air. I'm relieved we're not sitting face to face. If we were, I'd feel like I had to ask her why she said that. This way, she can move though the conversation at her own pace. Like John would.

I follow Lyla's gaze across to my mother's house. There's one light on in the kitchen. In the evening calm, I can hear the thud of a fridge door closing. My mother, hand to mouth, backlit at the window, walks and feeds. Lyla lays her head on her knees and stares.

"It would be nice to have Jurgen's reassurance that God is always with you. That someone loves you, isn't going to abandon you. I envy him that." She draws a long breath of moist evening air. "Me, I'm just angry with God. Beats the good right out of you, being angry. My mother used to tell me that." She pauses as long as it would take someone to smoke a cigarette. "I have a right to be angry. Don't I? First my father dies, then my mother ... you know ... changes." Lyla kneads her hands together. "And then even Claire dies." Lyla's voice sounds weepy even if there are no tears. "I keep trying to do good. I want to make up with God ... My friend in Kenya, whose child was killed, she never let the anger eat at her. Did I tell you about that? How their Land Rover broke down and how they were a long way from the city, afraid of bandits. Her husband went for help. He just started walking. The mother and children – she had three daughters – they were afraid to stay in the vehicle because they knew that men in trucks would stop in the middle of the night and rob them, and likely worse. Better, they figured, to let the bandits vandalize the vehicle than risk being caught inside so they set up a tent they were carrying in a small grove of trees. And then lions came and scratched on the tent and the mother told me she was thankful for the lions because she knew the lions would scare away the bandits. She thought God had sent the lions. Only the lions didn't leave and then the children woke up."

Lyla stops her story, turns her head slightly towards me. "Do you believe we're all put here for a purpose?"

"I don't know."

"You're too bright not to know or to have a plan. You need a plan," she says, staring again across the yard.

A minute passes. I ask her, "What happened? With the lions?"

"The lions smelled food or something in the tent and kept scratching until they ripped the fabric. Then my friend's seven-year-old, she got so scared that she bolted. Got up and ran. God only knows what made her do that. Usually people freeze when they're that afraid. And lions, they're just like big cats. One pounced on her, then grabbed her by the neck, like it was trying to play. Then it ate her, starting at the stomach. Can you imagine watching such a thing? By moonlight? And all my friend could do was hold her other two kids and wait." Lyla kneads her fist harder. "And you know what my friend told me about watching her child being eaten by lions?" Lyla's tone changes, from anger and despair to sarcasm. "She told me, 'But no bandits came.' And to this day, she thanks God for that." Lyla shivers. The cold air and the story working their way into her.

"I get a card from her now and again," Lyla tells me as stars appear in the blackness above us. "She's always asking me to help send shoeboxes of gifts to needy children at Christmas, especially needy Muslim kids. They put literature about the Bible in the boxes of toys people donate. It's propaganda, really. She think it's her duty but who's going to tell her different? It's like she's snatching other children's souls to get hers back. I don't know. I think she's just as angry as me but just won't admit it."

The light in my mother's kitchen stays on. Lyla says, "I used to be so sure about my religion. There's one good path, right? That's helping others. It was so straightforward. And straight, if you understand what I mean. Then my mother found her other side after my father died. She waited, of course, the selfish bitch. She never thought to wait until I was gone too. Think about how it made me feel. What was I supposed to think, then? Was I just an experiment and my father a bit of fun on the dark side?" Her sarcasm bites each word in half as they leave her mouth. "And then I have to put all her crap side by side on my plate with my beliefs. Like I'm some Hebrew expected to make a meal of milk and meat. You following me?" At that Lyla fades. What little heat had remained in her face drains from her lips and cheeks. Left are only wrinkles on a white pasty background caught in the weak glow of a small porch light. "Religion ...," she says, "I don't ... even have that now." Then she cries. Not forcefully, but with self-pity, sobs held back from fear of letting them loosen. She holds one hand up to her eyes while with the other she roots into her pants pocket to find a tissue. I make a lame gesture to search for one in mine, but don't find there anything of use. Don't touch her. I can do nothing but stand witness, mime concern. I am again an awkward little boy.

The cold soon chases Lyla's tears away. We go inside and I go down to my room. I'm feeling empty. Tease myself with thoughts of finding God by sitting in Lyla's chair and staring at the wall above my bed. Feign contemplation, something I know nothing about. I want to believe my life is something more than meaningless, but not like this. God's revenge, Lyla's revenge. Neither one is mine. I want my life to be something more than a leftover from the big bang, or some smaller bang that maybe knocked my mother to the ground while my father thrust into her. My cynical conception proportioned by nothing.

My thoughts continue to ramble as I slide down the other side of the kind of dream one dreams while still awake. Staring blankly, I wonder if God took Mary in the morning? And if he did was his beard prickly? Did he scratch her thighs giving her pleasure? Did it matter? Is God as self-centred and righteous as those who proclaim His name? Is the exercise of the spirit about pleasure, or about revenge? To my mind, those who think they are the givers are nothing but bedevilled parasites draining the needy of the one thing they can always give, their victimhood. Is this what God meant when he created sin? The real evil isn't the dramatic violence perpetrated by people like Jeremy, but the hidden intent of the do-gooder, the religious zealot, the community activist, the politician, the social worker. What kind of vengeful God would have had me taken from my home when I was just little, then put back? I doubt there was a higher purpose to serve. It was his baser need to rule over others that this paternal God understands. That we mimic with our policy and procedure manuals at my agency. If I'm bitter, I have good reason to be. What fiction was created to justify what I experienced at the hands of God's messengers? Social workers disguised as saints.

Before I can answer, there is more dreaming as I put my head down on my folded arms, resting myself on my knees. Downy-coated lions with soft nuzzles pull me towards them even as I try to draw back. A stranger pushes them away, then offers me a large breast to suckle, only my face is not that of a baby's but of a grown child. Prepubescent, smooth. And I oblige until I am scratched. Or is it until I scratch, or bite? Then I hear my mother's voice. She yells at me to stop. Then slaps me. Then there's running. Always running. While behind me, I can hear the lions pursuing. And at my side there's Stevie, who says, "I told you so," before he trips and falls. I don't look back. Keep running.

I stir and the overcast skies inside my head clear. It takes me a moment to remember where I am even as I sort into boxes lingering thoughts of hardened tissue, and the suppleness of youthful skin brushing up against it. No trace of either the dream or the message left. No stubble burn. Only scary thoughts lurking, not avoided, but intangible nonetheless.

Staring at nothing but an empty wall, I know I need facts. Need to know what happened when I was a child and why. I want to remember something other than this fiction. I lean back in my chair, resolved to what I need to do, but too fearful to convince myself it needs doing now. "There will be time," I tell myself. "Wait."

Upstairs I can hear Lyla getting her boys ready to leave. She's angry at one of them and the more she complains, the more I can hear his protests. I open my door a crack. Curious what she will do next to cajole him. Curious what a parent is supposed to do. His muffled cries just keep getting louder, and then I hear the familiar sounds of a child's feet being dragged forcibly across the floor and Lyla screaming, "Put on your coat now!" I can't believe she's yelling at him. I hug my legs tighter to avoid leaping from my chair and cursing back at her. Her anger is senseless. It's only a coat! But I don't go and yell or defend. Instead, I feel the tenacious grip of an old pattern. I want to run. I close my eyes and am surprised to feel tears squeeze out. So this is what families are. A thin sliver of decorum over annoyance and the pain we cause each other. I inhale silent sobs, then wipe my eyes on my pant leg.

Lyla needs my help, not my anger. Just like Vivian and Cameron and the rest of my clients need my help. A caring parent. Not one that snatches, or thinks baked cookies can heal. Not one that thinks she can do it alone, either, the arrogance of a sole parent whose mock independence is no better than the neglectful social worker who apprehends and forgets. It comes to me that parents, like social workers, are not numbers. One, or two, or three. More is simply more.

I realize what I really want to do is go upstairs and show Lyla I'm educated now. Make her understand children know things we adults have forgotten. But before I can rise from my chair, I catch the stinging *thwack* of Lyla's palm landing hard on a child's cheek. After that the boy hollers even louder and fear binds me in my sanctuary beneath the floor. I can hear Lou getting up from her seat, heavy footfalls as she tells Lyla she'll get the boy into the car.

"You go on," Lou tells Lyla, mopping up this mess just like she did my family's.

But Lyla will have none of it. "Stay out of this, Mother," she yells back. Then she grabs both boys. I can hear them straining to get away. I know how they feel. How much they want to bolt but can't.

"That hurts," the younger one complains, again and again, sobbing. But Lyla just keeps dragging her boys towards the door, little feet marched hurriedly to the front of the house and then outside. The front door slams closed and the last thing I hear is a few dull thuds as Lou returns to her study and resigns herself to her favourite chair.

thirty-two

THE LETTER ARRIVES A FEW DAYS LATER. It's a Department of Corrections envelope but the handwriting on the front isn't John's. It was addressed to my old address, next door. My mother must have dropped it in Lou's mailbox. It's the nicest thing she's done for me in years. The only thing she's done. I open it. There's a letter from John with a note stapled to the front. The note is from Clarence.

Dear Joey,

Thought he'd like you to have this, even if it isn't finished. If you need anything, just let me know. I'm here at the jail most days.

Clarence

Dear Joey,

Here in Adult it's hard to remain hopeful. I'm meeting too many of the little shits we didn't turn around when they were in the YO facility. I'm thinking we failed them every bit as much as they failed themselves. Like that friend of ours. Continuity is supposed to help, right? I'm not so sure any more. I've nothing to work with here. There's barely a teacher or book to be found in this place. Inmates' days are empty. I keep trying to believe that I'm helping someone, but to tell you the truth, most days I'm

*thinking I'm just more of the problem. We house them. That's all we do. I
feel like I'm in their prison instead of the other way around.*

*Still, I think he can be saved. It's just harder now. He's just never
understood what revenge is all about. He keeps messing up to get everyone's attention. It's all he knows. You taught me that. You also taught me
to hope for what everyone says is impossible.*

*Still, maybe it's my time to move on. I'm thinking that maybe next
year I'll go overseas again. Help patch people up in war zones, or work
with AIDS orphans. I'm not sure yet. What do you think? It's your turn
to give me some advice.*

There's a half page of blank space after the last period. No signature. I hold the paper up close to my face. I can tell it was written
in two sittings. The ink is from two different pens. The writing, here a
little darker, there lighter. John must have thought about me often. The
thought overwhelms me and I suddenly feel so safe I begin to weep
soggy tears that drip onto the paper, smearing John's plea for help.
This mingling of words and emotion is our last stiff handshake.

*   *   *

My computer at work is stained with the black crust of finger
grease, mine and Ellen's adding layers onto what was already there
long ago. It logs you out automatically after fifteen minutes to ensure
privacy. My password must be alphanumeric and no fewer than eight
digits. It's childish, I know, but "Fuckyou2" seems appropriate. Reminds
me to never forget why I'm really here.

The Integrated Client Management System, or as Shirley tells
me "ICMS," greets me with a dull green screen and ten choices. I
do my case notes first, regurgitating in detail everything Joan, Vivian,
and Mr. Jeffrey say each time we meet. The computer already has his
age, his family history, the length of time the family has received service. Income level. Who lives in the home. Who we suspect lives in the

home. A presenting problem. There's even a small space for strengths to be listed. I guess there's the expectation that there is something good to say about even the worst of our clients.

I update the file regularly. Note what the Jeffreys need. It's always the same. I hit enter and the computer asks me to verify my entry. Then flashes, "Do you wish to continue?" I have no choice. I update my statistics. Itemize my work. Then there's the report back to the Metro Housing Authority, the MHA as we call them. I should also send something to Cameron's school, and the school board, RSB for short. The appropriately dated releases of information are all in place. I check. Many more moves and Cameron will need an Individualized Education Plan. That's an IEP. Maybe a volunteer to help. I'll contact the Community Resources Volunteer Bureau. They refer to their agency as the CRVB. I'm pretty certain that should do it. The ICMS is complete and reports generated. Finally, I write to the Department of Community and Health Services, the DCHS, petitioning them for the IEP funding. Then I sign off.

My hot chocolate has long ago gone cold and I need another cup. As I mix myself one in the lunchroom, Shirley walks in and asks, "How's Vivian doing? And Mr. Jeffrey?"

"Fine," I tell her and she smiles warmly. She puts her cup out for me to pour her some hot water for her tea while I'm still holding the kettle.

"Nice of you to take them out," she says. I nod, feigning humility. Shirley buys none of it. "Really, it was a nice gesture. I'm sure it meant a lot to them seeing what was left." Then she leaves before I can say anything to take away from the confidence she's just shown in me.

When I get back to my desk Ellen is at the computer, Diet Coke in hand. "I'll just be a few minutes," she says.

She almost never looks me in the eye. She types away, hitting each key with the defined stroke of a carpenter. I've known her password for weeks. Been sending her anonymous short messages about sexy boys for hire. Deleted one of her case notes. She was astonished. I could hear her swearing when she discovered it was missing. "Stupid computer," she kept yelling. Knowing I was listening, she'd made her position clear. "I have a kid. Childcare. Things to worry about. I can't work overtime. I can't do these notes again." She solved the problem by dictating them, then made one of the secretaries downstairs type them after hours. The secretary has children at home. Ellen told her, "You have a husband. Make him look after the kids. I have to go home."

Ellen spends a lot of time at home. She rents box sets of television shows. Entire seasons, without commercials. Stays up all night watching them. She talks with the other staff a lot about this vicarious life. The late hours means she misses a lot of work. Tells us her little boy has a cold and uses her sick days to care for him. It's a bit hard to stomach the agency having to pay her to babysit her kid. Or her staying home to sleep. I think of Mr. Jeffrey and Joan. They should be so lucky to have someone paying them to do nothing.

A week later I can't resist the opportunity to stress Ellen further. I stay a bit late and again tinker with her files. This time I put in strange symbols. Randomly throughout her case notes. Make it look like her files are corrupting. Misspell words she has so meticulously typed.

The techs who look at the machine say they can't find anything but I know they think she's a nuisance. One of the techs asks her if she's hitting the save key when she's done. If she properly logs out. "I'm not that stupid," she roars. "And don't talk to me like I'm a woman!" I imagine the tech figures she's an idiot regardless of her gender. I feel sorry for him. My empathy makes me have mild regrets for what I've done. For inflicting her on him.

It's a warm day and I bicycle home afterwards. I have no special place to be so I pass through town and drive past Mr. Jeffrey's new place. Garbage is stacked several bags high outside. They'll have the health inspector on their case. Rats don't mix with children. I get off my bike and without knocking on Mr. Jeffrey's door pull the bags to the curb. There's a light on, but no one comes to the window to take a look.

The next day I enter the agency's intranet and mess up some of my files. Make it look like the computer problem has now gone beyond just Ellen's work. They'll suspect a hacker. At least I hope they do. Then I sign on again, this time as Ellen and then, as her, enter Mr. Jeffrey's file. I enter a request for a change in financial aid. Increase the number of dependants from two to three. It's a change that is unlikely to be caught for months. There are few audits on our work. A few keystrokes create a new life from the electronic void of bureaucracy. Then I give Mr. Jeffrey's newest offspring problems. I run amok with codes. There's no shortage of choices. School problems, psychiatric disorders, truancy. Exposure to violence. The child's violence. Sexual abuse. The computer practically cries as the sun sets outside and the building groans with silence.

I hit save and there it is before me. A life. I cackle, "It's alive," and the cleaner next door pokes his head in to see if everything's okay.

"Anyone else around?" I ask.

"Just Shirley, as usual," he says, and I nod.

I hit save one last time. Stretch. Look out the window at a grey evening sky. The view is of a parking lot, then tidy suburban homes. Pastel-coloured aluminum siding. Clean. My creature will walk and feed at the trough of their wallets. I promise myself I'll put things back to the way they should be in three months or so. Before anyone catches on. Meanwhile, Mr. Jeffrey will have some spare change. At least a portion of what Ellen earns babysitting her kid.

Two weeks later Shirley asks me again about Mr. Jeffrey and his family. Wonders if I'm putting in a lot of overtime. Asks about the computer problems. I joke amicably with her. "Everything's fine, nothing I can't handle." She knows about Vivian's pregnancy. Maybe she'll want another baby picture for her collection. A pang of guilt crosses my mind, but I quickly stuff it beneath layers of righteous contempt for the system. Contempt that I exclude Shirley from. I've grown to like her and the motherly way she cajoles me to be my best. Can't fault her for trying. Excuse her ignorance of why I'm really here. My coming through the glass front door duplicitous. The only time I feel unsure of my plan is when I'm standing next to Shirley. Then I feel a little naked. Like she understands more than she says.

Vivian has her baby that same week. "Wonderful news," Shirley says. "Say hello for me when you see her." How she can be happy that a sixteen-year-old just gave birth is beyond me. But what else can she say? Maybe in the privacy of her car later she will swear a half-muffled, "Jesus, Mary and Joseph." I imagine Shirley's like that. Perhaps she overlooks the obvious only in public. She too must know Vivian's life is a bent coin with two tails. A cycle of regrets and lost hopes. Her affirmation of life through birth something that will bring mostly pain. That's all Vivian will ever know. Lows and more lows. After the pain of retraining, re-educating, re-parenting, there is only the hope of experiencing deeper despair. Like my mother? Maybe even worse.

After Vivian's discharged from hospital, I go to see her in her new basement apartment. The place has been provided to her and her son, Sam. It was thought best that she didn't stay any longer with Joan and Mr. Jeffrey. Not with the baby. That would be too much stress on everyone. Instead, Sandy, our best homecare worker, goes to visit with Vivian a couple of times a week. And we give Vivian welfare. Like the rest of her family, she too begins surviving on the alms of our tax-based charity.

I get through the door after pounding on it for a long time. Then I stand idiot-like in the middle of her small living room. She bears her teeth when she speaks. "What do I have to do now?" she asks. "To keep him." She's tired. Emaciated, not emancipated.

"You have to attend the parenting course. You have to keep your place clean. You can't use. What else can I say? It has to be like that."

"Uh huh." Her tired expression worries me. I wonder if I sounded just as stupid when I talked like that. She asks, "If I do all that, then I can keep him?"

Sure, I tell her. Lies. If I were honest I'd tell her straight out, "Come on, Viv, get with the program. You don't want the fuckin' kid dead, do you?" She'll have to prove to everyone she's a worthy mom. But I hold my tongue.

Vivian nods. Slouches on her couch. The baby is in her slack arms. She gently plays with its hair. Absently. "When's the class?"

"Mondays. You can bring Sam. There's people to look after him. There'll be other mothers, too." I try to sound enthusiastic. She looks past me. I'm just a voice. I imagine her a circus animal. In training for some show she never believes I'll let her perform.

"And then they give him right back to me? No one is going to keep him?"

"You get him back. Every time."

She looks like she is willing to play along. The corners of her mouth crack a little grin that turns quickly into a yawn.

"Whatever."

I leave having never sat down. Make the arrangements. I even go back one morning and take a picture of Sam with a digital camera so the parent support workers can have one for their files. Identify the child easily in a group. I keep a copy for myself. Put it in my desk in the envelope with the pictures Joan gave me of Cameron and Vivian. Then I send the necessary documents to the support workers. All the appropriate forms are filled out. Taxi chits requisitioned. Vivian's welfare worker must agree with the plan. They're tight with money, but everyone says sweet things and plays nice together. Vivian gets her funding. Then I have to write up Vivian's case profile. And pass that electronically to the workers who provide the course. They'll call and interview me. They'll ask me to speak about Vivian's motivation. "Sure, highly motivated," I'll tell them. Then they'll ask about the baby and what kind of care he'll need. And about Vivian's other supports. Ask why she doesn't live with her mother and grandfather. About the arguing. I won't tell them about the dogs and how Joan helped them fuck. I won't tell them about Vivian being a child of the system, unless they ask. I won't tell them about how she has given up on us. Given up on them before she's even met them. I won't tell them how much I admire Vivian for her hating us. Envy her the quiet space she has found. Her peace, an apathetic salve on my incursion.

Vivian goes to each class. She knows she has no choice. The next time I see her, it's at her mother's. The baby is on a blanket on the floor. He's quiet but not in a good way. Sam's dark eyes are empty. He kicks feebly, looks from side to side. I'm there fifteen minutes at least before he makes a sound. I'll have to ask if that's normal. I thought babies complained more.

"How's it going?" I ask and Vivian yawns as usual. I smile at the innocence of the gesture meant to push me away.

"My baby's good. Those classes you sent me to, too fuckin' borin'. How long do I have to go?"

"Twelve weeks." No answer. "The other mothers? What are they like?"

"Losers, like me. Or am I not supposed to say that? Whaddaya expect? We're all like there because you think we can't fuckin' look after our kids, right? Right?"

I like this version of Vivian. A younger Joan. Spirited. It will help get her through the tough times ahead.

"Bang on," I tell her. Might as well admit it. Kindness is wasted here. In her own way, Vivian is smarter than any of us. We live in the illusion of utopia. Vivian is grounded. Her fuckin' kid is buried alive and she knows it. Her basement apartment a living tomb.

Joan comes in from the kitchen and adjusts her bra. She's put on more weight. Her big heavy breasts shift as she walks. She sniffs the air. "The baby needs changin', Viv," she says. She more energetic than I've seen her in months. Vivian doesn't move. She is not going to prove anything to me, today or the next.

"I know," she shouts, then snarls, "In a fuckin' minute."

Joan just sighs, and pulls a tissue from her sleeve and gives her nose a wipe. Slips the tissue back up her sleeve. "I 'ave to be out now. You need anythin'?"

Vivian says nothing. Her mother adjusts her bra one more time. "All right then. Nice to see you, Joey." Joan has been much nicer to me since I found her family the duplex. She picks up a black purse and leaves Vivian and me alone. I sit there for a few more minutes, waiting for Vivian to say something. Do something. She eventually gets up and picks up Sam.

"I'm goin' to change him. Just can't stand her tellin' me to do it."

"I understand," I say, and think I really do.

"I'll try. Really, I'll try. Now fuck off." She says this with a faint smile. The Vivian I met in my office months before now here again with me.

Back at the office, Shirley is unsure what to make of my story. "And the baby's okay?"

"Good enough." I don't like to bullshit with Shirley but I don't want to be the kind of social worker who intrudes. I'd promised myself I'd listen. I'd subvert the system. I'd put the client's voice first. In this case, that means leaving Vivian to raise her kid on her own. Taking her at her word. Vivian is doing the courses. The baby is still alive.

"I think we should give her a chance."

Shirley doesn't answer right away but looks at my notes, which are there on her computer screen. She has access to all our files. "You say little Sammy seems attached ... quiet. And Vivian isn't using?"

"No," I fudge. I was too scared to ask her.

I know Shirley's not buying much of this, but what can she say? Vivian has set up house like she was expected. Even the homecare worker has little to report, especially now that Vivian brings the baby home to Joan every so often. Joan knows how to raise a kid, at least when they're babies. "Sam is safe," I tell myself. The truth is somewhere buried beneath the facts.

"Well, then, I guess you can close the case after the parenting classes are done."

A shiver runs down my spine. I can actually get myself out of Vivian's life. Let her and the baby make their own way. I smile and Shirley touches my shoulder lightly. "Well done." She heads back to her office.

What have I done? After all these years, have I finally succeeded in helping someone break out of the system? Escape her social worker? I need to celebrate. I'll tell Sheila when I get to her place tonight. We'll order in Thai. Her favourite. I won't tell Sheila anything about what I've really done, except that I'm a good social worker. The best kind. The kind who knows when to find his way back to the front door and leave. The best social worker, I'll joke, is the one whose arse you're looking at. Definitely, this is what I wanted. I repeat that phrase over and over. "This is what I wanted." Then take a small bow, as if I'm picking up a pencil on my desk.

I'm on my way. Upended the entire dysfunctional system and proved how wrong they've all been. About Vivian, about Stevie, about me too. And yet, I'm surprised that I stand for a moment longer waiting for Shirley to change her mind. She doesn't and I'm left to look confident as I swallow hard and feel the crust of a dry throat betray my secret that there still remains a small part of me unconvinced by my own bullshit.

* * *

Riding my bicycle home I avoid Vivian's neighbourhood. I circle out through the suburbs. Feel the wonder of an even cadence. Glide the hills. I'm running from my thoughts and know it. My plan to see Sheila shreds. I'm actually not ready to celebrate at all. Sure, Vivian will get what she wants and I'll have won. But this mistake is mine alone to make.

The further I peddle, through suburban rows of townhouses, then down brick-front plaza strips of box stores, and finally onto forest paths, the more I realize this evangelical drive to liberate Vivian has little to do with what she or Sam needs. Maybe wants, but not what they need. It's been about me. I hate the hypocrisy but it's the truth. I choke on every phlegm-soaked part. For a moment I even consider confessing to Shirley. Ask her to put things right. Exonerate myself of my mistaken arrogance. But I can't. All I can do now is slow down Vivian's discharge. Or surreptitiously keep an eye on her. For my sake as well as hers. "Damn," I shout to no one but the sky and the trees that arch above me, "I thought I was better than those others. How could I have been so stupid?"

I pump my pedals harder but still can't shake either the shame or the fear. Both scents linger deep in my nostrils. No matter how fast or hard I move my body, there remains a putrid smell like the lingering presence of someone else when you enter a public toilet.

It was a lousy night full of dreams that chased me when I got back to Lou's. The next day I call in sick and sit on Lou's back steps. I need to stay put, focus. Hide. I'd curl up, only I'm too old now for that. I drink a cup of sad-tasting coffee. I make it with a paper filter stuck in a plastic funnel that I sit on my favourite mug. I want to be alert so I force myself to drink two bitter cups. Hot chocolate would taste better, but I need more caffeine. I sit looking again into my mother's backyard. Today, my life feels like an unfinished case file. I see whiteout where text should be.

It's my turn to rest my head on my knees. My life feels disordered. Out of sequence. Like my mother having me when she was just a bit older than Vivian. My cousin Kristine, my mother's older sister's eldest daughter, had already had her two girls by then, Jillian and Cathy. It was funny when we were all together. At seven, I would wrestle with nine-year-old Jillian. If she had me pinned, I'd tell her she had to respect me and get off because I was her uncle. Or at least I thought I was since her mother and I were first cousins. She'd just laugh, which only me made more angry, so I'd knee her in the stomach, which wasn't a good idea because she'd just started her period or something like that and was real tender. And then she ran and told my aunt, who boxed my ears so hard I could barely hear anything out the right side for the rest of the day. I never told my mother, though. She never had much time for fighting between kids. That was my dad's work before he died.

I learned about sex much the same way. At the wrong time. The winter my cousin Sean came to live with us I was just nine. It was only a few months after my father died. My father's younger brother Tommy was divorced. He had to go out west for a job. Needed my mother to take Sean for a few months while Tommy got himself set up. I never liked my uncle. He always looked crow-like, skeletal. I used to wonder why he just didn't eat more. Sean's mother wasn't much healthier. I learned later she was an intravenous drug user. Just as thin as my uncle. She looked old and brittle, though she was my mother's age. She moved jerkily like a robot, her words staccato.

Sean told me he was going to explain life to me. Mostly he talked about the sex part. At thirteen, that seemed to be all he knew. I knew he was telling me something I wasn't supposed to hear. It began with him showing me pictures of women, then men with huge hard-ons, impossibly long. Most of it seemed outright weird to me. But he liked it so I knew I should like it too.

He'd get hard looking at the pictures. I could see him adjusting his shorts. If he was sure no one was home he might even take them off and stand in front of me. "Not as big yet as those guys, but some day ...," he'd joke. I'd mostly keep looking at the pictures like I thought I was supposed to. Ignore what he was doing behind me.

Then he told me it would help him if someone pulled on it. "It'd feel good," he said. Help it grow. I wasn't sure. I felt sort of hot.

"I'll pay you. I'll get you a pop, really. Just put your hand there," he said, grabbing me and making me touch him.

It didn't bother me much. Even when he came it mostly went into his hand, not mine. And then he bought me a Fanta.

Later, he had me try new stuff to make the pulling more slippery. Jam, his mother's hand lotion. Sometimes when he used food, he'd ask me if I'd lick it off him, but I never did. I had it in my head I could get ill like that. Or maybe pregnant, though I knew boys weren't supposed to get pregnant. Besides, his come tasted all salty. I knew that from licking my fingers. I hated gargling salt water when I had a sore throat so couldn't see the sense of putting my mouth on him.

The social worker who'd taken us to live with the lady who made cookies came back to investigate. She placed Sean with another family. My mother caught him with Stevie. He'd used her face cream and had Stevie hide in the basement with him. My brother was promised much more than a Fanta. Sean was going to take Stevie with him when he went to a ball game with his dad, who was supposed to come for a visit. When the social worker came, she asked me lots of questions. I didn't tell her anything. I was afraid my mother would get into trouble, even though the social worker said it was my mother who'd called her. It was the only time I can remember my mother opening the house to a stranger. Of course, by that time the social worker wasn't really a stranger at all.

Thinking about it, that social worker must have been the same worker who came to our house when I was much younger. When Stevie was just a baby. She'd been the one who'd removed us from my family before my dad died, before we moved to the house next to Lou's, before Sean lived with us. It doesn't make sense, though. *Why would social workers have taken us when my father was still alive?* That thought races around inside my head like a hamster on a wheel. I can hear the rumble but it gets me nowhere.

I take another sip of coffee and shift my seat so I'm leaning up against the railing post. Across the yard, my mother's laundry is hanging. I know she'll have to come out to get it eventually. I can see rain clouds in the distance, coming in low over the pricey homes to the north. Yes, she'll have to come out soon. She'll see me on the steps. Maybe ask me why I'm home this time of day. Ask me if I'm feeling well. Why I'm not at work. Maybe congratulate me on having a job.

It would be just as John had promised. I'd being living my life and she'd see that I'd done great things without her. She'd apologize. And I'd have my revenge. I wouldn't be obnoxious about it either. I promise myself that.

But she doesn't come out to get her laundry. Even when teaspoon-size raindrops wash my hair flat to my head and the clothes begin to hang down heavy, still she doesn't come out. Just lets her hard work go to waste. Lets the rain ruin everything.

When I finally come inside, chilled, Lou hands me a towel from a pile of laundry she'd just done. "It's wet outside, eh?" is all she says. I wonder how long she's been watching me.

thirty-three

THERE'S SILENCE WHEN I ENTER Vivian's basement apartment two weeks later. Officially, her file's in the process of being closed. Unofficially, I've committed myself to finding some reason to keep it open. Convince myself I should speak to Shirley again. I thought a visit might help make up my mind. Only Vivian wouldn't answer the door. The basement half window has mouldy brown checkered curtains pulled half closed. I had peeked in when Vivian wouldn't come to the door when I knocked. I'd even knocked on the window. I could see her lying on the couch. Something about the limpness of her posture worried me. The Super should probably not have opened the door for me.

As I come in, the place smells mildly of stale beer and more pungently of pot smoke and stagnant dishwater. Vivian is passed out on the couch. The closer I get, the more I can smell the mix of drugs and booze. The couch is from Mr. Jeffrey's old place. An heirloom of sorts. One of Vivian's few attachments to her past.

I touch her shoulder. "Vivian," I say gently, leaning tenderly over her. I nudge her awake when she ignores me. Her dim dark pupils stare at me confused. Opaque. There is an emptiness there, a stoicism that makes me cold and the dinginess of the apartment appears like a

Dali-inspired vision of hell. Draped garments, soiled diapers in a pile, a sloping stack of dishes. Such is life in basement apartments where you can hear everyone else's lives as muffled steps above your head, while they hear nothing from you. Ignore you so much you can forget you exist as easily as they do. Thoughts like these rattle around inside my head as I rouse Vivian.

Vivian blinks, coughs, fumbles for a cigarette from an empty pack that she'd used as an ashtray. The green shag beneath my feet is stained grey with ash. Vivian yawns as if forgetting I'm there, rolls over. Her shoulders boney outcrops beneath a loose sweater.

There are no child's cries, though it's late enough in the morning to expect them. There's a crusty diaper on the floor by the kitchen garbage can, the bin overflowing next to it. The smell more pungent the closer I move towards the galley kitchen. There's a baby's milk bottle on the floor, another in a pot of cold water where it looks like Vivian had been sterilizing nipples just like she'd been told to do.

I pass all this on my way to the bedroom. The door's closed, which gives me some comfort for a moment. Maybe she'd thought enough to shield Sam from whatever had been going on last night and from the look of things, nights before that. I'd been trying to call her for days. The line had always been busy. I'd given her space, knowing that at times that can be what we need. I'd wanted to tell her that we were trying to close her file. Even though she'd missed a second appointment with the public health nurse, I was going to tell her I still thought she could be done with the department altogether. And me too. Very soon. Except, of course, I wouldn't mean it. I had sensed instead in the unravelling of my plan an opportunity to postpone disaster even if I could no more admit to Vivian I was wrong than I could to Shirley. I was stuck now finding more and more excuses to change my mind and insist I stay in Vivian's life. She'd be furious with me when she learned what I was up to. But I couldn't ignore what the Super had said. That a lot of people had come and gone the past few days, but that last night it had been quiet. He also said he wanted her out next month. Something about being threatened by her boyfriend when he told him to turn down the music.

Though I knew Vivian would see my intrusion as a violation, experience it physically in ways I could understand, I wanted to get to her before others noticed the risk to her child. Those others might insist I take Sam from her. I couldn't, wouldn't do that. So I came on my bicycle. Had her door opened as a friend. Parked my professionalism at the door. I wanted her to know that it was really me, not the cardboard cut-out she saw when she met me playing her social worker. I wanted Vivian to know I was still the boy I used to be. That I used to play with boys like Jeremy. And scheme with girls like Carrie. She could be my Carrie. My roots were the same as hers. My motivation to survive as vivid as hers. Playing at being good. By the time I get up the courage to open the door to the baby's room, I am desperate that Vivian understand what I am really doing. How I am protecting her.

There is no baby in the crib. I'm relieved. Relieved to be able to avoid the false front of the all-knowing social worker who would have to remind Vivian of her responsibilities. Put on the air of authority once again. Pure crap, all that was. She and I would both know that any mother who left her kid to rot in a crib while she got wasted on the couch was so messed up that there had to be consequences. Had to be an apprehension.

"Good news, Vivian," I mumble out loud. "You didn't fuck up this time." I leave the baby's room. Go back and lean over Vivian, who is still on the couch.

"Where's the baby, Viv?" I roll her over. Still the blank eyes and sallow smile that makes her lower lip appear to pucker. I can't tell if she is holding back tears or proud laughter at my foolish doubt.

She does nothing but look at me for a time, then as she rolls back on her side, pushing her face into the stained cushions, she tells me, "Clean, dirty, like what does it fuckin' matter."

"Say again, Viv? Where's Sam?"

"Just fuck off, would ya'." She rolls off the couch and stands up wobbly. Reaches for the dregs of a warm beer that looks like it might have been used as an ashtray too. She doesn't seem to care. Takes a swallow of what's left, then collapses back down on the couch. Closes her eyes and pulls her knees into her stomach.

I search the apartment once more. The bathroom, the bedroom, under the crib. No Sam. But my search reassures me. I begin to notice order where I'd seen only chaos. She must have given Sam to a neighbour or her mother. It even looks like she'd been trying to clean up. In the kitchen there was a large green garbage bag thrown in the corner. There was a faint smell of rot. She must have been cleaning the fridge. The fridge, when I look inside, is scrubbed white. Even the electric broom was out of its hideout in the corner closet, plugged in and waiting. The whole scene looks like someone had at the very moment of final commitment paused, decided that order was pointless after all. The effect is like some strange museum, postmodern youth circa early twenty-first century. An interpretation of what it means to be tidy. But nothing decisive. Vivian, the ultimate performance artist, one of those odd characters that gain our attention by sleeping on nails or wearing cow dung in the middle of exhibition halls to make a statement about what life really means. There was poetry in Vivian's defiance, if one chose to see it. Her disregard for our expectations a challenge to femininity. No fallen petticoats and mislaid lovers here. Just pathos and irony.

There is nothing more I can do except take out the garbage. Ask the Super to not evict her for a few more months. Beg him for a simple act of kindness. I will let Vivian sleep meanwhile and come back tomorrow. That is my plan, at least until I go to pick up the garbage with both hands and feel the dense weight of what is inside. My insides heave the brown remains of my breakfast onto the floor next to the bag where now a baby's fine crown bulges from the green plastic refuse.

thirty-four

Is what I do worthy of prime time? Would jiggling, sexless social work matrons ever become the next *Sex in the City*? Not without violence.

Lights. What does the camera see? A slow pan across the lineups at the food bank. Then fingers of social workers rapidly typing reports. A whole episode of keystrokes. Maybe John's stories as voice-over. Homeless boys with little dicks and able-bodied attendants with even bigger ones. That story's already been told, but not often enough. And never told by the ones who put the boys in harm's way. The social workers who apprehended, or didn't apprehend fast enough. Who placed the vulnerable among the venerated.

If it's to be prime time, it will need a bloodied cabbie.

Take two. A counselling office. That's the problem with any script a social worker pens. It keeps having to slow down. There is no E.R. pace to the work. Just lineups and emotional voyages. How can we ever make the dominoes of faces standing, waiting, sexy enough so people will care? Cut. Too ordinary. Too routine. Tonight's episode, "More Waiting." Stay tuned. Social insurance numbers scroll by like the otherworldly vision of *The Matrix*. Can we ever memorize so many

numbers? What kind of life must a person have to hold their social insurance number at the front of their consciousness? No one ever wants
to talk about that. About the lives that get audited by those whose jobs
it is to document. Investigators, forensics, capacity assessments, taxation,
skills audit, personality inventories, pre-disposition reports, records of
care and intervention. Stacks of documents telling the most mundane
of stories. The stories of lives lived invisibly.

Maybe we'd rather not be reminded who really lives next door.

Unless a social worker screws up. Then we have a story we all
want to know. We demand accountability. Say it was our community's
right that every child be kept alive. The village forms where there was
none before. A tent city in a sandstorm. Demanding to see the face behind the mistake. Refusing to accept that accidents happen. That people mean well. These others, on the other side of the television camera
that Shirley must stare into, they are so confident they could have done
better.

Drama needs great falls.

I'll learn later in a report from the police that Sam died because
Vivian let him drown. She didn't mean to. She was trying to give him
a bath.

The vision stabs me and I stop reading. I bring the palm of my
right hand up and press it to my forehead. I suddenly have a fierce
headache. I feel nauseous. Breathe deeply. When the pain subsides a
little, I pick up the report and read more, confused by what just happened. Vivian was cleaning, it says, boiling bottles. Vacuuming. I think
back to what I saw. Know she was determined to do something right.
This once. I imagine she carefully drew Sam's bath. That she tested the
water like she'd been shown. That she was committed to giving her son
this one pleasure. And then the phone rang? Or had the radio been on
and Vivian become distracted? Maybe she got lost in the music as she
danced around her kitchen with a broom for a partner? Slightly stoned.
Would a kid like Vivian do that? She'll never say. She just got busy.
That's what she told the police and the coroner. When she remembered
her son, it was too late. And the water too cold. He'd slipped from his
little terrycloth seat. He shouldn't have been able to move. She said
the nice ladies at the parenting classes had never said anything about

a baby being able to kick himself from his seat, slide himself under the water. But he had. Maybe he'd reached for the bright blue elephant toy that was floating next to his head. And for a moment, as the still warm water took him in, maybe he'd experienced the reverie of being flooded with memories of a safe womb and Vivian's steady heartbeat. Before the next breath choked him with the truth of his birth.

We'd all later feel the blame even if the coroner assigned no fault. No report will ever draw a line back through time to Vivian's birth. Or my own.

I put the report into my desk and know what I have to do. Something I committed to doing while sitting on Lou's back steps.

I request the key to Records. Tell Patsy who guards the front desk I have an investigation underway. She hands me the key without any intuition of how long and urgent my quest really is.

When I open the storage room door I smell the peculiar scent of thousands of old file folders. Captured lives. It takes me a while, but eventually I locate in an old ledger book kept by the door code numbers for each family seen over the years before computers made lives into pinpricks of electricity. Here lives are still weighed down by the paper they produce. Once I locate my family name and the year of investigation, I have a file number which leads me to a banker's box labelled with a sequence of black-marker numbers. I pull the box from its lower shelf, kneeling over the contents right there among the stacks. My family file takes up fully half the box. A story collected in chapters tabbed with blue markers and red inserts. Orderly, much more orderly than I remember it.

That's when Shirley comes in behind me. I hear the door open and know before I see her that the careful footsteps are hers. "Why don't you bring that upstairs," she says and without a word, I close the box and carry it behind her. Dutiful. The weight of the contents all but ignored.

When we get to Shirley's office she draws the blinds by her desk to block out the late afternoon sun, which at this time of year is low in the sky and blinding. She lets out a slow whistle. "That is quite a pile of paper, isn't it," she says as we remove my family's files from the box. Stack them on her desk. "I think they're all there. Usually are. If any are missing, we can try to requisition them from the other departments that were involved. Police, courts, coroner's office." The list worries me, but she says it all so matter-of-fact I feel confident I can handle whatever is in this pile. "It's yours to look over. Take your time. But I must tell you, there are things in those files that I'm ashamed of ever having written. I never imagined ..." She doesn't finish her sentence. Instead leaves me in her office, alone, staring at the board of faces hanging beside her desk. Staring at the two bright red squares of bristol board that lie empty next to the photos of all the other children she has known.

There're lots of legal documents and case notes in the file, but the closing summaries set the story in order. Shirley's neat, rounded script explains what happened the first time. No editorializing. Just the facts. As I would expect.

I was four. The hospital called Shirley on a Monday night. There'd been an accident. I had a baby sister. She died before she reached the hospital. She was three months old. My father had called an ambulance. Said the baby had drowned. In our bathtub. My mother was at bingo. I stop and read the sentence again. Unbelieving. My father said it was his fault. He wasn't good with kids. It was all there in a sworn affidavit in the file. He said he'd forgotten the baby until I'd run and told him the baby was floating in the bathtub. Told him the water was still on. Told him I didn't think my baby sister could swim. My dad had kept insisting it was all a mistake. Shirley writes that I seem confused, quiet. My words are not recorded. Only my father's. My voice strangely silent.

The doctors and nurses examined my sister and realized something wasn't quite as it seemed. The baby's neck showed bruising. An autopsy confirmed she'd been shaken before being placed in the bath. Experts testified they were certain she'd been unconscious before she drowned. The trauma to her neck would have been enough to disable her. My father was sentenced to six months for what he'd done. Shirley's note reports all this without emotion. It's only in the daily case notes that I find, in red, a note in the margins. An addition to the narrative, written obviously months later. "Bingo closed on Mondays." Nothing more.

My brother and I were placed in foster care for one year. With the same woman who would later bake us cookies again. And read us stories at bedtime. And tell us to not use foul language. And take us to church even though my mother told her not to. And it was with her that I would do strange things like want to suckle at her breast. Would ask her if she would rub my bum like my mother did. Would want to sleep beside her naked. Told her my mother liked it when I cuddled with her and she'd caress my cheeks and rock herself and make all these funny noises. We did this when my father wasn't home.

The foster parent told all this to Shirley, who documented everything. Shirley referred my mother to Dr. Dirk. He was new at the university then. Dirk even has a report in my family file. He confirmed what happened. From things my mother told him. He doesn't talk specifically about what she said. I know that's confidential. Another paper trail would lead there. He tells Shirley only that my mother has been using her children (my brother too?) for "sexually stimulated pleasure." His typed report is printed in twelve-point Courier on a dot matrix printer. His technology at the time as innovative as his theories. He notes that the "phenomenon has been overlooked." He encourages Children's Aid to be diligent protecting my brother and me from the threat posed to us.

When we were returned to my parents, there was a promise my mother would continue in treatment. By that time my father was out of prison. Shirley saw me for the last time a year later. My father was working at the warehouse. My mother had finished treatment. Or so she said.

"The children," Shirley wrote, "appear to have adjusted well to the transition back home. They show no signs of further trauma."

*   *   *

Shirley comes back two hours later. She finds me sitting by the window, one tattered yellow file folder in my hands. Numerous other documents are stacked on either side of me on the floor. I'm not looking at the pages in front of me any longer. I've opened the blinds and stare at the reddening sunset.

"Did you know who I was when you hired me?"

"Not until after the interview." She reaches into the top drawer of her desk and there in her hand are two pictures, a youthful Joey and baby Stevie, both of us without a care in the world. I am four years old. She hands me the photos.

"My mother? You gave us back to her?"

"We did what we did. Things weren't the same then." We don't talk about the sexual abuse. Instead, Shirley asks, "Your father ... he never said anything about what really happened? With the baby, I mean." Shirley is being gentle with her words. For my sake and for hers. I shake my head.

"You have to understand," she says, her face flushed, her voice breaking, "these things ... they were new. We weren't trained to look for them. We didn't really know. You boys were probably still safer at home than in care. More stable."

"Makes no difference," I say with a shrug. "She messed up. That's all."

Shirley looks at the bulletin board. "I never forget any child's story. That's not always a good thing, you know. Lots of nights, I can't sleep."

I put the file on the floor and can feel tears stinging my eyes from inside. This isn't the place for tears, I tell myself. I don't want this pain. I don't want to go backwards. I had thought it would be easy. It would all be academic. I was to be the object, subject, both at the same time. I was to flow over the case records. I'd have answers, but I wouldn't be scarred by the truth. There couldn't be a truth. It was easier when it was all dreams. With truth came pain and obligations to live beyond the pain.

"I know about the computer too," Shirley says, rupturing my self-absorption. "I changed things back. You know, made them the way they should be. I'm not upset with you." Her words ring in my ears. I can feel my sinuses swell. A nervous fog clouds my thoughts. I'm wondering if she will say anything about Mr. Jeffrey's house. But she doesn't. Instead, her voice goes very tender, more than it should for a colleague.

"I think you meant well. Didn't you? I couldn't see you getting into trouble. There's really no point, now is there? Not after all you've been through, all you've done to get yourself here."

Who did I think I was fooling? I am full of embarrassment knowing Shirley knows everything. Her playing by the rules easily trumping my youthful excesses.

"I can quit."

"I'd miss you too much." Her eyes are now as moist as mine. "But maybe take some time off. How about that? I'll make arrangements for a replacement. Just for a few weeks."

I want to stand up and go over to Shirley and be held. To bury my face in her large friendly bosom, the kind of bosom matriarchs should have. Must have. I want to have my hair stroked and playfully tousled, the way mothers are supposed to love their sons. I want to have someone take all this weight I carry and unburden me of it. Someone who can understand the sobs that haunt my hollow insides.

I do none of it.

I just sit there until Shirley touches me on my neck and I begin to sob like the child I never was. I reach up and hold her hand but I don't get up. Can't find my legs. Am too confused and flooded with grief to know how to stand. And my tears keep flowing. And I'm watching now, watching this release from somewhere else. I am at once both the director and the actor in my drama. And then the scene changes and it is me, the one crying, who is watching that other one, the one who prefers to just watch. And I can see him smiling. Confident. And the tears streak what I see until that other is washed away and there is just me and my wet hands pressed to my face to capture my tears. The well-deserved price of my revenge. I sob. That's when Shirley saves me from all my nonsense. Reaches over and draws me to her. Kisses the top of my head and brings me close like she knows she should. My wet face is tickled by her woolen sweater, making me laugh, self-conscious of my tears. Yet I remain fixed there with my head on her stomach. My ear pressed close to her womb. The dull echo of a beating heart somewhere nearby.

"You'll be okay," she says.

We stay like that for a few moments longer. Then I draw back. She accepts the rejection gently, shifts her weight and leans over to take the pictures of Stevie and me from my clenched fingers. Walks over to her bulletin board. Takes two green plastic pins from the lower corner and puts the pictures back where they belong. The pictures cover perfectly the bright red squares. Then she reaches out an index finger to the boy that is me before her and lightly touches his four-year-old face before she hurries from the office.

She doesn't come back. When I later go to look for her to lock things up for the night, she's gone. The cleaner tells me she left without saying a word. I return to Shirley's office, leave the pile of papers neatly stacked on her desk. Then go to my office. I suddenly miss John more than ever. If I could, I'd invite him to go for a walk. I'd say, "I have some things I need to tell you ..."

The thought makes me choke out more tears as I sit down and wait until the sun has completely set and all I can see outside my darkened window is my own reflection. The wood-framed glass showing me a young man sitting relaxed in an office chair. A social worker deep in thought. I reach into my desk drawer and take out the little brown envelope that holds three children's photos. Vivian, Cameron, Sam. I thumb through them, then reach for tacks and place each on the small bulletin board that hangs to the left of my desk. Then I relax back into my chair, my eyes moving back and forth between the photos and the image of the young man I see framed in the window. And I breathe, very deeply.

*   *   *

I ride to forget. Take my bike and head to Spring Garden Road where on warm Saturday nights like this partiers cruise in noisy cars with big stereos, young chrome-encased studs with testosterone in their tanks and enough girls along the sidewalk to notice. I wear spandex riding shorts now. I wave my ass in the air as I pass drivers stalled in the congested traffic. I only slow down to pick up tunes here and there from the booming sound systems of convertibles. When I hit a light, I do nothing more than stand up on my pedals, angle my front wheel and wait, my right pedal raised, ready for the traffic to clear. Then push off, moving forward. A half-mile later I reach the quieter streets where couples stroll. That's when I turn and race back to the suburbs.

The evening air is invigorating as I leave downtown, circle the rotary, climb up to Spryfield. I pedal without effort. Even uphill. The music is in me now. I soon reach the uppermost streets and a school parking lot with a view back down past the expensive houses to where I live with Lou. My mother's house is just another dark dot down there somewhere. Cool sweat clings to the inside of my t-shirt. Catching my breath, I watch teenagers groping, teasing. I laugh to myself and look at the lights as the chill slowly invades.

It's been three weeks since I've seen Shirley. I'm enjoying my leave.

I crook my head to the side. Stretch. For a moment the lights of the city appear like stars upside down. I look again for my mother's house. Indecision has been chasing me all night.

I get back on my bike and scream towards home. My mother's home. Ride so fast that the corners practically toss me from the road. I slipstream a Mustang for a few moments, allowing its sleekness to carve a path. The stereo surprising me with rap where I'd expect country.

Each time I brake, I think how little I want to stop. Porch lights strobe by through trees as one corner meets another until I am back on the busy roads I rode as a boy. I slip easily through the traffic knowing where I belong.

I ride to Lou's. I leave my bike in her backyard, then walk over to the fence separating Lou from my mother. I jump the fence. March right up to my mother's back door. The same door through which I left years before. I knock, though I know I could just walk in. My mother looks confused as she comes to the door. Before she sees me clearly. Then as she recognizes me, she looks afraid. I notice her hair is much greyer. The crow's feet around her eyes make her look well on the other side of middle age. I've seen her through her window many times but always in my mind, she looked the same. I was the only one changing.

She has to open the door. Just as I have to say, "Hi," like we haven't spoken for a few days instead of years.

"You can come in," she says, only a little defiant. Then she backs up. "I'll make a cup of tea." Her hands are shaking as she fills a tarnished kettle and puts it on the stove's back burner.

"I'll have one too, if that's okay?"

"All right, then." She shuffles her way between the sink and the stove again, this time filling the kettle for two. Then she turns the burner on high. The appliances are all the same ones she had years before. The cupboards, too. Nothing's changed. Only everything is duller than I remember. It's as if the one-hundred-watt bulb in the light fixture above me has had a forty put in instead. The polish is worn away from countertops that are chipped and marked with the rings of what I guess were hot pots placed by my inexperienced brother on the unprotected surface. Too little care taken by my mother to show him how to care for fragile things. The marks make me wince.

The house is quiet except for the sound of the kettle warming and my mother's wheezy breath.

"You ever hear from Stevie?" I ask.

"He's out west," she says. "Writes me every week. And calls too. Unlike some." I know from the way she speaks too quickly that she's lying.

I'm leaning against the kitchen table. She hasn't asked me to sit. I look at her, up and down. Notice how her stockings grip bulging calves. She wears no shoes or slippers. "I was just running a bath," she says. I can hear no water running. "I'll go turn it off." I wait in the kitchen as the kettle boils.

When my mother returns her breathing is more even. She pours the hot water into a small teapot, then puts in a single tea bag. Waits a moment, her back turned to me, then pours herself a cup. She places the pot on the small front burner of the stove to keep it warm. She forgets to pour me a cup. I say nothing about it. We both sit at the kitchen table.

"I'm a social worker now."

"Yes, I know," she says. I doubt she does, but I let her keep her dignity. The omniscience of the parent. "And you like it?"

I ignore the question. "I saw my file," I tell her. "The doctor's report. Everything." I promised myself in my head I'd stay calm, but the red flush of anger competes with tears. Tears that well from the fear I will do something to take away any hope I have of recovery. I tell her, "You know, I never really understood why we were taken away that first time."

She answers so quickly that she must have been rehearsing this moment for years. "They had no right to take you," she says angrily. "That Shirley woman ..." Then my mother startles me and starts to cry. It doesn't come easily. Only, I'm not sure if the tears are for us, her children, or for herself. Until she says, "She had no right to do that to me. She had no right."

"I was the one taken, not you!" I snap back.

Her tears dam as anger sparks. "Oh, and you know everything. Being accused like that. And your father in jail. I guess you know about your sister too, then." I remain silent. She leans across the table and stares at me hard. "I was all by myself. You can't understand what that's like." She bangs her fist down in front of her.

Beads of perspiration rain down my back. "You never told me I had a sister."

She stops looking at me. Holds her eyes so fixed on her tea that I look down with her into the pale brown liquid. "None of them, not one of them did nothing for me. Never. Except your father."

I can't keep up the pursuit. She looks too vulnerable. "I'm not here to fight," I say, my voice now attempting a caress.

"Yes you are. That's all you've ever done. Made me beat you. Made me out to be some old crow. Go on say it. I'm a bitch. Right? You always wanted to make me feel like that, didn't you?" And then she cries again, much harder than I've ever seen her cry before. Maybe that's because now it really is about her, and we both know it.

The tenderness I felt congeals into lumps of loathing. I want to scream, it's not all about you. Want to argue so hard she'll try to slap me again. Then I can have an excuse to grab her. But I just growl, "This isn't about you. Fuck, it's about me and what you did to me."

She looks up. "Your father wouldn't have let you to speak to me like that. If you came over for a fight, then just go back to Lou's. How she ever puts up with you and your filth is beyond me."

I push myself back from the table, gripping the edge hard. I can either throw it, or launch myself back, or get up and leave. Something must break the pull I feel to sit here and listen to this. My crusted feelings flake like a child's decaying scalp. Helpless. I grip harder, count to three, then release. Think, I need to fix this mess. I stand up and gather in my mother's look of surprise. I know what she expects me to do. To strike her. But instead I go over to her, get down on two knees and embrace her. Wrap my arms around her fleshy shell. Hold her close in the way saints embrace the ill. She is unsure what to do with me. Though she is nothing but loose pockets of skin, I feel her tense every muscle.

I hold on tight, even as she slips an arm from my embrace and presses her hand against the table to push herself away.

I hold on tighter, even as she shakes the table and strains to rise from her seat, her feet planted hard on the linoleum below us.

Still, I hold on.

When her tea tips over and the hot liquid pours down my back, I hold on.

When she says, "Now look what you've made me do," I keep holding even while big full tears push their way into my eyes and I feel her hand press down on my head as if anointing me, but really pushing herself up, lifting herself off her seat with me nothing more than a prop. Her hand still on my head as my tears stain her blouse. Her heavy chest, a place to rest only momentarily.

I finally must let go. She is standing now. Fully up and over me. Then she races to get a dishrag to wipe up the tea, leaving me there bent over her empty chair, as if at prayer.

I stand up slowly. Cough away my tears. "Shirley did what she had to do," I tell her. I wipe my eyes with my open palms, then look towards the back door. *No, not this time,* I think. "If you want to talk again, you know where to find me."

She says nothing. Keeps staring at the dishrag that she is now rinsing in the sink. Rinsing it over and over again. I walk backwards a few steps down the hall towards the living room and the front door while my mother remains at the sink with her back to me. The hot water sends moist steam to her face. I watch her wring the rag out several more times before I have the courage to say, "Bye Mom," and turn to leave. This time, though, I use the front door.

Acknowledgements

I WOULD LIKE VERY MUCH TO THANK a number of social workers who have taught me much of what I know about great practice. In particular, a special thanks to Shirley Morrison, Janet Anderson and John Picketts, who mentored me along the way. Without ever knowing it, their wisdom shaped these pages.

To craft ideas into a novel is not a solitary endeavour. I appreciated the guidance I received from David Adams Richards, who provided helpful comments on a very early draft of *The Social Worker*. Later drafts owe thanks to Chris Benjamin, who offered so many great suggestions while he was himself writing his first novel. Then there were the many readers of the drafts, people like Joyce Halpern, Robert Shephard, Rhonda Brophy, Normand Carrey and Nicholas Graham. More formal editing was first provided by Jane Ledwell, then by Julia Swan and Peggy Amirault from Pottersfield Press. Together, they made the work much better through their careful attention to detail.

I also want to thank my family. I was too afraid to let them read earlier drafts but they were still full of encouragement, and sometimes disbelief at the persistence it takes to get a novel published. I'm looking forward, finally, to hearing what they think.